The Prides of Sol
Book Two

A Nepenthean Solution

by

Rod Rogers

Acknowledgments

Many thanks to Todd Cardin, P. David Myerowitz, Judith and Markus Schatz, and especially to my wife and primary editor, Olivia Diamond. All contributed in no small part to turn a promising story into a good read.

The characters, places and events portrayed herein are fictional and any similarities to actual people and events are unintended. Many locations exist, although the details may be different. India and Pakistan became nuclear powers after the conclusion of this work. I can only hope the other events remain figments of my imagination.

Chapter One
May 4, In the Peruvian Andes
Fourteen years from now

Sayla Linneow eased Sam Weber's fevered lanky frame into the after cockpit of the Sikt. Gently touching his brow, she recalled a similar instance, long ago, with another man, another human, who was also near death. This time she would save her brother, a designation this one also had claimed by saving her life.

That his illness was curable seemed likely, although not in the time he had left if she was to isolate the pathogen and then synthesize its antagonist, which she could not accomplish while he rested in stasis. He needed human care and thus would receive it even though that requirement would likely turn this world upside down.

That was not the only reason for her decision.

Linneow climbed into the forward cockpit, pressed the icons that brought Sikt to life and hesitated. There was no undoing this next step.

While she slept through centuries, Earth slid to the precipice. Her analysis indicated that the tipping point was near, and her decision would likely precipitate disaster for humanity. Avoiding the fall was no longer an option. She had to act now, salvage what she could and begin again. But not at the beginning, for that was unthinkable.

The enemy is here. To further delay is to invite disaster.

She pressed the last icon. A digitized stream of instructions issued from the Sikt, instantly received by the mammoth vessel within which the smaller craft resided.

Massive engines stirred to life for the first time in more than forty million years. Anti-helium annihilated its opposite. Irresistible force moved the mountain enclosing the ancient starship as it bored through primeval granite ramparts as might an acetylene torch through a gossamer web. Kilometers in length, the ebony teardrop blasted out of the rainforest canopy and leapt skyward at an astounding rate. The heat and shock of departure seared the forest for tens of kilometers in every direction and registered on Richter Scales around the world. The ejection of the Sikt represented a minor event in a cataclysm humanity could not fail to notice.

Chapter Two
10:07 MDT, 4 May
Colorado Springs, CO

Marcus Ouilette addressed the ball, his mind slipping into autopilot and delivering his body to its direction as he began the backswing. With autonomous ease, he initiated his drive toward the seventeenth hole.

A solid shock in the graphite handle of the club.

A satisfying crack.

During his follow-through, he picked up the ball against the azure backdrop to the west. The tiny white dot climbed and arrowed directly down the fairway. His partner muttered a curse for this was a five hundred and ten yard, par five hole, and that stroke carried better than halfway to the green—a lot better than halfway.

Admiral Dell Petersham, director of the Combined Command Center, Cheyenne Mountain Air Station, still grumbled as he stepped forward, bent and planted his tee. He balanced a ball atop the small plastic pedestal and turned to Ouilette. "Where in hell did you learn to hit like that?"

The long-framed Deputy Director of Operations, National Security Agency, who was casually dressed in a long-sleeve polo shirt, khaki trousers and ball cap, dropped his driver into his bag. "Been working at it," he drawled.

Petersham, a stocky, older New Englander, bent over his ball and groused, "You've been sandbagging me." The admiral's full but normally orderly mass of gray-white hair had been blown into a state of disarray by the robust but fitful breeze since he wore no headgear. His gray flannel shirt and dark brown corduroy trousers offered little restraint when he began his swing with well-practiced ease.

Ouilette waited until his partner launched his drive before replying, "Nothing in the rules against practice, Admiral."

Petersham's ball fell well short of the native Virginian's and very close to the rough on the right. He dropped his driver into its pocket with a pained expression and hoisted his bag. This was in the rules. No caddies, no carts. Eighteen holes, straight up. Winner takes all. In this case, a cool grand, cheerfully donated to the charity of choice by the loser. 'Pete' Petersham had yet to lose to Marcus Ouilette in the four years since their private little spring ritual first began. His flawless record now seemed close to joining the endangered species list. Ouilette was up by two strokes and his last drive effectively choked Petersham's dwindling hopes for a comeback.

As the two men trudged across the fairway, Petersham glanced at his taller companion. "Marcus, I've been trying to figure how to say this for over an hour so now I'm just going to spit it out. I want you at 3C. Come back and work for me."

The request came as a total surprise and at first Ouilette could form no reply. At Petersham's expectant expression, he finally answered, "I'm flattered, Admiral, but I like the NSA...even with the current hiatus. I don't miss Navy compartmentalization even a little. Congress will soon work out the budget issues and we'll be back in business."

Petersham withdrew a two iron from his bag. He leaned over his ball and launched it toward the green. For several seconds it looked like a great shot, but the ball hooked and dropped into a trap. He picked up his bag, and said, "They've already cemented the budget."

"What are you telling me, Admiral?" Ouilette could not suppress the sudden hollow feeling in the pit of his stomach as they approached his ball. He withdrew a two iron and stood facing his partner, twirling the club in his fingers.

"No more operations," Petersham replied. "Not this year or next. Maybe never again."

"I find that hard to believe, sir. Why kill the NSA?"

"It's everybody, Marcus. No more operations. No more humint."

Ouilette digested the news, ruffling his sandy hair in exasperation. "I still have people outside...good people. What about them?"

"You need to call them in. The NSA and the CIA are to be dismantled...part of right-sizing the government. That's why I want you back. Take your shot, will you? The suspense is killing me."

Ouilette turned to his ball, muttering, "Who can think of golf at a time like this?"

"You can, Commander, or I wouldn't be asking you to join me."

Ouilette studied the lie, took a practice swing and stepped up behind his ball. He had barely started his swing when the phone burst to life. It wasn't his phone. Nestled in a side pouch of Petersham's golf bag, the little navy-blue device emitted a sophisticated warbling that was as unique as it was penetrating. Recognizing the sound, Ouilette twitched. The forest to the right of the fairway echoed to the repetitive crack and snap as his ball ricocheted among the trees.

He turned to find Petersham's broad grin and helpless shrug as the admiral retrieved his phone.

"You planned that, you heartless devil," Ouilette accused.

"Would that I could." Petersham opened its cover and punched in his code. The steady drone of a mechanical voice squawked, albeit too softly for Ouilette to make out any words. Petersham's smile vanished.

"When?"

The voice continued a moment longer.

Petersham answered, "Of course I'll take the chopper, damn it! I'm forty minutes away by car. Prepare two briefing packages." He looked up at Ouilette as the voice droned on. He shook his head impatiently as he replied, "I know the classification. Just do it."

When Petersham snapped the cover closed, Ouilette asked, "What's up?"

"Def Con Two. An inbound missile and the satellites read it as a nuke."

"What! Who launched it?"

"They couldn't say. Only one missile."

"What's the target?"

"They couldn't say that either. Mississippi Valley, anywhere from New Orleans to Chicago."

"How much time?"

"Not enough. We need your help, Marcus. This baby popped up out of the Peruvian rain forest. Right about where you held your last little party."

"I lost good people, maybe the best people, down there."

"Well, my friend, it's apparent we need to know a little more about that."

The sudden appearance of a Marine Sea Stallion effectively jumbled Ouilette's coalescing thoughts. The helicopter roared over the trees, spun in a tight circle and descended toward the fairway. Three marines in battle-dress uniforms dropped from its opened hatch even before it settled. They hurried forward, the lead man digging into his Kevlar vest. He withdrew two photos, glanced up and saluted. "Admiral Petersham?"

At Petersham's affirmation, the marine indicated his companions. "Sir, if you and Commander Ouilette will give these two men your keys, they'll return your vehicles and equipment to the mountain."

"The hell with that." Petersham motioned toward the aircraft. The marines turned without further word and sprinted toward the waiting helicopter, Ouilette and Petersham directly behind him. The five men hustled into its waiting maw. The turbines spun up and, like two silent vigils on a sea of green, both abandoned bags toppled from the rotor-wash. The Sea Stallion rebounded into the morning air, veered a hundred and eighty degrees and hurtled westward.

The aircraft skimmed over the countryside at a hundred and fifty knots, barely four hundred feet above the trees. Petersham leaned forward toward their escort, shouting above the whine of the turbines and the roar of the wind through the still-open hatch. "What's our ETA?"

"Eleven minutes, sir. We're cleared through the restricted zone so we'll drop you right at the east entrance. There'll be a vehicle waiting."

Petersham nodded and said nothing more.

Ouilette leaned back against the padded interior of the fuselage, his mind working through chaos, turning to recollections of the Brazilian affair of nearly a year ago.

The conclusion of the cold war at the end of the previous century did not reduce the need for precautions. In spite of the hopes and wishes of the global community, weary of decades of living under a nuclear threat, instant disarmament and lasting peace did not flourish. Admonitions by conservative factions warning of the emergence of some new nemesis, proved groundless. However, relaxation of Soviet-American tensions and attendant curtailment of active and covert surveillance offered an ideal environment for other players to enter upon the stage of mass destruction. Aside from the specter of a nuclear horror show, bio and chemical threats loomed at every turn. Friends seemed like enemies and long-standing enemies, friends. Violence erupted around the globe in random fashion. World leaders sought to discover the source, but the shadowy trails were clothed in deception and intrigue. They often led nowhere.

With ever-increasing budget constraints, North America's security depended on the only avenue left to avoid cataclysm. Elite teams were formed and organized for covert operations. They struck repeatedly at symptoms without ever isolating the cause. Recruited from the Navy by the past director of the National Security Agency, Ouilette had been selected for his experience, most specifically his seven years as commander of SEAL Team Six. His new task—focus upon the nuclear threat. Unfortunately, he had been prohibited from activating or utilizing entire SEAL teams because of the risk of exposure; a risk that neither the NSA nor its political overseers were willing to accept.

Thus limited, Ouilette chose among the remaining options. He recruited the best of the best. Matching a single ex-SEAL to a Marine sniper for backup, he formed elusive two-man teams that had managed exceptionally well until the previous year. That's when the problems began. Ouilette's boss retired and with his replacement arrived a new administrative staff and a different outlook. The N-missions received far more scrutiny than ever before. Ouilette felt that too many people knew about the operations but could not risk curtailing them.

Two missions in a row met with trouble. A hurried extraction prior to contact saved the first one. The second cost his best and most experienced team, along with a fifty-four-million-dollar experimental helicopter. The new director's decision to cut back came as a relief since Ouilette considered that the NSA might now have an internal security problem. Half of the teams were dissolved, the elements reassigned outside the NSA.

Congress removed all the choices when they pared funding for the NSA to the bone. The N-Team roster shrunk to four men, two of whom were missing in action; Sam Weber, a close personal friend, and Cliff Kaminski, the two-time Palma champion from Illinois, both lost during an emergency extraction. Without backup, Ouilette could not send the remaining team even if the director permitted it.

He sighed and shook his head, wondering how destruction of St. Louis or Chicago might be explained away with campaign rhetoric. A quick glance at the young marines in the cabin reminded him of something else. No family worries. No significant others. No wife and children to send scurrying to safety from a nuclear threat. His career had kept him aloof and free of marital or emotional entanglements...probably a blessing in times like these. The grim picture so occupied his mind that the Sea Stallion's sudden pitch to the right and subsequent descent toward Cheyenne Mountain escaped his attention.

10:38, Combined Intelligence Center, Cheyenne AS, CO

Doctor Stanley Wozniak did not look like a possible savior of the human race. Nor did he resemble any reasonable expectation of a hero. Almost six feet tall and possessed of a broad frame that supported his excess mass well enough, he certainly did not match the cut expected of a fit and muscular champion. The off-white shirt and dark brown sweater vest struggled in vain to contain his bulging belly. A wide canvas belt dipped low under the protruding mass, obviously dependant on a pair of navy-blue suspenders to keep his dark gray slacks from sliding southward. The pudgy fingers of his left hand flew over the keyboard while his right precariously balanced the tattered remains of a sausage and biscuit. Crumbs tumbled unseen onto Wozniak's belly as he hunched toward the thirty-seven inch flat-panel screen. His myopia insufficiently aided by the oversized display and his *coke bottle* glasses, he scrunched his eyes to double-check the command line. He struck the return key and lurched back into his chair whispering, "Go baby, go!"

The door to the subterranean satellite command center hissed open but he remained oblivious to his visitors until a raspy voice broke through his concentration.

"What the hell's taking so long, Wozniak?"

Although startled by the sudden intrusion, the scientist focused his attention on the results of the new configuration. He effectively compartmentalized the interruption and evinced no reaction. *Nerves of steel.* He replied aloud,

"Saving mankind from destruction." Turning in his chair, he added, "Sir!"

That humorless round face had been all too familiar of late. Agate-hard pale blue eyes, an eagle's beak for a nose, and a thin harsh line that slashed across below it. *The man has no lips!* Major-General Henry Pigott, director of air-defense operations, stood in front of an unusually subdued and sweaty-faced retinue, a row of dominos dressed in air-force blue uniforms.

A tinge of red crept up Pigott's throat. His eyes narrowed and not for the first time Wozniak sensed the general's disdain for a civilian contractor usurping what he obviously considered as military eminent domain.

"*Mister* Wozniak, you tagged an inbound missile as nuclear. Instead of feeding your face and playing games, how about a professional effort worthy of the reputation that preceded your arrival in our mountain."

A renowned scientist, Wozniak owed no deference to the military but his sense of inferiority in the presence of fit and vigorous officers and enlisted men diminished his characteristic sarcasm. Pigott's remark swept away this restraint.

"This *game* employs a cluster of six 9400 mainframes. Each has thirty-two Epsilon petaflop processors." His exuberance spewed particles of the biscuit in a fan shaped pattern. With an almost imperceptible delay while he did the math in his head, he glanced at his watch and added, "Seven hundred and sixty-eight thousand trillion missed opportunities, General, while I explain this to you. What's on your mind?"

Disgust shaping his features, Pigott backed a step. Wozniak knew that the general was unlikely to engage him in a technical discussion, one he would surely lose and might appear stupid in the process, and after a moment's hesitation, the officer lifted his chin and replied, "Answers to remaining questions, that's what. What about the trajectory change? What's the impending target? How much time to impact? The director needs those answers. The President expects those answers. Can you find them, Mister Wozniak?"

"Freed from pleonastic questions...of course." Wozniak swung back to his screen. The emerging patterns were entirely unexpected.

"Hello...?" he murmured. He dismissed the party behind him and waved off further intrusion.

Pigott retreated to the elevator where he called out, "Five more minutes, Wozniak. Five!" The general and his aides retreated inside the lift and the door swept shut behind them.

Absorbed in reentering his command lines, the scientist took no notice of their departure. He watched a second pattern emerge and swore, "Not frigging possible!" He struck the cancel button and added four more filter programs, reconfiguring his search of the incoming satellite data. Again, the pattern began to trace. This time it was different but still unexpected.

Wozniak recognized several unusual features, elements heretofore seen only in advanced simulation programs. His astonishment soon turned to fascination. Balancing the last remnant of his breakfast on the narrow upper edge of the monitor, he canceled his previous configuration and restarted the analyses employing some intuitive guesswork. Trace after trace confirmed his presentiments.

To verify a developing hypothesis, he issued commands to all three of the tracking satellites, directing them to increase gain and refine focus. The signal strength of the probes trebled. He watched as the ancient KH16 and the two new LR-38s boosted their output. The result startled him. The traces and the patterns they defined vanished.

"You ineffable little snit!" Wozniak muttered.

He reissued the commands to no avail. The satellites could no longer *see* the incoming bogey. And, he no longer thought of it as a missile.

"God bless!" Wozniak rocked back in his seat, his thoughts disordered by a sense of alarm until he noticed the nature of the loss of contact. It matched, precisely, the order and timing with which he had boosted the satellite transmitters' gain. He canceled the tracking subroutine and picked up the red phone to the director's office. Cutting off Petersham's assistant in the middle of her greeting, he blurted, "Sheila, get the Admiral."

"Sorry Doc, but Admiral Petersham is not available."

"Break into whatever he's doing. It's critical."

"Doc, you always say that."

Wozniak hesitated. It was true. Failure to find a more demanding superlative evoked a sense of remorse at his prior indiscretions. In a communication window that opened automatically on his screen when Wozniak made the connection, Sheila Wellsley appeared nervous, no doubt frazzled by the current situation. "Listen Doc, he's inbound by helicopter. How about if I call you when he arrives?"

Wozniak nodded and then realized she couldn't see him. Her workstation would not be included in the video loop. "My gratitude shall be boundless," he added.

"No problemo." She turned suddenly to her left. "Oh wait! He's just arrived, but the brass is all over him."

"I'm coming up. Pass me through to the war room."

Sheila confirmed she would and the window collapsed. Wozniak heaved his bulk out of the seat and trundled toward the elevator.

When he reached the main floor and passed through security to the war room, as the missile-tracking center of Air Defense Operations was frequently called, he found Petersham. Along with another man he did not recognize, and several generals, including Pigott, the Admiral stood by a series of consoles that displayed the SEW line, the recently deployed Southern Early Warning radar picket.

One of the technicians raised his voice. "Acquisition on four!" He stabbed the keyboard, bringing more transmitters online. The occupants of the war room gathered around the displays, which consisted of several large screens showing the track of the inbound. The rapidly moving red dot left the coast of Venezuela, hurtling out over the Gulf of Mexico.

Petersham spoke first. "I'd have thought it would be approaching apogee by now. And a hell of a lot closer." He glanced at the Air Force officers. "It's ballistic, right?"

Wozniak interjected, "Initial trajectory said so, Admiral. The target climbed to an altitude of eighty miles before arcing over. It's been descending ever since."

A ray of hope brushed Petersham's features. "A dud?"

Wozniak demurred, his mouth open to add more when Pigott cut in. "It doesn't matter. With a cruise missile profile, we can deploy *Starlance*. A squadron of F-27s is scrambling right now."

Alarm flooded Wozniak at the mention of the anti-missile weapons. The admiral needed his data.

Pigott continued, "We've time enough and a solid lock on the missile."

Wozniak shook his head and said, "Not for long."

Pigott bristled, but Petersham looked away from the screen, cutting off the General's retort. "What do you mean, Doctor? What do you know?"

"Admiral...I hoped we could...I need to discuss something in private."

"What do you know?" Petersham repeated.

"It's more hypothesis than certain knowledge, Admiral."

Pigott said with a sneer, "He can't add anything. We're in control."

Wozniak was about to reply when someone shouted, "Sir! We've lost acquisition!" The technician who spoke jumped from his seat and shoved another operator from a nearby display. He reconnected to the SEW line. A second later, he raised his face. "The damn thing vanished."

Petersham swiveled to the Air Force advisors. "A stealthy missile? I didn't know anyone had that capability."

The sandy-haired officer beside Petersham drawled, "The hell of it is, Admiral, who's to say how many are inbound?"

Wozniak cleared his throat. "Admiral, I really need to talk to you."

Petersham's eyes narrowed. He appeared to consider an unspoken message before he turned to Pigott. "General, launch your fighters. Vector them on the last known position and go for visual. Get everything in the air that can shoot. I want a screen a gnat couldn't fly through." He faced Wozniak and pointed toward an adjacent conference room. "Let's talk, Doctor."

Wozniak hastened toward the indicated room. The admiral's companion entered the room behind Petersham, who slipped into a chair across from Wozniak. The stranger closed the door and leaned against it from the inside.

Wozniak studied the sandy-haired newcomer. The hard eyes and unruffled expression spoke of a warrior with confidence—with an unflappable demeanor most probably born of a long and successful career. His angular, sun-bronzed features were unreadable and Wozniak decided he needed allies at this particular moment, but when the scientist glanced back at Petersham, the Admiral preempted his reluctance. "This is Commander Marcus Ouilette, lately deputy-director of operations at NSA. He now works for me. Commander Ouilette ran an operation to infiltrate and destroy a clandestine nuclear weapons lab not twenty miles from where our current threat originated." The admiral glanced at Ouilette and nodded his head toward Wozniak.

"Marcus, meet Doctor Stanley Wozniak, professor emeritus, on loan from Los Alamos Laboratories' Theoretical Division."

Ouilette shook Wozniak's hand and said. "Professor Emeritus. Damn near deserves a salute."

Wozniak felt uncertain whether that was compliment or jest. Petersham cut into his thoughts before he could decide.

"Tell us about the nuke, Doctor."

"It's not a nuke, Admiral," Wozniak blurted. "It's not a missile either."

Petersham gazed steadfastly at Wozniak. Ouilette said nothing. Wozniak swiveled from one to the other then back again. He mistook their silence for disbelief. He spread his hands on the table.

"Okay! I tagged the nuke designation. I'm sorry for that. I believed the computer's projection, especially with the neutrino flux at the launch site. It even looked like an ICBM in the infrared scan. You've seen my analysis in the briefing package?"

Petersham nodded as Ouilette replied. "What's changed?"

"Size! This object, whatever it is, was, or may be…it's too large; even after it split."

Ouilette stiffened. "A MIRV?"

"Not a multiple independent re-entry vehicle. A smaller craft ejected from the larger one. The big one went straight up."

Petersham asked, "How far up? Where's it headed?"

Wozniak shrugged. At the looks of exasperation on the faces of his companions, he hastily added, "The larger section reflects no radiated energy. It's the smaller piece we detected and that only for a short time."

"If it had stealth technology, how could you know it exists? How big was it?" Ouilette asked. Petersham inclined his head, indicating his interest in the answers.

"Indirect analysis of air wave deflections, projections of thermal loading in the lower atmosphere during launch and boost among a host of other things," Wozniak answered. "I'd estimate the mass at close to three hundred metric tons."

Petersham let out a nearly soundless whistle before he replied. "About the size of an airliner. How big is the smaller section?"

Wozniak blinked in surprise and then answered, "Admiral, that is the smaller section. The big piece was at least three orders of magnitude larger."

This time Ouilette moved away from the door, disbelief in his eyes. "Impossible!"

Wozniak leaned back in his chair with a knowing smile. "I'll tell you something else that's impossible. I've a strong signature on the motive source for the smaller object. It's a Thorfield Engine—a superbly efficient variation of a fullerene design using air for reaction mass. Pop C60 molecules filled with deuterium atoms into a magnetic containment chamber and crush them with a laser. You know what you get?"

At the blank stares he received, he answered his own question, "Heat, gentlemen. An incredible amount of heat. And, of course, some helium."

Ouilette responded, "Fusion?"

Wozniak nodded with a self-satisfied grin, which prompted Petersham to ask, "Are you certain? Who could have built something like this?"

Wozniak met the challenge straight on. "I can call up the treatise from classified documents at Los Alamos in less than five minutes. You can compare them to these." The software engineer reached into his lab coat and withdrew a sheaf of printouts from his last analysis scan. They'll be damn near a perfect match."

Ouilette repeated the Admiral's second question. "So who built it?"

Wozniak blew a burst of air from his lips that sounded much like a noisy fart. He followed it with an exclamation. "Well, we sure as hell didn't!"

Petersham replied, "We better find out which country did and quickly. This weapon is aimed at us."

Wozniak leaned forward. "Admiral, you still don't get it. When I said *we couldn't* I meant *we* as in the human race." As comprehension dawned in both men, he added, "We can manage the theory just fine. The material sciences still elude us."

Petersham stood and pivoted away, facing the wall. After ten seconds, he turned back to Wozniak. "Order up those documents, Doctor. Put your reflections in logical order. It will be up to you to provide the initial briefing. Code black, gentlemen. We three are it until I add additional staff." Petersham turned toward the door and then paused. "Marcus, you better call off Pigott and his Black Widow squadron."

"Bad idea, Admiral. Doctor Wozniak's confirmed nothing yet, and national security's at stake."

"Not to worry, Admiral," Wozniak said.

"Doctor, assuming you're right, I'd hate to destroy the evidence."

He replied, "My analysis, gentlemen. Assuming it is hostile, our uninvited guest will soon be deep in enemy territory. It knows we are vigorous and vigilant. But, compared to their likely level of technology, we're armed only with rotten apples." Wozniak showed his teeth.

Petersham simply shook his head and closed the door behind him.

"Rotten apples?" Ouilette asked with a smile.

"Or a functional equivalent thereof." Wozniak glanced around the room. "How am I supposed to get those documents the admiral wanted?"

Ouilette lifted a handset off the wall near the door and touched a number. He spoke quickly and quietly and then handed the handset to Wozniak. "Delegate Doctor. Sheila will handle the necessary legwork."

That task completed, Wozniak hung up the phone. He turned to Ouilette and said, "Willet? Is that French?"

Ouilette spelled it out. "Close enough. Champenois actually. Since you're not military, just make it Marcus. I'm okay with that. And since you're not military, what brings you to this subterranean domain?"

"Ah, well...I guess I can talk about that. A special project I've been working on regarding social dynamics on a planetary scale. My antiquated network in Los Alamos wasn't up to the task so they let me borrow time up here. Hey, didn't the admiral say you were involved in the Peruvian thing a while ago?" At Ouilette's affirmation, Wozniak added, "That's the kind of event I've been analyzing."

"The development of clandestine nuclear labs?"

"Not just that. Every destructive event. Every threatening trend. All of it. Where it's going and why? What's so funny?"

Ouilette's smile faded. "Coincidence. Believe it or not, we've been in the same business, you and I, except that my end had more emphasis on corrective action rather than analysis of cause and effect."

"Yeah? Well, good luck with that, because if the most likely hypothesis proves valid, your approach hasn't a chance of success."

"Something I should know, Doc?"

"Most definitely. We're learning about it now. Together." Wozniak's eyebrows flicked up and down.

Chapter Three
12:02 CDT, 4 May
Pensacola Naval Air Station, FL

Commander Ed Baylor, call sign *Whistler*, turned his F-27 Black Widow onto the taxiway behind his flight leader. The world's most advanced interceptors rolled swiftly over the expansion joints in the taxiway with stiff-legged jolts. Slung under each wing, an AMM-56 Starlance anti-missile weapon in brilliant white contrasted with the dull black surfaces of the aircraft.

Both fighters swung right onto the active runway and paused. The whine of the powerful turbines and the high-frequency vibrations emanating through the airframe sizzled beneath Baylor's concentration. Despite extensive training, his heart hammered and sweat beaded his brow.

This was the real McCoy! If Breaker Flight didn't nail this target, a city somewhere might fry in nuclear flame.

Baylor released the throttles and stick to shake the tingling sensation out of his fingertips. The metallic voice of departure control issued from the earphones in his helmet.

"*Breaker Flight* cleared for immediate departure. Vector to one-nine-oh and climb to angels forty. Check in with *Gunslinger* on tac-two."

Commander Joe Griffin, call sign *Grayfin*, in the lead fighter replied, "Roger, that. Vector one-ninety, angels four-oh. *Gunslinger* on tac-two." The lead fighter began to move even before Griffin added, "*Breaker One* rolling."

Baylor responded, "Two." He released the brakes and pressed the throttles forward, slipping into afterburner. Ninety-six thousand pounds of thrust from the two Pratt & Whitney F140 turbines hurled his craft forward like a tail-scorched eagle, slamming him into the seat. He switched off his transmitter and eased the stick back. Airspeed rocketed past three hundred knots and the F-27 arrowed skyward nearly a thousand meters behind his flight leader. With his left hand, he detached his facemask and howled into the cockpit. "Yee-haw!"

The tension gripping him subsided and a second later, a laconic voice buzzed in his ears. "Now that you've got that out of your system, how 'bout joining up with me."

Baylor glanced at his transmitter. The switch was off. He flicked it on and said, "What?"

"Whistler, I know what dead air means on climb out."

"Uh-huh. Okay boss, here I come."

Baylor overtook the lead aircraft as his altimeter passed thirty-eight thousand feet. Griffin had already dropped back into super-cruise, allowing his wingman to close the distance. They leveled off at forty thousand feet and slipped past the sound barrier. At nine hundred and sixty-five knots ground speed, the two fighters hurtled south-southwest over the Gulf of Mexico.

Griffin switched to tactical channel two and keyed his mike. "Ah, Gunslinger, Breaker Flight at altitude and heading."

"Roger, Breaker. Turn to two-zero-zero and light 'em up. Drop to level twenty. We need you here pronto."

"Affirmative, turning to two-oh-oh. Going to burner. Descending to level two-zero."

Baylor watched his speed indicator slip past nineteen hundred knots then finally hover around twenty-one-eighty. "I hope there's a Texaco up ahead," he said.

As if they read his mind, the AWACS positioned over Grand Cayman broke in. "Breaker One-Two, ETA with the tanker in nine mike. Eleven mike to refuel in tandem. Breaker One-Two is lead-off batter."

At two miles every three seconds, the Gulf of Mexico is a small place. Breaker flight found their tanker and slowed. They lined up on the trailing drogues of the KC-10 and refueled simultaneously. Taking on just enough for the intercept, they concluded within the allotted time and were directed southwards once again.

"Breaker Flight, this is Gunslinger. Vector is two-zero-two. Angels two. Maximum speed."

Griffin replied, "Gunslinger, Breaker Leader. Say again flight level."

The AWACS controller complied. "Breaker flight will intercept at flight level two."

"Acknowledged. Heat is on. Coming to two-oh-two, descending to level two."

Baylor toggled his transmitter to inter-plane. "I don't get it, Grayfin. Why carry Starlance if this is a low-level intercept?"

"Someone botched the call." Griffin added, "Are you painting the target?"

"Negative."

Tension evident in his voice, Griffin replied, "Come up on my left. Let's spread out and go for visual." Griffin then switched back to tactical frequency. "Gunslinger, where's the bogey? My systems show no contact."

"Breaker, the target has stealth technology. You'll have to utilize the IR tracking and acquisition mode of the AMM-56."

A few seconds of pensive silence filled the air as the interceptor pilots digested this latest information. Griffin replied, "Gunslinger, how do you know where it is?"

"We're receiving IR telemetry via satellite. The target is emitting a substantial heat trail."

"Great!" Baylor said. "They don't know where it is either, only where it's been."

Griffin clicked the mike to signify understanding. He switched back to tactical. "Gunslinger, Breaker Flight at level two. We're eighteen minutes to bingo. How about a little situational data?"

"Breaker, target is dead ahead of you, speed nine hundred knots, altitude not precisely known, but should be below you. Range, seventy miles."

"Roger that." Griffin switched back to inter plane. "Open it up a little more, *Whistler*. We'll turn into it and close from a better angle."

Two thousand miles away, tension in the Air Defense Center mounted as every word between the aircraft and the controllers aboard the AWACS rolled out of the multi-channel receivers. Wozniak was particularly fascinated, having never before participated in such an event.

Computer projections highlighted the positions of the interceptor flights as they slipped into a *defense-in-depth* arrangement. If Breaker flight should fail to destroy the oncoming target, several other assets had moved into position to try. General Pigott approached Admiral Petersham. "I'd like to back them up, sir." Petersham nodded without speaking, and Pigott lifted a handset. He spoke quickly and quietly.

Within seconds, another controller aboard the AWACS added, "*Cue ball*, this is Gunslinger. You're on deck. Turn to vector one-seven-eight, level two. Maximum speed."

In a west-Texas drawl, a new voice replied, "Cue ball copies, heading one-seven-eight, burners lit."

"Two."

"Three."

"And four."

Wozniak turned to Ouilette. "What does that mean?"

Ouilette whispered, "Cue ball is a flight of four F-22 Raptors. They're carrying heat seekers to draw off any defensive systems our target might have. Breaker might need to take more than one shot."

Petersham broke into their conversation, peering at Wozniak. "Your computers are still trying to communicate with the intruder?"

Wozniak nodded. "No replies, Admiral, on any frequency. But we finally have some satellite pictures." He passed a package to Petersham. The Admiral opened a folder and peered within.

His head came up with a snap. "Is this some kind of joke?"

Slipping over an empty blue sea at twelve hundred meters per second provided for an amazing sense of velocity. While he scanned a fan-shaped sector ahead of them, Ed Baylor reflected that he was traveling faster than a speeding bullet—a modern age superman in his invincible flying machine. Any time now. The rate of closure was formidable.

Griffin's vision was keen but Baylor saw it first. "Contact! Grayfin, I have visual. Come left five degrees."

"Roger that. Coming out of burner. Weapons tuning," Griffin added. "Selecting missile one."

Baylor slipped behind and to the right of his flight leader. "Check it out, Grayfin! It looks like a duck!"

"More like a goose. A big, black goose. How weird is that!"

"Big ain't lying. Maybe it's a good thing we carry Starlance after all."

"Gunslinger to Breaker Flight. Verify that your cameras are activated."

"Roger Gunslinger, Breaker One verifies camera rolling."

"Two."

"Whistler, slip to the right for a good angle on my launch. Gunslinger, missile one is armed and locked on."

In the ADC, Pigott turned to the admiral, who reluctantly nodded. The general leaned over and spoke to a controller. A second later the speakers burst to life.

"Gunslinger to Breaker, you are cleared to launch."

"Breaker One, commencing attack."

Commander Griffin continued his commentary as he approached an apparently docile target. "Bogey is maintaining course and speed about two hundred meters altitude. Range to target, twenty-seven hundred meters. I'm easing onto its six."

Griffin's voice continued. "Still closing, Sixteen hundred meters."

Wozniak asked, "What does he mean, *easing onto its six?*"

When Ouilette portrayed the maneuver with one hand moving behind the other, the scientist said with sudden alarm, "Oh, no, no! Tell him to get out of there! He's in danger!"

Breaker leader hesitated, then added in a higher pitch, "Got a problem here. I'm losing my left engine! Gunslinger, I'm declaring an emergency! I have fires in both engines. I'm breaking off the atta—"

The speakers filled with static.

Wozniak shouted. "Get him out of there! Now!"

Another voice erupted. "May Day! May Day! May Day! Breaker Two! Breaker leader has fire-balled. Commencing attack. Fox two! Fox two! Weapon's away. Locking on with second missile. Fox four! Both missiles away."

After a few tense words from Wozniak, Petersham passed his message to Pigott. The general conferred with his controllers.

"Breaker Two, this is Gunslinger. Do not, I repeat, do not assume a trailing position on the target."

"Roger that! Target's maneuvering! It's going ballistic!"

Petersham spoke to Pigott, raising his voice above the speakers. "Get the backup in there. Breaker Two has no other weapons!"

"Gunslinger to Cue ball, commence attack. Be advised, under no circumstances should you approach from behind."

"Cue ball copies."

"Gunslinger, Breaker Two. Target has opened fire! Missile one is destroyed! Crap! He got the second one too! What the hell is this thing?"

"Breaker two, this is Gunslinger. I have four Raptors on the way in. Squawk your IFF so they can identify you."

"Cue ball to Gunslinger. Where's the target? Is it destroyed?"

"Negative, Cue ball. It's stealthed. Switch to tac-two and vector on Breaker Two. He's in close proximity."

Baylor's voice interrupted. "Shit-fire, can this baby maneuver! I'm at angels thirty-two and climbing. Still in burner. The bogey just reversed on me. Executed a twenty-gee turn."

"Gunslinger to Breaker Two, are your cameras rolling?"

"Damn straight! Okay, we're going for the deck now. Damn! Gunslinger, I've passed bingo. Better get a Texaco out here, pronto!"

Petersham leaned forward and spoke quickly to Pigott who relayed his message to the AWACS controller.

"Breaker Two, this is Gunslinger. Get out of burner now! You are to preserve your aircraft at all costs. Turn to vector zero-three-zero and ease throttles to thirty percent. We have a tanker on the way."

"Negative Gunslinger. We'll lose the bogey. It's headed for the deck. I'll hang on until Cue ball arrives."

"Breaker Two, Cue ball. Do as the man says. Cue ball One commencing attack."

Baylor lifted his fighter's nose and banked away. He backed out of afterburner and slowed to two hundred knots. His heart sank when he glanced at his remaining fuel. Well, at least it's not the Arctic Ocean. A few seconds later, his radar picked up the approaching tanker, a KA-6 barreling toward him at full throttle. He dismissed the dwindling fuel reserves from his mind and focused on the radio traffic from the situation behind him.

"I got him, *Wizard*! I got him! Break left!"

Commander Red Somms, unable to turn with his target, slammed his stick to the left, swearing as his Raptor slid away from the bogie.

"Do it, *Ghost-man*. I'm out of here."

"Fox two! Missile away. Good God! Look at that thing climb!"

Somms twisted his head nearly backwards as he shoved the throttles to the stops. With a satisfying kick in the pants, his Raptor leapt forward and spun to the right as it accelerated. The target climbed vertically at an impossible rate.

"Got it boxed, *Ghost-man*," a third voice chimed in. "Fox two!"

"*Rustler*, *Wizard*. I'm backing you. *Joker*, stand off in case this puppy breaks loose. Get on it, *Rustler*. *Ghost-man's* blocking the low road." Somms leveled his fighter and lined up on the twisting pair in front of him. The target was ahead of and turning sharply inside of *Rustler's* pursuing fighter.

"It's coming right! Coming right! Can't stay with it! Sorry, boss. It's yours."

Somms engaged his gun camera and acquired missile lock on the turning bogey. "No sweat *Rustler*, I'm on it. Target is opening fire! Got your missile, *Rustler*. Yours too, *Ghost-man*."

The intruder straightened from its turn and accelerated. Somms slammed his stick hard to the left and forward, barely able to keep his pair of Sidewinders locked on the target. He found an opening and squeezed the trigger twice. Somms noticed that he was coming perilously close to the lethal exhaust stream and banked away.

"I'm out! Who's in?"

"*Wizard, Ghost-man*! I'm on it."

As Somms turned his fighter in a tightening circle, he could see Cue ball Two in afterburner, climbing straight up under the bogey.

"Target's firing again. Got both your missiles, *Wizard*."

"Balls! Two left, but I have this sudden feeling…"

"What is that red stuff, a laser beam or something?"

"Worry about it later, *Joker*! *Ghost-man*, you in or out?"

"On it...Fox two! Going right up the stovepipe...Gawddamn!"

For several seconds silence reigned.

Somms keyed his comm. "You get a shot, *Joker*?"

"Negative."

"I guess that's it, then."

It was the voice of Cue ball leader, Commander Somms.

"Gunslinger to Cue ball, is the target destroyed?"

"Ah...negative, Gunslinger. It got on the burners and left town."

"Standby Cue ball, we're getting new telemetry."

On inter-plane, Cue ball Two queried, "What the hell? There's no way..."

"Can it, Ghost-man. They'll figure it out."

"Two."

"Gunslinger, Cue ball is standing down. You have a Texaco for us?"

A hundred miles to the north, Ed Baylor dropped away from his tanker. He banked toward the west as he keyed his mike. "Cue ball, Breaker Two. Give me the scoop."

"Roger, Breaker. You guys paid the bill. The target's returned to its original course and altitude. I'd estimate the velocity as mach six."

"Say again, Cue ball!"

"Breaker Two, Gunslinger. Come to three-five-zero. Climb to level thirty-three, maximum speed. Say state."

"All systems green. Fuel is twelve-two. No weapons."

"Roger, Breaker Two. You are now designated *Watchdog*. We will vector another tanker as you approach CONUS."

"Acknowledged. Watchdog climbing to level three-three. Heading three-five-oh."

At the ADC, Pigott's face reddened. "I can't believe this, Admiral! You're going to let it overfly the U.S.?"

"General, this intruder can outmaneuver, outshoot and outrun everything you have, including the Black Widows. Tell me how to prevent it."

"Sir, a pilot is dead, an aircraft destroyed."

Wozniak responded, "General, that wasn't an attack. In fact it was our mistake...could even be called my mistake."

"What are you talking about, Wozniak?"

"The craft utilizes fusion drive. Its exhaust is expended plasma, probably a few thousand degrees in temperature for a mile or more aft. If our aircraft ingest those gases..." Wozniak shrugged.

"Why the hell didn't you warn us about this?"

Wozniak dropped his gaze. "I didn't know how a fighter aircraft attacks targets. I didn't see the danger."

"For God's sake, a man is dead—"

"A time of learning for us all," Petersham cut in. "Our air defenses are ineffectual, so we'll keep Watchdog in contact with the intruder. We'll play it by ear from here on in."

Pigott crossed his arms and turned away. Petersham faced Wozniak. "Prepare your briefing, Doctor. Commander Ouilette will be your liaison. You've half an hour."

Wozniak nodded, his eyes downcast and his face pained. Ouilette nudged his elbow. "Like you said, Doctor. Rotten apples."

12:25 MDT, ADC auditorium

Admiral Petersham moved to the front of the room where he stood beside Stanley Wozniak, who had lost control of his briefing. An emergency technical team thrown together less than fifteen minutes previously included scientists, Air Force and Navy pilots, Intelligence and State department personnel. Now, a half dozen separate conversations erupted, the voices of the participants growing steadily in volume as each sought to overcome interference from all the others.

Petersham shouted, "Hey!"

In the sudden silence, he continued, "Stay on track! We're here to discuss what we know from a technical perspective and from that, to draw some preliminary conclusions. Until we finish with what we know, shut up and listen."

Kurt Voelmer, an under-secretary from the state department, objected. "Admiral, we need to discuss the political aspects. Your satellite data can help by giving us some clues about the reactions of the rest of the world. The dog-fight in the Gulf didn't exactly pass unnoticed."

"Mister Voelmer, the political discussion is scheduled for 14:00 at the White House. If we don't stay on track here, we'll not be prepared for the questions that are sure to come." Petersham turned back to Wozniak. "From the top, Doctor."

As Petersham leaned against the table facing his audience, Wozniak felt the weight of the Admiral's presence as an ally and his confidence surged. He pointed to a computer-generated slide displayed by a digital projector.

"By the time our *intruder* separated into two pieces, we had established the mass of the entire object as in excess of three hundred thousand metric tons. Once the fighter portion split off and began its descent, the satellites lost all trace of the larger object."

"Wait a minute," an intelligence officer interrupted. "How did you ever mistake something the size of a battleship for an ICBM?"

"Good question. This information was derived in later analysis of non-reflected energy. The larger piece of whatever this is does not reflect any energy. The minimal return of the smaller piece, plus the massive amount of heat at launch, suggested a multiple ICBM liftoff. The computers tagged it so and well, that got our attention. Only when the anomalies appeared did we reexamine our assumptions.

"Whatever the drive source, the carrier emits no heat. We've plotted its projected course based upon the last known trajectory, but have been unable to detect any trace of its presence. In short, we have no idea where it is."

Ouilette raised his hand. "Why call it a carrier, Doctor?"

"It seemed appropriate since the larger object launched the fighter with which we now contend."

Another scientist said, "You've called the smaller object a *fighter* twice now."

Wozniak smiled. "I love a straight man." He clicked a button on his infrared remote control. The view changed to a plot line showing the convergence of the first two interceptors and the target.

"We're reasonably certain this craft displays all aspects of a combat vehicle. It stealthed when we irradiated it." He pointed to the loss of signal and the timing that matched his satellite commands. He followed with the SEW-line loss of acquisition.

"When engaged by our most capable air defense units, it possessed counter-fire effective enough to destroy their weapons. Please note that the aircraft themselves were never fired upon, in either engagement."

"But we lost one of them," a voice from the back of the room objected.

"An accident I shall now explain. We've determined the nature of the drive on the fighter. Fusion powered, the drive emits high temperature expended plasma—ionized gases extremely destructive to internal combustion engines such as jet turbines. Unaware of the danger, one of our pilots entered this fatal zone and his craft was destroyed."

"Could that have been an offensive tactic, to hose down our fighter with its own exhaust?" one of the aviation officers asked.

Wozniak smiled again. "You guys are good." He changed pictures. "These are actual aerial combat photos sent by microwave as soon as Cue ball flight was retrieved aboard the carrier, *Abraham Lincoln*. I've selected a series of eleven photos that show exactly the opposite."

"I'd like to discuss the weaponry," Eugene Thompson, an engineer from Fermi Labs interjected. He pointed at the photo where two streaks of ruby light intersected a brilliant ball, the atomized remains of a Sidewinder missile.

"We'll get to that next. Note these series of pictures. In each case, an F-22 Raptor comes close to entering the fatal zone. In every case, the very next photo shows a radical change in the aspect of the intruder, all of them vectoring exhaust away from our fighters." Wozniak thumped the wall on each photo for emphasis. His enraptured audience got the point.

Ouilette mused, "So the pilot, assuming there is one, was flying in combat fashion to avoid the easy shot, turning at each opportunity to destroy the missiles we launched, and protecting our aircraft from the hazards generated by its own exhaust?"

"Exactly."

Murmurs arose in the audience. Petersham derailed them with a question. "How, Doctor Wozniak? How could that heavy craft maneuver so effectively?"

Wozniak rubbed his nose before he replied. "Our aircraft maneuver by high-velocity deflected airflow over control surfaces or with two-dimensional thrust vectoring. To turn quickly, you need both."

One of the Air Force officers at the back of the room quipped, "Speed is life!"

Wozniak shook his head and continued, "Not necessary for our intruder. This craft ingests vast quantities of air, heats it to...I don't know...maybe thirty thousand degrees." Wozniak thumbed his control.

"Look at these photos showing intense maneuver, specifically these jets of gas from the shark-gill ports on the upper surfaces of the wings. There's no doubt about the engine exhaust ports and, from the underside, you also see substantial heat-wave distortion. I'd be willing to bet the intruder could hover and maybe even fly backward."

The Air Force officer spoke again. "Like a *Harrier*, only better. But this next page says that the intruder departed the combat area in excess of forty-seven hundred knots."

Wozniak turned to the Navy officers present. "Recall the advancement in capability of the submarine when it switched from battery power to nuclear propulsion. This is the same order of magnitude, only in an aircraft. We estimate the mass of this fighter to be in excess of two hundred and fifty tons. Most of that mass is probably structure to support the stress that the power system is capable of producing." Wozniak clicked to a different picture.

"Here we see evidence of incredible G-loads. At this juncture, the intruder turned a double loop inside of a Black Widow that managed nine Gs. Our analysis tells us that the pilot of this vehicle withstood twenty-six Gs for over seven seconds."

"Shit!" one ex-fighter pilot exclaimed.

"They might have," another replied, "if they're built like us."

Wozniak didn't follow the comment and so ignored it. "Any questions on the airframe?"

"Just one," Doctor Iszak Rabinowicz, from JPL raised his hand. "In your opinion, is this craft space-capable?"

Wozniak glanced at two or three of the engineers he'd discussed this subject with prior to the meeting. He turned to

Rabinowicz. "It's our opinion that it is not. We feel this design is optimized in favor of stupendous performance in the lower atmosphere. Drive and airframe seem to suggest that it is an air superiority design or maybe a top-notch ground-attack platform. All that mass in the airframe offers no advantage in a vacuum. The area of the maneuvering ports also indicates extremely large volume which can only be used to overcome aerodynamic aspects of low level flight."

"Then," Rabinowicz added, "the *carrier* must return."

"We hope so. If there are no other questions, we'll move on." Wozniak clicked to a different series of pictures.

"Okay, weapons." Everyone leaned forward as he continued, "Not laser beams! I know they look like it, but they're not. In the Cue ball engagement photos, the flight leader, Commander Somms, carried a high-speed digital camera. Capable of one thousand frames per second, this camera gave us some valuable clues." He turned to Ouilette, who stood near the door. "Lights please, Commander."

Once the room darkened, Wozniak continued, "The following five frames are selected from a series that Commander Somms captured as he was launching two Sidewinders at the target." Wozniak pressed the button five times. In each picture, a lance of red energy advanced about forty feet toward an approaching Sidewinder that seemed to be suspended in space. Wozniak repeated the sequence several times then called for the lights.

"Before everyone reaches for their calculators, let me say that the missile moves about twenty feet in total, while the counter-fire advances about ten times that or about two hundred feet. Light travels almost two hundred miles in a thousandth of a second, so a laser's out.

"We believe we're seeing a mass driver, probably ejecting a glass coated metallic pellet at forty thousand feet per second, the energy of which would be impressive in its own right."

Wozniak selected another picture.

"Note here a different geometry on the angle of fire as related to the target craft. Computer enhancement indicates that this protrusion, under the…the…"

"The bill of the goose…" Someone at the back of the room quipped.

"Okay...anyway, it can articulate. It tracks its target independently of the aircraft's attitude and direction."

One of the Navy pilots let out a low whistle and shook his head. Several other flyers nodded without comment. The Navy man asked, "What's the range of this mass driver?"

Wozniak shrugged. "Depends on the thickness and makeup of the silica coating on the pellet. It might last as long as a second."

"So a range of forty thousand feet?"

"I don't think that's beyond the realm of possibility."

"If that's true, Doctor Wozniak, then there's nothing on this planet that can successfully attack or defend against this aircraft. I may be a flyboy, but my major was physics. One shot by that weapon might blow an Abrams tank to fragments. It has a range of eight miles and a time of flight measured in milliseconds. Until you brain-boys come up with a counter for this mass driver, I'd suggest you rethink any more air-intercepts."

Petersham stood. "Commander, the objective of this intruder is unknown. Until we establish communication, we cannot afford to dismiss any options. But, we will consider what we've learned."

In the pensive silence after Petersham's words, the red phone on the wall next to the door chirped. Startled, Ouilette plucked the receiver off its hook. He listened for a few seconds and then held it out to Petersham.

"Admiral, Gunslinger wants to patch Watchdog through to you."

Chapter Four
13:56 CDT - Over northern Arkansas

Little Rock receded in the distance. Baylor's F-27 Black Widow paced the intruder while both craft swept northward over the Mississippi Valley. At five hundred knots and four thousand feet of altitude, he speculated about the havoc they were creating with the commercial air lanes. The air traffic controllers couldn't see the intruder and, while he was squawking his transponder continuously, Admiral Petersham had imposed radio silence.

Over New Orleans, Baylor had taken on enough reserves to reach Hudson Bay but had a hunch they wouldn't be traveling that far. During the flight north, he had gradually closed on the other craft until less than fifty meters separated them. In the last few minutes, he had risked several trial approaches, none of which prompted any response.

He swallowed away the lump in his throat. *No guts, no glory.* He eased his stick forward and to the right, sliding toward and beneath the exotic, droop-winged craft.

Nudging the throttles, Baylor moved forward until his canopy was meters beneath the nose of his companion. He glanced over his shoulder into the gaping maw of its intakes. This close, the aircraft lost all likeness to any animate object.

Baylor studied the turret-like construction under the goose-head, which was flattened, streamlined, and attached to the under-surface of the *bill.* He verified its capability to articulate or track targets independently of the direction and movements of the aircraft. Not unlike the chin turrets of bombers half a century old, four tube-like projections protruded from the forward edge, the inner diameter of which seemed similar to that of 20mm cannons.

Baylor retarded his throttles, letting his fighter slowly drop back a few meters, his attention now focused on the massive ball-in-socket joints in the neck of the craft. There were two, the forward one just behind and attached to the goose-head. The rearmost formed the base of the neck. These two joints were clearly capable of raising and lowering the nose of the craft similar to the Concorde. Unlike the supersonic airliner, the second joint would allow the nose of the craft to remain parallel with its body, albeit on a different plane.

Baylor eased his stick forward, gaining some separation and dropped back another few meters until he was under the body. He examined a large pod slung between the two intakes. Flattened and roughly rectangular, but with graceful curves that softened the angles and formed an efficient aerodynamic shape. Aft of the intakes, he could make out long panels that appeared to be hatches. Doors for landing gear?

The pod also exhibited hatches in its underside. It had weapons stamped all over the design. He could see two areas that looked like hard-points for the attachment of external stores on each wing.

Dropping back even farther, his aircraft entered the periphery of turbulence from the massive vehicle over his head. Despite the buffeting, he could see the ravening distortion of the exhaust, lethal but colorless against the bright blue sky above.

After his extended inspection of the intruder, Baylor arrived at the conclusion that a pilot, if there was one, must reside in the goose-head. Returning his fighter to its original position, above, slightly aft and twenty meters to the right, Baylor considered the unearthly nature of the aircraft's construction. Fifteen years of studying military hardware by every nation on the planet taught him how designers thought. Human designers, he reflected, just didn't build things this way.

No canopy, for instance, meant that whoever or whatever was flying this vehicle could not directly see from within. Obviously, there were sensors of some type, as this craft had no trouble in destroying his missiles. Furthermore, Baylor could find no manner of egress from, or entry into, the goose-head. It appeared to be seamless in construction. He could not imagine that someone would enter into one of the hatches in the body and wiggle their way through the neck. Those joints at either end could not possibly allow passage for a body of any significant size. The goose-head itself was not likely to hold more than two passengers, assuming they were similar in size and shape to humans.

Baylor suspected he must avoid including assumptions in his reasoning. For all he knew, the pilot could be an intelligent snake, or a pack of rodents or a swarm of insects. Perhaps it was not organic at all. What if a robotic brain controlled this craft, an inorganic intelligence built into the framework by some distant engineer? All of these possibilities chilled him, and made it especially hard to control his rage at Joe Griffin's senseless death. He reasoned that the pilot of this craft was not responsible but his anger, fueled by fear of the unknown, remained fixed on the intruder.

Without realizing his transmitter was still switched to inter-plane mode, he spoke aloud. "What the hell are you?"

A throaty, sibilant voice whispered in reply, "I am named Linneow. I regret the death of your companion." The name was pronounced as *L'neo*.

Baylor was too stunned to reply. He nearly missed the second phrase that whispered into his helmet on inter-plane frequencies.

"You...speak English?"

"I've had opportunity to learn."

"What country are you from?"

"Not from a country, Pilot Whistler, nor from your world."

Holy shit! One assumption confirmed! Baylor decided to break radio silence and switched to tactical. "Gunslinger, Watchdog. Do you copy?"

"Roger, Watchdog."

"Gunslinger, I'm in contact with the intruder. The pilot speaks English."

Silence followed for several seconds. "Watchdog, I'm patching you through to the ADC. Standby."

Moments later, a new voice queried, "Watchdog, can you hear me?"

"Affirmative. Who's this?"

"I'm Admiral Petersham. It is vitally important to ascertain the purpose of the intruder's visit. It's also urgent we establish communications between the intruder and the ADC. Can you manage these two items?"

"Sir, I can try. About the intruder's origin, Admiral. It told me—"

"Some things speak for themselves, Commander."

"Aye, Sir. Watchdog out." Baylor switched back to the inter-plane frequency. He tried to remember what the other pilot called itself, but could not. He did remember that it knew his call sign, however.

"This is Whistler. Can you hear me?"

"Linneow listens. Will Pilot Whistler forgive Linneow?"

"We'll talk about that later. I'm instructed to ask you about your purpose for intrusion into United States airspace."

"Linneow wishes to save a life...a human life."

Sensation enveloped him...softness of voice, emotions of regret, the need for absolution, an offer of apology; all touched human engrams that seemed somewhat feminine. He could not ignore them.

"Are you a woman?"

"Woman is human female. Linneow is female but not human."

Confirmation of his instincts established an emotional contact, a bridgehead from which his logic began to work.

"What happened to my wingman?"

"Linneow believed earth fliers to be automated drones. Seemed too small for human pilot. Must avoid *Sikt* exhaust."

Baylor considered this revelation and how it fit with what he remembered of the original intercept. Still there was the pertinent question. "Whose life have you come to save?"

"Sam Weber. He is near death."

"Who's Sam Weber?"

"Linneow owes Weber a life debt."

This was a complicated subject. Baylor changed his line of questioning. "Why didn't you communicate with us before?"

"Sikt remains in battle mode. A coherent light communication link is required."

A laser link! A sure bet the ADC didn't think of that one. "How are you sending to me now?"

"Linneow modulates concealment energy. It is capable of low power transmission only."

"Where are you headed, Linneow?"

"Linneow does not understand."

"What's your destination?"

"Chicago."

Good grief! I don't think so! Aloud he said, "I must confer with my commander."

"Linneow awaits."

At the ADC, uproar raged in the auditorium. Technicians hurriedly installed a phone on the table at the front where Petersham sat. They patched it into the audio system so the admiral could broadcast the next conversation. As word spread about contact with the intruder, the auditorium filled within the space of minutes. Petersham had barely assumed his seat when the phone rang again.

Baylor asked, "Gunslinger, Watchdog. Am I still patched through to the Admiral?"

"This is Petersham, Commander. Give us a moment."

Petersham punched a button on his phone and continued, his voice booming out on the speakers and accompanied by a feedback squeal. "Go ahead, Commander. Our technical teams can hear you now as well."

While the technicians turned down the gain, Baylor replied. "Sir, the intruder is bound for Chicago. The purpose is a rescue mission."

A moment of silence followed. Petersham finally responded, shaking his head. "Out of the question, Commander. Who needs saving in Chicago?"

"The pilot, a female named Linneow, transports a man named Sam Weber whom she said might be dying. I guess she's taking him to Chicago."

Uproar ensued so Petersham swiftly muted his speakerphone, stood and raised his voice. "Hold it down!" With order restored, he turned to Ouilette. "Marcus, take over this liaison with the intruder. Tell him to persuade our visitor to avoid Chicago airspace. I'll establish a controlled environment somewhere else."

As Petersham hurried from the auditorium, Ouilette punched the mute button, opening the channel to Baylor. "Watchdog, this is Commander Ouilette. Sam Weber is a Navy SEAL who currently lives in Chicago. Your intruder must be taking him home. We're planning an alternate location. Convince your contact that we can provide life-saving care in a different place. Tell her about the difficulties of approaching Chicago."

"Affirmative, Watchdog out."

Baylor switched back to inter plane. "Linneow, can you hear me?"

"Linneow listens."

"We must avoid Chicago or we would disrupt and endanger many lives. We can provide better care for Sam Weber at a different location."

After several seconds of silence, the throaty whisper returned. "Does Pilot Whistler forgive Linneow?"

Surprisingly, Baylor felt no enmity and realized Linneow was looking for a measure of trust. He keyed his mike. "Linneow, my human name is Ed Baylor. Whistler is a call sign. You're not responsible for my friend's death. After all, we attacked you."

"Linneow is saddened that Ed Baylor loses a friend. For Chao, friendship and trust bond those who fly together. Do we fly together, Ed Baylor?"

"You bet!"

"Linneow understands. Sam says this when he agrees. Linneow will follow."

Ouilette turned to Wozniak. "Doctor, I want you to organize this crowd."

"In what way, commander? I've no authority here."

"I'll handle the command and control part. Put together a logical structure of technology, medical, and linguistics teams. Think of what expertise we'll need in all pertinent areas. Contact anyone you need."

"There are some really sharp folks at Los Alamos."

"Wherever you find them," Ouilette replied. "Just keep a lid on it."

"Where should I send them?"

"Send the civilian types to Denver International and any military people you happen to select, to Peterson AFB."

"Peterson? Where's that?"

"Just outside of Colorado Springs." Ouilette touched an Air Force captain on the shoulder and, as the man turned, read his nametag. "Captain Russell will be your liaison. He'll arrange your lines of communication and help you with traveling instructions for your team members."

When Russell nodded, Ouilette continued, "While you're in the selection process, I'm going to start working on logistics." Ouilette did not wait for acceptance. He slipped past the two men and made his way to the phone where he connected with Petersham's secretary, Sheila. He spoke rapidly, cataloging the reactions while Wozniak wound his way from group to group.

The scientist led the majority of the crowd to a huge white board at the side of the auditorium. He drew a checkerboard in multiple colors with erasable markers and, with calls and shouts from his audience, scribed in titles and subtitles. He had nearly filled all his boxes when Petersham re-entered the auditorium. The Admiral had changed into his khaki service uniform. He strode to the back of the crowd, spent a few minutes gaining some insight into the process underway and then scanned the room until he found Ouilette. He slipped away from the raucous mass at the white-board and approached.

Petersham waited until Ouilette hung up. "Looks like selection is under control. What about logistics?"

"Just finished. Question is...where to?"

Petersham glanced back at the crowd around Wozniak. "I've established another link with Watchdog. This one is encrypted, at least to the AWACS. Let's leave these guys alone and send a message to our visitor and her escort." Over his shoulder, he added, "Since you'll be with us for the duration, I've sent someone to retrieve your uniforms and gear from your hotel."

"Thank you for that, sir."

Ouilette followed Petersham down a long corridor and through two security doors where the Admiral swiped his card to gain entrance. They turned right to enter a wide, darkened room with a low ceiling. In the center, encircled by a maze of flickering workstations, they found General Pigott hunched over a console along with three technicians and communications officers. All four looked tense.

Petersham approached and asked, "New developments?"

"We're stressing the commercial airways, sir," the general replied. "We need to rethink our strategy."

"Explain."

"Traffic is backing up all around the Great Lakes. We need to move our intruder out of that air corridor."

"Do it. I've arranged a reception team at Minot. We'll use the facilities of the old 5th Bomb Wing. The controllers of the 91st Missile Wing can assist our logistics train once it's inbound. Henry, I'd like you up there to run the show from an operations point of view."

Pigott nodded. "What about Air Defense?"

"Pick someone. The way I see it, this is the most important thing on our plate. Take whatever and whomever you need. We've a green light from the Secretary."

Petersham turned to Ouilette. "Marcus, I want you to take care of security. Use everything you need to seal it tight."

Ouilette spread his palms. "I'm caught out, Admiral. All my resources are back in Washington."

Petersham dug into his breast pocket and pulled out his security card, which he handed to Ouilette. "No time to dial you in. Sheila will show you to my office. Shiloh64 is the authentication key on the workstation. You'll have access to every string. Pull them all."

"What about you, Admiral?" Pigott asked.

"I'm in the back seat of an Eagle from Peterson as soon as we send Watchdog and his charge toward Minot. Have you opened a comm link to Baylor yet?"

"Yes, sir. I can divert him at any time."

"Then let's get started. As soon as your plan is launched, I'll expect you on-site in North Dakota. Any comments?"

Ouilette said with a smile, "At least you picked the right season, sir."

"Don't plan on a summer picnic, Marcus. We'll still be at it when the snow flies." Petersham turned away and loped from the room. Ouilette tapped the card on his left index finger and then said to Pigott, "You need anything from me, sir?"

Pigott folded his arms and shook his head once.

Ouilette wondered at the sudden ice in the General's demeanor. He turned away, cleared his mind, and began to grapple with the problems of establishing security around the most important happenstance in modern history.

"Watchdog, Gunslinger. Advise your consort of a new destination. Climb to level 54 and turn left to 288."

"Roger, Gunslinger. 288 on 54. Where to?"

"Sorry, Watchdog."

"Understood." Baylor switched to inter-plane. "Linneow, we're to change course and climb above the commercial traffic. Our new bearing is..." He hesitated, confronted with the problem of passing human-specific information in terms an off-world visitor might understand.

"Linneow, how do you reference bearing and altitude?"

"Measure with coherent light. Navigation base six. Programmable."

"We use base ten. Our current altitude is forty-one hundred Earth units above sea level. Subdivide the surface of the planet pole to pole by three-sixty. Same for relative bearings. Understand?"

A light hiss issued through the comm link. After a moment's delay, she replied, "Linneow knows feet and degrees, Pilot Baylor. After seventy million years on your planet, Linneow knows many things."

Baylor felt a flush creep into his cheeks. *Seventy million years...Jehoshaphat!* He replied, "Current bearing is 010. Come left to 288. We'll climb to 54,000 feet."

"Linneow will comply."

Baylor switched back to tactical. "Gunslinger, Watchdog. Executing turn and climb." He keyed his inter plane. "Linneow, we are to change course and altitude now." He rolled his Black Widow smoothly to the left, pitched the nose up and advanced the throttles. The F-27 leapt skyward. As they approached the mach-limit, he dialed off the power and craned his neck to peer over his left shoulder. The Sikt remained stationary relative to his craft, about twenty meters distant and slightly aft. In less than a minute, he leveled off and keyed his tactical.

"Gunslinger, Watchdog flight at altitude and bearing."

"Ah ... roger, Watchdog. We thank you. Chicago Center thanks you."

Baylor double clicked his mike and switched back to inter-plane. "You said seventy million years, Linneow. Is your race immortal?" Once again, he heard a light hiss.

"Linneow is amused. Sometime I feel like immortal being. Span of life five hundred and eighty Earth years. Linneow has lived three-ninety-four."

"But you said seventy million—"

Linneow does not count stasis time. Sixty billion years in stasis."

"Whoa! Wait a minute! The universe isn't that old."

Several seconds of silence passed.

"Linneow comes from a previous expression into your universe."

The concept snapped into his mind. He stammered, "Y-you mean like the big bang and all that?" Baylor let the image flow through his mind. "How did you... No, wait. Let me get this sorted out. Your people, Linneow, what are they called?"

"We are Chao."

"Tell me about your world, Linneow. Was it like Earth?"

"All gone now. Destroyed by an ancient enemy."

Whoa! That was like a punch in the gut. It stopped him until he decided he still wanted to learn more about her. "Tell me about it anyway, if you want to."

She did not immediately reply. When she did, her voice was lower and softer. "Two worlds were home for Chao. Sethke and Leia. They occupied the same orbit around our star, Cha. Pilot Baylor understands this?"

"Call me Ed, Linneow. Your people must have originated on only one of those planets, though."

"On Cha'Sethke. Chao build sun-powered ships. For many seasons, no Chao returned. Finally, Chao build strong ships and flew to Leia."

"Damn," Baylor whispered. And we haven't yet made it to Mars. "How long did it take you to develop interstellar flight?"

"Chao built slow ships. Many, many years to reach next star."

"Slow ships? Yeah, I get it. Slower than light. Like us trying for Alpha Centauri, if we ever get that far." Baylor's laugh was filled with envy. "What a trip that would be. What did you find?"

"Chao find a dwarf star."

"No planets? No uninhabited paradise?"

"Only fragments in orbit of the star. Chao mine for metals."

"Like the asteroids!" Baylor glanced at his companion's craft. Her voice was alluring and he fought the urge to see her as a babe from some distant time and place. More likely, she looked like a squid. Or a hairy-legged arthropod.

"Linneow does not understand Asteroids."

"Sure you do. The belt of rocks beyond Mars."

Several seconds of silence passed before she replied, "Linneow is sorry. That word was not known. The fragment belt known."

Baylor laughed again. "No problem. Some theories say it was a small moon ripped apart by the tidal stress from Jupiter."

"The gas giant did not destroy Tassone. Oo'ahan destroy Tassone, and try to destroy Earth at the same time."

It was as if she had suddenly changed the subject. "What! Who is Tassone? What's Hu-wa-hahn?"

"Oo'ahan are the enemy. Tassone was a Vithri fortress world. Oo'ahan destroyed Tassone sixty-five million Earth years before now. Try to destroy Earth same time. Chao and Vithri ships destroy Oo'ahan vessels first. A sad battle for Linneow. Lose mate. Lose friends."

A void loomed before him. *What the hell was all this?* He recalled what she had said about her own world.

"Did the Oo'ahan destroy your world? Are they your ancient enemy?"

"Oo'ahan Collective exist as the oldest living race. They were not always an enemy. Mizorca destroy Cha in Great War against Oo'ahan."

"Mizorca!" Baylor tumbled the new word in his mind. He felt as if he had just walked into a barroom fight with everybody swinging at him and he didn't know why. "Let me get this straight. The Mizorca were enemies and the Oo'ahan at least neutral, if not allies. Now your people are fighting the Oo'ahan? And they want to destroy Earth?"

"Mizorca were very powerful. Like Oo'ahan. They lost the war but defeated Oo'ahan grand plan. Oo'ahan try again. This time they eliminate competitors."

"The Chao are competitors? What about us? Surely we're no threat."

"Chao population is small, like Human, but not so weak. Chao ally with Vithra, a people stronger than Chao but not numerous as Oo'ahan."

"What about the Mizorca?"

"All dead. How you say? Extinct?"

A chill coursed his spine. "Linneow, why did you come to Earth?"

"Pilot Baylor is—"

"Call me Ed. Ed is my name like yours is Linneow."

"Linneow wonders about source of name."

"Ed is short for Eduardo. My father was a tenant farmer. He wanted a famous son and thought a famous name might make him so. He called me Eduardo when I was born. Rumor has it I'm named after a famous cigar."

"What is a famous cigar, Pilot Ed?"

"Oh God, we could spend the rest of the day on that one. Let's just say it's a rolled-up leaf, stuffed with a plant called tobacco. You ignite one end and inhale."

"Linneow knows about tobacco. Why are you named after tobacco?"

Baylor laughed. "I was the son of an ignorant man, Linneow. As you probably know from seventy million years of hanging around Earth, humans are seldom peaceful types. We tend to focus on differences in our endless disputes, things like the color of our skins."

"Linneow believes religion is foremost divisive factor."

"Yeah, religion is another one. Anyway, my pop was a black man in a white-skinned society. In his time, it meant more than today and it still means something now. My pop thought he could give me a lift with a famous name. On the day I was born, the landowner where he worked handed him a cigar and told him that it was from Havana. So he named me after it."

"Linneow understands. Baylor is a family name. Chao custom similar. Linneow is my family name. Chao use only family names unless mate or sibling."

"No kidding? Out of curiosity, what's your given name?"

For several seconds only silence followed. Her answer, when it came, was husky and soft. "Sayla, Pilot Ed." She pronounced it with the accent on the second syllable. "Linneow is sad. Not heard this name for many years."

He toggled off the switch for inter plane. *Shit, Baylor! Sometimes you ask the dumbest questions.*

Chapter Five
13:41 MDT, 4 May, Cheyenne AS, CO

Ouilette rubbed his aching eyes and closed the door to Petersham's office behind him. He flicked off the overhead light, tread soundlessly across an expanse of silver-gray carpet and slid behind a polished mahogany desk. Enough light penetrated the entryway's frosted glass pane to outline a large flat-panel display in one corner. The screen was dark and a magnetic strip reader protruded from the right side of the monitor's frame. He dragged Petersham's security card through it.

The screen flashed once and gradually brightened, depicting a scarlet field dominated by the number thirty in block white characters. A second later, the number changed to twenty-nine and then again to twenty-eight. Beneath the edge of the desk, a tray contained the keyboard. He grasped the tray, swung it upward, and it snapped into place.

On the monitor, twenty-four faded to twenty-three as he typed shiloh 64 and struck the return.

"Invalid."

The phrase faded, replaced by the number twenty.

He tried again with shiloh64.

"Invalid."

Thirteen changed to a twelve. *Case sensitive*? He typed Shiloh64 with a return. The number eight disappeared and the screen displayed an intricate site map. Without exception, every security agency he knew and some he had never heard of were listed in little boxes. At the top, a flashing cursor hovered beside the question: Classification?

Ouilette typed in Black and only a quarter of the listings remained. He glanced at his notes, making some decisions. First the launch data, then the intercept, and finally the intrusion.

He began to build a layered plan of misinformation. At the first level, he created dozens of conflicting stories and then sent them to various agencies for *release*. Specific commands eradicated the real data from any non-secure or marginally secure repository. Special algorithms reshaped reams of false, old, and non-essential files from the system archives into unique, vibrant, and entirely irrelevant excerpts. He sent the files to drop boxes that would deploy the information to both domestic and international wire-lines.

With the offensive plan in motion, Ouilette turned toward the defensive strategy. He initiated an immediate lock-down at Minot. Leaves, tours, VIP visitations—all canceled. Twenty new security teams from the Pentagon's sensitive areas in Nevada were reassigned to the North Dakota air base. He requisitioned a dozen mobile homes for the technical staff and rotated in two companies of marines.

Satellite schedules indicated at least twenty-eight hours remained before Minot could be scanned from orbit. That much time was a gift. Ouilette sourced and scheduled both prefabricated butler buildings and high-density camouflage netting. He finished his list, and after some moments of reflection, signed onto his NSA system through the remote link. Ouilette wondered if the security measures he had personally installed would detect this intrusion. The worm employed by Petersham's system blew through the NSA firewall as if it did not exist. In less than five seconds, most-secret files trickled out onto his screen.

My God! What could you not accomplish with this kind of power. He keyed in two phrases and activated the code word launching *Night Tiger*. The covert program was probably overkill but an ace-in-the-hole never hurt. The shredder routine destroyed the files as they executed. A few seconds later, the screen went blank and an error message displayed.

"System not accessible. Files not found."

Satisfied the destruction of files on his personal workstation at the NSA had continued, Ouilette signed out of the system.

A light knock sounded on the door. When he opened it, a slim brunette, Sheila Wickham waved a sheet of paper at him and said, "A message from Admiral Petersham. I thought you might want it right away."

The admiral had taken the chopper to the Academy where he caught a shuttle to Peterson. His F-15 Eagle should be rolling at this moment. The admiral had jotted some notes, highlighting his concerns as he flew to the Academy. Ouilette had anticipated all save one.

Petersham wanted a fast-mover on standby at Minot for quick transit to Washington once they had the situation at

Minot in hand—meaning getting the XT craft down and secured.

"Thanks. This helps a lot." He closed the door and returned to the workstation where he connected to another system.

Two hours later, Ouilette leaned back into the plush confines of the chair and reviewed the complex strategy he had initiated. Looking for holes, for forgotten elements. There seemed to be few of either.

During this moment of reflection, the monitor changed in hue from scarlet to solid black. A complex glyph grew from a dot to fill the center of the screen. The glyph pixel-faded and was replaced by the word *Genghi*s. Six streams of characters filled the screen, flickering from right to left at tremendous speed.

Ouilette recognized few of the alphanumeric sequences, and most appeared to be gibberish. He leaned forward and steepled his fingers in front of his lips.

What the hell is this?

He could detect neither pattern nor meaning. The entire incident lasted less than two minutes and after the screen cleared of characters, it remained black. Ouilette struck the enter key a couple of times with no response.

He shrugged, stood, and stretched. The XT vehicle should be just about home. Ouilette strode to the door, opened it, and stood face to face with two strangers wearing anxious expressions.

"Who the hell are you?" the foremost asked.

"The name's Ouilette, Captain. Who wants to know?"

"Sorry, sir. I'm Decker, the officer in charge of communication security. I need to see the Admiral. He's in his office?" Decker craned his neck, trying to peer past Ouilette into the darkened room.

Ouilette retreated, flipped on the lights and gestured Decker and the second officer into the room. "I'm afraid you've missed him," he replied. "Maybe I can help."

The second officer said, "I'm Lieutenant Hodragian, sir. We're here to report a serious breach of security. I think we need to speak with the Admiral."

Ouilette turned and sat on the edge of Petersham's desk. "Gentlemen, he has just appointed me to head his security team. So how can I help?"

Decker frowned. "No offense, sir, but it would be nice if we can get him to confirm that."

"Not possible. He's off-site and may not return for days or even weeks. Since this is a security matter, I'd suggest that we deal with it now."

Decker glanced at his assistant and then replied, "We've incurred an unauthorized intrusion, Commander. Our information repositories have been invaded, and we're in the process of implementing a *sweep and compare* that will take hours."

"When did this happen?"

"About ten minutes ago," Hodragian replied. He added, "Commander Ouilette, were you using this workstation by any chance, sir?"

Ouilette plucked Petersham's security card from his pocket and waved it. "I was. I've not yet been assigned an office, so the Admiral lent me his and this card."

"Highly unorthodox, Commander," Decker replied.

"I'd agree, if the circumstances were different. Have you located the source of the intrusion?"

Hodragian replied, "It was a bi-directional assault, sir. From outside, a wireless mobile transmission. Internally, we think it came—"

Decker cut him off. "We are not sure of the internal source yet, sir. Procedure requires that we refrain from offering conjecture until the investigation is concluded."

Hodragian nodded again. "We still need to know, sir, if you saw anything unusual while you were logged in."

"As a matter-of-fact, I did. A high-speed data stream with complex and unreadable characters."

"Would you please power up this workstation, sir?" Hodragian asked.

Ouilette stepped around to face the screen and swiped the card as he had done the first time. In this instance, there was no response. After a moment's delay, he swiped it again. Still nothing.

"I don't get it. This sequence worked the first time."

"If you'll permit me, sir?"

Ouilette passed the card. Hodragian swiped it while depressing the shift and control key together. A stream of characters slowly marched across the screen.

EEPROM ERASED…REPROGRAM EEPROM

"What does that mean?" Ouilette asked.

Hodragian glanced up from the scrolling stream. "This workstation's data files have been destroyed. I'll need access to this system for the investigation, sir."

Ouilette retrieved and pocketed the card. "I'm departing for another site tonight. I'll leave this card with the Admiral's secretary. I assume you know her." With Decker's nod, he continued, "Enter your request by the book and I'm sure she'll cooperate."

Over western North Dakota

The final leg. Baylor flexed his back muscles and rotated his head to loosen the kinks in his neck. Minot's control tower finished relaying their instructions, so he toggled his tactical comm switch and replied, "Roger, approach control. Descend to 8000, speed 350. Advise when crossing the next highway." He switched back to inter-plane.

"Linneow, we must discuss the landing. Tell me about your speed and angle requirements."

"Linneow needs only a barrier to deflect exhaust."

Baylor considered a moment before replying, "I don't think there are barriers at Minot. Only aprons."

"Not know word aprons."

"An open field, covered with reinforced concrete for heavy aircraft."

"Acceptable. Sikt should not land near other craft. Exhaust temperature…too high."

When his aircraft slipped over the highway, Baylor toggled his comm unit again. "Approach Control, Watchdog is crossing the highway."

"Acknowledged. Turn to zero-zero-five, descend to 2000. Maintain speed. Advise when you have the runway on visual."

"Roger. Oh-oh-five, level two." Baylor toggled back to inter-plane. "Linneow, you should land first. As soon as you're down, I'll join you."

"Linneow complies." She hesitated and then added, "Pilot Ed, will America imprison Linneow for the death of Pilot Grayfin?"

"No way!" The full ramifications of what was happening began to emerge. Would the U.S. Military let a highly advanced, extra-terrestrial craft drop off a sick human and fly away? *Not a chance.*

"Linneow, our people will need to talk with you. They'll want to know everything about you and where you come from. They'll want to know why you're here. They may not wish for you to leave until they know all of these things."

"Linneow can stay twenty-four Earth days. Dangerous to remain longer."

"Dangerous? What...oops, hold a minute." Baylor switched back to the tower. "Approach Control, Watchdog. I've visual on the runway. Be advised that the... the craft I'm escorting should land first. Direct us to a vacant pad, well away from buildings or other aircraft."

"Roger, Watchdog. Standby."

A few seconds passed.

"Watchdog, an active taxiway intersects the runway at its midpoint with a thirty-degree left turn. At the end of the taxiway is a vacant alert pad large enough for several heavy bombers. We'll send medical and rescue teams in advance."

"Negative on the advance teams, Approach Control. The exhaust of the visitor is..." *How the hell do I say this?* He re-engaged his comm. "Just wait until we're down and cool. Copy?"

A second voice broke in. "Approach Control, Queen's Rook entering the pattern at level eight and thirty clicks out. Whatever Watchdog needs, he's got it."

"Acknowledged, Queen's Rook. Watchdog, Approach Control, the pattern is clear. Advise when you're down and cool."

Who the hell was that? Baylor switched back to inter-plane. "Linneow, we've been given clearance. I'll bank over the apron they want us to use. If it's suitable, begin your landing."

"Linneow complies."

Baylor cut his power to thirty percent. He *dirtied* up the F-27 with flaps and landing gear. The Black Widow flashed over the end of the runway as it dropped to within three hundred feet of the tarmac. Baylor banked at the intersection and flew above the active taxiway. At the far end, he could see the apron. When he scanned both sides of the runway, hundreds of people streamed out of every building around the edges of the field. "Linneow, if you're ready, let's land now."

"Linneow complies."

Baylor banked sharply over the apron and turned back toward the slowing Sikt. The heavy, black craft had descended until it was ten meters from the taxiway surface. Its speed had dropped to less than fifty knots. As Baylor turned another one-eighty, approaching the Sikt from behind, two long runners deployed from each of the hatches that he had guessed contained landing gear. Like a helicopter! Skids make more sense than wheels.

"Apron is acceptable, Pilot Ed. Land soon?"

"You bet!" Baylor retarded his throttles and the Black Widow sank into ground effect, flared, and touched down. He popped the drogues to scrub velocity before he turned up the taxiway. The aircraft's speed tapered to eighty knots then slowed further as he approached the apron.

The Sikt had grounded directly in the middle of the concrete expanse.

Despite his previous inspection, the flexibility of the extra-terrestrial airframe amazed him. Its double-jointed neck had articulated, drooping from the fuselage. The forward joint reversed the angle so that the *goose-head* was parallel with and resting upon the concrete surface. Clouds of superheated dust and vapor rose from the apron around the craft. Baylor taxied his F-27 to within fifty meters and shut down both engines.

With no chocks for the wheels, he set the brakes electrically and hoped the battery was up to the task. He raised the canopy and clambered over the sill. When his left foot found the first toehold, a ladder automatically extended. In seconds, he was standing on the ground. He doffed his helmet and placed it on the pavement beside the Black Widow's nose-gear.

Time to make history, Eduardo. Baylor desperately tried to think of some enduring aphorism like "One small step for a man..." but nothing would come. He took several paces toward the Sikt and stopped twenty meters away. The heat radiating from the surrounding pavement denied a closer approach.

The high-pitched whine of jet engines drew him around. An F-15E Strike Eagle taxied onto the pad and parked next to his fighter. Its left engine shut down and the canopy opened. A stocky-framed man in a flight-suit with no insignia clambered out of the rear cockpit, descended to the pavement and approached.

Baylor extended his hand. "Queen's Rook?"

"'Fraid not. That's the Air Force call sign for the driver. I'm Petersham."

"Admiral Petersham?"

"The same." Petersham released Baylor's hand. He peered at the immense alien craft as he continued, "Heck of a job up there today, Commander. Have you learned much about our visitor?"

"A drop in the bucket, sir. Some folks are going to be busy."

Petersham glanced at Baylor. "No doubt. Anyone in particular?"

Baylor did not take his eyes from the Sikt. "Historians. I have a feeling that much of what they've written is wrong."

"Enlighten me, Commander?"

Baylor wrenched his eyes from the Sikt to meet Petersham's challenge. "Admiral, she's on a mission. And she's been at it for seventy million years."

Petersham's only reaction was a quick blink. After several seconds, he glanced back toward the Sikt. "Imagine that."

A screeching hiss accompanied an electrical whine and the upper half of the goose-head cracked away from its base. Hinged at the rear, it revealed two helmeted heads, one behind the other. The forward head swiveled toward them. No tentacles, or segmented chitinous appendages, but what was definitely an arm reached up and touched the helmet.

Both Petersham and Baylor immediately snapped a salute in reply. Petersham said, "Now that's encouraging."

The visitor reached over her head, grasped the edge of the canopy and lifted herself out of the cockpit. A moment later, she stood on the pavement.

"Jehoshaphat!" Baylor muttered.

"Affirmative!" Petersham replied.

The being facing them stood about five and a half feet in height. She was bipedal with two slim, short arms and a diminutive waistline. More than half her height was in her legs. The fact she was female would have been an inescapable conclusion for any human male. Her light gray, seamless flight-suit conformed to an hourglass figure that was almost a caricature of the human feminine form.

Baylor whispered out of the corner of his mouth, "I surrender."

Petersham chuckled.

When Linneow turned away and attended the figure in the rear of the Sikt's cockpit, Baylor started forward. "I think she could use some help."

"If you make contact, Commander, you'll be quarantined for an indefinite period." Petersham turned to the F-15, put his fist to his cheek to simulate a phone call then circled his hand over his head. The F-15 pilot nodded.

Baylor replied, "I'll take that chance, sir."

"One of us should and I can't afford to," Petersham said.

Baylor had nearly crossed the distance when Linneow turned toward him. In her arms, she carried a human male. Baylor hesitated, struck by the incongruity of the image. A relatively small and lightly built creature handling with ease a bulky form that probably out-massed her two to one.

He increased his pace. "Mister Weber, I presume."

Although muffled by her helmet, her voice sounded little different from the conversation over the airwaves. "My first American friend. Of America, and your language, I learned from him." Linneow passed Weber to Baylor who staggered under the load.

"Lord! He weighs a ton! Baylor hobbled twenty paces from the Sikt before he lowered Weber to the pavement and removed his helmet. He discovered a dark haired man in his early forties whose pale complexion was bathed in sweat. Baylor touched Weber's brow and felt for a pulse at his throat. "He's burning up with fever and his pulse is fast and weak." In the distance, sirens grew ever louder. "Fortunately, here come the medics."

Baylor turned back toward Linneow and received a second shock. She had removed her helmet.

He stood transfixed. So this is the Chao! Her slender neck supported a large head dominated by two huge almond-shaped, amber eyes. Conical half-shells that could only be ears branched from either side of the top of her skull. Tuffs of the golden fur that covered her face, neck, and head, rendered these delicate, mobile ears similar to those of a lynx.

Baylor wrested his gaze from the captivating eyes. High cheekbones, and fine-boned brows. A full mane, like a lion, with amber fur tipped with russet hues. A delicate heart-shaped face, a small triangular nose, and the canines of a carnivore.

Most striking of all—a familiar but elusive spicy scent that made him realize he hadn't eaten since yesterday.

Linneow breathed, "Pilot Ed finds the Chao repulsive?"

"Not hardly."

With a roar of engines, several dozen vehicles charged onto the apron. They encircled the three aircraft in the inverse manner of a wagon train entrapping the Indians. Baylor was not surprised to see marines leap from several vehicles. The troops hastily erected a perimeter over a hundred meters beyond the trucks. Two medical vans, with huge red crosses emblazoned upon their sides, nosed forward toward the Sikt. When they stopped, a dozen specialists in grade five bio-suits emerged and approached. One led several others directly toward Baylor and Linneow.

"Commander Baylor, Visitor Linneow, I'm Doctor Richard Weiss. I've been charged with medical sciences during contact. These vehicles will transport both you and Mister Weber to the labs we've prepared. In order to avoid the consequences of bio-contamination, I need the two of you to step into the van on the right. We'll be moving Weber in the second one."

Linneow motioned toward Weiss. "Weiss is a life-sciences engineer?"

"A what?"

"Sorry. Linneow means physician?"

"Yes, ma'am. Specializing in microbiology."

Linneow inclined her head. "Weber says tetanus."

"That one we can handle." Weiss passed the information to two of his assistants as they carried Weber toward the second van. Linneow fixed her immense eyes upon Weiss.

"Save Weber's life. It is important to America, to your world and to me."

"Yes, ma'am. We'll take care of him. Are you ready to come with us?"

"Soon." Linneow turned back toward her Sikt with a graceful but unnatural gait that seemed odd until Baylor identified the reason. She powered her stride from her ankles, a second joint that articulated in opposition to her knees. After a moment, Baylor realized it equated to the human heel. The Chao stood and walked on their toes.

When Linneow reached her craft, she opened an access panel in the fuselage behind the left nacelle and removed two small devices. She backed away from the Sikt and lifted one to her mouth. Baylor could not hear a reply and wondered to whom or what she was communicating.

Immediately, the upper half of the cockpit began to descend. In the seconds before it closed, Linneow scooped both helmets, hers and Weber's, from the concrete and tossed them inside. Baylor could hear the latch cycle with a whine and a thump. She clipped the retrieved devices to the collar of her flight-suit and returned.

"Linneow is ready."

Baylor swept an arm before him and toward the medical van.

"Age before beau...er...I'll follow you."

Chapter Six
11:20 CDT, 7 May, Minot AFB, ND

Ouilette paused in the doorway of Weber's room at the base infirmary. "For an old coot, you're hard to kill," he said. Dressed in his khaki service uniform, he took a seat on a corner at the foot of the bed.

Weber closed the report he had been reading and placed it on the side table. "I might take umbrage at that appellation if I wasn't so glad to be here. You turn up in the darndest places, Marcus. This thing," he tapped the report with a forefinger, "says that you're head of security here. What about our gig at NSA?"

"Ancient history, Sam. Ever since you popped out of a Peruvian grave and zipped home in an extra-terrestrial craft. Changes everything, as you might well guess. Anybody ever mention that your methods tend toward the sublime?"

"Not in those words." Weber nodded toward the report and added, "Far as I can tell from reading this thing, that Wozniak fellow got a hell of a lot right. Not bad for mostly conjecture and unsupported conclusion...his words. You should keep him around."

Ouilette smiled and said, "Not my decision...but I think Petersham has that in mind."

"Your old boss? He's running the show?"

"That's why I'm here...and why you're here also. Right in the center of it all...as usual."

Weber sighed. "Can't say it was by choice." He glanced up at his friend. "You hear from Barbara?"

"Oh, yeah. More than once. A lot more."

"I can imagine."

"About five months ago, she called with a new address to send your paychecks. Security procedure meant we had to...well, you know the drill. She set up house with her dentist friend in Libertyville. I believe she's going to have a baby in a few months."

Weber glanced away. "Bully for her. She file yet?"

"Seems like that's not part of her plan. She wanted me to list you as KIA so she could access your pension. Had a lawyer working on it, and that guy's been a pain in the butt. I suspect you've saved me a lot of grief now."

"You're welcome."

Ouilette laughed. "How did you ever hook up with a Canadian, Sam?"

Weber's steel-gray eyes focused on Ouilette. "Your fault, you old coot!"

Ouilette laughed again. Weber's forty-one years and his thirty-six might indeed make them ancient relics in their chosen field. In truth, departure from intelligence work, both analysis and operations had become a consideration after Weber went missing. This new event did indeed change everything. "My fault?"

"That forced medical leave after the Guatemalan affair a few years back."

Ouilette snorted. "Sam, we took four bullets and a dozen fragments out of you. You were out of the game until you recovered. How's that make it my fault?"

"Got tired of laying around Eureka so I drove up north. Met her at a shindig at the Calgary Stampede. Suborned by a pretty face, I guess." He laughed and added, "Truth is, I thought we were on the same page as far as my job was concerned, but I guess she expected something else...like maybe I would quit and raise a family."

Ouilette shrugged. "Lot to be said for that. What we do is not work for a family man."

"Ancient history, Marcus. No kids, so I should've cut my losses years ago and saved us both a bunch of grief. You read my report?"

Ouilette shifted position at the change of subject. Weber was not a man to dwell long on personal affairs and that time was now over. "Somewhat sparse for eight months in the field," he replied. "If you were wounded two months ago and the infection set in a week later, how come you're still among the living?"

"Sayla called it a stasis cell. That's Linneow's given name, but you folks should refrain from using that. Chao customs and all."

"Got that." Ouilette crossed his arms, resting his chin on one curled up fist. "What happened after the failed extraction?"

"A mighty long story, amigo."

"Humor me. How did you meet her?"

Weber leaned back against the headboard and stared at the ceiling. "That came later. Started our egress in the chopper, but it took a missile. When it came apart in the trees, I figured I might be cashing in. But, we just hung in the limbs, two dead men and me."

"You climbed down," Ouilette guessed.

"Spent the rest of the daylight hours burying Kaminski and the chopper pilot. I still don't know his name—black mission and no tags."

"Eric Jorgenson. Married, two kids."

"Sonofabitch," Weber murmured. "Like you said...wrong line of work for married folks." He continued. "Well, nine weeks later, I was eating bugs and leaves. Things starting to look grim. Walking out in that country isn't for the faint of heart. Wasn't much later I found a cave, a monster hole in the ground. Ten feet inside, the walls were smooth and symmetrical. Two hundred paces in, it was pitch-black and me without a light. A dozen thick cables running along the floor of the shaft. Someone was piping serious power into this place."

"I'll be damned," Ouilette whispered. "What did you think?"

"Figured it had to be another clandestine lab. Still had seven or eight pounds of C7 left in my pack, so I scouted the area and then laid low for a few weeks to see what developed."

"Above and beyond, Sam."

"Yeah. Eventually, patience ran out and I decided to force the issue by packing half a pound of C7 around a couple of the cables."

"Had to gain someone's attention," Ouilette offered.

"Folks came running, but not from the direction of the cave. Damned cartel patrol evidently detected the detonation."

"Out of the frying pan and into the fire. Must be your motto."

"It gets better. About a dozen shooters came into the bush after me. I worked around their flank and back toward the cave entrance before nightfall. The next morning, I awoke to gunfire. Sporadic shooting to the east and later, to the north."

"Wouldn't it have been smarter to get out, Sam? Let us know what you'd found?"

Weber shifted to meet Ouilette's gaze. "No food, no comm gear, one gun, nine bullets. I wanted to blow that lab. To even the score for Kam's death, the loss of the chopper and crew."

Ouilette slowly shook his head. "I don't know how you made it."

"Hadn't counted on help. Twenty minutes later, I found the first bodies. Necks broken. Weapons empty and expended cases all around. Fifty yards away, I found two more.

"Half hour later, three of them. Two had their throats ripped out. Clawed clear back to the spine, Marcus. Gave me the willies. A minute later, two men burst out of the growth. They were running right at me, paying more attention to their back-trail than where they were going. We all got into a gunfight and those boys lost."

Ouilette chuckled and shook his head. Weber continued.

"Shooting draws crowds, so I left the trail and moved into deep cover. The lab was still my target. I moved south and found a shallow gully. The angle of the mountain face told me I was approaching the entrance. With two hundred paces to go, I started to climb out of the gully when the scent hit me...apple pie!"

Ouilette laughed. "Deep hunger has some unusual side effects."

"It was no illusion. Cinnamon! I turned around, lost my footing, and fell on my ass. Something launched out of the brush, inhumanly quick. I rolled with the fall, turned and drew my pistol in the same move.

"We stood facing each other, but I didn't know what I was looking at. She was butt-naked, wearing nothing but the fur on her back. She stood as if waiting for me to make a decision. When I holstered the pistol, she relaxed and said, *Quitase Usted! Ahorita!* Spanish, and with perfect inflection."

"Which means?"

"Get out of here! Right now! I thought I was losing it, Marcus. I'm up to my neck in bad boys and this fur-covered *something* is telling me to get lost in Spanish."

"What happened next, Sam?"

"She vanished in the bush. I wanted that lab, but I didn't want to run into this cat creature in the dark. I figured I'd hole up for the night and have another go at the lab in the morning. "The next day, an old Havoc roars over the ridge. I had a sinking feeling that reinforcements just arrived. The chopper had door gunners but no troops. An officer climbed out and bent to inspect the cables. He beckoned one of his gunners to get out and enter the cave.

"Before the troop could oblige him, a squad started down the opposite slope. The rearmost went down with a scream. The others sprayed the side of the hill.

"The Havoc lifted just as the last two shooters limped into the ravine. The chopper must have had an infrared detector because they zeroed on the Chao pretty quick.

"Those boys on the ground never saw me coming and I dropped them pronto. Retrieved one of their weapons and sprayed the Havoc as it passed overhead. Smoke poured from the exhausts as it swung around and headed straight for me. I aimed for the pilot's windscreen and cut loose. When the slide locked back on empty, I figured it was *adios*."

"That's where you picked up all the metal?"

"Damn straight. The chopper exploded. I couldn't get clear and part of the damn thing fell on me. Lights out.

"From that point...well...imagine waking up in an interstellar cruiser as big as a battleship that had been buried underground for millions of years. Imagine you're lying on a pedestal with something digging into your backside while being fully conscious and without a trace of pain. The Chao stood beside me and now she was clothed. When she realized I was awake she asked if I spoke Spanish."

I told her my English was better. She asked me if I was an Englishman. Marcus, she had never heard of America. She had come out of stasis when I blew up the power conduits. She figured the drug czar's force was the enemy who tried to wreck her power plant and so she launched a counterattack."

"Naked and unarmed?"

"Well, she made hay even so. I learned later she was surprised by our level of technology. The last time she was out, we fought with edged weapons and rode horses."

"When was this?"

"The rest of this story is a doozie and that part is not in my report."

"Why not?"

"Have you debriefed Linneow?"

"That begins in twenty minutes. The medical team found no trace of bio-threat. They cannot ascertain the risk to her."

"The risk for her is chemical in nature."

"How so?"

"She'll tell you in the briefing. Anyway, the last time the Chao played a hand was in England a thousand years ago. Her side won and she hopped back into stasis."

"She must have expected some advancement in the interval."

"Look at history, Marcus. Sayla had been jumping forward in four, five and six century leaps. Each time she comes out, we ride horses and fight with edged weapons. She helped the Arabs, the Romans, the Greeks, the Macedonians, the Egyptians, the Assyrians, the Sumerians, and who knows else before that. In six thousand years, not a lot had changed."

Ouilette scratched his neck. "Come to think of it, what we call the Renaissance was a damn peculiar spurt."

"Hold on to your hat, amigo. Sayla attributes it to cumulative effect over the millennia."

"Effect of what?"

"Genetic engineering. Human husbandry. Supported by the Chao-Vithra alliance on behalf of the human race."

Ouilette stood and paced to the end of the room. He turned. "I get the general picture, Sam, and I can't say I like it."

"It doesn't get better. They have an opponent in this struggle and the alliance looks to us as a future resource. That's why she popped me into stasis...so she could catch up on developments over the last ten centuries. We're in it up to our necks already."

"I like that even less. Why get mixed up in someone else's conflict? Maybe we should be talking with the other side."

"The other side wants us dead. They've been here before and Linneow believes we sent an invitation to come again."

"What the hell does that mean?"

The door to the room burst open and in strode a tall, middle-aged nurse pushing a cart. Ouilette guessed her brisk manner, bright smile and lustrous eyes meant Weber's magic had been restored.

She maneuvered the cart alongside his bed. "Lunchtime, Sam. How are you feeling today?"

"Top of the world, darlin'. 'Specially when you come calling." Weber quickly passed the report to Ouilette, who folded it and thrust it into a hip pocket.

She patted his arm and hung a bag of colorless solution on a pole beside the bed. Glancing at Ouilette, she sniffed and said, "Who's courting whom? And if I gave a hint of interest, this hospital would witness the most miraculous recovery known to mankind."

"You might be surprised, sweetheart. What are you feeding me today?"

"Last of the antibiotics and then a real lunch–turkey on rye and a milkshake."

"What's the occasion?"

Her expression turned dour. "They're kicking out my favorite patient because he won't pay the rent."

"And here I thought I was getting by on my good looks." He patted her rump when she bent for the tray. "You been holding out on me, Molly darlin?"

She set the tray down hard and straightened, hands on her hips. "Mister Weber! Behave yourself, you hear me?" The expression of disapproval never reached her eyes.

Ouilette checked his watch and moved to the foot of the bed. "Sam, about that invitation…."

Weber shook his head minutely as the nurse turned toward the window and drew the blinds. Over her shoulder she said, "It's nice outside today. Would you like some fresh air?"

Ouilette lifted his wrist and tapped his watch.

"Tell you what, Darlin'," Weber drawled. "My boss has a pressing engagement. How 'bout you come back in a few and tell me more about Tennessee?"

She swept toward the door, winked and said, "It will be a pleasure, *Darling*."

When the door closed, Ouilette shook his head and said, "Some things never change."

"It's been nine months, amigo. What if I lost my touch?"

"We wouldn't want that, I guess. About this invitation…"

"The opposition are folks called the Oo'ahan. They placed sensors to detect electromagnetic emanations. The Chao swept the system, but she says the alliance can never find them all. Especially out beyond the Oort cloud. When a civilization reaches the point where it can broadcast radio waves or detonate a nuclear device, it sends a calling card to the Oo'ahan to come and rectify the situation."

"Good God, Sam, we started down that path over a century ago. Where are these Oo'ahan? Can we believe the Chao?"

"Your boss will have to decide that one."

"Petersham left this morning for Omaha," Ouilette explained. "He'll be traveling to Washington to brief the President, but he doesn't have any of this stuff."

"Just as well, don't you think?"

"I don't know what to think. When did the Oo'ahan visit us last?"

"Well..." Weber began, "what we're sure of is this. The Chao-Vithri alliance lost a major contest in this system. They had established a fortress on a moon called Tassone to serve as a base of operations, which existed for almost five million years before the Oo'ahan turned it into rubble. Those bad boys bombarded Earth at the same time. The alliance managed to destroy the assault force before this planet suffered the same fate. Got the dinosaurs though. The Chao says they used small moons from Jupiter as bombs launched toward Earth. The alliance had to hit them hard and often and a few chunks got through. That's how they took out Tassone."

Ouilette let out a long, low whistle. "These folks play in a different league. I fail to see how we could help or hinder either side."

Weber replied, "The Chao were once like us, Marcus. Single-planet ground dwellers. They had only one war in their entire history. The arrival of the Vithri ended that conflict. There's a lot I left out of my report."

Ouilette approached and sat on the edge of Weber's bed again. "Why not tell it all?"

Weber locked eyes with his former commander. "There's some nasty shit coming our way. Certain measures need to be taken. Strong, eleventh-hour measures."

"Already done, Sam."

Weber snorted. "You started it already? How'd you know?"

"Just a hunch. Three days ago."

"They'll need me, you know."

"Probably...but not for a while. Your profile is too high at the moment. I'll send you under when the time comes."

Ouilette left the medical ward and dropped two levels into the administrative center. His mind aboil from the session with Weber, he failed to notice a large ambulant figure approaching from the opposite direction.

"Collision alert, Commander! You're off course."

Ouilette glanced up and veered. "Sorry, Doctor Wozniak. Off course? The briefing isn't scheduled for the amphitheater?"

"Oh, but it is! You passed the entrance thirty paces back."

Ouilette sighed and turned. "Too much on my mind." At the entrance, he said, "Why do you scientific types need a military officer for this session?"

Wozniak reached for the door handle but hesitated. "Everyone in the next room has a specialty. Each will cast a particular slant on what we're about to learn. None will agree on direction. That's your job. All of us trust that someone on high will see the total picture and make a decision. I hope you're up to it, Commander."

Ouilette slapped Wozniak on the back. "So do I, Doctor. So do I."

They entered together. As Ouilette marched down the center aisle and climbed the steps to the stage, ideas flitted through his mind. One in particular stood forward. Given what he had learned from Sam Weber, they must avoid endless technical trivia before the real message became clear.

He approached the podium, stood behind its imposing bulk and tapped the microphone. Two loud thumps filled the spacious room. He placed Sam's report on the podium and straightened his tie.

"Good Afternoon. Some of you know me, some not. For the ignorant, I'm Marcus Ouilette, human, from planet Earth."

After a few chuckles from the audience, he continued. "Titles and positions are less important today as all of us here are collectively the human organism. We must now reach beyond our experience, and must for this challenge, overcome physical differences, emotional or cultural nuances, psychological and intellectual dissimilarities.

"Some of you will be our eyes. Others, our ears. Some will smell, taste or touch. Others will calculate and analyze. Like all organisms, we have a goal, which begets a strategy, which requires objectives. Each of you have different tasks but keep in mind the goal requires every objective be pursued...and met.

"I'm the goal-keeper."

Again more laughs.

"I won't keep score, but everything must move in a common direction."

At that moment, the Chao entered the far right wing of the stage. Ouilette turned toward her and added, "Humanity is poised on a new threshold and it's time to climb out of the cradle. It's time to establish an enduring relationship with the Chao-Vithri alliance. Please welcome the Chao ambassador to Earth, the honorable S. Linneow."

Ouilette extended his left arm toward Linneow and she took the stage to a standing ovation. Still wearing her silvered flight-suit, she moved with fluid grace and a mesmerizing stride. His gaze lingered involuntarily on her torso and hips as she approached, and he banished a sensation of guilt only with the rationalization that she would be unaware of human non-verbal cues.

He covered the microphone with his right hand when she stood close to him. "Welcome, Linneow."

Her eyes remained fixed on his. "Ouilette finds the Chao attractive. We are much alike, yes?"

Caught looking, Marcus. Embarrassed, he laughed lightly, guilty of having forgotten about her seventy million years on earth.

She tilted her head toward the audience. "They honor me?"

"They do," he replied, grateful for the change of subject.

"Ouilette takes risks, I think. Can he speak for all of Earth, or even all of America?"

He laughed again. "No. But, it's important we start with the right point of view."

Linneow inclined her head. "I think Ouilette also honors me. My brother has spoken highly of his commander. I am pleasured, now, to know the reasons for his opinion."

As the applause died away, and members of the audience took their seats, Ouilette bowed and replied, "Honor for honor, Madam Ambassador. Your mastery of our language is astounding."

Linneow touched an object clipped to the collar of her tunic. "An intelligent device has learned the language of America. To me, it teaches subliminally in times of rest. Today, I think, will still present a challenge, yes?"

Ouilette agreed. "I'll be in the back if you need me." He withdrew and found a seat alongside Wozniak in the last row.

Linneow leaned close to the microphone. Her amplified voice, low, sibilant and husky, silenced the room. "I would start with questions you must surely have. A good idea, yes?"

About two score voices agreed and at least as many hands were raised. Finally, everybody stood, each with several questions. She leaned toward the microphone again.

"This is a test for a Chao, yes? To demonstrate that Linneow can think like a human...like an American human. So in America, when many humans wish a single resource, by what method is the first chosen?"

Someone in the audience shouted, "We form a line."

Linneow inclined her head. "This American custom is sound, I think. It is logical. First in line is first to come." She swept her arm toward the front row. "Or most brave. Each has equal merit, yes?"

A smattering of applause grew to a crescendo. She waited until it died, then continued, "We will try an American plan. I would start in the first row on this side and work across. One question to each. Each row that follows is the same until we begin again. How is Linneow's first American plan?"

The room erupted in applause and Wozniak leaned close. "She's a natural."

A good start, Ouilette agreed, on a long and rocky road. In spite of the new information being revealed in this session, Weber's disclosure gave him no peace. After several minutes, he leaned closer to Wozniak, who was scribbling shorthand notes on a tablet, evidently jotting down Linneow's answers to various questions.

"Forgive the intrusion, Doctor," he said, "but there's some things beyond all this I should know more about."

Wozniak paused, shifted his glasses on his nose and peered at Ouilette. "Of course." He leaned forward, toward the row ahead and tapped one of his colleagues on his shoulder. "Take notes for me, will you Barry?" When the other agreed, Wozniak passed forward his notebook and gestured toward the exit. "Let's find a quiet spot."

The two men made their way to the base cafeteria, where Wozniak selected a pastry, an apple and a waxed paper cup, which he filled with raspberry tea. Ouilette procured a cup of black coffee. They found a table in a corner near the windows facing the flight-line and took seats opposite one another.

Wozniak studied the naval officer for a few seconds, noting the intelligent blue eyes, the square jaw-line and broad forehead. Champenois, he had said, which probably meant Norman influence, and possibly a Danish heritage, which fit the facial construction and sandy hair. Unlike Petersham, whose aura of command prompted immediate respect, or Pigott, who demanded that whether he deserved it or not, Ouilette's persona seemed understated and reserved. A thinking man, then, and in Wozniak's experience, somewhat of a rarity in mid-grade military officers.

"What's on your mind?" he asked.

"You mentioned earlier," Ouilette began, "that you were analyzing social events on a macro scale...a planetary scale, I believe you said."

"Indeed."

"Was this your line of work at Los Alamos?"

"Not at all. I'm a physicist at heart and by training. An astrophysicist by preference. My true calling takes me to the heart of the cosmos...when I can find a suitable project, that is."

"How long have you been there...at Los Alamos?"

"In the Theoretical Division? Eight years. On the campus, eleven...ever since I left M.I.T."

"What does the Theoretical Division do, exactly?"

"Ah...what not?" Wozniak leaned forward. "Whatever is difficult, we do. Theoretical science and physics, applied mathematics, chemistry, biology, and engineering...from fundamental issues to complex systems in both basic research and application."

"Social science was not on that list."

"Indeed not. It began as a little distraction...," Wozniak motioned to the side with one hand, "a bit of a detour, I guess. Once I began my research, it became more interesting than that."

Ouilette considered the man across the table. Physical appearance aside, there seemed to be a formidable intellect residing behind the deep brown eyes. Many people associated obesity with slovenly habits, but Ouilette was inclined to discard such casual surface assumptions. The fact that the scientist had recognized an in-depth conversation might be necessary gave evidence of an ordered mind and deep intellectual curiosity. "The name Wozniak is Polish."

"Babie Doly. Third generation." At Ouilette's perplexed and somewhat amused expression, Wozniak laughed and added, "Strikes most people that way. It's a small village north of Gdynia, right on the Baltic Sea. Never been there of course, but my great grandparents came over to America just before World War Two. I'm the last of that branch of the family, and you might say the culmination of all their efforts in America."

"Meaning what?" Ouilette said with a frown.

"Meaning that the degree of education invested in me represents most of what they acquired in America. Oh, I've done well enough since the fellowships at Cal Tech, but before then...well, there wasn't much left to go around."

"Brothers and sisters?"

"None. A couple of cousins, but we're not very close. How about you? Large family?"

"Two sisters," Ouilette replied. "Both older and both married. I've five nephews and nieces with more on the way."

"In Virginia?"

"San Diego. My dad was navy also. It's were I went through my SEAL training."

"You're a SEAL?" Wozniak's raised eyebrows imparted a sense of surprise.

"Was. That was before the NSA and before my most recent...ah...responsibility."

"Meaning the containment of the problems facing humanity around the world?"

Ouilette chuckled. "That might be overstating it a little. Seemed more like band-aids to me."

"And that's probably understating it, Commander. SEALS are elite people, I'm told."

Ouilette laughed this time. "We probably rank below the Theoretical Division, though."

Wozniak bowed his head. "Thank you for that. Not many in your line of work hold such respect for what I do...especially when it comes to hypotheses concerning social sciences. I've not been able to arouse the slightest interest in the conclusions I've been developing."

"Until now."

"A remarkable exception," Wozniak replied. "That alone tells me you may have some access to knowledge I lack."

"What prompted your interest in the social sciences direction, if I may ask?"

"Ockham's razor."

"Come again?"

Wozniak sighed. "Too many bad things were happening to too many diverse peoples. I wanted to test what was then a rather dubious hypothesis as to the source of all the trouble."

"What about the razor?"

"From a Franciscan friar of the same name, then expressed in Latin as *Lex parsimoniae*, or the law of parsimony. Among competing hypotheses, that with the least assumptions wins. Trouble was, I couldn't accept that one back then."

"Why not?"

"It seemed to indicate an off-world influence as the source for all the problems."

Ouilette sat back in his seat, surprised.

"Thought it might strike you that way," Wozniak added. "So...quid pro quo, Commander. What do you know?"

Ouilette drew a deep breath. "There's evidence to support that hypothesis, I'm afraid. I'm not sure about what to do next."

"I am."

"Enlighten me, Doctor. Please."

Wozniak mimicked his companion's posture. Then he shrugged. "What every good scientist does, my friend. We make some predictions. Should they bear fruit, we move to the next level."

Ouilette lifted one eyebrow. "Predictions?"

"I'll make one," Wozniak said. "Soon, very soon, things will take a turn for the worse."

"Why should they?"

"Because our antagonist must believe we're on to him...or them...or it." The scientist heaved his bulk from his chair and stood. "I should get back."

Seemingly distracted by other considerations, Ouilette only nodded and murmured, "Later then, Doctor. I'm sure we'll talk more on this."

After Wozniak departed, he turned his chair to face the exterior windows. Dark clouds and a wall of rain raced toward him from across the prairie landscape, soon eclipsing distant hills, closer trees and then the perimeter buildings to the east of the base. Minutes later, rain pelted concrete and window alike with a snapping hiss, rendering everything beyond fifty meters invisible.

Something disturbed him, but he could not quite quantify what it was. Peterson had mentioned Baylor's statement. A mission, the flyer had called it. Of seventy million years' duration. Weber said something about genetic engineering and human husbandry and how their visitor had been influencing the past. For seventy million years? Seemed such a prodigious investment. To what purpose? Why begin so long ago? Something here remained hidden. Something important, but he had not the knowledge to identify what.

Chapter Seven
09:16 EDT, 8 May
Outside Reagan International Airport, Washington, DC

A pale yellow dump truck, rust burgeoning from cancerous scabs all over its heavy body, sat alongside a curb not far from the airport exit, with two large men seemingly jammed together inside the narrow cab. The driver, a sallow-skinned, lanky man in his early forties, fidgeted with his lighter, unsuccessfully trying to ignite a mangled cigarette dangling from his lips. Across the cab, his partner peered through the bug splattered and dusty windshield with a pair of binoculars. Both men wore dark overcoats; the one with the field glasses, a gray fedora as well.

The driver finally managed to coax flame from the nearly empty Bic. He dragged heartily on his cigarette and expelled a plume of smoke into the sweltering confines of the cab. His partner coughed, waved his hand in front of his face and groaned, "For God's sake, roll down the window, will you?"

The driver turned toward him, belligerence building in his eyes. "Roll down yours if you don't like it."

The man with the fedora lowered his glasses. He turned to look at his partner, an exasperated expression on his face. "What's with you?"

"Shut up and watch the road."

The second man's face tightened with anger but he did not reply. After a moment, he raised his glasses again. His anger evaporated and he sat forward suddenly. "Got him! It's the Blazer."

"'Bout damn time." The driver twisted the key with his gloved hand. The road-weary truck shook itself to life, spewing an oily cloud curbside. The driver jammed the shifter into low range and eased out the clutch, spinning the wheel to negotiate a U-turn across the highway. He slammed the heel of his hand into the hub, his curse synchronized with the horn as an impatient motorist tried to cut him off. Dribbling bits of rust and debris, the truck swung neatly into line behind the Blazer.

"Are you sure it's the right dude?" the driver asked.

"I got a good look as he passed. It's the right vehicle too. The plates match."

"Okay, let's do it."

The passenger shook his head as he dug into the pocket of his coat. He retrieved the transmitter as he spoke. "Not yet. Wait 'til we hit a red light. Don't let anybody get between us and him."

"I know my part," the driver snarled.

Fortune rode with the Blazer for the first three lights, but dissipated at the fourth. The light turned yellow and the white 4x4 slowed to a stop.

The driver of the aging city vehicle did not slow. He mashed his foot down on the accelerator instead. His partner placed his thumb over the button on the transmitter. Simultaneously with the impact, he pushed downward.

The rear end of the blazer folded like an accordion. Glass blew out of the rear quarter panels as the heavy truck propelled the smaller vehicle into the intersection.

Beneath the Blazer, a tiny receiver decoded a string of radio pulses. Satisfied with the result, it closed a relay, igniting a shaped charge that ripped a six-inch hole in the Blazer's gas tank and churned most of the contents into a fine mist. Thirty milliseconds later fourteen gallons of vaporized gasoline detonated.

The Blazer turned a half somersault in place. It smashed down on its roof, engulfed in flame. The lone occupant made no effort to escape. Both men in the dump truck threw open the doors and fled the raging pyre in the center of the street.

08:29 CDT, Minot AFB, North Dakota

Baylor wrenched open the door to his quarters to find Ouilette immediately outside with his hand lifted to knock. "Good morning, sir!" he boomed.

"Good morning yourself. You seem in high spirits." Ouilette backed a step and gestured down the hall. Baylor fell in beside him. Both men wore naval service khakis.

"Yes, sir! I'm back on active status as of today. The tyrants of scalpel and scissors have set me free."

Ouilette laughed. They turned a corner and he asked, "What's next, Commander? The admiral has expressed an interest."

"Altitude, sir. And afterburner! If you know what I mean?"

"'Fraid not. Only thing I've flown recently is a desk."

"Hey! I can fix that. We'll find you a suit, sir. You could be singing to the angels by lunchtime. The Black Widow is single seat, but the Eagle's still in town, right?"

"You fly Eagles also?"

"Yes, sir! Good ship down low and in a scrap. But I do look forward to my main ride."

Ouilette broke his stride. "Sorry, you've just reminded me. The F-27 was retrieved by your squadron two days ago."

"Who the hell authorized that? Someone has their head up their butt."

Ouilette's expression cooled. "I signed the release, Commander. I believed we could do without the F-27 for now."

Embarrassment flooded him and Baylor lowered his gaze. "Sorry, sir. I have a big mouth."

"Apology accepted. You didn't answer my question."

"Well, sir, I guess it's back to Pensacola. Sittin' in the hot-shack waiting for the call. It will seem dull after this little jaunt. I'll miss Griffin too. I'll have to break in a new flight-leader."

"You could skip all that, you know."

"A figure of speech, sir. I have some habits that take getting used to."

"I meant you could remain at Minot…as part of our contact team."

Baylor frowned. "Doing what, sir?"

With a small smile, Ouilette said, "The admiral will need a quick ride from time to time, among some other things."

The offer was not compelling. "I didn't sign on to be a chauffeur, sir."

Before Ouilette could respond, the Chao emerged from an intersecting corridor, flanked by a pair of marines. She still wore her silvered flight suit, the marines dressed in khaki and green. The ponderous form of Stanley Wozniak trundled close behind, the scientist dressed in brown corduroys, an off-white shirt and a gray sweater vest and navy-blue suspenders.

"Linneow!" Baylor hooted, "Hot damn! A good morning indeed."

The Chao changed direction and ducked behind one of her escorts. She moved close and grasped Baylor's arm. Her hand was small, possessing only three long, slender fingers. No thumb. A trio of bony ridges lined the back of her palm. His fascination dissipated when she shook his arm.

"Pilot Ed sleeps again."

"Sorry, Linneow. I'm distracted by the loss of my ride."

Her huge eyes remained fastened to his. She blinked and a nictitating membrane swept past her pupils. "Of no concern, this is. One craft is enough, yes?"

"Sure. But, I'll miss the Widow. I only had one to lose."

She hissed and tugged his arm. "Sometimes, I think you are purposely dense. What matters another craft when you are flying the Sikt?"

Baylor stopped in his tracks and swung Linneow around to face him. "What!"

Linneow glanced toward Ouilette and back. "Of this, we spoke yesterday, Ouilette and I. He agreed you should test with the Sikt. The future may require humans to fly our vessels."

"Whoa! Drive your ship?"

Linneow dipped her head.

Baylor swung to Ouilette. "I'm to fly the Sikt?"

"Among other things."

"YES!" Baylor shouted.

Linneow's ears flattened at the volume of his voice and Ouilette chuckled. "The reason for your participation in this conference. May we get on with it?"

Wozniak fell in beside Baylor. "Doctor Stanley Wozniak, Major." The scientist thrust out his hand.

Baylor returned his grip. "Ed Baylor. I'm Navy, so it's commander, not major. Call me Ed."

"I'll never understand these insignia," Wozniak complained.

"Don't worry about it, Doc. It's all the same."

Ouilette turned suddenly and indicated a hobbling figure with a cane approaching from the opposite direction. "Doctor, here's someone I want you to meet."

Linneow sprang away from Baylor's side and hurtled past Ouilette. About halfway to Weber, she paused and assumed a crouching stance.

"*Setti, colanga-aash tommack!*"

Dressed in jeans and boots, blue plaid flannel shirt and leather vest, Weber looked like someone who might have just stepped out of a stagecoach. He chuckled but did not otherwise reply. He closed the distance to less than ten feet from Linneow and said, "*Setti, tommacka-con desshud!*" He swung the cane at her head.

Linneow recoiled with extraordinary speed and easily avoided the blow.

Ouilette and Wozniak froze with shock.

Baylor growled, "What the hell!"

Both marines reached for their pistols.

In the next moment, Linneow hissed and walked into Weber's open arms. He pointed to the side of his throat and said, "Sayla darlin', I need a kiss."

She embraced him and lightly nipped his throat directly over his jugular.

Shit! He called her Sayla. Perplexed, Baylor followed Wozniak forward as the marines relaxed.

"What was that all about?" Ouilette asked.

"This is my brother," Linneow replied. "He saved my life and I have now saved his. In Chao custom, we are bonded."

Weber glanced down at her as she nestled in his arm. "I'm a lucky man, wouldn't you say, Marcus?"

"I'd say so", Baylor murmured.

Ouilette replied, "You gave us a start, my friend. Was that some kind of Chao greeting?"

"Yessir. A challenge between friends and hunters, long parted. She called me a vile, old cripple. I called her dumb and ugly. I had to swing at her to prove I wasn't crippled. I offered my throat to prove that she still has my trust."

Wozniak softly said, "Fascinating! Where did you learn all that?"

Ouilette turned to the scientist. "Doctor, meet Sam Weber, the man, rapidly becoming legend, who started all of this. Sam, this is Doctor Stanley Wozniak, the lead advisor on the science team."

Weber extended his hand. "Welcome to the posse, Doc."

Wozniak blinked. "Posse?"

Ouilette chuckled and said, "Don't let his cowboy manner fool you, Doctor. Weber may be from Montana, but he's mostly civilized by now."

"You're sure about that, Marcus?"

"Not entirely." Ouilette indicated the conference room only five paces away. "Since we've arrived at the proper place, let's get started."

As they entered the room, Linneow remarked, "Sam is from Montana? Not America?"

"Montana is part of America, although we're sometimes slow to admit it."

Baylor found a seat next to Linneow. "I thought you were from Chicago?"

Weber looked away. "Been there too."

Ouilette approached the head of the table, waited until everyone was seated, and said, "I've come to an epiphany of sorts and since the admiral is offsite, I'll have to go it alone for now. Both Sam and Doctor Wozniak recently provided detail that dovetails and thereby forces a reluctant conclusion. And so...we need a special committee to address issues above and central to all that's happened. That would be us."

"Why a separate group?" Wozniak asked.

"Different issues, Doctor. Today, we'll discuss our opponent and the threat they pose."

Wozniak stiffened but Baylor spoke first. "Wait a minute. I don't know what you're talking about."

"Would that I could say the same," Wozniak murmured.

"We'll rectify that in a moment. First, this is secret beyond classification. No storage or dissemination of information by any means. Because of the problems with electronic security, no phones, no—"

Wozniak interrupted. "What kind of problems?"

"It started with a large scale breach at 3C we could neither stop nor prevent. An investigation is underway, but it's clear the information repositories have been penetrated."

"Through the firewall? How's that possible?"

"Doctor, it was a tunnel through the firewall, and over a gigabit wide. The intruder suborned all the control systems."

"When did this happen?"

"The same day Linneow launched her cruiser towards Saturn—"

"Whoa, whoa, whoa!" Baylor broke in. "Cruiser! Towards Saturn?"

Ouilette thumped the table with his knuckles. He quietly continued, "For the moment, let the information flow. You can catch up off-line with any of us later. We haven't much time and there's a lot to cover. Did I get the security message across?"

At the collective nod, Ouilette turned to Linneow. "You've detected them in system? What threat do they pose?"

Linneow inclined her head. "Ouilette speaks now of the Oo'ahan. Forerunners have arrived. Two far out in your system and one in orbit of Earth. *Ammonte* now engages all three."

"*Ammonte* is a Chao warship," Ouilette offered, "an automated, intelligent interstellar cruiser."

Linneow continued, "Earth orbit is decontaminated, but the outer system will take more time. Oo'ahan can be difficult to locate if they have time to prepare." She shifted her posture and moved closer to Ouilette. "My friend, Oo'ahan ships arrive while Linneow lies in stasis. Possibility exists Oo'ahan have landed already. If true, we are endangered."

"Why? Our government is strong enough to deal with a few infiltrators."

Weber broke in. "We'll never find them soon enough, Marcus. In the meantime, they'll subvert our systems, our command chain, and even our government. They'll use that strength you mentioned against anyone and everyone who tries to organize against the real threat."

Several seconds of silence passed before Wozniak said, "I'm sorry, I need a huge amount of data before I can help."

"C'mon, Doc," Baylor chided him. "It's simple. We've a real enemy for the first time in decades."

"Whom do you shoot, sky-pilot? How, when and where. And with what?" The scientist leaned back in his seat. "I see no effective strategy."

"Lighten up, man. You have to think positive." Baylor turned to Linneow. "Any more fighters like the Sikt on that warship of yours?"

Linneow inclined her head. "*Ammonte* contains one other Sikt assault ship and two Saark space-capable supremacy fighters."

Weber and Ouilette glanced at each other then at Linneow. "Darlin, seems you didn't tell me everything," Weber drawled.

"Sam, we speak continuously for one human month. Much remains unsaid."

Baylor beamed. "There you go, Doc. Things are looking up already. We thought the Sikt was a bad-ass machine, but the phrase *supremacy fighter* absolutely gives me a woody."

"Sorry to let it down, Commander," Ouilette said with a small smile, "but those additional assets are out beyond Mars and headed toward Saturn. You'll not see them soon."

Baylor frowned but Wozniak remained obdurate. "Commander, in every contest since the beginning of time the most important rule of engagement has been to know your opponent. What do we know?"

Linneow fixed her eyes upon the scientist until he flushed and looked away. She removed one of the two objects clipped to her collar. It immediately emitted a soft beep and a compartment opened on one end. Linneow extended the device toward Wozniak and upended it. A pale blue, pea-sized crystal bounced on the table's surface. It spun for a few seconds, reflecting ribbons of light.

Wozniak leaned forward, squinting. He drew a pen from his vest pocket and pushed the crystal closer. Multi-faceted, it appeared as two cones joined at the base. After a moment, he asked, "What's this?"

"A data repository of one hundred and sixty petabytes. A stylized record. A historical rendition."

"What's it made of?"

"Carbon crystal, laced with ytterbium throughout the lattice. You must build a device to retrieve the data." She touched the object that had contained the crystal. "This one is tuned to my mind and is of no use to humans."

"Means of extraction?"

"Apply a sinusoidal signal to the equator. With increasing frequencies, sequential streams of digital data will emit from the poles. Vary the frequency for random access."

"Cool!" Wozniak pulled a kerchief from his pocket and pushed the crystal into it with his pen.

"We would be very interested in that data, Doctor," Ouilette remarked. "How long will it take to build a reader?"

Wozniak shrugged. "Depends on the format and type of code. Downloading the data is the easy part. Interpreting it is another matter."

With a hiss, Linneow said, "Chao science is advanced, Scholar Wozniak. You will find the visual stream pixel oriented. The aural stream is Earth standard, in English."

"No kidding!" Wozniak turned to Ouilette. "In that case, Commander, give me two weeks. Maybe less."

"Excellent, Doctor." Ouilette swung to face Linneow. "If the Oo'ahan have already landed, how can we counter them?"

Linneow inclined her head, her eyes wide and unblinking. "A great problem this is. Oo'ahan remain elusive until risk is low and victory assured. Chao and Vithri learn to wait…to let Oo'ahan succeed until the enemy believes triumph is imminent."

Weber asked, "Where do they hide, Sayla. Underground?"

Using a human method of expression, Linneow slowly shook her head. "No, my brother. In your mind."

"What!" Baylor said.

Linneow turned to the flyer. "Truth I speak, Pilot Ed. When linked in group-mind, Oo'ahan can deceive our senses. We cannot see or hear them, nor detect them through any physical means."

Wozniak said, "But you've learned to defeat them."

Linneow turned toward the scientist. "Chao analyze data from Oo'ahan activity. When close to victory, Oo'ahan become more active. Sensors detect epicenter of command stream. Chao respond with force."

"What kind of force?" Baylor asked.

Linneow bowed to the flyer. "Fusion warhead is effective."

Baylor thumped the table with his fist. "Now you're talking. I was worried we might need some kind of hypnotic ray."

"Prevention is better than the cure," Ouilette said, "especially if the cure is a fusion weapon. How can we prevent subversion, Linneow?"

She turned toward him. "You speak of penetration. Did Ouilette see evidence of this?"

"I was probably the only one who did. Gibberish flying across my screen. The investigation still continues."

"Investigators will find nothing, if Oo'ahan are responsible. Any trace of presence is designed to delude." Linneow hesitated. "Most often Oo'ahan communication begins with keyword. Symbols of the controlling group-mind. Does Ouilette remember a keyword?"

"Hell, no. Most of the characters weren't alphanumeric at all."

Linneow moved closer to Ouilette. Before he could react, she placed a three-fingered hand at the side of his neck. Her index finger curled under his chin and the second two gently massaged the base of his skull.

Ouilette stiffened and started to raise his arm when Weber murmured, "Easy, swimmer. I've been there."

Ouilette swallowed and nodded.

Linneow stretched upward on her toes until she could whisper in his ear. "Ouilette remembers the sign before the code. It swells to fill the void. It swells to fill the mind. He, who sends the sign, encompasses your mind. Remember his call. Serve him and remember. Remember his sign."

Ouilette jumped violently backward. He pushed Linneow away, his eyes wild and his face twisted with hate.

"Stand down, SEAL!" Weber shouted.

Ouilette sagged and grasped a chair for support. His entire body was trembling. "What the hell..." he began weakly.

Linneow moved to help him sit. She glanced at the others. "Ouilette has met the Oo'ahan. The group-mind impressed a command string into his mind. If he did not belong to the group-mind, he was to forget everything of consequence. The Oo'ahan control those who have seen the command string by using extreme emotions to guard the message from detection. Chao have learned to release the guardians and discover the message."

She turned back to Ouilette. "Now, Ouilette must draw the sign."

Wozniak pushed paper and a pen across the table. The commander curled his lip and swallowed. "God, I don't want to do this. Hate it and dread it at the same time."

"But you remember?" Linneow asked.

"Yes, damn it." Ouilette grabbed the paper and scrawled the design. His stomach heaved as he refined it. Bile rose in his throat, followed by a strong urge to vomit. He finished, stood and walked to the window where he wiped his sleeve across his forehead.

Weber eased out of his chair and moved to stand beside him. "Amigo?"

Ouilette nodded and glanced at Weber. "We're in big trouble."

"I can see that."

They both turned at a small cry from behind. Linneow leaned against the far wall, her head back against its surface. Baylor moved toward the Chao but she ignored him. Her eyes remained closed but husky whispers in a long-dead language filled the room.

Ouilette glanced at Weber. "You know what she's saying?"

"Hell, no. What I know of Chao is hello and goodbye."

Linneow straightened. At first, she couldn't seem to focus but she found Ouilette and moved toward him. "It cannot be. Not again."

"What's wrong, Sayla?" Weber asked.

"The sign of Genkhus falls upon this world. Genkhus destroyed Tassone. Genkhus defeated the Vithri in the Great Ringed Nebula of Draika. Genkhus is of the most powerful of Oo'ahan. Earth is not prepared to face such as him."

"Genghis! That was the name I saw in English," Ouilette remarked.

Linneow inclined her head. "We must plan for a long campaign." She removed the second device from her collar then held out her hand, palm up. Both Weber and Ouilette focused upon the callused knob at the edge of that palm. It served as a brace for her fingers to restrain whatever she chose to grasp.

"To my brother Sam, I offer my neck in exchange for his hand."

Weber grimaced but did not hesitate. He extended his arm.

Linneow lowered her device and pressed it against his palm. Weber felt a sharp jab and a burning sensation. He clamped his jaw but did not move otherwise. She released his hand and turned to Ouilette who raised an eyebrow at Weber.

"A little sting is all," the agent replied to the unspoken question.

Ouilette bared his teeth but remained as still as Weber had. Another figure loomed close behind Linneow's shoulder.

"I'm next." Baylor offered his hand to Linneow.

She hissed as she placed the device into his palm. Baylor gave no indication that the device had any effect. "Thanks," he said. "Do you want to bite my neck now?"

Ouilette shook his head and Weber chuckled as he studied the floor.

Linneow hissed laughter. "Pilot Ed must know that him I trust without such proof. We fly together and what can be more proof than that?"

"Damn straight!" He lowered his voice. "Can I call you Sayla?"

She shook her head in the human fashion. "Our bond is strong but not yet so intimate."

Baylor raised his chin. "But Weber can."

Linneow lowered her voice until it was nearly a whisper. "Sam Weber earned the right when he stepped before my death and turned it upon himself."

"I would do the same."

She inclined her head. "Linneow believes this to be true."

"I guess that's good enough for now." He turned away.

The sweating face of Wozniak was next in line. "I hate pain. Especially pain from needles. It that a needle?"

Weber coughed and said, "Felt like it to me."

"Why does it have to be a needle? Did it hurt a lot?"

Weber held out his hand and waggled it. Ouilette turned away to hide his grin. Weber continued. "Look at it this way, Doc. It's like a Purple Heart in advance. You're doing the honorable thing."

Wozniak held out his hand and closed his eyes. "What's honor got to do with it? Pain is pain and I hate it. Ow-ow-ow!" His feet wiggled as Linneow completed her task, but his arm held steady. He snatched back his palm as if expecting the worst. There was only a tiny spot of blood. "The scientist in me has to ask. What was that all about?"

"Linneow collects blood and tissue samples for design of biote."

"For what?"

She hissed. "Linneow will explain later when design is done. Scholar Wozniak must trust Linneow. Shall I offer my throat to Wozniak?"

The heavy scientist flushed bright crimson and stuttered, "N-no. No need. Didn't hurt that much." He shambled back to the table and sat down. Weber joined him.

Ouilette was about to speak when interrupted by a knock on the door. Before anyone could answer, a marine thrust in his head.

"Sir! Most urgent. A message about the Admiral." He handed in a slip of paper.

About, not from. With a sense of foreboding, Ouilette received the sheet and scanned it. He closed his eyes and released his breath. When he reopened them, the marine had departed.

To Wozniak, he said, "As much as I hate to say it, your prediction was accurate, Doctor." To the others, he added, "Petersham is dead. Killed in a hit and run accident. He never made it to the White House."

Several seconds of silence filled the room.

"It's started," Weber finally said.

"Fraid so." Ouilette paced across the room. When he reached the far side, he turned to Baylor. "Take the Eagle, Commander. Hightail it to Washington. Retrieve General Pigott before anything befalls him. We'll handle the communications from this end and stack the tankers as soon as we've finished here. You wanted afterburner, son. You've got it!"

"Yes, sir!" Baylor jumped up and dashed out of the conference room.

Wozniak glanced after him. "We might all be at risk...him too."

Weber shook his head. "Don't think so, Doc. Baylor wasn't on the inside when this Genghis character breached the CCC. You, on the other hand, and Marcus here, are better targets."

"You're not?" Ouilette asked, turning to Weber.

"Dunno. Depends on what leaked about me in the Sikt. What about the deep program? Any chance that's been jeopardized?"

Ouilette thought through the order of events. "My system at the NSA was junk before the intrusion began. I think we're okay." He turned to Wozniak. "Earlier, you mentioned taking things to the next level. What exactly did you mean by that?"

Chapter Eight
14:24 EDT, 8 May
The White House

Chief of Staff Russell Dougherty strode across the foyer toward the settee near the far wall where General Pigott sat reading the morning paper. When he paused and cleared his throat, the general glanced up. Dougherty said, "Sorry about the delay. He seemed fine until a few minutes ago. If you'll give us another half hour..."

Pigott folded the paper. "Not to worry, Russ. I've nothing more important than meeting with my commander-in-chief."

"Stomach flu or something. His physician believes he'll soon recover."

"Glad to hear it. We've a hell of a mess, with Petersham and all."

"An unfortunate affair, General. I hope he didn't suffer."

Pigott's eyes turned cool and distant. "Death by fire, Russ."

Dougherty blanched and muttered something unintelligible. He added, "I-I'll check on the President, General. Be back to you soon."

Pigott nodded and returned to his paper.

14:41 EDT, Andrews AFB, Maryland

Baylor paced the narrow corridor between the snack bar and the dispatch center. He had grounded his F-15 over an hour earlier and the Eagle now sat refueled and ready. All that remained was to locate the general, impel him up the ladder and climb out of this muggy swamp they called an air base.

None of his phone messages to Pigott's hotel, his aides, or his second in command at Cheyenne Air Station had been returned. Evidently, Commander Ouilette was no more successful. A terse note had been waiting when Baylor arrived. He scanned it again.

Unable to locate Gen. Pigott. Remain in place at Andrews.
M. Ouilette, Comdr., USN

"Commander Baylor?" the dispatcher called.

"That's me," Baylor turned and loped to the desk.

"A call for you, sir. Take it there." The dispatcher pointed to a black handset sitting on a circular table.

"Right."

When the handset purred, he lifted the receiver. "Baylor."

Weber's voice replied, "Ace, find a room for the night. Marcus can't locate Pigott but we know he's in Washington. Call me when you're settled." Weber reeled off a string of numbers.

"Yes, sir ... hey, Weber! Are you military?"

"Was. This stuff's from Marcus anyway."

"Okay, man. Got it. Call you later."

The phone went dead with a click. Baylor peered at the receiver. *You're a cold dude, Sam Weber.*

He replaced the phone and asked the dispatcher for information on transient housing.

The White House, 15:01 EDT

"The President will see you now, General."

Pigott folded the magazine, stood and smiled. "Of course."

He followed the Chief of Staff down the corridor, through the double doors and into the Oval Office.

The President of the United States, Bernard Lowry sat at his desk. A lanky man of modest height, with heavy brows and a prominent hawk's beak nose. An uncanny resemblance to a raptor, well past its last meal. His dark gray suit appeared rumpled and a thin sheen of perspiration lined his forehead and upper lip. Regardless of his earlier infirmity, he now appeared both alert and attentive.

"Will you need me, sir?" Dougherty asked.

"No, Russell. We're fine. If we run long, keep the wolves at bay."

"Yessir, Mr. President."

After the Chief of Staff slipped through the door, Lowry turned toward Pigott. He indicated a chair before his desk. As soon as the general claimed the seat, Lowry said, "I'll get right to the point, General. I accepted your request for an audience because we've a problem to solve."

"Sir?"

"This ruckus the late Admiral Petersham has brought down upon our heads. It's causing me grief in the international arena. What are you going to do about it?"

"Me, Mr. President?"

"You were Petersham's second-in-command."

"Yes, sir. At 3C, in Cheyenne Mountain."

"Well, then."

Pigott leaned backward and steepled his fingers in front of his lips. "Sir, my role as second-in-command to Admiral Petersham entailed air defense of the United States. It did not extend to this situation, sir. I believe he picked someone else for the job."

"Who?"

"A man named Ouilette, sir. A Navy Commander."

"I know that name. NSA. He botched some operation in Brazil about a year ago."

"I know nothing of the matter, Mr. President, but I think this is the same man."

Lowry rocked backward in his chair. "I won't have it, General. Since Petersham is out of the picture, anything less than the best is unacceptable."

"What do you intend, sir?"

"I don't know. I just don't know."

Pigott leaned forward. "Since you agreed to see me, Sir, I find that hard to accept. I believe you have everything you need to make a decision. All you need to do is to think about it."

Lowry gazed at the General for several seconds, and then he too leaned forward, and said, "Take charge of this alien spaceship matter. Make it go away."

"Go away, sir?"

Lowry jabbed the blotter on his desk with a forefinger. "Bury it. So deep no one will ever find it. I want to deny this whole matter without worrying that some leak will make me look incompetent or stupid."

"There's valuable technology at stake, Mr. President."

"I know that. Put good people on it and lock them away for however long it takes to get results. But completely buried, understood?"

"You're talking about a full time job, sir."

"Appoint someone to oversee defense of our airspace. You deal with this other problem. Am I understood?"

"I understand your words, Mr. President. But, my authority does not extend that far. Appointing a successor for 3C is a task for the JCS."

Lowry thumped his desk. "No, goddammit! I'm the Commander-in-Chief. I make the rules. You manage it. Do I have your support, General?"

"To the hilt, sir."

Lowry waved his hand, indicating dismissal. "Tell Russell I want him on your way out."

Pigott stood, turned and strode through the exit. As he passed Dougherty, he quipped over his shoulder, "Your master beckons."

Pigott climbed into his limousine with satisfaction welling within him. Time to make some changes. He rapped on the glass and the driver rolled down the barrier. "Sir?"

"Messages?"

"About twenty, sir. Most from North Dakota. Three from Andrews AFB, and six or sev—"

"Andrews?"

"A Navy officer named Baylor. Says he's holding your ride back to Minot."

Pigott sniffed. "I don't think so. We'll take the Gulfstream." The general passed a list forward. "Call these people and tell them to meet me at Dulles. They'll know where. Book a flight plan to the Academy and, from there, another one to Minot tomorrow morning."

The driver reviewed the list. "Sir, that's a lot of people for the Gulfstream. We'll be flying heavy."

"Tell them to pack light."

"Yes, sir. What about the Navy pilot at Andrews?"

"Ignore him. Any more questions?"

"No, sir."

"Then, take me to my hotel."

19:20 EDT, BOQ531, Transient, Andrews AFB

"C'mon, answer the damn thing." A few seconds later Baylor slammed the receiver down and stood. His frustration continued to grow. The lack of answer from Minot produced a sodden burning sensation under his breastbone. His nerves felt jangled and the room seemed to shrink.

He glanced at the small bag that contained sweats and his running shoes. About five miles should do it. Baylor kicked off his aviator's gear and struggled into the rumpled sweats. He burst out the door while thrusting his head through the neck of the jersey. He picked up speed and turned in the direction of the flight-line.

While Baylor's pace ate up the distance, his heart and lungs pumped the tension out of his body. When sweat trickled into his eyes, he felt a whole lot better. Physically, anyway.

He could be in a jam. He was a thousand miles out of place, sent on a mission without written orders by a man recently appointed to the job by an Admiral who was now dead. At least both Petersham and Ouilette were Navy. Cross-service chain of command would have made it worse. But, he was flying an Air Force fighter that did not belong to him while his own craft was *who-knew-the-hell-where. Perhaps, I should call my CO at Pensacola and get a read on this muck-up.*

Twenty-four hours. It would be tough to sit around for another day, but if it passed without contact from Ouilette or definitive orders, he would call Pensacola.

With sudden surprise, Baylor noticed that he had completed his five-mile lap already. He checked his watch. Twenty-eight minutes—not bad. One more lap.

At eight-thirty, Baylor tried the number again. Someone lifted the phone on the first ring. "Yo!"

"Weber?"

"Where you been, hotshot?"

"Hey, I called. Nobody answered."

"Couldn't be helped. What's your number?"

Baylor read the number from the phone then asked, "Can I speak to Commander Ouilette?"

"'Fraid not. He's meeting with a Pentagon team investigating the breach at Cheyenne," Weber replied.

"Ouch! Better him than me."

"Any word on Pigott?"

"No, damn it! I finally got through to his driver but no reply yet."

"Better trail than we've managed. I'll call back tomorrow."

Baylor started to hang up, then hesitated. "Hey, Weber!"

"Yeah?"

"Thanks for waiting around."

A few seconds of silence elapsed. "No sweat, pardner. Stay chilled."

"Yes, sir. Later."

The line went dead from the other end before he could hang up.

09:09 CDT, 9 May, Minot AFB, North Dakota

"Good morning, Doctor."

Wozniak glanced up from his notes. Ouilette stood beside his table. Sandy hair ruffled. Pallor beneath the sun-weathered complexion, and red-rimmed eyes. On the naval officer's tray sat a single English muffin and a large Styrofoam cup filled with black coffee.

When Ouilette slid into a seat across from the scientist, Wozniak said, "Super! I was hoping we could hook up this morning, Commander. I need to catch a plane to New Mexico."

"And I hoped we might have a word or too also." Ouilette paused as he sipped his coffee. "What's in New Mexico?"

"I've recently learned I'm getting a bank of the best hardware money can buy, courtesy of Los Alamos Laboratory grants. I've sketched out some ideas but I need that bandwidth to put them into practice."

"Would your computers reduce the time you need?"

"The ones I have make it possible. The new ones...absolutely."

"How can I argue? Military transport suitable?"

"If it's leaving soon."

"There's a C-130 bound for Holloman in less than an hour."

"That'll be great, Commander. Holloman's only three hours from Santa Fe. Thank you, sir."

"Quid pro quo, Doctor?"

Wozniak leaned back in his chair with a smile. "Absolutely. What's on your mind?"

"A mission of seventy million years duration." When the scientist blinked, he added, "When did humans first appear?"

"Modern humans or early hominids?

"The early version."

Wozniak shrugged. "Two million years ago...give or take. What's that about seventy million years?"

"What possible objective would have required them to start so early? Eradication of the dinosaurs?"

"An impactor took care of the lizards, Commander. Sixty-five million years ago. Who is them?"

"The K-T extinction event. I've heard of that." Ouilette leaned forward. "So they were here before then. Why wait around so long afterward?"

Wozniak leaned forward. "Them...They.... Are we talking about the Chao and her Vithri friends?" When Ouilette nodded, he said, "Maybe you should ask her."

The Navy officer drew a deep breath and downed the rest of his coffee. "Maybe I should." He finished off his muffin, stood and added, "Let's drop by my office and I'll generate your travel papers."

In a matter of minutes, Wozniak and Ouilette had completed the paperwork. As they both left Ouilette's office, Wozniak said, "You look a little peaked, Commander. Long hours?"

"Been reviewing that firewall breach with the Pentagon boys. Some anomalies we can't explain."

"Such as?"

"It seems to have originated in two points, one of them internal."

"A spy? A foreign collaborator?"

Ouilette shrugged. "Unknown. What's worse, the inside link is logged to Admiral Petersham's account, the same one I was using while the break occurred."

Wozniak paused. "Remember what Linneow said about false trails."

"Hardly something I can talk about with the Pentagon. Makes for a bit of delicate maneuvering on my part. And for long nights."

"I don't envy you commander. Good luck with it."

"Takes more than luck, Doctor, as I'm sure you know. You apply the same stuff to your problem and let me know when you have results."

The Gulfstream landed behind a departing C-130 Hercules. While the executive jet taxied in toward Minot's transportation services center, Pigott turned to his deputies. "Phil, assume direct control of security. Close the base. Nobody on or off by air or surface."

"Yes, sir." replied the sandy-haired colonel.

"Jim, the alien's your responsibility. I want no divided loyalties on this so change the guard first. When you're ready, I'll take care of the executive team."

"Who exactly are they, sir, with Petersham dead?"

"A Navy commander and one of his cronies."

"Expecting trouble, sir?"

"These boys are ex-SEALs, which means they can be unpredictable. First task is to reduce their options. Everybody set?"

When he received affirmation, Pigott pivoted toward the crew deck and said, "Unbutton us."

In the briefing room, Ouilette drew a deep breath and replied in the negative—again. "That's not how it happened. The last action was to withdraw from my NSA workstation. The anomaly began afterward."

"Sir, are you aware that your NSA system suffered catastrophic failure?" The Pentagon officer glanced at his notes. "The disk is wiped. Could the intrusion under the Admiral's account have triggered this reaction?"

Ouilette shrugged. "It's conceivable, but the system was fine when I logged out. Look at your time stamps. We've been over this before."

"Yes, sir. And we'll need to go over it again until it starts to make sense. The major point is that the intruder was aided by software engaged under Petersham's account."

"Can you trace it to the admiral's workstation?"

"No, sir. Theoretically any of several workstations could have established the session, but only if the operator knew both the account and password."

"Sounds like an insolvable problem, Lieutenant."

One of the clerks from the administrative section approached the table where all the readout and log reports where spread. "Commander Ouilette," she said, "General Pigott would like to speak with you."

"About time. A recess, Lieutenant. This is a call I have to take."

Ouilette followed the clerk from the conference room. Once in the hallway, he asked, "Can you pipe the call to my office? I'd like a little privacy."

"No need, sir. General Pigott is in your office."

"What! He's here, on base?" At her nod, Ouilette muttered, "Stranger and stranger."

He loped down the hall toward the cubbyhole Weber used as an office and stepped inside, hoping to find his friend. Pigott was sure to want confirmation of what he was about to learn. The room was occupied only by an NCO to whom the agent had been dictating all he knew of the Chao's manner, habits, and social behaviors.

"Where's Weber?" Ouilette asked.

"Sorry, Commander Ouilette. Mister Weber hit the rack some time ago. He'd been up almost thirty hours and was feeling a little bushed. Shall I roust him?"

"Not advisable. When Weber says he needs some shuteye, let him be."

The noncom nodded and added, "Sir, there's some messages from a Commander Baylor. He's been trying to get in touch with Weber or you."

Ouilette paused. Baylor was way out in left field and the play had just come to home plate. "When Sam awakens, have him tell Baylor to plan his own refueling, but to make best possible speed back to Minot."

"Yes, sir."

Ouilette left Weber's office and, within a few seconds, reached his own and pushed open the door. Seated in his chair, Pigott lifted his eyes and said, "I'll have to call you back." He hung up and pointed to a chair opposite. "Commander Ouilette! You look like you've had a long night. Take a seat."

"Thank you, sir. We're mighty glad you've returned. Ever since the Admiral's death, we've been worried."

"A horrible accident, Commander. Tell me...Marcus, correct?" At Ouilette's nod, Pigott continued, "Do you miss field work?"

Where was this leading? "Sometimes, sir. I miss the clarity of purpose most of all."

"Understood. You should know I met with the President, Commander. He wants a change of direction on this XT affair."

"That's fortunate, sir. We've some new and highly sensitive information. He might want to mobilize a large portion of our defenses when he learns of the danger."

"He's taking the opposite tack. We're to downplay this affair until we know more. I happen to agree."

"Begging your pardon sir, but neither of you have been briefed. There's a lot you don't know."

"I don't doubt it, Commander. But, you can't have a much better picture." When Ouilette started to object, Pigott overrode him. "I know you've made a good start but you can't jump to conclusions. We now have a full research team on board, one that can take this whole thing apart, right down to the smallest component."

"Sir, I'm not talking about XT hardware."

"Neither am I. I'm speaking of a cultural, biological, and technological dissection that gives us every iota of information available. Cross-checked, catalogued and constructed behind a double-blind research program."

Ouilette stood. "That sounds like you plan to dissect both the Sikt and the Chao."

"Whatever it takes."

"What!" He repeated, "What? She's a living entity, a visitor, a potential ally!"

"That's your problem, Commander. Your scope is too narrow. You're too close to it. The president is looking at this from a global perspective."

"The President is out of touch!" Ouilette objected, letting anger overcome caution. "And so are you, sir. The Chao brought us data that depicts a calamitous threat to the planet, to the entire human race. How's that for a broad perspective?"

"Confirmed? And how?"

"A terabyte-wide hole blown through the firewall at 3C while the Chao approached. It was driven by a non-human source."

"Which you've isolated?"

"No, sir. Just identified. But—"

"Exactly my point, you're reaching for conclusions from an uncertain perspective. The President has charged me with full responsibility for managing this program. Which means that—"

"Wait a minute, sir. The President's acting without full knowledge. Don't you think we should at least lay out what we've discovered to date?"

Pigott tapped the table with an index finger. "Until I know enough to provide an adequate briefing—"

Ouilette crossed his arms and said, "You've no intention of presenting this danger to the President, have you General."

Pigott also stood. "We're done here, Commander. I had hoped that we could establish a workable arrangement. I see now it isn't possible, so let me say it straight out. You're out of the XT affair. You'll surrender any notes you might have. As of this moment, you're restricted from all contact with or entry into any of the testing laboratories. You'll have no further contact with the XT. Have I made myself clear?"

Ouilette found his anger surging. He forced himself to breathe deeply and clamped his jaws to prevent a retort.

"Do you understand, Commander Ouilette?" Pigott repeated.

"Understood. But, with respect, sir, your actions endanger the nation and the government I've sworn to protect. Accordingly, I've no recourse but to seek redress through my chain of command. Eventually the President will receive my data."

"And when he does, Commander, it will be old, obsolete and worthless. For I expect that we will now learn the real reason why this alien has come among us."

"As you will, sir. Since you've no use for my services, I'm on my way to Washington."

"The base is closed to traffic, Commander. In or out."

Ouilette took a step forward. Pigott straightened but did not retreat.

"Don't try to stop me, General. Your authority does not extend that far."

Pigott glared but said nothing. Ouilette turned and strode from the office.

After Ouilette departed, Pigott sat on the edge of the desk, letting his emotion evaporate. He leafed through several folders stacked in the in-basket. While he was examining them, one of his aides, Captain James Forster, knocked on the doorjamb.

"General, can you spare a minute?"

"Sure, Jim. What have you got?"

"We've closed the base down and assumed control of communications. Here's a note from Commander Ouilette to one of his deputies. It's supposed to be sent to an officer named Baylor...a Navy pilot who's currently at Andrews."

"Ah, yes. The flyer who escorted the Chao. Listen Jim, Baylor is a bit-player but he could become tangled underfoot if he returns to Minot. I want you to immobilize him. Be creative but subtle. I want Mr. Baylor to have other things on his mind. Where's Weber?"

"Sleeping, sir."

"Excellent. Let's keep it that way."

"No sweat, General. What about the Chao?"

"Tomorrow. We'll deal with it tomorrow when we have better control."

"Sir!" Forster saluted and stepped away.

A second officer knocked, a lieutenant whom Pigott did not recognize.

"What is it, lieutenant?"

"Sorry, sir. I was looking for Commander Ouilette. We're supposed to conclude our work today...if possible."

"What work, Lieutenant? I'm assuming most of Ouilette's responsibilities."

"Well, sir, I'm afraid this involves him personally. Can you tell me where he is?"

"Look, son, you'd better let me in on it. Ouilette has left, I'm afraid."

"That's most irregular, sir. The commander is a key figure in the breach at Cheyenne Mountain. We're unlikely to make serious progress without him. My team flew all the way from the Pentagon to interview him."

"Let's visit your team and you can fill me in on the way."

Twenty minutes later, Pigott's cellular phone buzzed.

"Pigott."

"General, sir, this is Sergeant Evans at the front gate. I've detained a Navy officer who says he means to pass. He told me to call you, sir. What should I do?"

Pigott absent-mindedly tapped the report he had received from the Pentagon team. After a moment, he said, "Advise this officer that the base commander has established quarantine and that if he breaks it, he does so in violation of those orders. Understood, Sergeant?"

"Yes, sir. And if he still departs?"

"Log it, Sergeant. Name, rank and serial number."

"Yes, sir. Thank you, sir."

Pigott hung up and headed down the hall for the staff meeting he had scheduled at 16:00.

At the same moment, two men stealthily slipped into Sam Weber's room. Weber lay on his back, his mouth open and snoring lightly. The first man moved to Weber's right. Once they were positioned on either side, the second man opened a small bottle and poured its contents into a towel. After a moment, he dropped the towel over Weber's mouth and clamped it down with his hand. Simultaneously, both men threw their full weight onto the sleeping agent.

Weber reacted violently, arching his back, while he thrashed his head. Unfortunately, his assailants had timed their move to perfection. Weber received a full dose of the chloroform on his first breath. In ten seconds he was out. The two men relaxed.

"Easier than I thought. Wasn't this guy supposed to be a SEAL?"

"Shut up and finish it. We still have a lot to do."

The second man withdrew a vial from his coat and inserted a hypodermic needle. He drew off several CCs, squeezed out the air and then found the vein in Weber's left arm and injected the contents of the needle.

"That's it," he said.

His partner patted Weber on his shoulder and said, "Night, night."

They pocketed the towel, the vials, then turned and left the room.

07:25 CDT, 10 May

Captain Jim Forster checked the charge in the stunner for the fourth time. He glanced at Lieutenant Wasnich and the pair of burley enlisted men behind him. Each of them held cattle prods and wore full body armor with face shields. Forster handed the stunner to Wasnich.

"We'll lock the door behind you. If you're overcome, we'll gas the entire suite. Try not to let that happen."

Wasnich peered at his two companions. "No problem, Captain." He motioned the noncoms to stand aside and unlocked the door. He stepped back and handed the key to Forster. The two men pushed open the door and burst through the entrance, Wasnich right on their heels. Forster pulled it shut behind them and locked it.

The antechamber was darkened and empty. Visible through the passageway to the room beyond a double bed was placed with one end up against the wall on the right. The creature reclined with its legs toward the wall, head and arm hanging over the foot of the bed. It turned the pages of a large book on the floor.

At the rustle and thump of their entry, it lifted its head and swung its legs over the side of the bed. Wasnich was the third man through the passageway. The noncoms spread out to block any attempt at escape. The creature seemed confused, but for only a moment. It leapt backward, placing the bed between them and it.

"Close in a little, I don't want this thing getting by us," Wasnich growled.

"Yes, sir," the man on the left replied.

His partner snorted and jiggled his prod as he called, "Here kitty, kitty."

"Shut up, Anderson. It understands English."

"So what, sir. Who cares?"

The XT's gaze followed each comment in turn. When it next glanced at Wasnich, he had a sudden sinking feeling in his gut. "Watch it!" he started.

Too late.

The being transformed into a blur of brown and gold.

It bounded over the bed and raked Anderson across his chest before he could react. His prod flew from his grasp as he crashed to the floor.

Without hesitating, the beast charged for Wasnich who back-pedaled furiously.

"Childs!" Wasnich thrust his stunner forward.

Childs brushed the creature's thigh as it passed. The prod discharged and the XT shrieked when its leg collapsed. It staggered sideways and struck the wall. Bracing itself with its upper limbs, the creature lashed out with its good leg.

Childs backed out of reach. He followed it as it hopped toward the far corner of the room, finally touching its remaining leg with the prod. This time it did not cry out but simply collapsed against the wall.

As Wasnich eased forward with his stunner held foremost, the Chao reached up and pressed a stud on one of the objects clipped to its collar.

"Delanka-ami, Caama-tesch. Staa!"

"What the hell's it doing?" Wasnich asked.

"Speaking into some device," Childs replied.

The XT tossed the object into the corner of the room, unclipped the second one and tossed it away also. Wasnich closed to within two paces and then reached out with his toe to touch one of the beast's feet and then the other. Both legs twitched but it was obvious that the Chao could no longer control them. Wasnich squatted and reached with the stunner.

"Why?" the beast asked, its tone husky and soft.

He pressed the stunner to its flesh. With a buzzing sound, the weapon discharged. The creature's eyes closed and its head lolled. It fell onto its side, unconscious or lifeless.

"Check this out!" Childs exclaimed, pointing into the corner of the room where the Chao had tossed the devices.

Wasnich glanced over to find a shattered pile of smoking ruin. "What happened?"

"I don't know. They just melted."

"To hell with that. Check out Anderson while I bring in the captain." Wasnich stumped toward the entrance and thumped the door. "Open up! It's over."

Forster unlocked the door and stepped inside. "Well?"

"Close one. One man down. Childs, how's Anderson?"

"He's OK. Lieutenant, you've got to see this."

Wasnich and Forster entered the second room to find Anderson on his feet. He was running his fingers through three long slashes in the laminated Kevlar of his body armor. Only a single layer remained intact.

Anderson swallowed and said, "Are you sure that thing's out?"

Forster replied, "Let's not take chances. Bring in the gurney. Tie it in and we'll head for the lab."

A few minutes later, while the XT was wheeled from the room, Forster turned to his aide. "What's the matter, Harry? Why so glum?"

"Don't know, sir. I hope we're doing the right thing."

"Ours not to reason why, Lieutenant."

"Yessir, I know," Wasnich replied. "But it was like zapping my kid sister."

Chapter Nine
13:15 EDT, 10 May, Andrews AFB, Maryland

Baylor quickened his pace as he approached his quarters. An air-force blue sedan sat in the driveway. A noncom was standing by the door.

"Can I help you?" Baylor called as he loped across the yard from the sidewalk.

"Commander Baylor?"

"That's me."

"I'm sorry, sir. I have to ask you to vacate these quarters. As you know when you registered with us, we could only allow two days."

Baylor sighed and said, "I remember. There's been a delay. Can I stay a little longer?"

"Not possible, sir. We've assigned personnel arriving this afternoon. When can you vacate, sir? We need to send in the housekeepers."

"I really have no place to go."

"You could try the Holiday Inn."

"Yeah. Great. Give me thirty minutes to shower and pack my stuff then it's all yours."

"Thank you, sir. Sorry for the inconvenience."

Baylor used only twenty minutes of the allotted time. He flagged a shuttle and caught a ride to the Holiday Inn, which was located on the base just inside the main gate. When he checked with the registration desk, the clerk informed him that the inn still had vacancy. Baylor laid his government credit card on the counter to begin the registration process.

While the clerk filled out the paperwork, Baylor picked up the phone on the desk and called Weber. After a dozen rings, he gave it up and called a second number he had for Commander Ouilette. A woman's voice answered.

"General Pigott's office, may I help you?"

"Pigott! The general has an office at Minot?"

"Yes, sir. Do you wish to speak to the general, sir?"

"He's there? On base?"

"Yes, sir. Whom shall I say is calling?"

The hotel clerk broke into his conversation. "Commander Baylor, I'm sorry, sir. This credit card is coming up as invalid."

Baylor clapped a hand over the receiver. "Try it again. It's a government card."

"I know, sir. I've tried several times. I'm sorry, sir, but you'll have to use another card."

Baylor spoke into the receiver. "Just a minute, please." He dug into his wallet, fished out his personal VISA and handed it to the clerk. He then turned his back to the reception desk and spoke into the phone.

"This is Commander Baylor. Let me speak to the general."

Several seconds passed before the voice returned. "I'm sorry, sir. General Pigott is not available. Perhaps if you tried again later."

"All right. Put me through to Commander Ouilette, then. That's the number I tried to dial anyway."

"I'm sorry, sir. Commander Ouilette has left the base."

Baylor held the phone away from his ear and stared at the receiver for a moment. He shook his head and asked, "When will Commander Ouilette return?"

"The Commander did not leave word."

"How about Weber? Can you at least find him?"

"Weber, sir?"

"Yeah, Sam Weber. Ouilette's right-hand man. Tall guy, salt and pepper hair."

"I'm sorry, sir. I've no record of a man named Sam Weber. Perhaps you should ... oh, wait. Yes, sir. One of my assistants tells me that a man named Sam Weber has been admitted to the base hospital. He's in critical condition. Shall I put you through to the hospital, sir?"

A hollow premonition developed deep in his chest. "No. That's not necessary." Baylor hung up. Something was terribly wrong at Minot. He rolled his wrist to look at his watch. There wasn't enough time to put a flight plan together, let alone schedule a departure for North Dakota.

First thing in the morning. He turned when the clerk tapped his shoulder.

"I'm very sorry, Commander Baylor. But this card comes up invalid also."

"You've got to be kidding! Let me see the damn thing."

Baylor took the card, turned it over and called the 800 number on the back. When the administrator answered, she told him that the account had been closed weeks before. If he wished to reopen the account, she would send him an application. Baylor hung up and tried the service number for his American Express card. He found the same story and struggled against a veritable tide of bad news that was probably all connected. *Stay focused. Push forward.* He put down the phone and turned to the clerk.

"How much in cash?"

"For one night, sir?"

"Yeah, one night. Non-smoking, if you have it."

"Seventy-nine dollars, sir, plus tax. Will you wish to use the phone?"

"Damn straight. There seems to be an awful lot wrong with the world at the moment."

"I'll need another twenty dollars as a deposit on the phone, sir."

Baylor fished a hundred and ten from his wallet. With the change he received from the hotel clerk, he had only a little over thirty dollars remaining. He accepted his key, lifted his bag and stepped into the elevator.

Once in his room, Baylor tossed his gym bag on the diminutive desk, sat on the edge of the bed and called his bank in Pensacola. He asked for customer service and reached Janet Wallace, a middle-aged lady he remembered from previous visits.

"Hello, Commander Baylor. How can I be of service today?"

"Mrs. Wallace, you'll save my life if you'll wire about a thousand dollars to the Holiday Inn at Andrews AFB, in Maryland. There's some snafu with my credit card and I'm caught short."

"Why sure, Commander Baylor. We would be glad to help. Do you have your account number handy?"

"Yes, ma'am." Baylor rattled off the string of numbers from memory. Over the clicking of a keyboard in the background, he heard her breathe, "Why, that's not right." A moment later she said, "Just a minute, Commander. I'll be back with you shortly."

She soon returned. "I'm very sorry, Commander. There must be some mistake. The IRS has issued a levy on your checking account. The assets are frozen and I cannot access your funds."

Baylor rocked on the bed as he considered the unfolding picture.

"Commander Baylor, are you there?"

"Sorry to bother you, Mrs. Wallace. Goodbye."

Baylor lay back upon the bed and peered at the ceiling. He knew he must fight the frustration and chaos that threatened to overwhelm his thinking. He did his best to dampen the emotions. He imagined himself at forty thousand feet, under attack by several adversaries. His opponents had launched their missiles first. They were trying to isolate him. Pin him down. Eliminate his maneuverability.

Baylor sat up suddenly and dialed the number of a lawyer in Little Rock who had managed his father's estate. The image of air-to-air combat persisted. He was ducking the missiles—losing energy, speed and altitude. His enemies didn't care if they destroyed him. They just wanted him low and slow.

Baylor hung up before the phone was answered. *That was it*! The purpose of this charade was to tie him up in knots. *Why*?

It didn't make a lot of sense, but, he considered what he knew—Ouilette missing. Weber suddenly sick. The situation resembled a broad attack on the entire team.

What if I take the hit? The missile he was dodging was not fatal. What if he ignored it and turned his energy to attack instead? The idea appealed to him as it was opposite of what his unknown antagonist wanted or expected.

He considered an offensive. Where were his resources? He had transportation. Or did he? Was the Eagle still available? To his mind, that was the obvious move. The credit cards and bank account were far more subtle. A quick call to base operations confirmed that the F-15 had departed for its home base in Colorado at 0800 in the morning.

In a way, the news settled him. He was guessing at an unknown enemy's strategy and analyzing it correctly. What about Pensacola? Could they block that avenue also? He dialed the number for his squadron's operations officer.

13:55 CDT, Minot AFB, North Dakota

Pigott directed the driver of his humvee to swerve to the right as the ambulance charged past them, its lights flashing and sirens wailing.

"That's the third one in the last ten minutes," the driver said.

"Step on it. Let's see what the devil is happening."

Pigott's vehicle arrived at the alert pad where a score of marines were hastily erecting a barricade around the Sikt. As the humvee approached, a marine turned toward them and raised his arm, palm forward. When the driver braked to a stop, the marine stepped up to the hummer and snapped a smart salute.

Pigott returned it. "Who needs the ambulances?"

"We've a dozen men down, sir."

"How?"

"It's the XT craft, General. A patrol of two dropped first. When our guys rushed in to help, they toppled also. So did the first pair of medics on the scene."

"How are you getting them out of there?"

"Grappling hook, sir. We snag their clothes and drag them beyond the barricade. Sixty meters appears to be the safe limit."

"How bad?"

"They're comatose, sir. The medics think it'll pass in a few hours."

"Thanks, soldier. Stay alert."

When the marine returned to the perimeter, Pigott turned to his aide in the back seat. "Phil, I've been through all the data in Ouilette's office. There's nothing mentioned about this problem in the transcripts of the science meeting three days ago."

Colonel Philip Rotts removed his cap and rubbed his forehead. "Sir, there was another meeting with no transcript, at least we've not found one."

"The meeting with Ouilette, Weber, Baylor and Wozniak?"

"Yes, sir. On the morning of Petersham's death. Those four met with the Chao. All morning long, sir."

"All right, Phil. Find out what they know."

"Sir, Ouilette's not on the base. Neither is Baylor or Wozniak. Weber is drugged to his ears. I doubt the Chao would talk to us even if it could."

"Not to worry, Phil. I've put a plan in motion against Ouilette. He should be in custody shortly after he arrives in Washington. You call Baylor at his hotel. Find out if he knows anything. Are you sure he's still there?"

"Yes, sir. We've got him pinned. He can only go where he's willing to walk. We have a tail on him he's not likely to shake. Professionals."

"Good work, Phil. When you call..."

"Yes, sir?"

"Don't let Baylor know who or where you are."

"Yes, sir. What about this civilian, Wozniak?"

"Leave him be. If we discover that he knows something important, we'll pursue it."

Pigott turned to the driver. "Take us back." The hummer gathered speed and he glanced to his aide and added, "I want to move Weber to a secure location. One with iron bars."

16:10 EDT, Ronald Reagan International Airport

Ouilette climbed into the back seat of the cab. He dropped his suit bag on the seat beside him and propped his briefcase on the floor by his leg.

"Where to, suh?" The cabby, a black man with a Jamaican accent, was wearing a bright Hawaiian shirt and dark glasses.

"The Regency."

"Yes, suh." The cabby flipped down the meter's flag and shifted into gear. Ouilette settled into the seat, trying to put order to the chaos. In hindsight, he now wished he'd not ordered Baylor to return from Andrews. The F-15 might come in handy if he managed to reverse the situation at Minot. He was troubled about his inability to reach Weber all morning. His call to Baylor confirmed that the flyer had already left the BOQ.

Equally troubling was the inability to reach any of the upper levels at the NSA. Officially, he was still the deputy-director of operations. Only six days had passed since he departed for Colorado Springs and a week's vacation. He was not due back until tomorrow.

It remained a surprise therefore, when his boss, or even Rear Admiral Jervison, who ran the NSA, could not take his calls. Time to try again. Ouilette switched on his cell phone. It immediately beeped with an incoming call.

"Ouilette."

"Left Claw Four. See the clown at 10th and Pennsylvania. Turn off your phone."

With a click, the line went dead. For a dozen seconds, Ouilette sat in place, replaying the message in his mind. *It's over the top!* He shook his head and then flipped the switch on the cell phone to the off position.

He rapped on the Plexiglas partition. "Changed my mind. Take me to 10th Street and Pennsylvania."

"That be a good idea, mon. You be gettin' no rest in that hotel."

Up ahead, with lights flashing, a dozen police cars lined the street in front of the Regency. Officers had blocked the street from both directions and were directing traffic away from the hotel. As the cab swerved down a side street, Ouilette watched the scene from the rear window, wondering what the disturbance was all about.

Ten minutes later, the cab sidled up to the curb at the juncture of tenth and Pennsylvania. True to expectations, a clown in a red and blue suit, bearing a balloon with the *March of Dimes* logo emblazoned upon it, approached the cab. Ouilette rolled down his window. The man in the clown suit, bent low, but said nothing.

"I'd like to make a donation," Ouilette said.

The clown nodded vigorously, still silent. Ouilette fished a ten-dollar bill from his wallet and handed it to the clown who then handed him an envelope. The clown straightened and turned away. A few seconds later, he had disappeared in the crowd.

Ouilette carefully tore the end off the envelope, discovering inside a hotel key and a note.

Leave the cab. Walk to 12th and find the cab. Lic#245523.

Ouilette paid his fare and hiked the required two blocks. He found a Checker cab with the correct plate number and climbed into the rear seat. On the seat was a green gym bag. The cabby, a Caucasian in a straw hat and wrap-around dark glasses, grinned in the rear-view mirror. "You might want to change out of that uniform, sir. It's hot in Washington this time of year. Especially for Navy Commanders."

Ouilette nodded without replying. As the cab pulled away from the curb, he began a rapid change of clothes. Along with the civvies and shoes in the green gym bag, he found another wallet, a new cell phone and a Glock in .40 S&W. He racked the slide back. A full magazine.

"Welcome to the bush," the driver said.

Ouilette leaned back against the seat. *Night Tiger.* He relaxed and emptied his mind. Once the *tiger* swallowed him, his old life and all its expectations vanished. He knew for certain the reason for their action would be exceptionally astute.

20:15 EDT, Holiday Inn, Andrews AFB, Maryland

Baylor nodded when the waitress asked him if he was finished. He watched her whisk away the remains of his meal, along with almost half of his remaining funds. He leaned back in the chair and sipped another glass of the *bottomless* iced tea that had been a feature of the meal. Tonight, he figured, had to be the *Last Supper.* Unless things turned around in a hurry, he'd be in tough shape by this time tomorrow. The call to Pensacola had been a disaster. The operations officer and squadron commander had both been reassigned. No one named Ed Baylor was listed on the squadron roster and, according to the computer, there never had been. A call to base personnel uncovered empty file folders for records of a Commander Baylor, but that officer had been reassigned and his records shipped off to the new location. They would not tell him where.

His unseen enemy had gone to extraordinary lengths to mess up his life and for a purpose still unknown to him. The net sum? He was stuck in a hotel, at least for one more night, and had no access to transportation or resources. Sixteen dollars and forty-three cents would not fund much of an offense.

The restaurant became crowded when a busload of tourists visiting the base stopped for an evening meal. The waitress wanted his table for another patron, so Baylor levered himself out of his chair and ambled into the lounge.

He chose a booth set back from the bar, where he had a good view of the television, and ordered a pitcher of beer. The barmaid brought a basket of chips as well. The lounge was also busy, but with a different type of clientele. This crowd seemed content to sit and chat, and watch the early season ball game on TV. Baylor watched also and thus did not see her approach.

"Hey, Navy. Mind if I join you?"

She stood a couple of inches taller than average and was wearing a white blouse and designer jeans. Fit, athletic, with an auburn cluster of coils styled as a modified Afro. She had a pixie face, but Baylor could see the African roots in her heritage despite the light color of her skin.

"Sit and be welcomed," he replied. As she slid into the opposite side of the booth, he added, "What makes you think I'm Navy?"

She smiled, exposing a perfect set of bright white teeth. "Could be the salt in your hair. Sea-green eyes, that sort of thing."

Baylor laughed, enjoying the first pleasant happenstance in almost three days. "I must have been reincarnated without my knowledge. Or maybe you're pulling my leg."

"Hon, I never pull a stranger's leg." She extended her left hand, pushing her knuckles against his before adding, "Maybe it's the jewelry you wear."

On her third finger and across from his, glittered an identical though smaller Naval Academy ring. Baylor shook his head. "I'm slow tonight." He stuck out his hand. "Ed Baylor, Lieutenant Commander."

She wrapped a long-fingered delicate hand in his. "Adele Reeves, Lieutenant. Don't expect any salutes tonight, Commander Baylor."

"Why not? And call me Ed."

"Okay, Ed. Because for a little while the Navy doesn't exist."

"You must be on vacation or something."

"Something like that. What about you?"

"Right now, I'm not sure."

"Are you in trouble with the Navy?"

"It's a complex situation. Let me pour you a beer."

"The beer and pizza's on me," she said with a dazzling smile. "After all, I did crash your party, such as it was. Why so glum?"

"I've already eaten."

"Well, I'm half starved. You can keep the leftovers for tomorrow."

Baylor leaned back and watched as she ordered. Her movements were quick and animated—her eyes full of life. When the waitress left, she lifted her glass to sip her beer and said, "You didn't answer my question."

Baylor studied her for a moment. "I've no way back."

"Where's back and why do you want to go?"

He shook his head. "Sorry, Lieutenant. Security. If I told you, I'd have…

"to kill me," she chimed in, matching his words. "I get the picture."

"This one's not for public consumption, Adele."

"In that case, tell me about you. Unless you're not for public consumption either, and from where I sit that would be a shame."

She said that with bright eyes and a smile that left Baylor momentarily bedazzled. When he could gather his wits, he said, "What would you like to know?"

"What do you do in the Navy?"

"I fly fighter jets."

Adele threw back her head and laughed. "Not very original, Ed."

"I do!"

"Yeah, right. What type?"

"Black Widow."

"Of course. The meanest and fastest there is." She leaned forward, her face suddenly wearing a dead-serious expression. "Get this wrong, and I'm gone. What's the service ceiling?"

"That's classified."

"The maximum duration at super-cruise?"

"That's classified also. Ask me something I can answer."

"Fourth item on the checklist after engine shut-down?"

Baylor blinked. "Electric brakes." He laughed and added, "Like you would know if that was bullshit or not."

"And then you safe the seat," she replied.

His smile vanished. "Just what the hell do you do, Lieutenant? I think I know every Widow pilot there is, so it can't be that."

"War college instructor. I know a lot."

"No shit! How did you get into that prestigious gig?"

"I'm good at what I do. But this is supposed to be about you. How long have you been driving Widows?"

"Eighteen months."

"And before that?"

"Raptors on the Reagan air wing."

"And before that?"

Baylor laughed. "You want my service history or my life story?"

"Yes."

He leaned back in his seat. "Maybe I should start at the beginning then, instead of walking backward." At a little toss of her head, which he took for an affirmative, he said, "Where to start?"

"Where did you grow up?"

"Near Clarksdale, a little town in northwest Mississippi. What about you?"

"In the mid-west." She jabbed a slim forefinger in his direction. "Stay on track. Brothers, sisters?"

"None. Ma did not survive childbirth, and so it was just me and my pop."

"What did he do? Did you guys get along well? Is he still living in Mississippi?"

Baylor laughed again. "This feels like a job interview. We got along great, whenever I saw him, which was not often. He was a foreman on one of those mobile combine units that travelled all over the states and through western Canada during spring, summer and fall, so he made a pretty good wage for a guy with no high-school education. He always said his primary goal in life was to make sure I had a good education, and so I lived with his sister, my aunt, until I graduated from high school. Pop lobbied with one of our senators until he secured my billet at the academy. He died of a heart attack during my last year, but I'm pretty sure he passed knowing he had accomplished his life's goal. How many of us can say that?"

"Not many," Adele quietly said. "That's a nice story."

"So...quid pro quo...what about yours?"

"Not for public consumption, Ed. Not yet."

"What! You're not going to tell me anything?" At the pert shake of her head, he added, "How's that fair?"

"It's not, but that's the way it is until I know you better."

Baylor shrugged and said, "Well...if we've run the gauntlet on me...and you won't talk about you...then where do we go from here?"

"Where would you like to go? Other than the *back* you can't talk about?"

"I'd like to forget about that right now."

"In that case, let's have some fun instead."

"Like what?"

She lifted both hands shoulder high and clenched her fists. "Boogie!"

"Dancing? Dressed like this?" Baylor was still wearing his sweats.

"Is that all you have?"

"Next to my flight suit."

"Don't you guys ever pack for the unexpected? Forget it! I know the answer. Wear what you've got on. If you wore a flight suit, people would think you're a plumber."

Adele had wolfed three pieces of the pizza while they talked. Baylor leaned against the edge of the booth, considering. It could be a set-up—part of the campaign to isolate and confuse him. If so, certainly the best part so far. "I hate to be a spoilsport, but there's another problem," he added. "No wheels."

"I've got the wheels part covered. Are you ready?"

"Right now?"

"Let's go, Mister Navy Pilot Ed. Before I think all the stuff I've heard about hotshot flyers is just a bunch of hooey."

"What have you heard?" Baylor asked with a grin.

"Uh-uh!" Her curls bounced delightfully when she shook her head. "No self-fulfilling prophecies from this woman. Are you planning to sit in a bar all night feeling sorry for yourself?"

Charade or not, her offer was much better than that. The decision took two seconds. "Not guilty, ma'am."

"All right, then. Let's go."

Baylor followed her out of the lobby and into the parking lot. They turned to the left and skimmed the trees edging the asphalt. Halfway across she turned suddenly. "Oops! Forgot my coat. Will you wait?"

"I'll get it."

Adele reached into her pocketbook and fished out her keys. "You're driving. You can warm it up."

Baylor squinted at the keys. He couldn't make out the emblem in the darkness. "Warm what up?"

She lanced one slim arm across his chest and pointed toward a nearby white Porsche 911SC. Baylor glanced at the sports car and then back to the woman. But, Adele had already begun her sprint across the lot and toward the lobby entrance.

He watched the symmetry of her hips sway as she ran. *Nice butt.* He walked to the car, bent to unlock the door but noticed a flashing red light of an alarm inside and decided to wait until she returned.

Adele soon reappeared. She started across the lot but then turned toward the trees. Baylor could make out the figure of a man standing almost inside the tree line. Adele approached him and he turned toward her. Suddenly they were grappling.

"Hey!" Baylor shouted.

"Hey!" he repeated as he raced across the lot. Before he had covered half the distance, Adele's arms flailed and she skipped backward. The man pitched forward on his face and lay still. Baylor reached her in the next moment.

"Are you okay?"

"Yeah." She was breathing heavily. "The creep calls out like he's sick and then goes for a grope."

Baylor knelt beside the fallen man and felt for a pulse. "He's out cold. Want me to call the cops?"

"And spend the evening at some dreary police station?"

"He'll come around in a while. Headache for sure tomorrow." Baylor stood and turned toward her. "You know how to take care of yourself, Lieutenant."

"Adele."

"Adele." Baylor offered his arm. "Remind me not to try a grope," he added.

"You think you'd suffer the same fate?"

"Are you saying I wouldn't?"

"I'm saying nothing of the sort, Pilot Ed."

The words hit him like a blow.

"What's wrong?" she asked."

They climbed into her car and he put the key in the ignition before replying. "Nothing. For a second you reminded me of someone else."

"Another woman, right?"

Baylor ducked his head. "Well, sort of."

"If it's a wife, the groper will have company on the sidewalk."

Baylor laughed. "I'm not married. Nor engaged."

"I'm glad. Start the car and let's go."

He did. They entered the beltway and headed for Georgetown before she brought the subject up again. "So this other woman, Ed. What's she like?"

"Let's forget about her. It's just you and me tonight."

"Smooth, Ed, but it doesn't work that way. You tell a woman, namely me, that I remind you of another woman. So now, I've got to know why the woman of the second part, namely me, reminds you about the woman of the first part. Am I making myself clear? Turn here."

Grinning, he dropped into third gear and the Porsche deftly swerved to the right. "Uh, not exactly. Could you repeat the first and second part stuff?"

Adele elbowed him. "You're stalling, coward! Out with it. What's she like?"

Baylor rubbed his ribs where she struck him. "She's about your height, big eyes…"

"What color?"

"Uh, Yellowish. Amber. Something like that."

"What color's her hair?"

Baylor chuckled and said, "Which hair? You'll have to be more specific."

"Rat! I didn't ask if you were intimate. The hair on her head!"

"No! I didn't mean that. It's just that she has a lot of hair. The hair on her head is golden."

"A lot of hair? Like where? On her arms or face?"

"Yes."

"Yes to which?"

"To all and she weighs about two hundred pounds."

"Eeuuww! Now you better be careful, Ed. Why is it, exactly, that I remind you of this woman?"

"Well, she's super intelligent and very engaging. Also, it's the way she phrases questions and she called me Pilot Ed."

Adele folded her arms and leaned back in her seat. After a second, she nodded. "I like that. You were comparing my mind instead of looking at my ass. You're okay, Ed."

Baylor mentally offered a prayer of thanks and then turned into the club she indicated. He switched off the Porsche's throaty snarl, climbed out and opened her door.

"You're okay too, Adele. However, I cannot tell a lie. Your butt did not escape inspection."

She leaned close and jabbed a forefinger into his chest. "The important question is, did it pass?"

"Oh, yeah."

Adele smiled and stepped away. "Let's go dancin'!" she shouted into the sky. She began a series of dance steps toward the entrance of the club. Baylor followed in her serpentine wake.

Back at the Holiday Inn, the man who had grappled with Adele climbed to his feet and shook his head. With a hand clutched to the side of his face, he shuffled to a nondescript sedan. He unlocked the door, climbed in and drove away. A few seconds later, a second man stepped from another vehicle, this one a black Dodge Ram 4x4. He walked casually into the lobby and up to the desk.

"You've an envelope for me? Name's Taskill." A crisp twenty-dollar bill followed the question.

The clerked nodded and pocketed the twenty. He glanced at the robustly framed man with a beard, dark glasses and a baseball cap pulled down over his eyes. He reached into his mail basket and drew out the envelope.

"Here you are."

The bearded man retrieved the envelope and turned away. He stepped into a nearby phone booth and dialed a number. It rang once before someone picked up the other end. The caller said, "Right Claw Two retrieved the package while the shadow slept." He hung up and left the Inn. He didn't open the envelope until he reached the 4x4 and had climbed inside.

He tore off the end and dumped out a micro-cassette. This, he inserted into a pocket player and listened all the way to the end, rewound it and played it again.

Finally, he switched on his cellular phone, dialed another number and said, "Phase two." He switched off his phone, started the turbo-diesel engine and eased the truck away from the Inn.

Chapter Ten
01:12 EDT, 11 May, Georgetown, MD

Baylor strolled toward the Porsche, enjoying the sensation of the woman's body pressed close to his. His arm encircled her waist and she leaned her head on his shoulder as they walked. "Had enough for one night?" he asked.

"Mmmmm." Her reply oozed contentment.

Baylor unlocked the passenger's door and she slipped into her seat. He climbed in opposite and thrust the keys in the ignition. "Where to? Coffee?"

Resting her head against the seat back, she turned toward him, her eyes soft and luminous. "I'm taking you home."

"Just like that? Not that I object, mind you."

"I think so. Start the car, I'll give you directions as we drive."

They crossed the river into Virginia and turned northwest. In three or four miles, she told him to exit from the highway and turn left on Route 120. A couple of minutes later they turned right onto Highway 29. About a mile up the road, Baylor could see the flashing hazard lights of a large truck pulled over on the shoulder. He downshifted and veered toward the center to pass when Adele laid her hand atop his on the shifter.

"Pull in behind the truck."

He eased off the gas, shifted down and braked to a stop. He engaged the emergency brake and left the Porsche idling in neutral. Adele unclipped her belt and surged across the seat toward him. Her lips were soft and warm on his cheek. She breathed into his ear. "Here we are."

When she retreated, Baylor glanced around. There was nothing but the truck in front of them. "Your home is a semi?"

Adele retreated to her side of the car. "I said I was taking *you* home."

Baylor leaned back against his window. "What gives, Adele? What's going on?"

"You're a target, Commander Baylor, and an enemy of the United States has decided to eliminate you from the field. They've been gentle so far but that probably won't last, so I'm taking you out of their line of fire. While you'll no longer appear in *their* sights, you may become the hunter. All you need to know is to remember your oath and to follow your conscience."

Baylor nodded. "You've summed up my predicament without telling me a damn thing. You're also offering me the means to strike back. I was trying to think of something like this back in that bar. What you haven't told me is who you are and what you're part of."

She grinned mischievously. "If I told you, I'd have to..."

"Kill me..." he echoed with a laugh. "All right, I can accept the need for security. Are you really Navy, Adele? Or is that part of a masquerade?"

"I was, Ed. And might become so again."

"Depending on what?"

"On how goes the battle. It's likely to be a long one."

He pursed his lips. "I think maybe this is all related. This stuff you're doing and what I was involved in."

She simply sat watching him.

"Still, it requires a long leap of faith, Adele. I wish I had time to think this over."

"I can understand why you feel that way. But this enemy of ours has you pinned to the ground. You've no transportation and no resources. Right now, the enemy doesn't know where you are. If you return to the hotel, you'll have no options. If you decide to join us, every decision you make will be your own."

Baylor drew a deep breath, and then nodded. "If you're playing me for a fool, I have to admit I'm enjoying it. I'm in."

She leaned forward and honked the horn. The rear door to the truck began to lift and a pair of ramps extended. Adele opened her door and climbed out of the Porsche. She shut the door and walked around to his side while Baylor rolled down the window. She bent close and said, "Drive inside, Ed. Keep your mind and ears open. You've a lifetime of training ahead of you."

"Will I see you again?"

She smiled wistfully. "It's less than likely, but tonight was fun, and I won't forget you. Go on, now. We're exposed with the truck open."

Baylor jammed the gearshift into first and drove up the ramp and into the truck. The semi immediately lurched forward while the ramps retracted and the door started to descend. In the rearview mirror, Adele's slim outline retreated in the distance. She stood in the middle of the road, alone.

17:40 MDT, Los Alamos Laboratories, NM

Wozniak patched in two more fiber-channels, bringing the total to an even dozen. He reset the simulation and started it again. This time the data-search was far faster.

"Got you, you little bugger."

For two days, the bottleneck had eluded him, his software extraction routine bogging down until the screen froze. He tackled it bit by bit, line by line, until he had usurped the computational capability of the entire campus. CPU horsepower had not solved the problem. It was the data rate of the infernal crystal. His first test had shown that nothing currently on the market could accept data at the speed the crystal dumped it.

Instead of trying to slow the crystal, which he wasn't sure was possible, he opened parallel paths to every buffer his lab's cluster could offer. The next problem was to empty the buffers in an organized manner. The new super-spiders from Altavista Software had solved that problem. Operating over twelve-terabit enhanced optical channels, the spiders snatched the data, organized it, linked it, indexed it and filed it on the cluster's disk farm. Volume was still going to be a problem. He had access to only about a quarter of the space he'd need to download the entire contents of the crystal.

The simulation concluded successfully.

"That's my baby," he whispered and snatched his phone from its cradle. He punched in four digits and when the other end picked up, said, "It works, Tim. Build it."

"Great, Doc! Day after tomorrow?"

"To tell the truth, Timmy, I'm salivating. Can you finish it sooner?"

"Hey Doc, hardware isn't the same as software. I can't whack out a few strokes on the keyboard and *voila*! Instead, I need to acid etch multiple layers of PCB. I need to bake the layers together in an oven. Then comes insertion and wave soldering."

"I get the point. Soonest then."

"You bet."

Wozniak put the phone down and it rang immediately.

He picked it up again. "What now?"

"Hey, Doctor Wozniak. You got a minute?" It was not the hardware engineer, Tim Reynolds. The voice sounded familiar, however. "Excuse me, I thought you were someone else."

"C'mon Doc. It's Baylor. I thought we were on the same team."

"Sorry, Commander Baylor. I didn't recognize your voice. Where are you calling from?"

"Out east, Doc. I was hoping you could help me out here."

Wozniak grabbed a sheet of paper and wrote the time and Baylor's name under it. "I'm kind of under the gun. Deadlines, you know. What do you need?"

"Well, Doc, it's like this. I've been out of touch with Weber and Ouilette for several days. I can't get either of them to call me back. I've been stuck in a hotel with no place to go and no way to get there. You know what I mean?"

Wozniak began to feel uncomfortable. He twiddled his pen through Baylor's last question. "Like I said, Commander, How can I help? What do you want me to do?"

"You've had a few days to think about everything. How do you feel about it now? You still believe all this crap? I know I'm having second thoughts."

Wozniak frowned. "All what crap? Come on, Commander. Get to the point. I need to get back to the crystal." He felt a tiny flare of alarm. *Uh-oh, shouldn't have said that.*

Baylor's voice replied, "You know ... all that stuff the alien told us about her mission and the breach at 3C."

Now the scientist was truly alarmed. Baylor knew better than to discuss this over the phone. He was also unlikely to call Linneow *the alien*. Wozniak hung up.

Minot AFB, Communications Center

"Ingenious, Phil. Simply amazing."

"I think he caught on at the end, sir."

"Maybe he did, maybe he didn't. He'll have doubts in any regard. If Baylor does try to contact him, he's likely to refuse the call. How does this work?" Pigott indicated a nearby computer system.

Rotts explained, "We recorded all of Baylor's outgoing calls and digitized the analog signal, thereby constructing a database. When I speak into the handset, my words are converted to text and then, the text to speech, choosing words from Baylor's database. The software modifies inflection according to context and all at a speed that makes it seem natural."

"It seemed so to me. You started to tell me about Baylor."

"Yes, sir. We lost him and Commander Ouilette. I could accept the disappearance of Ouilette. He was a SEAL, and they can be resourceful. However, Baylor did not react as expected. He didn't raise hell with the bank, call the IRS, or a lawyer. He went out on a date with a woman and promptly disappeared."

"What about our tail?"

"Ex-CIA operative and a good one. Baylor's date, a college-girl type, put his lights out."

"Can he ID her? Maybe we can track Baylor through the woman."

He's on the computer now, sir. We've started a search a half an hour ago." Rotts added, "We traced Ouilette via a cab to tenth and Pennsylvania. That's where the cabby said he got out."

"Could Ouilette be running an op?"

Rotts shook his head. "Don't think so, sir. Everyone at the NSA is accounted for."

"You've worked miracles so far, Phil. We need to visit New Mexico, I think. I don't like the sound of that crystal Wozniak's working on."

"What's on your mind, sir? Shakedown?"

"Too complicated. An accident, perhaps."

"Escalation, sir? Is it appropriate?"

"Spoken like a good tactical officer. The answer is...I'm not sure. But I don't want these guys gaining traction. See to it."

Los Alamos Laboratories, NM

The phone rang again. Wozniak had been sitting, staring at it for the last five minutes. He tried to assess the nature and meaning of the previous call. After the fifth ring, he picked up the receiver. "H-hello?"

"Dr. Wozniak, this is Director Levine. I'm calling on behalf of my systems administrator who is unable to complete her job because you're not cooperating."

Wozniak rolled his eyes. "I know she feels that way, Director. But it's the work schedule. I cannot release the cluster to the IT team for another week without setting us back weeks, maybe even months."

"Doctor, there are six brand new systems in receiving—upgrades that have six times the power of the units you're using. We've processed them already. Which means the warranty has started and we will be required to pay for them in less than three weeks. I don't want to pay for hardware that I haven't even tested. Does that make it clearer, Doctor?"

"Director Levine, I know all that. I also know that your IT team will take one to two weeks to complete the testing during which the cluster will be unavailable to me. Since the testing takes place here, my lab will also become unavailable to me. If you interrupt the process of my programs at this time, a hundred machines, ten times as fast, will not help."

Resigned and cold, Levine's voice dropped an octave. "Doctor, you've five more days. Use them well." The line went dead.

Oh, shit! Wozniak pressed the flash button and dialed Tim Reynolds' number.

"Whaaaat! No, they're not ready!"

"How'd you know it was me?"

"Who else? What do you want?"

"Listen buddy, pal, old friend…"

"Oh, no. No-no-no. Whatever it is, keep me out of it."

"Hey, I lose my cluster in five days. I need that reader."

Reynolds sighed. "Levine, right?"

"Yup."

"Time to make a deal, Doc. What's the reader supposed to read?"

"I can't tell you."

"If you want it to read anything this month, you will."

"Look, buddy. It's government stuff. Really black stuff."

"Well, I guessed that already. Why else all the bandwidth? Let me be part of the program when I'm done with the hardware. I'll have to tune it real-time anyway. I'll see the data then."

"You may wish you'd kept your nose out of it."

"Not a chance. What's the subject? Surely you can tell me that much."

Wozniak paused a moment before he replied, "The beginning of the universe. How's that grab you?"

Several seconds of silence followed. Reynolds' voice came back subdued. "I'll buy if you fly. Everything but anchovies."

Wozniak chuckled and patted his considerable stomach. "We'll need two."

"Bullshit! More like three. I know you, Stan."

Wozniak laughed outright and hung up. He would start on the hardware drivers immediately. Using the bulk of the code he'd written for the simulators, he might be finished by midnight or even sooner.

19:10 CDT, Interstate 70, Topeka, Kansas

The driver topped his tanks and vaulted back into the cab of the semi. When he saw his partner lope toward the truck from the truck-stop office, he started the diesel and shifted into low range. Ouilette climbed into the far side of the cab. "Let's roll."

The old Peterbuilt cab-over eased out onto the highway, gaining speed at a good clip due to the light load. Ouilette punched the intercom buzzer. A few seconds later, a voice replied, "Sir?"

"How's our passenger?"

"Sleeping like a baby. How he does it beat's me. Hell of a racket back here."

"Give him an hour and then wake him up and feed him. We're going to put him to work."

Ouilette broke the connection and turned to the driver.

"Any deserted ramp...say in about sixty miles. We're going to turn our package loose."

"You aren't taking him to the installation, sir?"

Ouilette shook his head. "Too soon. He doesn't have the conditioning to carry him so deep."

"It's tough working in the dark, sir."

"Are you speaking for our guest or yourself, commando?"

"A little of both, sir. We're all on our toes, but without a mission profile, one of us could make a mistake. I'm surprised it hasn't happened already."

Ouilette paused before replying, "We've assumed a defensive posture and we'll need to sustain it for some time yet. Lifting me off the hook and helping Baylor out of his jam was good thinking. We'll need information before we can act and that's where Baylor comes in."

"What's our mission with the truck, sir? After we separate from Baylor?"

"Same as before, mister. Another load of food to Utah."

"Sort of thought so, sir. Just checking."

Ouilette clapped the commando on his shoulder. "You weren't hoping for contact were you, son?"

About an hour later, Baylor awoke to someone thumping on the roof of the Porsche. He straightened with a jerk, banging his head on the liner. For an instant, he could not determine where he was. As the images of the previous day flooded into his mind, he picked out the faint traces of perfume from the interior of the sports car.

Baylor opened the door and slipped through the narrow space afforded by the lack of clearance; the Porsche wasn't all that much smaller than the interior width of the semi-trailer. Two odors triggered his mind and stomach into action.

Bacon and coffee.

The inside of the trailer was illuminated and, near its forward end, a table and a Sterno stove had been erected. The cook, a compact man with a mustache, waved him onward.

"C'mon and eat. Not much time left." The other man wore jeans, a flannel shirt with a canvas vest and a ball cap. Military-style chukka boots adorned his feet.

Baylor eased forward, matching his movements to the natural sway of the trailer. "Before what?"

"The boss's cutting you loose."

Baylor only nodded. He gulped down scrambled eggs and bacon and followed it with coffee. The man across from him watched him eat with an intensity that bordered on obsession. Baylor just stared back.

Finally, the other shrugged and said, "You keep your trap shut, I'll give you that."

Baylor grinned and replied, "The lady said to keep my ears and mind open. She said nothing about my mouth." He extended his hand. "I'm Baylor."

"Not any more. Your new name's Ryerson." The commando shook his hand anyway. Then he swiped at his own face up near his cheekbone. "You got a...a target on your face. That Long Rifle might be marking herself a new man."

"Huh?" Baylor said.

The commando passed a paper towel. "Lipstick, man. A perfect zero in red."

Baylor wiped the towel across his face. It came away with red smudges. He chuckled. "Damn! That was my only souvenir. What did you call her? A long rifle?"

The commando's eyes closed down. "Forget it." He stood and began to clear away the remnants of the meal. As soon as Baylor stood, the folding table and chairs followed the stove and dishes. The truck slowed abruptly and gently swerved to the right. It pitched down a gradual incline and bounced to a stop.

The commando pointed to the Porsche. "Climb in. Wait until I open the gate then fire it up and back out. No lights."

"Got it. Where in hell are we, anyway."

"Not in hell, at least not yet. Kansas."

No Shit! Baylor clambered into the Porsche. The lights inside the trailer flicked off and when the door rumbled upward, he started the engine. Backing slowly, while keeping the wheel straight, he eased down the ramp without incident. He switched off the engine and climbed out.

As he leaned against the side of the car, a tall lanky gentleman in western garb sauntered back toward him from the direction of the cab. The newcomer wore dark glasses and a full beard under his straw cowboy hat. "Mr. Ryerson, I presume?" he said.

Baylor could swear he'd never seen this man before, but his voice sounded hauntingly familiar. "That's me. Who are you?"

"Call me Grant. I've something that belongs to you."

Recognition flooded Baylor. "Thank God! Comman—"

"No!" Ouilette waved his forefinger. "Just Grant. We're among friends at the moment, Mr. Ryerson. It will not always be so. Learn to go with the flow." Ouilette dropped a newspaper on the hood of the Porsche.

"Interesting reading, don't you think?"

Baylor picked up the newspaper and opened it. The headlines, in one-inch block letters, screamed, *Assassin still at large*. As Baylor scanned the page, he found shock after shock. Finally, he glanced up at Ouilette.

"My God, sir! He was your friend and they're saying you killed him."

"And planned to kill the President. And that I'm responsible for a security breach at 3C. A clever web of deception."

"That's why you—"

"I've not reacted to this affair. Just as you, so correctly, did not react to the nest of lies they built around your life. My team pulled me undercover at the right time, just as they were trained to do. You also."

Baylor nodded. "In my case, very smoothly done, Mr. Grant. My compliments to your agent." Baylor rubbed his chin. "Nice beard."

"I'll pass it along." Ouilette scratched his throat, ignoring the aviator's second comment.

"I was hoping you would. Now, you have a task for me, I've heard."

Ouilette nodded. "I'm sending you down to see Wozniak. He's at Los Alamos Laboratory near Santa Fe." Ouilette reached into his jacket and pulled out a cell phone.

"Use this to contact him. Turn it on, use it and turn it off."

"Saving batteries?"

"You can be tracked through your cell phone."

"Got it. What do I tell Wozniak?"

"Make an appointment. You'll have to be clever as he's working all out on our project and will not welcome interruptions. I want you to support him. Back him up if trouble comes his way. We need his data badly, Mr. Ryerson. And we need his help to locate Weber."

"Why me?"

Ouilette smiled. "You ask because you're not trained as an agent or a commando and you think I've a lot of resources who are better qualified?" When Baylor nodded, Ouilette continued, "For precisely those reasons. The operatives in this program are irreplaceable. I can't risk even one unless the results demand it. I'm afraid you're the most expendable at the moment."

Baylor nodded. "Think you might ever need a jet jockey?"

"If so, your stock will increase accordingly." Ouilette held his hand out. "Your wallet please."

Baylor passed it to Ouilette and received another in exchange, one that appeared as battered and worn as his own. He opened it. It was filled with currency, mostly twenties and fifties.

Baylor lifted his eyes. "Looks like I got a raise."

"Operating capital. Conserve it as if it were your own."

Baylor stuck the wallet in his hip pocket. He scooped up the newspaper, folded it and thrust it into the Porsche. He turned back to Ouilette.

"What about Linneow, sir? How does she figure into all this?"

"She is the purpose of all this, my friend. If we cannot remove the threat to her life...if she dies, then we've lost before we've begun." Ouilette unfolded a map from his hip pocket and marked their present location. He circled the city of Los Alamos on the map and thumped it with the tip of his pen.

"Any questions?"

"Two, sir. Hardware and clothing? If someone moves against Wozniak, I need to defend him, and my sweats are beginning to ripen."

Ouilette considered the question for a moment. "Your best bet, Mr. Ryerson, would be to run like hell and then call our ops center. Here's the number. If things get really tense, you'll find some tools in the trunk of the Porsche, alongside a suitcase filled with proper attire. Anything else?"

"No, sir. Thanks for the classy ride."

"Don't thank me. The car belongs to the lady. If I were you, I'd take mighty good care of it." Ouilette turned away, loped to the front of the truck and climbed inside. A few seconds later, the semi wound up through its gears, heading west. Soon, Baylor stood alone on the silent vastness of the Kansas prairie.

09:20 MDT, 12 May, Los Alamos, NM

"I need your driver's license, vehicle registration and proof of insurance, Mr. Ryerson." The security guard at the gate stuck out his hand. Baylor dug out the documents, wondering why it was that women saved empty gum wrappers. The glove box was full of them.

"The vehicle does not belong to you, sir?"

"Ah, no. It's my fiancée's. Mine's in the shop."

"What's the name of the host, Mr. Ryerson?"

Baylor blinked. "The host?"

"Whom are you visiting?"

"Oh! Doctor Wozniak. Stanley Wozniak."

"He's expecting you, sir."

Baylor adopted a bonhomie voice. "Stan has been on my case all week for my company's software routines. We just couldn't get them here in time. They arrived late last night and I drove up to Denver to pick them up. I haven't been able to reach Doctor Wozniak yet to let him know I was on my way."

The guard signed the visitor form and passed it to Baylor. "Put this in the left corner of your windshield. Do you know where the Theoretical Division is located, sir?"

Baylor grinned. "It's been a while, and this place is huge."

"Yes, sir. Well, stay on Research Drive until you reach the second intersection. Turn right and follow the road around to the left. The Theoretical Division is a cluster of ivory buildings in a cul-de-sac. You can't miss it. Dr. Wozniak's lab is located in building fourteen. You'll need to stop at the lobby and wait for an escort."

"Thanks a lot. You've been a big help."

The guard lifted the barrier and Baylor accelerated through the gates. About a hundred yards up the road he wiped his brow and muttered, "Man, this stuff is a bitch. How come James Bond never worked up a sweat?"

10:34 CDT, Minot AFB, North Dakota

"Her name is Karen Adele Royce. She's twenty-eight and a graduate of the Naval Academy. According to the information source, which is almost two years old, she's a Lieutenant, j.g., serving on the USS Vincennes as an assistant fire control officer." Rotts looked up from his report. "The problem, sir, is that this article says she was reassigned from that post to the War College in DC as an instructor in electronic countermeasures more than eighteen months ago. She is not at the War College."

Pigott tilted his head. "So where is she?"

"Sir, she doesn't exist, according to Navy records."

The general frowned. "Where did you get all this stuff then?"

"This information comes from an article in the Washington Post. They did a write-up that included a picture," Rotts passed a facsimile of the picture to Pigott, "and the information about her new posting."

Pigott read the article. "Second place in National High Power? A rifleman?"

"Yes sir, a long-range specialist. The details on the scoring shows that she set records in speed and precision during the eight hundred and nine hundred meter contests."

Pigott studied the picture. "Cute. Doesn't look like a rifleman." He glanced up. "Why does the Navy say she no longer exists?"

"Clarification, sir. They say she never existed. No academy records, no service aboard the Vincennes, no records, period."

"How do you explain this, Phil?"

Rotts grinned and said, "You knew I had an explanation, sir?"

"You've served me long enough to anticipate my questions. And long enough to know that I expect answers to them. So what's the answer?"

Rotts shook his head. "A damn clever one, sir. We decided to review the War College records. We thoroughly scanned their computers, including the backups. When we found no trace, we checked the log files. Of the several anomalies we discovered, one was very interesting. There is no log file for May 4th, eight days ago. The file for that date has been deleted."

"So a lot of stuff happened to their computer and the log of what happened was erased," Pigott restated.

"Yes, sir. We can guess that Royce was also being erased. When we followed her trail backward to the other Navy systems, we see the same pattern. The log files all took a hit on that same day. My analyst went a step further, sir. All branches of the service show similar traits in their master systems."

Pigott stiffened. "Recruiting?"

"It looks that way, sir."

The General stood and paced around the room. He paused. "Phil, this is damn disturbing. I want to know how many, who they are, and what their skills are."

Rotts shook his head. "I don't think that's possible, sir. We got lucky on Royce because we knew what she looked like. The hard-copy article gave us a break on the rest. Unless we knew what to look for, we could be searching for twenty or thirty people in a service population of almost two million. The odds of finding one of them is about a hundred thousand to one, against."

"Why can't you visit each personnel office on every base or ship and ask who transferred out that same day?"

Rotts grinned. "I've a test for you, Sir. If you can pass it, I'll be surprised." Rotts passed over a list with the names of the General's team on Minot. "This is a listing of all of our folks at Minot, about a hundred, sir. Do you recognize each and every name?"

Pigott scanned the list. "Of course, so what?"

Rotts handed him a second list. "Sir, one of our guys has the flu and could not report for duty today. This is today's duty roster. Pick out who's missing."

Pigott scanned it, frowned and then checked off each name. After a minute, he passed it back. "Point taken."

Rotts nodded. "I also have to reverse my previous position, sir. I now think Ouilette is running an operation. How extensive or capable is unknown."

Pigott considered for a moment and then said, "Find Royce, Phil. Move on her family. Tap their phones. Invent a story about her and make it public. Drive her to contact them and when she does, nail her to the ground. We'll pick her mind apart until we find what we need. And Phil?"

"Yes, sir?"

"This means you need to accelerate the plan for Wozniak. If Ouilette's putting together an organization, he's only had since the 4th to get it running. Let's make sure that he cannot gain more resources than he already has."

Chapter Eleven
09:54 MDT, 12 May, Los Alamos Laboratories, NM

"I'm sorry, Mr. Ryerson. Doctor Wozniak told me explicitly that he was not to be disturbed. He's been working all night, you know." The receptionist at the Theoretical Division lobby, a middle-aged brunette with rectangular rimless glasses and a beehive hairdo, would not budge in her defense of Wozniak's privacy.

Baylor replied, "I drove all the way from Denver with these computer tapes so he wouldn't need to work again tonight. Just buzz him and let me talk to him. I'm sure he'll be glad you did."

She leaned forward and whispered, "I can't. He told me not to ring him even if Director Levine calls again. He stressed, 'On pain of death, Marla.'"

Baylor laughed. "What could he do, Marla? Sit on you?"

She rocked back in her seat, her eyes wide with delight, hand over her mouth. Baylor followed up his success. "Look, he won't be mad at you. If anything he'll be mad at me for not arriving yesterday."

She was still shaking her head when a door chimed behind her. She glanced over her shoulder and then quickly turned back to Baylor and winked. "I have a solution."

She called out to the newcomer in a singsong voice, "Oh, Tim? Are you going down to Stanley's lab again?"

The wiry man dressed in blue jeans, a flannel shirt and boat shoes with no socks, straightened from pushing his cart.

"Yep. One more trip."

"Can you escort Mr. Ryerson down to the Lab. Doctor Wozniak's expecting him."

Tim Reynolds looked dubious. "I'm not sure, Marla. Stan's working on some highly classified stuff for the government."

Baylor smiled. "I'm with the government, and if you're referring to the crystal, then that's my project."

"Holy Smoke! C'mon then. You can give me a hand."

When they reached the end of the sidewalk, Reynolds lifted two of the gray metal boxes from the cart. He pointed at the third with his chin. "Can you manage that last one, Mister...er, I forgot your name. Sorry."

"Ed Ryerson. Sure." Baylor laid his briefcase on the last box and lifted them both. About the size of a shoebox, the metal case seemed relatively dense.

"What's in these things? They didn't look this heavy."

Tim mumbled through the key that he held clenched in his teeth. "Power supplies, oscillators, ROM chips, and one big whopper of a gate array."

"Is that what weighs so much?"

"Hell, no! The silicon weighs just a few ounces. I thought you were in the computer end of things."

The two men approached a featureless one-story, flat-roofed building. Reynolds asked, "Can you get the door?"

"Sure." Baylor picked up the previous thread. "I know squat about hardware. We worked up some software routines for Doctor Wozniak."

Reynolds indicated the door at the far end of the hallway. "Use this key to unlock the elevator we're going to use."

"The lab is below ground?"

"Four floors down. The stuff they play with in here needs bedrock for shielding. Keeps them from causing a ruckus in campus communications and vice-versa. That's also why my boxes are so heavy. Some of the freqs I use could be heard in Singapore otherwise."

Both men stepped into the elevator. Reynolds pressed the level five button. The elevator dropped swiftly and then abruptly slowed its descent. The doors slid back and Baylor led the engineer into a cavernous room filled with bulky shapes and flickering shadows.

"Wow, can't see a thing," Baylor remarked.

"Hey, Stan! How about some lights?" Reynolds called. In a softer tone he added, "Wozniak never keeps the lights on. These software types seldom do. Beat's me why."

The lights flickered overhead and suddenly the shapes resolved themselves into rows of computer cabinetry. Baylor could hear the hiss of air-conditioning against a backdrop of whining fans.

Wozniak stuck his head around a corner. He withdrew and then abruptly leaned back again, exclaiming, "What the heck! Tim you can't…"

Wozniak then obviously recognized the man standing in front of Reynolds. His face filled with surprise and alarm. He lurched to his feet and lumbered toward them.

Baylor held up a hand. "Before you say anything, let me tell you that Ouilette sent me. He said it's urgent that I contact you here."

Wozniak turned to Reynolds. "Tim, the hookup is just around the corner. I need to talk with my buddy here a moment."

Reynolds bobbed his head. "Yup. Government secrets and all. No sweat. I'll get started." He tramped off in the direction Wozniak had indicated. After making sure he was out of earshot, Wozniak turned back to Baylor. "What the hell, Commander Baylor?" he whispered.

"It's Ryerson while I'm here, Doc. That's the name Ouilette assigned me."

Wozniak blinked. "I thought you were a flyer...not a secret agent."

"Well, things are confused at the moment. I guess I'm supposed to be an agent for now."

"You sure scared the hell out of me with that call."

"What call?"

"You called yesterday evening, between five and six."

"No, sir. I did not. I was out like a light. Riding in a semi across the Kansas prairie. What makes you think it was me?"

"You told me so. With the very same voice you're speaking with now."

"Shit! That's impossible, Doc. I didn't even know where you were."

Wozniak became agitated. "What's going on? Whoever it was even mentioned Ouilette and Weber by name. Seemed like a real breach of security to me. I hung up."

"Damn good idea. Someone was scamming you, Doc. What did he want?"

"He asked if I still believed in all this crap. Those exact words."

Baylor nodded. "Trying to pump you. Did this impostor mention anything specific?"

"No. That's what spooked me. That and he called Linneow, *the alien*. Since you have the hots for her, I didn't think you would refer to her in such a cavalier manner."

Baylor flushed to the extent that color was visible even through his darker complexion. "Jeez, Doc. She's from another planet."

"Whatever. It seemed very wrong, so I hung up."

Baylor shook his head. "That's disgusting, Doc."

"Why?"

"Why what?"

"Why is it disgusting? I mean, from a scientific point of view, she looks like a human woman, within limits. She has a great figure from a man's point of view."

"Doc! We don't even know if all those curves mean the same as they would in a human woman."

"Well, they do, to a degree. I sat in the medical briefing. She's mammalian, bears live young, and in approximately the same way a human female does. One can assume the Chao are impregnated similarly. She acts like a woman socially or did you miss that?" When Baylor shook his head, Wozniak added, "I thought not."

"But, Doc, she's an extra-terrestrial."

"So what. You think she's sexy but you won't admit it."

"Look Doc, let's change the subject, all right?"

"Very well. Why, exactly, are you here?"

Baylor was thankful for the shift. "Ouilette. By the way, his name is Grant now. I'm supposed to be your guardian angel."

"Carrying this spy stuff a little far aren't we?"

Baylor opened his briefcase and pulled out the paper Ouilette had given him. "Don't you check the news, Doc?"

Wozniak studied the headlines for most of a minute. He lifted his face. "This is a pack of lies. Who would believe this crap?"

"The truth isn't being told, Doc. And the bad boys who leaked this stuff are out to make sure that anyone who could, won't. Like you and me."

Wozniak appeared flustered. "What're we to do? How can we compete with the national media when our people are being painted as mega-villains?"

"Doc, we do what we can. You finish your reader. That gives us data. Ouilette wants us to track down Weber because something's happened to him. He was in the Minot base hospital but the other side has moved him somewhere else. He was hoping you could locate him."

"I can. Or rather you—"

"Hey, you guys!" Tim Reynolds hollered from the next aisle. "Are you going to jawbone all day? I'm hooked up and ready to tune unit number one."

As they walked toward the laboratory's test center, Wozniak hurriedly added, "You can run the search, while I'm programming the application into the ROMs."

"Me? I know squat about computers."

"Time to learn, Agent Ryerson. I'll set up the search engine and you type in text questions. The software does the rest."

"Sure! Like *Where is Sam Weber*? I'll bet not!"

"You'd lose that bet." Wozniak scribbled on a notepad. "It's Boolean math, you remember that."

"Faintly."

"Good. Type this, *double quotation, Sam Weber, plus sign, new location, end quotation*. Anything inside the double quotation is searched for an exact match. If those two phrases occur on any document anywhere accessible to the web, you'll come up with a hit. The software ranks the hits in order of relevance."

Baylor nodded. "I can handle that. Where do I work?"

"Let me get Tim started and I'll show you."

Wozniak scuttled away to the table where the hardware engineer had patched in all the cables to his first prototype reader. Soon their heads were inches apart as they carefully completed the programming of the ROMs and downloaded the reader console into flash memory. After twenty minutes, Wozniak returned to Baylor.

"Er … first name still Ed?"

"Yep, that's right."

"Good, I'm glad Mr. *Grant* didn't make it overly complicated. You ever surf the Web?"

"Sure, who doesn't?"

"Great, this is the same thing only on a larger scale. We've higher clearance than the typical web browser so you get into systems that would never be accessible from the public domain. C'mon, I'll log you on."

Wozniak led Baylor into an office about fifteen paces down the hall. He snapped on the lights and powered up the workstation sitting in the center of the desk. He scrolled through the startup routines and then connected to the resident search engine on campus.

"We have our own search server. It's a high-powered variant of the latest Google Iridium engine. Since this is a weekend, you should have the total capacity all to yourself. I'd suggest configuring the search before you begin. That isn't difficult since the tools are self-explanatory."

"If I have a question, I'll holler."

Wozniak nodded and ducked out of the office.

Baylor laid his hand on the mouse, circled the cursor a couple of times to get the feel and then clicked on tools. In the pop-up box, he checked most of the choices, all priorities, security levels, and ancillary search engines. He considered the reporting menu and finally decided on the full report selection. When he was satisfied, he clicked *OK* and typed in Sam Weber + new location. An hourglass icon appeared. A few seconds later, a box popped up with the message, *you have selected full reporting. This feature will greatly extend the search time required. Estimated time of completion for your request is 71 hours. Do you wish to continue?*

"No way!" Baylor muttered as he clicked on *No*. He changed the feature in the tool menu to *Data* reports *only* and then typed in the original selection again. This time the information box said *Estimated time to completion is 16 minutes.*

Much better. As the minutes ticked away, a bar showing progress crawled across the screen. The search concluded before the estimated time, but it still took almost twelve minutes. A summary screen appeared that said, *802,767 selections: Sam = 47,252; Weber = 20,915; New = 633,521; Location = 101,079.*

Baylor groaned. It took him a minute to see his mistake. He'd forgotten the double quotations. He reentered his request, prepared to spend another quarter hour waiting on the results. Instead, the message flashed directly back, *0 matches.*

Baylor leaned back in his chair. This was not going to be so simple. It looked like he would need to keep track of what he entered. He searched the desk for a pen and a pad but before he located them, he noticed the printer in the corner of the room. He switched it on and, within a minute, it beeped, ready light illuminated. With the mouse, Baylor selected print on the screen. To his satisfaction, the laser printer softly whirred then ejected a sheet of paper with the screen's content.

"Time to rock and roll," he muttered.

In the lab's work-center, Wozniak rubbed his chin. Reynolds glanced up at him. "What's wrong?"

"I don't know."

"You said the programs worked, right?"

"The simulations worked, Tim. It's not the same thing. That's why they're called simulations."

"So what's different between the reader and the simulations?"

Wozniak grinned. "The sixty-four thousand dollar question! Your gate array is the most significant difference. Let's work through it, buffer by buffer. Maybe I missed something in the code."

Four and a half hours later, Wozniak leaned back in his chair.

"That's all of them and every single one looks perfect to me. You did a great job, my friend."

Reynolds wiped his face. "Except none of them work. We tried all three boxes with the same results. They hang in the first few steps of initialization."

Wozniak nodded. "That should be a clue in and of itself. I need a break. Let's grab lunch and kick it around for a while."

Reynolds rolled his wrist over to check his watch. "You mean dinner."

"What time is it anyway?"

"Quarter to five."

"No wonder I'm hungry."

Baylor appeared by the entryway to the work area, waving a sheet of paper. "Hey, Doc! I found something."

Wozniak beckoned him over. The scientist retrieved the printout and scanned it. The key phrases seemed to jump off the paper at him.

New cell assignments: 10May, Block B. Maximum security.

About a third of the way down the list, the entry *Weber, S., male, cauc.* appeared across from cell number 2011A. Wozniak glanced at the header and then up at Baylor.

"This looks promising. Turn on full reporting and run this entry again. Add in the cell number and you should have the location cold. It could be a Steven Weber, or Stuart or Sylvester or anything but this is a pretty good lead."

"Sylvester Weber? Who'd name a kid that?" Baylor asked with a smile.

Wozniak grinned in return. "You'd be surprised. If the cell turns out to be part of a county jail in Podunk, Missouri, then you'll know it's probably not the one you're seeking."

"With a cell number like 2011A, I think it must be a huge prison," Baylor countered.

"Could be you're right," Wozniak agreed. "But the scientist in me avoids conclusions like the plague. It could also imply cell 1-A in the courthouse at 201 Main Street in Podunk."

Baylor nodded. "I'll run it again."

Wozniak replied, "Just start it, Ed. We're going to dinner and you're invited. That report will be waiting for you by the time we return."

The three men rode the elevator to the surface and piled into Wozniak's Jeep. A half an hour's drive brought them into the village of Los Alamos, where Wozniak picked out a Mexican restaurant of local renown.

Reynolds was bubbling with questions. He hardly waited until the three of them were seated.

"So what are we going to see once it's finished? The Big Bang or something different? Where did the Crystal come from?"

Baylor nodded toward the engineer while looking at Wozniak. "What did you tell him?"

Wozniak grimaced. "Probably enough to get his and my goose cooked. Can't be helped though. He's essential to the start-up."

"Hey, guys! Talk to me."

Baylor smiled. "Sorry, Tim. I wasn't trying to be rude."

"No problem, sir. I just wanted…"

"And, let's drop the *sir* stuff. I'm Ed, he's the Doc, and you're Tim. Got it?"

"Fine by me. Can you answer my question?"

Baylor pursed his lips. "I'll answer part of it. The rest you'll have to be smart enough to pick up on your own."

Reynolds' head bobbed, so Baylor continued. "The Crystal comes from Deneb, a bright star in the constellation Cygnus and over eighteen hundred light-years from Earth. There's a museum of sorts circling Deneb. I gather that it's on a planet or something but I don't have those facts. Anyway the museum is called the Deneb Crystal Archives and it's one of many."

"Holy Smoke! How'd it get here?"

"A visitor brought it. I can't tell you more than that. The crystal contains data about the beginning of the universe and a history of the oldest species in existence."

"Why...?" Reynolds began but Baylor cut him off by holding up his hand. Their waitress approached and conversation turned to food. After they had ordered, Baylor leaned forward. "I can't tell about why, Tim. This stuff is all classified to the gills. Just watch and know that you are getting a view of reality that is far from what they teach in school. Any school."

When the meal was served, communication tapered off as the three men assuaged their ravenous appetites. As they cleared their plates, Reynolds asked, "Did you get to meet this visitor personally, Ed?"

"Yes, I did. So did the Doc, here. We can't talk about it though. Orders from on high."

Reynolds glanced from one to the other. "You guys are lucky sons—"

Wozniak interrupted. "Hey Ed, why did Mr. Grant want you to run the search for Weber from here? Why not just implement it on his own systems?"

Baylor shrugged. "I received the distinct impression that Mr. Grant is resource poor at the moment. He wants to establish a direct and permanent link to you and your systems. Can you arrange that?"

Wozniak frowned. "Normally, not a problem. But I lose my cluster in three days for an upgrade. The new systems won't be ready for at least three weeks."

Reynolds snorted. "Those guys are laggards. I could plug that cluster together and have it whistling Dixie in twenty-four hours."

Wozniak turned to Reynolds. "Yeah, Professor. And that's why they pay you big bucks and the IT team minimum wage!"

Baylor jerked his head backward. "Minimum wage?"

"A figure of speech. They make more than that, but certainly nothing compared to this overpaid layabout."

"In your eye, Stan! It's not me who's holding things up. My hardware is working fine. How come it's the software that's marking time?"

Wozniak sat back, a startled expression on his face. His mouth opened part way and his eyes focused on the far wall. Reynolds turned to Baylor.

"What'd I say?"

Baylor shook his head. "Dunno. Maybe Doc needs the Heimlich maneuver."

Wozniak blinked then turned toward Reynolds with a grin. "You did it again, you little twerp. How come you always say the right thing at the right time?"

"What?"

Wozniak turned towards Baylor as he jerked his thumb at Reynolds. "This guy knows zilch about software. But he has a way of putting things that really helps a complex mind like mine. He said my software is marking time and that's exactly what's wrong with the program. Wozniak turned to the engineer. "Tim, you built the reader synchronous or asynchronous?"

"Synchronous, of course. The data rates demand it."

Wozniak nodded. "But I set the timing loops on my simulator to trigger by event. That way I can troubleshoot the software efficiently. When I transported the code, I forgot to link the routines to the clock. The software is waiting for the reader to initialize instead of looking at the clock. And the reader is waiting for software to load packets from the crystal at each clock tick. Duh!"

Baylor shrugged and glanced at Reynolds. "Sounds good to me."

Wozniak lurched up from the table. "Somebody pay the bill, we have to get back. History is waiting."

Baylor shelled out the cash and left the tip. He had never seen the ponderous scientist move with more alacrity. Both men had already climbed into the Jeep by the time he emerged from the restaurant. Wozniak didn't even wait for Baylor to close his door before mashing his foot on the accelerator. The Jeep spun out of the lot with chirping tires and flying gravel.

The half-hour ride back to the lab only took twenty-two minutes as Wozniak trashed every speed law in the state of New Mexico. When he turned onto Research Drive, he nearly sideswiped the first of two gray Suburbans coming the other way in a manner that was almost as reckless.

"Assholes!" Wozniak groused as he jerked the wheel to the right and then counter-steered when the Cherokee got a little sideways.

"Them or us?" Baylor quipped. He glanced through the rear window but the two other vehicles neither slowed nor stopped.

Aside from Reynolds' battered Escort at the edge of the lot, and Baylor's Porsche near the entrance, there were no other vehicles. Wozniak parked alongside the sports car. He wondered, for a moment, if some primitive herding instinct had driven him...an action linked to the premise of safety in numbers. When the three men approached the door to the laboratory building, the scientist slowed, fishing in his pocket for his keys. Baylor, leading the trio, didn't hesitate. He whisked open the door and stepped back, intending to let them pass.

Wozniak paused, keys in hand. "Extraordinary! The door wasn't locked?" he asked, glancing first at Baylor and then at Reynolds.

The engineer shrugged. "I guess not. They usually latch automatically." Reynolds pulled the door shut behind them and then pushed it open again. He bent to peer at the latch.

"It's jammed. Who knows how long it's been like this?"

"I do," Wozniak countered. "I had to unlock it this morning." He reached forward and twisted the deadbolt. "I'll have to call security when we leave. For now, this will suffice."

They stepped into the elevator where Reynolds pressed the five button and the lift dropped to the lowest level. When the doors drew back, Wozniak sniffed.

"Something smells strange," he commented.

Reynolds nodded. "I smell it too. Paint?"

Baylor drew a deep breath. "Kind of sweet, like rotten fruit?"

"Yeah. Maybe I left an apple or something somewhere." Wozniak shrugged and led the way to the two tables where the three prototype readers rested. He stood over the unit that was hooked up to his workstation.

"Let me reconfigure the driver and then we'll try this one again." With both Baylor and Reynolds watching, Wozniak plopped into the chair in front of his monitor, called up the console editing tools and began his changes. Since there were many, the task required several minutes to complete. He turned to his audience. "Cross your fingers," he said as he stabbed at the return key. The screen immediately turned red and a note in C sharp issued from the speakers. Wozniak struck the return key again and the screen shifted to orange while the note crept up the scale. On the third key strike, the color changed to yellow, and the audio pitch continued to climb but this time the sound was scratchy and broken.

"Oops! A synchronization problem." He punched the escape key and then turned to Reynolds. "Any ideas on what would cause a mismatch?"

The hardware engineer shrugged. "Component tolerance. Etch transmission characteristics. Array drain impedance. Could be any one of a number of factors. Set the audio as the higher priority since the circuits serving the sound channels are the slowest."

Wozniak nodded and made the suggested changes. He tapped a few keys and struck the return again. This time, the screen flashed through the spectrum, while a series of notes issued from the speakers.

The scientist spun in his chair and raised his thumb. "Ta-da!"

"All right!" Reynolds grinned.

Baylor snorted. "That's it? That's the data from the crystal?"

Wozniak glanced at Baylor like he'd fallen off a truck. "This is our test pattern. It just tells us that the reader circuits are working correctly." He turned to Reynolds. "Let's tune the other two and then we'll tackle the real job."

The engineer nodded. "Should only take a minute or two now."

The job took a lot longer as the second unit proved to be a trial to tune. Wozniak was very close to calling it a dud, when Reynolds found the magic combination and it played the test pattern in perfect sequence. The third and final reader executed the pattern on the first pass, without any changes.

Wozniak shut down the reader, and then his workstation. He turned to face both Baylor and Reynolds. "Show time, gentlemen." He reached into his pocket and withdrew a metal cigarette case. He opened it and unfolded the cotton batting within. From its center, he withdrew the crystal. He opened a two-inch square portal on the top of the reader and unclipped the upper hemisphere of a hollow, faceted ball in the center of the cavity.

"What are all the springs for?" Baylor asked, leaning over the cavity.

Reynolds shrugged. "There might be different size crystals."

Wozniak nodded. "That's a perceptive thought. I'd hate to build another one of these just because of the physical size of the storage media." Wozniak placed the crystal inside the sphere and closed it. He reset the access panel to the cavity and powered up the reader. He turned his workstation back on and logged in. Finally, he typed in a command line and then whispered, "Here goes nothing," before striking return.

The screen turned black. After a moment, a series of complex and unrecognizable symbols appeared in the upper left corner. For a moment, nothing further happened. Suddenly, a bright dot in the center of the screen expanded in a flash of light and a fury of sound. In less than a second, the image, a chaotic representation of brilliance, froze in place, the sound steadied to a discordant roar.

For several seconds, neither scientist moved. Baylor looked from one to the other, puzzled at the expression on their faces.

Reynolds broke the spell first. "Awesome, Doc. That was just awesome."

Wozniak nodded and replied, "I am humbled."

"What the heck are you guys talking about?" Baylor asked.

Wozniak pointed at the screen. "We are the first humans ever to witness what some people call the *Big Bang*. While a terrible misnomer, that appellation is reasonable shorthand for 'brane interaction, which is what really happened. I know this is not an actual recording. If you'll remember, Linneow told us that. Even so, it is a rendering by people who know what they are talking about."

"It happened so fast," Baylor complained. "How can you ever expect to see any details?"

Wozniak glanced at Reynolds. "How much memory?"

"I installed five hundred terabytes."

"Why so little?"

Reynolds shrugged. "You said you wanted it soon, so I kept it simple. Besides, we could never add enough to make a real difference. You've got to go to PNA." For Baylor's sake, he added, "Parallel Neural Array – fastest large scale storage there is."

Wozniak nodded. "Yeah, you're right. The workstation has a second drive. It's forty P so that should give us about two minutes worth of storage."

"Can you compress the audio, while expanding the video?"

Wozniak frowned. "Why would ... oh, I get it. Slow-motion video with natural audio. Yeah, that should be easy." His fingers flew over the keyboard.

"Here we go again."

Wozniak struck return but nothing happened. After five seconds, he frowned. After ten, he muttered, "What the heck?"

Reynolds pointed to the reader. "It's idle. The workstation's not querying."

When Wozniak glanced back at the workstation's monitor he could see a single line at the bottom of the screen.

Format 4% complete.

The number changed to five as he watched.

"God Bless America! The damn thing's formatting the hard drive."

"Why would that happen? The data would overwrite any files that might have been present." Reynolds was perplexed.

"Not the data drive, the friggin' system drive. The one that contains the application code."

"Can you stop it?"

"Too late. The index and boot sectors are the first to go." Wozniak stood in front of the screen considering the problem. He shook his head. "I don't get it. The reader could not have sent the format command. It must have come from the cluster." He walked over to the cluster's command console and glanced at the screen.

"I'll be damned. It's a memory resident batch job. Look here. When I initiated the transfer, this job woke up and pre-empted my command. It's going to format the hard drive and then reload the system. That will take about an hour. Where in hell did this program come from?"

Baylor spoke into the silence that followed Wozniak's rhetorical question. "I've a feeling that you should stop it. Can you shut down whatever it's doing?"

Wozniak peered at him. "Sure. Good idea, too. I have a current backup flash of the system disk. A restore would only take about fifteen minutes." Wozniak leaned over the console keyboard and struck a few characters. He repeated them once and then pounded on the return key a few times."

"Damn thing must have come unplugged. Hey, Tim. Hand me a screw driver will you?" Wozniak eased his bulk around to the back of the cluster cabinet.

"What are you going to do?" Baylor asked.

"Plug in the keyboard wireless interface so that I can cancel that TSR. Hey, this thing is already open. Forget the screwdriver." A few seconds of silence passed before Wozniak spoke again. This time his voice contained a quaver.

"Ed, would you come here a minute?"

"Sure." Baylor slipped into the cramped space beside Wozniak who pointed inside the cabinet.

"Is this what I think it is?"

Baylor blinked, his mind refusing to accept what his eyes presented. The sweet smell they had noticed previously emanated from inside the cabinet, thick and cloying now that the source was so close.

"We need to get out of here."

Taped inside the cabinet were more than fifty blocks of C7 high explosive. Wozniak reached for the electrical detonator cords. "Why not just pull these out? Obviously whoever put this in here didn't expect us to find this stuff."

Baylor shook his head. "Bad assumption, Doc. Look here, on each bundle of cords. What do you see?"

Wozniak squinted. "A tiny glass sphere filled with...with...it looks like mercury."

"Right. In anti-terrorist training, they call it a tremble switch. You'd have to secure every single one of them. What do you suppose sets this mess off?"

Wozniak traced the wires backward. "Each harness goes to a disk drive on this node. Maybe we could just unplug this node. Crash it."

"Check the others, Doc." Baylor stepped around to the console again.

"The same! They're all the same! There must be a thousand pounds of explosive."

Baylor swallowed. "I guess that means we can't hide in the other room. Doc, you said this program will reload the system files onto the workstation, right?"

Wozniak joined him. Reynolds, who had remained speechless, stood on Baylor's opposite side.

"Yes, that will happen as soon as the format is complete."

"And the system files will come from the cluster disks?"

"Yes! So the format is the timer to the bomb! We need to prevent the disk from completing its reformat."

Reynolds grabbed the harness behind the monitor. "Just rip this out?"

Wozniak shook his head. "NO! That's only the monitor. The system is buried in one of these cabinets." Wozniak pointed at the four pedestals that lined the underside of the workbench. He glanced at the screen.

Format 26% complete.

"Thank God for big drives." Wozniak wrenched off the covers to the pedestals. There were three bays in every pedestal, each with a bundle of cables as thick as his wrist. The bundles merged at the top of the pedestal and ran along a tray to the end where they dropped down and passed through the flooring in the direction of the cluster of systems. Worst of all, at least a dozen tremble switches had been woven into the cables.

Wozniak glanced toward Baylor and said, "End game."

Baylor nodded to Reynolds. "Time to leave. Let's each grab one of the readers and hightail it out of here." He turned to Wozniak. "Don't forget your backup chip."

Both scientists were galvanized by his words. They wrenched the cables from the readers and trotted toward the elevator. Baylor pushed the button and then placed his reader on the floor. "Almost forgot. That report about Weber should be printed by now. Hold the elevator for me."

Without waiting for an answer, he loped back to the office he had been using and scooped three new pages from the printer's output tray. On the way back, he glanced at Wozniak's workstation.

Format 37% complete.

They still had plenty of time.

"Something's wrong with the elevator," Wozniak said, sweat beginning to form on his forehead. "I can see the lights of the lift but the doors won't open. Maybe a pry bar?"

"Forget it!" Baylor replied. "We'll take the stairs. There are stairs aren't there?"

"Yeah, this way," Reynolds nodded toward his left. When Baylor tried the door, he couldn't move the latch. "It's locked."

Wozniak grinned, holding the key up before his face. His smile disappeared when he shoved it into its receptacle. It turned but the door still wouldn't budge.

Baylor pounded on the door. "Damn it!" He shook his head. "Thorough bastards, aren't they? Back to the elevator."

Each man placed his reader before the elevator doors. Baylor tried to grasp their edges with his fingers but could not gain a grip. He turned to Wozniak. "You mentioned a pry bar?"

"It was a conceptual thought. I've no idea where to find one."

"I do!" Reynolds chirped. He dashed over to a nearby desk, peered at it and then trotted to the next and finally a third. At the last, he bent over and yanked at the center drawer, which was locked. He dropped to his knee and fished his hand behind the drawer. Baylor could hear metal rattle. Reynolds grunted and heaved a few times and then he suddenly fell backward, a bar of galvanized steel about an eighth of an inch thick in his fist. He stood and brought it to Baylor.

"Damn thing was always falling out on my desk."

Baylor hefted it. "It's a little light. Can you find another? Better yet, three."

Reynolds nodded and began his search. Baylor jammed the bar into the gap and pried. He made some early gains but then the bar bent. When Reynolds showed up with two more, Wozniak said, "I wonder how much time..."

"I don't want to know," Baylor replied. He wedged a second bar along side the first and finally was able to lever the doors far enough apart to stick his fingers in the opening. With the assistance of Wozniak and Reynolds, he forced them even farther apart until he could slip in between them and use his back to good advantage.

The inner doors yielded more swiftly. All three men trundled into the cab and Baylor jabbed the *1* button several times. Nothing happened. He reached over to the control panel and flicked the main power switch a couple of times. He pushed the alarm button. There was no sound.

"It's dead. Where's the fuses for this thing?"

Reynolds pointed upward. "Topside. In the maintenance cabinet."

Baylor reached up but could only just touch the upper surface of the lift. He turned toward Reynolds. "Give me a boost, will you?"

Reynolds formed a stirrup with his interlocked hands and Baylor climbed into it. He ripped away the decorative grillwork and then pushed upward on the hatch over his head. It swung upward and then fell back with a thump. He thrust again with the same results. With a curse fueled by fear and frustration, his next shove was sufficient to send it over backward. Baylor thrust his head through the opening. He could see nothing in the total darkness of the shaft. He bent his head toward the scientists.

"Do we have a flashlight?"

Wozniak started to shake his head then paused. "Wait! The emergency lights!"

Baylor stepped down and nodded. "This qualifies as an emergency, I'd say. Where?"

Wozniak led the other two men to the stairway doors. Above them was a small platform with a self-contained emergency light plugged into an AC socket. Reynolds formed the stirrup again and Baylor climbed up and unsnapped the restraining harness. As soon as he unplugged the AC power, the lamp lit. He jumped down and, once back in the elevator, handed the light to Wozniak. With Reynolds' help, he pulled himself through the opening and then reached down for the light. Wozniak passed it up to him.

Baylor played the beam from the lantern upward inside the elevator's shaft. Power harnesses draped the sides and the steel lift cables ran directly to the top, more than forty meters above his head.

"You think we can climb the cables?" Reynolds asked, watching through the opening as Baylor illuminated that path to safety.

Wozniak shook his head even as Baylor replied, "I don't think that'll work. They're covered with grease."

Wozniak added, "Gentlemen, there is no way I'm ever going to get out of this elevator. I couldn't climb out and the both of you couldn't lift me, even if I could fit through that tiny hole."

Baylor clamped his jaw and replied, "Doc, it's all or none. We aren't leaving you."

"A noble sentiment, Ed, but consider what's at stake."

"I am, Doc. Without you, none of this stuff is much use." Baylor had been shining the light around the shaft as he talked. He bent down again.

"Hand up those pry bars will you?"

Reynolds did so and Baylor added, "Give Tim a hand up, Doc. I need some help." When Baylor dragged Reynolds through the opening, Wozniak shouted, "I should pass up the readers and you guys should get the heck out of here."

"Make another stirrup, Tim. Over here by the front wall," Baylor muttered. As he climbed onto Reynolds' hand, he shouted toward the hole. "Make sense, Doc. How are we going to carry the readers while we're climbing?" Baylor grunted as he grabbed a power harness and pulled himself upward, hand over hand. He bent down to Reynolds.

"Shine the light up here."

Reynolds did so, illuminating a pair of elevator doors on the floor above. Baylor found the barest foothold on the retraction mechanism for the doors. He bent over again.

"Toss up one of those pry bars." Baylor caught it on the first try and jammed it into the crack between the doors. He worked at prying the doors open but his progress was slow because he had no leverage. He gained about an inch when the bar slipped from his fingers, bounced from the top of the lift with a clang and disappeared down into the space between the lift and the shaft wall.

"SHIT!" Baylor cursed.

"What's happening?" Wozniak called out, the increased pitch in his voice underscoring his tension.

"Another one," Baylor hissed extending his free hand. The light from below distorted his vision. Reynolds had to toss it up a couple of times before Baylor caught the bar.

Reynolds leaned over the opening. "He's trying to open the door on the next level," he shouted down to Wozniak.

Baylor inserted the bar into the widened crack, levered it further then turned it sideways and gained a three-inch gap. He jammed his foot into the opening and bellowed as he heaved.

The door slid backward more then two feet and Baylor swung through the opening.

"He's got it!" Reynolds yelled. The engineer dropped back through the opening into the elevator. Each scientist picked up a reader and hurried to the stairway door. They heard muffled thumps and thuds coming from the other side. Reynolds retraced his steps to retrieve the last unit. He placed it on top of the others just as the door burst open.

Behind a smiling Baylor lay a pile of scattered two by fours and duct tape.

Wozniak grinned. "I taught Critical Thinking and Analysis at the University of New Mexico, Mr. Ryerson. I think you've just earned an honorary degree."

Reynolds nervously injected, "Unless you plan to have it awarded posthumously, I'd suggest we get a move on. Seventy-four percent."

Baylor's grin disappeared. He bent to pick up one reader and then turned to Wozniak. "Doc, this is no time for pride. Hand me your unit. We've got a long climb."

Wozniak nodded and complied. Baylor bounded up the first landing, Reynolds directly behind him. By far the most fit, and despite his heavier load, Baylor reached the lobby almost a minute ahead of the lanky engineer. He placed his readers by the front door and sprinted back toward the stairwell. He met Reynolds as the scientist started up the last flight of stairs.

"I've got the keys to the Jeep," Reynolds called as Baylor passed him, bounding down the stairs.

"Load the readers and back away from the building. I'll help the Doc up and we'll take the Porsche."

Baylor found Wozniak on the fifth landing, bent over and gasping. He lifted the doctor's arm over his shoulder and jerked him forward.

"C'mon, Doc. You'll feel a lot worse if we delay."

By the time they reached the eighth landing, Wozniak's legs had turned to rubber. Despite his obvious distress, the scientist did not complain or slacken his efforts.

"Two more, Doc. Can you make it?"

Wozniak's only reply was a nod and a gasp. He trudged upward. Twice, on the last landing, he slipped to his knees. Baylor redoubled his effort, bearing even more of Wozniak's ponderous weight. Finally, they staggered through the upper door of the stairwell into the lobby. Two of the readers remained by the front door. There was no sign of Reynolds.

"What the heck? I told him to..." Baylor began, as he stepped up to the door.

With a solid whack, the heavy safety-glass pane starred, stopping the bullet safely on the far side. Reynolds lay motionless about halfway to the Jeep, the reader he had been carrying, not far from his outstretched arms.

Two more bullets struck the door, further weakening the glass. Baylor pulled Wozniak away from the doorway and into safety behind the brick wall of the lobby.

Still traumatized from his exertions, Wozniak had not noticed that he had been the target of unseen gunmen. "What are we waiting for?" he gasped.

"More bad news, Doc. There are guys out there with guns who want to keep us inside. Reynolds is hit but I can't tell how bad."

"I didn't hear any shots!"

Baylor nodded. "Neither did I. Must be silenced weapons. I can't see them but they have to be close." Baylor ducked his head around the edge of the nearest window and immediately drew fire. He also detected a flash of motion behind Reynolds' Escort at the far edge of the parking lot.

"I got 'em. Two men behind the Ford." Baylor chanced another look, judging distances. This time he withdrew before the gunmen could fire again.

"Listen, Doc. We can't stay here. When a half-ton of C7 detonates, it's going to dig a damn big hole. I'm going to draw their fire. When I do, you get out of here. Leave the readers. You guys can build them again."

Wozniak was breathing slightly easier. "How will you protect yourself?"

Baylor fished the keys to the Porsche out of his pocket. On the keyless entry pendant was a button engraved with a symbol for the trunk. "I was told by our friends that the tools of the trade reside in my car. I'm going to take it on faith that they were right."

"It's two to one, Ed. Are you a good shot?"

Baylor grinned. "At the range, I'm known as an ace with guns." He clapped the scientist on his shoulder and sprinted through the door without telling him that the gun he typically used had an aircraft wrapped around it.

Baylor spent no time zigzagging. He dug in his toes and drove for the Porsche with his best forty-yard effort, expecting the burning stab of a bullet every step of the way. He leapt and sprawled in the dust behind the sports car's bulk. He rolled onto his back and pointed the pendant toward the rear-end of the car and punched the button. He had not yet figured how he was going to gain access to the trunk when it was completely exposed to his assailants' fire.

The *clunk* of the released latch came from the opposite end of the car. Baylor silently offered a prayer to the god of rear-engined vehicles as he scurried on his knees to the forward end of the Porsche. Reaching up while crouching behind the front fender, he lifted what would be the hood on a normal car.

The side glass shattered and dozens of thumps and clanks echoed around him as a hail of bullets struck the car. Baylor curled his fingers around the familiar shape of the pistol grip on a long gun. He yanked his hand backward as the windshield exploded and fountains of dust burst from the gravel surface of the parking lot. A streak of fire lanced across his shoulder.

A huge dose of adrenaline saturated his bloodstream while he heard running footsteps race toward him from across the parking lot. Baylor rolled over onto his knees, working the action of his weapon. His anger surpassed any level he had previously experienced.

"THAT'S JUST ABOUT ENOUGH!" he shouted, leaping to his feet. He squeezed the trigger of the weapon as he swung it towards the first man to come into view. The firearm bucked in his grasp, driving an impressive cloud of dust from the ground in front of the assailant.

"Shotgun!" the man yelled. He attempted to change direction but Baylor cycled the action and corrected his aim.

The blast caught the gunman in mid-stride, hurling him backwards.

"THAT'S RIGHT!" Baylor shouted, swinging to his left.

His third blast struck the second man as he veered for the cover of the Jeep. It spun him around and he stumbled to his knees, desperately trying to bring his weapon to bear. Baylor cycled the action and beat him to the punch.

The magnum load of buckshot smashed the gunman backward, his chest a bloody ruin. Baylor advanced, racking the action again.

"THAT'S RIGHT! SHOTGUN!" he shouted. "THAT'S RIGHT!" He strode to first one and then the second assailant. They were both dead. He stood breathing heavily, trying to cope with the raging emotions that swirled in his brain when Wozniak approached and stood by his side.

"Are you okay, Ed? You're bleeding."

"Huh?"

"Are you all right?"

Baylor nodded, and lowered the muzzle of the shotgun and shivered. "I don't know, Doc. I never killed anyone before. But they made me so damned mad."

"Ed. We've got to get clear. The bomb in the lab...."

Baylor shook himself. "Get the keys to the Jeep."

"I have them. Reynolds is still alive. A bullet grazed his skull."

"You drive. I'll fetch Tim."

Wozniak unlocked the Cherokee and climbed inside. He started the Jeep as Baylor lifted Reynolds' unconscious form and carried him to the rear door on the passenger's side. Baylor dumped Reynolds unceremoniously into the back seat and then opened the lift-gate. He grabbed the reader Reynolds had dropped and hurled it inside. Without a second's delay, he raced back to the doorway of the laboratory and clutched the last two readers. He tumbled them in beside the first one, followed them with the shotgun, and turned toward the Porsche. Baylor lifted his cell-phone from the seat of the Porsche and shook it free of shattered glass.

The Porsche would not start, its engine crippled by gunfire. Baylor leapt out and climbed into the Jeep.

"GO! GO! GO!"

Wozniak yanked the shifter back into reverse and stomped the pedal. He had thoughtfully shifted into four-wheel drive so the Cherokee rocketed backward, all four tires spewing dust and gravel. They bounced over the body of one of the gunmen and had almost reached the far end of the lot when a low rumble drowned out the sound of the engine.

Wozniak reversed the wheel, spinning the Jeep. He jammed the shifter into drive and tromped the gas pedal again. Sheets of flame lanced skyward behind them. A wall of air, compressed nearly solid from the concussion, slammed into the Jeep. Wozniak was hard pressed to keep it upright. About two hundred yards away he stopped.

Baylor and Wozniak climbed out. A monstrous smoking hole claimed nearly half the parking lot. Reynolds' Escort lay on it's side, aflame. The entire front wall of the main lobby had been smashed to kindling. There was no trace of either gunman, or of the Porsche.

"She's going to kill me," Baylor whispered.

Chapter Twelve
18:50 MDT, 12 May
Desert Range Experimental Station, UT

Ouilette turned away from the glorious splash of color on the western horizon. He strode toward the only man-made structure in sight, a large, long Butler building with a door in its southern end that was of a size large enough to admit a semi. Soon after sunset, the next loads would arrive. As he approached the building, the great door began its descent, settling on the concrete floor with a thump and a clang. A six-foot high crest, painted on the exterior, announced to any curious trespasser that this property belonged to the U.S. Forest Service and visitors were not welcome. Recessed into the wall, just to the left of the truck entrance, a smaller door opened and a short but muscular man in a forest-service, brown coverall stepped through. He seemed relieved to find Ouilette so close at hand.

"Commander, it's Ryerson on line six. He says he has a problem, sir."

Why doesn't that surprise me? Ouilette followed his aide, Andy Meisner, into the building. They hustled down a flight of stairs and into his makeshift office. He punched a flashing button for the indicated line.

"Good Evening, Mr. Ryerson."

"No, sir. It's not."

"Say no more. You have mobility?"

"At the moment, sir."

"Find a pay-phone and call again." Ouilette hung up. He punched another button.

"Who've we got near Santa Fe?" he asked.

"There's two trucks inbound from Texas, sir. They're scheduled to use Interstate 70 but we could divert them," Meisner responded.

"Too slow. Anybody else?"

"No, sir. All other units are engaged until 0400 tomorrow."

"Thanks, Andy. Call me if anything changes."

19:04 MDT, Los Alamos, NM

Baylor pulled into a gas station and twisted his neck to peer into the back seat. "How is he?"

"I think he must have a concussion. We really should take him to a hospital," Wozniak replied.

"Under normal circumstances, I'd agree, Doc. But we don't know why these people are using us for target practice."

"I think you're wrong, Ed. I'd bet that we've engaged Linneow's enemy. Everything that's happened, to us, to you, to Commander Ouilette and Sam Weber, all points to the same thing. We're under attack and the enemy is this Genkhus fellow Linneow fears."

Baylor frowned. "Doc, say you're right. How do you know who's working for him and who's not? I don't think we can risk a hospital. Both Tim and I have gunshot wounds. There would be a million questions we couldn't answer...wouldn't want to answer."

"So what's next?"

"Ouilette wants me to call him back on a pay-phone," Baylor pointed at the telephone immediately adjacent to where he had parked the Jeep. "We'll call in the cavalry, I guess."

Wozniak nodded his assent. Baylor turned and rolled down the Jeep's window. He lifted the handset and dialed the number Ouilette had given him. Ouilette picked up immediately and Baylor spent about a dozen minutes outlining the situation. A moment later he turned in his seat and said, "Doc, Ouilette wants to talk to you." Baylor pushed the phone into the back seat. The cord was short, forcing Wozniak to stretch his neck over the seat back.

"Doctor, Mr. Ryerson tells me your facility is out of order."

"He understates the situation," Wozniak replied.

"The loss of those resources is significant, perhaps even catastrophic. Do you know how we might locate alternative assistance?"

About to reply in the negative, an idea popped into his mind. "Command—"

"Mr. Grant! Please."

"Sorry, sir. I'm not used to all this...this tomfoolery."

"Believe me, Doctor, it is necessary."

Wozniak sighed. "It is possible to replace my computers." He delved into his briefcase, which he'd left in the back seat of the Jeep since morning. "Send a payment of $372,406.00. Make sure the check arrives tomorrow."

"It will be a stretch, Doctor. To whom do I send the check?"

"Make it out to the Labs in Los Alamos. Care of Director Harvey Levine."

"And the computers, Doctor? Where will Director Levine find them?"

Wozniak chuckled. "He already has them, Mr. Grant. Ed and I are going to buy them from him...sort of."

There was silence for several moments. Ouilette finally replied, "My compliments to you and Mr. Ryerson. You're both more resourceful than I expected. Please tell Mr. Ryerson that his stock has risen." The phone clicked and the line went dead.

Wozniak handed the phone back to Baylor.

"He said your stock is rising, whatever that means."

Baylor sighed. "I suspect it means more of the same kind of fun as we experienced tonight. What's this about buying computers?"

Wozniak grimaced. "Well, sort of...eventually. Only trouble is, we don't have the money right now and the owner probably wouldn't sell anyway."

"Let me guess. We are going to steal them first and pay for them tomorrow."

"Something like that."

"See what I mean? Even you're planning this stuff."

Wozniak nodded. "I'll tell you what, Ed. I don't feel like sitting around on the sidelines with a big, fat, target painted on my forehead."

"I'm with you, Doc." Baylor hung up the phone, rolled up his window and shifted into gear.

"Where to?"

"Back to the lab, but not through the front gate. We'll use the automated entrance on the west side."

"Show me the way."

Following Wozniak's directions, Baylor turned out of the gas station and headed west.

20:07 CDT, Minot AFB, North Dakota

Rotts, aware of the knotted muscles in his neck and shoulders, tried to relax. He failed. He had never seen General Pigott so enraged. The Brigade Intelligence officer debriefing them both hesitated, and then his monologue stuttered to a halt.

"They escaped!" Pigott snarled.

"Ah...it's not certain that—"

"Bullshit! You've two men missing, and the security guard logged Wozniak's Jeep out of the compound ten minutes after they should have been blown to atoms."

"Sir, he could be mistaken."

"Don't peddle sunshine, you jackass! They've escaped. Until you confirm their bodies in little pieces, I will not accept any other version of your story."

"Yes, sir."

"Get your teams back to Los Alamos. Find that Jeep. Find its occupants and finish the job. Is that clear enough?"

"Yes, sir!"

"Good. Get out of my sight."

As soon as the intelligence agent had left, Pigott strode to a table beside his desk, picked up a chair and hurled it against the wall.

"DAMN IT ALL TO HELL!" he roared.

Rotts flinched and sidestepped the flying pieces but otherwise did not react.

Pigott turned toward the Colonel. "Why, Phil? Why in hell are these people beating us? Are we using imbeciles?"

"No, sir. We're not. But I think maybe our people are underestimating the opposition, sir."

"Why is that happening, Phil?"

"Sir, our SOG unit had a good plan. I reviewed it. There is no way an overweight scientist should have beaten it. I don't think he was alone. The plate on the Porsche tells us this Royce woman was involved again, which means Ouilette had cover on the Doctor. Our people didn't know that and came up short because of it."

Pigott considered for a moment. "There's nothing in her file that suggests she is so capable. What's the story on Royce? Do you have the program working on her yet?"

"It airs tonight, sir. Late news. Full coverage on all major networks. Royce will lose her freedom to act in public and she'll be moved to call her parents."

Pigott stepped closer to Rotts and stabbed a finger into the colonel's chest. "No more screw-ups, Phil. I've had enough bad news to last a lifetime."

"No, sir. I believe we have it covered."

Pigott grimaced. "You think you have it covered. I hope you're right for both our sakes. I have to report this fiasco now. See that I'm not disturbed for at least half an hour."

Rotts nodded and hurried out of the office. Pigott's gaze remained fixed on the door after his aide had closed it. He wished he could follow the colonel instead of facing the task ahead. After a moment or two more, he spun toward his workstation, plopped down in the chair before the monitor and struck the keystrokes required to log onto a secure, high-speed command channel.

Nearly an hour passed before Pigott emerged from his office. His complexion was pale, his features taut with tension. Damp circles under each armpit and a streak down the center of his back provided evidence of the grueling session he had just completed. He seethed on a slow boil, directing his anger into his plan to turn events in a more favorable direction. He stalked the hall toward the medical section, entering the laboratories where his staff had confined the creature.

Pigott burst through the double doors to the administrative hall and strode up to the sealed inner doors of the X-ray lab. He grasped a handle and pulled but the door was locked. He turned toward the administration desk where he noticed two people, clerks or orderlies, he could not tell which, who stared at him with dumbfounded expressions.

"Open it!" he commanded.

One of the administrators approached with a key in his fist. His staff coat displayed double silver bars on his collar. A loose facemask dangled around his neck.

"Sir, that's a sealed room. You're not protected from contamin—"

"Shut up and open it."

"Yes, sir," the captain scurried to the door and twisted his key. He slipped his mask up and over his mouth and nose before pulling the door open. Pigott strode through and walked directly toward a cluster of people surrounding a table upon which was strapped the fur-covered form of the Chao. Each second, the motorized platform connected directly to an immense X-ray system stepped slowly inward, carrying its passenger farther beneath a massive panel-shaped device suspended over the subject.

The creature's head turned at his approach. It was conscious. Pigott glanced at the four monitors hanging on either side of the motorized table. He scanned the faces of the medical staff watching them in fascinated concentration. "Shut it down."

One of the scientists standing toward the front of the group pivoted toward him. "We'll have to finish this scan first." The scientist returned to his monitor, dismissing the general as if he were an errant child.

Pigott turned toward a cabinet adjacent to the X-ray system. Through a glass door emblazoned with an insignia of an Olympic figure hoisting a globe upon its shoulders, were several rack-mounted computers. On the upper shelf, above a box marked *Image Data Controller* was a second one that read, *Table Positioner*. A red button, with a flickering lamp embedded within it, was designated with the words *Emergency Extraction*. Pigott opened the glass door and punched this button.

The effects were immediate. A loud buzzer sounded and all four screens turned dark. The motorized table retracted at a rapid pace. Pigott backed away from the cabinet and turned to face the agitated scientists.

"What the hell do you think you're doing!" This from the same scientist who had cavalierly dismissed him a moment ago. He pushed his way through the group and advanced on Pigott with angry eyes and the limited expanse of his exposed face flushed with emotion.

Pigott calmly unclipped the flap to his holster and drew out his Beretta. He pointed to the ceiling, and pulled the trigger. The crack of the 9mm round was absurdly loud in the confined space of the laboratory. The physician staggered backward, his bravado instantly replaced by fear. The scientists huddled, convinced that they faced a madman with a gun.

Pigott lowered the pistol and examined the smoking muzzle for a moment. He dropped his arm to his side as the door burst open behind him, two marines entering with weapons drawn.

The marines spread to either side of the room and advanced two or three paces. One of them recognized the officer with the weapon.

"Sir! Is there a problem?"

Pigott holstered his weapon. "Not any more. Stick around a moment."

"Yes, sir!"

Pigott stepped toward the scientists and they huddled a little closer at his approach.

He spoke in soft, quiet tones. "This laboratory and the entire installation has been and remains in a state of emergency and governed by martial law where a military order assumes priority over everything else. As the ranking officer, and one who has been directly charged by the President of the United States, my authority exceeds anything you can conceive of. When I give an order, or even make a suggestion, it is to be acted upon immediately."

Pigott paused and scanned their faces.

"IS THAT CLEAR!" he shouted.

A sea of nodding heads waved with comprehension.

Pigott stood to one side and pointed at the door.

"Get out." At first, no one moved. Pigott touched his hand to his pistol and raised his voice. "Now!"

The scientists stampeded through the exit, the marines tracking them with their eyes and restrained smiles on their faces. When the door shut behind them, the marine who had spoken earlier eased from his defensive position and snapped to attention.

"Sir!"

"You boys wait outside. See that I'm not disturbed."

"Yes, sir!"

The marines hustled through the exit. Through the frosted safety glass of the doors, Pigott could see them assume a stance of parade rest, side by side. He spun on his heel and walked back toward the X-ray machine. The Chao watched him approach, intelligence and awareness in her huge, liquid eyes.

"It's time we had a little discussion, you and I." When the creature did not reply, he walked around the platform on which it rested, looking for a switch he had seen used before. He found it, a lever mounted near the floor. He depressed it with his toe. With a hydraulic whine, the table extended even farther. The foot of its surface dropped and the far end lifted as the table began to incline. Within a few seconds, it reached a nearly vertical position, its occupant still securely strapped against the surface.

Pigott stepped around until he faced the XT. It stared back at him without making a sound. He concluded it was an attractive creature in an exotic sort of way.

"I'm General Pigott. I know that you understand me. I also know you can speak my language. As the supreme military commander of this base, I'm charged by the leader of this nation to oversee all aspects of your intrusion. You have nothing to gain and much to lose by recalcitrance."

The creature said nothing. It only stared at him. Pigott wondered if maybe it had suffered mentally from the trauma of its capture. Could the electric shock of the prods or stunner have inflicted some serious damage to its mind? The reports he had reviewed implied there was no such injury. Could they be wrong?

The question was answered in the next moment as the creature replied, its voice low, soft and husky.

"Linneow is recalcitrant because she is restrained. Only my enemy would attack and bind me in this manner. Chao do not engage in conversation with an enemy."

Pigott smiled. "You're restrained because we must make certain you present no danger to our people. There's much more to be discovered about you and your purpose before we can allow even limited freedom."

Linneow cocked her head to the right. "You do not accept the judgment of Sam Weber or Marcus Ouilette? You cannot believe the scientific data I give to Stanley Wozniak? You did not speak to Ed Baylor? Are not these humans reliable guides for your decisions?"

"Sam Weber is very ill and cannot speak with anyone. Your Ed Baylor seems to have run amok. He is implicated in the conspiracy to kill our President. A conspiracy which began with the death of Admiral Petersham. A crime in which conclusive evidence points to Marcus Ouilette as the perpetrator. Doctor Wozniak's laboratory has been destroyed and it appears he has perished in the explosion. Your allies are dubious supporters at best. At worst, your interaction with them implicates you in the actions they have taken or the effects they have suffered."

Linneow blinked several times in rapid succession, an action that Pigott correctly analyzed as emotional distress. She finally inclined her head toward the floor.

"Linneow is fearful. These humans are not enemies to Earth, of this I am certain." She studied Pigott as she said, "This is work of the Oo'ahan. Of the group-mind known as Genkhus, who target humans who cannot be controlled and represent a danger to the designs of the Collective. This danger exists also for General Pigott and the President of the United States."

Pigott shook his head. "I'm not willing to accept that statement without proof. So far as we can determine, you are the only intruder. We find no evidence that supports the existence of any other life-forms."

"General Pigott has not seen the data from the crystal which I gave to Scholar Wozniak?"

Pigott shook his head. "We learned of the crystal only this morning. If Wozniak had it, then it must have perished with him."

Linneow inclined her head again. "For a crystal archive, destruction is difficult. Even if Scholar Wozniak has perished, the crystal remains intact unless the heat of fusion is employed. Other data remains."

"Such as?"

"*Ammonte* returns. The cruiser has destroyed Oo'ahan forerunner ships in this system. The ship will provide the evidence you seek."

Pigott stiffened. This was the important data he must procure. He wracked his memory for the proper information to form his questions.

"When?"

"Three Earth days from now. Will Pigott release Linneow?"

"Not yet. Can you communicate with the cruiser?"

"Linneow cannot without my AID. The Sikt speaks to the cruiser. Linneow destroyed the links to the Sikt when she was assaulted by humans."

"But you could still command the Sikt to communicate with the cruiser?"

Linneow inclined her head. "Sikt intelligence recognizes Sethkean speech."

Pigott recalled what he had read from Weber's notes and from the scientific symposium earlier in the week. The pieces fell together and formed a plan.

"You could also speak with the cruiser, yes?"

Linneow inclined her head a third time. "It also recognizes Sethkean speech although the ship is not equipped for sonic reception."

Pigott pressed. "But you could use the I-link to send in code."

Her head snapped up and her eyes closed to slits. A light trembling in her frame was the only indication of a prodigious effort to break free of her restraints. The straps creaked but held. Motion in her hands drew his eyes to them just in time to see her claws retract.

"*Mescoot pesta bistaasch!*"

Instead of the previous soft, husky tones, these words were spat rather than spoken. To his surprise, he understood them. She had called him a vile and traitorous worm. Pigott clamped his jaw in irritation. Where had he misstepped? He shook his head. The puzzle was not relevant. He needed this data and he would have it.

"You will not provide the I-link codes?"

She turned her head away, said nothing.

Pigott tried once more. "If you truly want human cooperation, you could ensure it by such action."

Her head whipped back to him. "Linneow speaks no longer to Oo'ahan puppet. You are mindless without your master."

Pigott turned away. He walked across to the cabinets on the far side of the room and pulled open several drawers until he found what he needed. He uncapped a hypodermic needle and inserted the end into a bottle of Merbromin, drawing off enough to fill the cavity of the reservoir. After recapping the needle, he placed it into his shirt pocket and slipped the sleeve from a scalpel. He then returned to stand in front of Linneow.

"I'm doing this of my own free will. This is General Pigott, not some mindless puppet."

He reached down between her legs, grabbed a handful of fur and skin and squeezed as hard as he could. Her breath exploded from her lungs. Her head snapped back and rapped sharply against the metal platform to which she was fastened. Her back arched and she trembled, her eyes tightly closed. He kept the pressure constant until she drew a second breath and let it out with a faint keening sound. He released her and stepped back. She sagged in the harness.

"As you see," Pigott said. "I know a great deal about the Chao. Where your pleasure and pain centers are, the latter of which I've just demonstrated. I know about your wonderful digestive system, how you can completely metabolize just about everything you ingest. With certain notable exceptions, that is."

Pigott moved toward Linneow's right side. "There are some things that remain a mystery, however and this might be an opportunity for discovery. He extended the tip of the scalpel until he touched the rounded mound high on the right side of her chest.

"For example...contrary to appearances this is not a mammary gland. The Chao do not suckle their young. I believe you call it a crèche.

"But..." Pigott paused as he drew the scalpel downward, slicing through the fur and into the underlying tissue near the tip of the mound. Bright orange fluid welled upward out of a shallow inch-long incision. He watched her reaction and found only stoic silence. He continued, "...this is a uniquely feminine characteristic for your species. Would you become emotionally eviscerated by its removal as would a human female?"

He shook his head. "I wish I had time to find out."

Pigott withdrew the hypodermic needle and uncapped it. He depressed the plunger until a drop of dark brown fluid appeared at the tip. He lifted his gaze to find her eyes on the needle.

"I intend to assault your mind. Rest assured that you will be de-clawed, physically, emotionally, and mentally, before we've finished. This is a simple antiseptic. We call it Mercurochrome. Harmless enough to humans, although it contains a dangerous element. That's the crux of the matter for you, however.

"You see, I know about the effect heavy metals have on the mind of the Chao. The metallic salts in this injection will slowly cross-link your neural patterns. Confusion, uncertainty, anxiety, depression are the initial effects. Paranoia, dementia, and senility follow. Finally coma, convulsions and death. You have no defense. Your people never evolved a liver or kidneys or any such biological filtering. *The only weakness of a closed metabolic system* is how our physicians described it."

Pigott's eyes bored into hers. "So you have a choice. The I-link codes, willingly or unwillingly?"

She turned her face away.

"So be it," he said. He plunged the needle into her shoulder and injected its contents.

She leaned her head back upon the surface of the platform, her eyes closed. Pigott tossed the tainted scalpel and empty needle into a waste bin. He turned away and walked to the door. He opened it and paused.

"You and I will continue this conversation tomorrow. I think you will be more cooperative. And, if not, there is always the day after."

22:45 MDT, Los Alamos Laboratories, NM

"How's he doing, Doc?" Baylor asked after braking the forklift to a stop.

"I'm not sure. His pulse is strong and his pupils react as they should, but he's still unconscious. How about you? You look like you've lost a lot of blood."

"Not really...a two inch furrow to brag to my grand-kids about."

"Provided you live long enough to have any."

Baylor laughed. "There is that."

"Is this the last one?" Wozniak asked, pointing to the six-foot crate on the forklift.

"One more. Hey, Doc. I was thinking. You should bring the Jeep up the ramp over there and we could load it behind these crates. We might need it down the road."

Wozniak nodded. "Good idea. We better leave pretty soon, though. The whole campus is stirred up and everybody's running over to Theoretical. It won't be long before someone gets the idea to close down the labs." He turned away and waddled toward the stairway leading down to the parking lot.

Baylor switched on the electric powered forklift and drove the crate into the forty-foot semi-trailer where he dropped it immediately behind the first four systems. He backed out and started after the final pallet.

When he returned, Wozniak stood beside the Jeep looking into the interior of the trailer. Baylor drove the last crate in, set it in place and backed out again. He shut down the forklift and trotted over to Wozniak. "I think I should drive it in. I can climb into the back seat and exit out through the lift gate."

Wozniak nodded. "I'll tend to Reynolds while you're finishing up here."

Baylor opened the lift-gate and leapt into the Jeep. He backed it up, lined it up with the trailer and then drove it in until the front bumper kissed the rearmost crates. He shifted into park and set the emergency brake before clambering out of the Cherokee and closing the lift-gate. Finally, he latched and secured the trailer doors, switched out the warehouse lights and climbed down beside the trailer. He pushed the close button on the bay door.

Fortune had smiled earlier when they found a late-model Kenworth tractor-trailer backed up against the loading dock, and with the keys above the visor. Baylor loped to the cab and climbed up into the driver's seat.

"Here goes nothing," he said as he turned the key. The engine spun reluctantly before it fired up into a clattering rumble typical of a big diesel. The sound seemed abnormally loud in the middle of the night.

Baylor jabbed the clutch in and shifted a lever into low range. He juggled a second one into low gear. He would start cautiously until he got the hang of the big Kenworth. He let the clutch out slowly until the engine labored. The cab twisted on its frame and bucked. Before the engine stalled, Baylor threw the clutch in again.

"What's wrong?" Wozniak asked.

"Not sure. We seem to have the brakes set somehow. Ah! Here!" Baylor flicked a switch marked parking brakes to off. A gasp of released air sounded from behind the cab and the truck rolled away from the building slightly. Baylor eased the clutch out again. The nose of the cab shuddered and lifted slightly, but the semi pulled smoothly away from the loading dock. He wound up the diesel and shifted into third. By the time he reached the street, the semi was up to fifteen miles an hour and Baylor shifted into the second range. He glanced over at the scientist in the opposite seat and grinned.

"Piece of cake."

"Yeah? What happens if you have to turn around?"

Baylor sobered. "That we should avoid. Do we use the automated gate again?"

Wozniak nodded. "I think we'd better. This is a weird time for trucks to be running in or out of the laboratory."

Baylor turned the truck up the grade, downshifted and, within five minutes, arrived at the west gate. Wozniak climbed down and shuffled over to the card reader. He swiped his card and the gate slid away to the left. Baylor eased the truck through and the scientist hauled his bulk back into the cab.

Baylor indicated the plastic ID card the scientist clutched. "You've left a trail with that thing."

"Can't be helped. Let's hurry. The farther and faster we travel, the harder it will be to find us."

Baylor turned left onto Route 4 and, a few miles later, right onto Highway 126. The road was a deserted but treacherous stretch of highway for a semi, especially at night. Only the fact that the truck was lightly loaded saved him from disaster during his clumsy negotiation of several difficult switchbacks. By the time they reached the village of Cuba on US 44, both Baylor and Wozniak were exhausted, all enthusiasm from their successful escape burned away by the tense ride through the mountains.

Wozniak leaned over and peered at the instruments. He tapped the fuel gauge. "How far can this thing travel on a tank of fuel?"

Baylor shrugged. "I don't know. I think it should average around five miles per gallon, but I doubt we've managed that in the mountains. The tanks probably hold sixty to seventy gallons each, so figure seven hundred miles at the most. The gauge says half full so we can keep rolling for another three or four hours." Baylor pointed to a pouch on the passenger's door. "I saw some maps in there. Why not plan us a route."

Wozniak reached in and drew out an atlas. He scanned through it until he found New Mexico. He lifted his face. "Which direction?"

Baylor shrugged again as he shifted into fifth. "Lets keep moving north and west. What's the next big town?"

"Farmington to the west, Durango to the north."

"Durango? Colorado?" At Wozniak's nod he continued, "Can we make it that far?"

Wozniak measured the distance. "It's about two hundred miles. So I guess the answer is yes."

"Durango it is then."

"What happens when we arrive?" Wozniak asked.

"We'll call Ouilette and see where he wants us to deliver the goods. After that, who knows?"

Baylor tapped the tip of the nozzle against the tank's neck, replaced the handle and screwed on the gas cap. The meter read $429.00. He slipped between the pumps and strode toward the service island, digging into his hip pocket for his wallet. After paying the attendant, Baylor moved the truck slowly toward the end of the lot, muttering under his breath the entire distance.

"What's your complaint?" Wozniak asked as Baylor engaged the brakes and shut down the engine.

"This is not a cheap way to travel. It cost me over four hundred bucks to fill the tanks and we only drove a couple of hundred miles. How's Reynolds?"

"I'm awake," the engineer mumbled from his horizontal position in the sleeper.

"Hey, Tim! Welcome to the land of the living!"

"Could have fooled me," Reynolds replied.

Wozniak added, "He has a whopper of a headache and double vision. I gave him some Dramamine for his nausea."

Baylor nodded. "Still, I'm glad he's improved. Tim, consider how lucky you are. Might be the first Purple Heart in the war of the worlds."

"That's not funny," Wozniak countered.

"A little levity can't hurt when you're down." Baylor pulled his cell phone out of his vest pocket and then thought better of using it. Who knew how long the batteries would last.

When he shoved open the door, Wozniak asked, "Are you calling Mr. Grant?"

"That's the plan."

"I'm worried about staying with this truck. Somebody is sure to be searching for it by the end of the day."

Baylor agreed, closed the cab's door and hustled toward the trucker's lounge. He found a vacant phone booth and dialed the number. A man's voice answered on the first ring.

"Base."

"Ryerson. I need to speak with Grant."

"One moment."

Nearly half a minute passed before Ouilette answered.

"Mr. Ryerson, I'm glad you called. In relation to your point of departure, where are you? State general direction and distance only."

"A couple of hundred miles to the northwest, sir."

"You've crossed the state line?"

"Yes, sir."

"Excellent. Three-six-oh, one-nine-one. Watch for pacesetter and follow their instructions. Monitor one-six on charlie-baker. Got it?"

"Wilco, sir."

"I trust the Doctor is still with you?"

"Yes, sir. Also a hardware engineer named Reynolds."

Several seconds of silence greeted Baylor's disclosure.

"An unfortunate complication. Can you leave him behind at your present location?"

"Reynolds has a head-wound that needs attention and he was instrumental in getting the hardware in Doc's device to work."

"Please understand, Mr. Ryerson. If Reynolds remains in company with you, he may not see his family or friends again. Willingly or unwillingly, he'll be with us for the duration."

"Is that the way it is with me, sir?"

"You're still outside, Mr. Ryerson. We'll not bring you in until we're sure that we can let you out again. The same applies to the Doctor. Your injured friend, however, requires assistance we can provide only at this base. Once we bring him here, he's in for good. Make sure he understands this."

"I understand, sir. You had a message for the Doc?"

"A question. Has he made any progress on that search we talked about? I know you've had distractions but our need is critical."

Distractions! Baylor's thinking was derailed for a couple of seconds. The web search for Weber popped into his mind.

"Some progress. We haven't had time to follow up because of all the...the distractions, as you put it."

"Can you continue to work on the problem?"

Baylor considered the question then said, "It will be difficult to pick up the trail as long as we're traveling, sir. Also, we have none of the necessary equipment."

"What do you need?"

Baylor reflected upon what Wozniak had told him. "A browser, sir. And a point of connection with some deep access."

"Understood." There was a click and the line went dead.

Baylor hung up the phone and returned to the Kenworth. He spent several minutes reviewing his conversation with Ouilette for Wozniak and Reynolds.

"What the heck is a pacesetter? And what do all those numbers mean?" Wozniak asked.

"Let's assume the pacesetter part will become obvious. I read the numbers as compass direction and route. Check the map." Baylor faced Reynolds. "How about it, Tim? You're the one with a decision to make."

Reynolds leaned forward holding a damp rag to his scalp. "Do you think they'll find a use for my skills and training, or will I become a janitor?"

Baylor laughed. "I can't speak for Grant, Tim. I'm still on the outside. And, I'm a jet-jockey who will probably never fly again. But I'm certainly not bored."

Wozniak added, "I think we'll be addressing some cutting edge problems, Tim. But who's to say?"

Reynolds nodded. "Well, I'm divorced and Rita, my ex-wife, would surely receive survivor's benefits if they say I'm dead. My parents died years ago. I've no ties, I guess. I'll stick with you guys, if you don't mind."

With a shake of his head, Baylor said, "I've a feeling the Doc and I won't be going with you. Remember what Grant said. He's keeping us out until he's sure about us."

"How can Mr. Grant be sure about me?"

"He's not. He's taking you inside, whatever that means, under duress. Whatever Grant's planning for us must be more than an injured man can face."

Reynolds pursed his lips, his face clouding with concern. Suddenly, he brightened. "You said you loaded the cluster upgrade into this truck."

"That's right," Baylor replied.

"Well, if you guys head out toward the sunset, then it'll be up to me to get the stuff installed and running, right?"

Wozniak grinned and said, "I believe the phrase was 'whistling Dixie in twenty-four hours'."

Reynolds laughed, then gripped his head with both hands. "Ouch! Anyway, I could begin with installing the cluster."

"Sounds good to me," Baylor said. "I'd be willing to bet that Mr. Grant will find that idea exceptionally appealing."

"I'm in." Reynolds flopped backward onto the sleeper's mattress and swung his feet up.

Baylor started the diesel, shifted into gear and pulled out onto highway one-sixty, headed west.

09:33 CDT, 13 May, Minot AFB, North Dakota

Standing under a cloudless sky and a brilliant morning sun, Captain Forster lifted the right cup of his protective muffs.

"Say again!"

One of the scientists raised his voice even higher, trying to overcome the persistent roar of the turbine-driven ground power units arranged in a semi-circle around the Sikt.

"We're all set, sir."

"Great! Give me a minute to start the telemetry."

Forster replaced his muffs and trotted to an air-conditioned trailer fifty yards back from the *drop zone* periphery. He entered and closed the door behind him. He whipped off his earmuffs, but before he could order the technicians to start the telemetry tapes, one of his aides called out.

"General Pigott, on line two. He's been waiting for several minutes, sir."

"Damn it, Freddie. Why didn't you send someone to get me?"

"I did, sir. Corporal Barnes tried to tell you, but you waved him off."

Forster remembered the moment, which had occurred while the technical team was arguing over some checklist procedures. He picked up the phone.

"Captain Forster, sir. Sorry about the delay."

"Not a problem, Captain, as long as you are making progress. Are you?"

Forster bared his teeth and winced. "Not exactly, sir. The voice synthesis system worked at first, but we ran into a problem. The Sikt's AI responded to the audible commands as expected. It recognized our synthesis of the Chao's speech patterns. The hitch is a key phrase, sir. We tried several times to bypass it without success. We even tried the Chao native speech routines you provided. The ship replied in native speech, sir. Your database translated the imperatives and it comes down to the phrase again."

"So now what?" Pigott asked.

"We're about to try the shielded suits, sir. We've analyzed the frequencies used to incapacitate our people and we think we have them blocked."

Pigott's reply was delayed for several seconds.

"Captain, if you reach the hull of the craft, you'll find a panel halfway up and about a meter behind the starboard intake. Inside this panel is a device called an interrogator. Attain it and you'll gain full control over the Sikt. Understood?"

"Yes, sir. That's what we'll try for."

"Listen to me, Captain. If you're successful, press the left upper button and repeat the following phrase. *Delanka-ami, Codetts-ka, Staa*! Have you got that?"

"Say again, sir."

"Write it down, Captain." Pigott repeated the phrase.

"Got it, sir." Forster wondered where the general came up with this stuff.

"Good! Let me know when the craft is powered down and approachable." Pigott hung up.

Forster exited the trailer and trotted across the concrete toward the scientific crew. He approached the team leader and tapped him on the shoulder. The man lifted the visor to his helmet, which resembled a fiberglass bowl encased in a mesh of interwoven wires.

"Captain?"

Forster pointed toward the Sikt's right nacelle. "The access panel is your primary goal, Lou. Unplug the device inside and I can disable the barrier field." Forster had to shout over the roar of multiple dash-sixty wolverine auxiliary power units.

"Yes, sir."

The team leader whipped the cable attached to his helmet forward until he retrieved the end of the cord. He plugged the umbilical cable into a socket on the panel of a universal field computer and typed in the start command. The scientist then lowered his helmet, stepped forward and clapped his two assistants, likewise encased in suits and helmets, on their shoulders. When they turned toward him, he pointed at the Sikt and started walking toward it, dragging his umbilical behind him.

All three men crossed the line marking the limits of the *drop zone* without ill effect. Three or four paces past the line, the team leader raised his fist, thumb extended, over his head.

"All right!" Forster mumbled. He covered his ears with his hands, realizing that he had left his muffs in the trailer.

The trio of scientists had reached the midway point to their objective when the first eddies of dust swirled around the skids supporting the XT craft. Before they could take three more steps, the swirling dust swelled into a driven stream of incandescent gases blasting against the surface under the Sikt. All three men turned to flee. They started too late and moved too slowly. Exhaust temperatures far beyond the melting point of their protective gear struck, knocking them flat. Their clothing and bodies flashed into flame.

With a voluminous roar that outstripped the power units, the XT craft surged into motion. The Sikt's double-jointed neck articulated, lifting its uniquely shaped nose from the concrete. To Forster's horror, the mass driver under the goose-head's bill pivoted, swinging his way. Four tiny openings in its leading edge flickered with angry red pulses.

A streak of light passed over his head. The shock wave of its passage slapped him backwards. He landed on his backside upon the surface of the apron. To his right, two of the power units soundlessly exploded, filling the air with debris that scythed down a score of marines and technicians.

Accompanied with a wave of heat, a second concussion pummeled him from behind when he tried to sit up. Before Forster could glance around to discover its cause, a spreading sea of flames reached for him from his left. The remaining two power units had also exploded. Forster rolled away from the expanding pool of ignited jet fuel. He climbed to his feet and sprinted directly away from the craft for nearly two hundred yards.

Gasping for breath and bent nearly double from the cramps in his side, he staggered to a stop. When he turned around, the trailer was a flaming ruin, its center sagging toward the pavement with the ends still brightly burning. One of the marines stood and opened fire with his rifle from the far side of the off-world craft. Immediately, the pod under the bill swung around and replied in kind.

Forster felt the ground leap under his feet from the impact. Bright flashes of light and detonations similar to heavy artillery staggered him. He dropped to the surface, covering his neck and head with his arms. Pebbles and chunks of concrete rained down all about him. Under his arms, everything was eerily quiet. At that moment, he realized the entire episode had been soundless, apart from the painful crack of the first burst of light over his head.

Forster did not move for several minutes. Eventually, someone tugged at his arm and then tried to roll him over. He climbed to his feet, much to the relief of the marine who had tried to assist him. In utter silence, the man mouthed some words. When Forster tried to reply, he found his voice as absent as the marine's. He slapped his ears with no effect. He knew the problem was serious when his fingers came away soaked with blood. Forster could hear nothing, not even the screaming sirens charging down the taxiway toward the apron.

When the medics tugged him toward one of the ambulances, he glanced over his shoulder at the Sikt. It was as motionless as before, its nose planted upon the concrete as if nothing had happened. The XT craft was the only undamaged object on the battlefield plateau of a short and vicious war.

Two hours later, Colonel Rotts joined Pigott as the general briefed his base security teams. The general lifted his eyes as Rotts entered the room.

"How is he?"

"Ruptured eardrums, sir. Some middle-ear damage that the physician says is not permanent. His team was wiped out, though. We also lost about half the marine contingent around the craft," Rotts replied.

"Your analysis, Colonel."

"Defensive action, sir. I'm impressed by the degree of control during the response. It eliminated all of our resources in the immediate vicinity, punished only those who continued what it recognized as an assault and then shut down. Everybody who was passive like Forster survived."

"Then the craft poses no further danger, in your opinion?"

"I'd say not, sir. If we were to escalate, say send a tank or something, its response might assume a different nature. I think we should just leave it alone until we have the means to control it."

Pigott nodded. "I'll work on that, Phil. Now join us in this other matter, will you?"

"What other matter?" Rotts asked, taking a seat.

"We need to stockpile this base with fuel and food. Enough to act independently for the foreseeable future."

Rotts' eyes narrowed. "Ambiguous term, sir. Are we talking about weeks or months?"

"I'm thinking years."

12:20 MDT, On US 191, south of Moab, UT

The only village they had seen in thirty miles faded in the rearview mirror. The Kenworth toiled up a long, gradual incline, leaving the Lisbon Valley behind. Whenever Baylor turned down the squelch, nothing but static issued from the CB radio.

"About twenty-five miles to go," Wozniak muttered, peering into the atlas.

"What's that?" Baylor called, raising his voice over the rumble of the diesel.

"Less than a half hour to go." Wozniak replied, matching his volume.

"To Moab?" When the scientist nodded, Baylor added, "I hope they're not lost. Hell, I hope we're not lost." He shifted into high range as they crested the hill and started down the other side. Baylor wound the transmission through several gears as the semi gained speed. They swept around a bend in the highway and spotted a roadside turnout about a half-mile ahead. Another truck had pulled off the road, its four-way flashers flickering in the distance.

"I'll be damned! The human race still exists!" Baylor joked as they charged toward the parking area.

Wozniak gazed at the truck as they approached. Suddenly, he tensed. "Hey! The trailer on that truck!"

"I see it," Baylor replied. The Kenworth flashed past the roadside where a bright white tractor, hooked to an equally white trailer with the word Pacesetter emblazoned on its sides, stood parked.

The CB crackled. "Mr. Ryerson, I presume?"

Baylor reached up and grasped the mike. He toggled the switch and replied, "Affirmative."

"Good. You'll find another roadside in three miles. Pull off at the far end and shut down your rig. Remember to engage the parking brakes."

"Roger." Baylor replied. He hung up the mike and grinned at Wozniak. "I think our trucking days are over."

By the time Baylor found the roadside, he had decreased his speed to less than thirty miles an hour. The parking area was a natural overlook encompassing both sides of the road. Baylor pulled over, drove to the far end as instructed and shut down the engine. He set the brakes and turned to Wozniak and Reynolds.

"End of the line. Everybody out."

The three men had just climbed down from the cab when the second semi eased around the corner. Instead of turning into the parking area, the rig passed slowly by and, at the last moment, turned into the parking space across the road. Using the full width of the road and the parking area, the truck completed a U-turn and started back the way it had come. About a hundred yards up the road, it shuddered to a stop and began to back up. As it edged closer, Baylor nudged Wozniak.

"Load transfer. What do you want to bet?"

Wozniak frowned. "I don't see how..." He paused, puzzled by the problem.

When less than twenty feet remained between the trailers, the second semi's brakes hissed and it jerked to a stop. Two men jumped down from the cab of the truck and walked back toward them. At a range of fifteen feet one of them drew a pistol, pointed it at Tim Reynolds' chest and pulled the trigger.

The weapon chuffed. Reynolds, with no time to react, crumpled. Wozniak turned to run, but Baylor gathered his legs to charge, knowing he could never outrun a handgun.

"Don't!" the man with the gun warned. His words and the fact that he leveled the gun on Baylor froze both the pilot and the scientist.

The gunman suddenly smiled, lifted his weapon and broke open the pistol. He held it up and announced, "Tranq gun. Your buddy's just taking a nap."

"Jehoshaphat!" Baylor muttered. He slouched against the rear of his truck and added, "You could have said something."

"Like what? Hold still while I shoot you?" the gunman sardonically replied.

The gunman's assistant bent and lifted Reynolds in a fireman's carry. He started back toward the other truck's cab. As he passed, the gunman handed his weapon to him and then gestured at the back doors of Baylor's trailer.

"Open up. I'll butt this trailer to yours and we'll unload your vehicle first."

Baylor let the relief wash through him and found the strength to open the trailer doors. He glanced at Wozniak.

"You all right, Doc?"

The Scientist shook his head. "Death's been chasing me for two days now and it's becoming tiresome."

The other truck eased backward until the trailers clanged together. Baylor nodded. "A mirage, Doc. We've a while to live yet."

"How can you be so sure?"

"Just a feeling, Doc. But I've never been wrong yet. You'll have to trust me on this."

Wozniak grinned. "It's a deal. Now tell me how we unload my Jeep."

"This way," the erstwhile gunman called. He pointed to a regular-sized door in the side of his trailer.

"Climb in."

After both Wozniak and Baylor entered the trailer, the gunman continued.

"My name's Hal. My buddy is Parker. We'll tend to your friend all the way to the base. Mr. Grant says he's welcome. You two have another job to do."

Hal handed an envelope to Baylor and a large briefcase to Wozniak.

"There's directions in the envelope. I don't know what's in the briefcase but Mr. Grant said it contained tools for the job."

Wozniak hefted the fabric-sided case. It had a strap so he slipped it onto his left shoulder.

Hal pointed to the Jeep at the far end of the opposite trailer. "Parker is changing the plates on your Jeep. Afterward, he'll install ramps between the trucks. Back your vehicle into this trailer. I'll pull forward and we'll extend the ramps to let you down." He grinned at Baylor. "I've heard you're experienced at this type of thing."

Baylor nodded. He walked down the length of the trailers and opened the Cherokee's lift gate. In less than a minute, he had it started and backed the Jeep into the second trailer. A few minutes later, the vehicle was parked alongside the Kenworth, Minnesota license plates and all.

Once the ramps were retracted, Hal backed the trailers together again and used a forklift to transfer the six computer systems into the Pacesetter trailer. In fifteen minutes, the Kenworth stood empty.

The man named Parker closed the trailer doors, leapt up into the Kenworth and eased out of the parking lot. Within a few seconds, the semi disappeared down the road.

"Where's he going?" Baylor asked.

Hal turned toward him. "Salt Lake City. He'll abandon that rig at a truck stop. It'll likely be a month before someone notices it. You boys take off. I'll manage Mr. Reynolds and the cargo from here on in."

Baylor nodded and turned toward the Jeep. Wozniak had his hand out for the keys.

"My turn to drive. You play navigator for a while."

12:50 MDT, Desert Range Experimental Station, UT

"Good news!" Ouilette announced. He had just entered the communications section of his new domain. The area, a large subterranean room measuring almost forty feet in both directions, scarcely rated the designation. There were wires and connectors tumbling from openings in the walls and dribbling in assorted bundles of colored conductors from the ceiling. Optical cables, coax, multi-stranded phone lines, broadband networking backbones and at least a dozen flexible wave-guides were visible. The trouble was most of them hooked to nothing at all. A few phones were operable and only one satellite dish. Two television monitors flickered in the darkened room. At least a dozen people stood around them.

Several faces turned toward him, more than one incredulous at his announcement.

"Sir?" one of the specialists asked.

Ouilette became absorbed in the drama unfolding on the screen. A CNN correspondent spoke rapidly while dodging scrambling figures as they hurried past the cameraman. Ouilette could make out military garb on almost all of the passersby. Very few had weapons and many showed signs of injury. All were filthy and it was obvious that discipline was non-existent. Ouilette picked up on the words overwhelmed, panic, and defeated.

"Where is this?" he asked.

"Pakistan, sir. These are Indian troops. They're in full retreat."

Another voice added, "That's no retreat, Eddy. It's a rout."

Ouilette frowned. "When did this begin?"

"Last night, sir. Calcutta sent three divisions into Pakistan. The Chinese jumped into the game and the Indians got their butts kicked."

Ouilette replied, "I'll be damned. You can't sleep a minute without something ugly happening. What started this ruckus?"

The man named Eddy turned. "No one seems to know, Commander. Like the other fracas, it's a complete mystery."

"What other fracas?"

Eddy jumped up and changed the channel. This time the scene depicted a middle-eastern city. At first, Ouilette could not tell which one, but within seconds, Arabic symbols scrolled past at the bottom of the screen. They were followed by script announcing in French that the city was Riyadh. But, instead of pristine thoroughfares filled with bustling traffic,

Ouilette witnessed an aerial view of streaming mobs, overturned automobiles, and entire city blocks aflame.

The commentator spoke in French but a translator was interpreting the monologue as rapidly as possible. Eddy turned back toward Ouilette. "This one started this morning, sir. The electrical grid in the city failed and two hours later everyone went berserk."

Ouilette crossed his arms. "Anything else?"

"Nothing on this scale, sir."

After a moment, Ouilette decided. "Eddy, call everybody in. Start them all home. Ask Andy to help."

"Immediately, sir?"

"When you contact each team, tell them to finish their current operation and start in. I want everybody home in three days."

"Yes, sir."

When Ouilette turned to leave, the other specialist, known only as Rourke, called out.

"Sir! You said something about good news. I've a hunch you weren't referring to this mess."

Ouilette nodded. "We've located our computers. An Altair 9770 cluster, courtesy of some quick thinking in the field. I understand there's a computer engineer with them who will help with the installation. You guys need to make this place ready."

Two of the specialists looked at each other and then simultaneously jumped to their feet. A wide grin plastered to his face, Rourke replied, "Sir, that is great news. We've been feeling ... well, kind of disconnected down here."

"No longer," Ouilette replied. "Andy will bring down some plans for the auditorium. I'll want you two to pipe in some of the news feeds for my global briefing. You've seventy-two hours to square it away."

Ouilette left his communications team pouring over the architectural plans for the computer room. As he walked back to his office, he considered that one of the field teams might need a little more time than most of the others.

17:14 MDT, Denver, CO

"You're sure this is the right hotel?" Wozniak asked.

"The directions say the Rest-Awhile on North Laramie. This has to be the place."

Wozniak curled his lip. "What a dump! Surely the government can afford better than this."

"Of which government do you speak?" Baylor asked as he folded the maps.

"You have a point. I'll make you a deal. You check in and I'll keep the car running."

"Why is that a deal?"

Wozniak grinned. "If the riffraff in this place matches the decor, you may come out running."

"You mean, you don't want to get out of the air conditioning and cart bags into the hotel."

"What bags?"

Baylor jerked his door open. "A figure of speech. I'll be right back."

"Grab a paper, will you? I'd like to catch up on the world while I wait."

Baylor dropped two quarters into the paper stand and fetched a copy. He was about to hand it to Wozniak, when he paused and whistled.

"What's up?" the scientist asked.

Baylor passed the paper into the Jeep. "I thought traveling by truck was expensive before. Look at this. There's a fundamentalist revolution underway in Saudi Arabia. I think that means big trouble for the U.S. of A."

Wozniak took the paper, a sudden weight descending into his ample stomach. After he scanned the front page, he looked up at Baylor.

"You weren't wrong before, my friend. Remember when you said to Reynolds that he was a casualty in a war between the worlds? I think these are the opening moves."

Chapter Fourteen
17:46 MDT, 13 May, Denver, CO

"Your boss has outdone himself," Wozniak said as he glanced up from the laptop computer. The scientist had requisitioned the only piece of furniture in the room that could serve as a desk. He had pulled the three-drawer dresser away from the wall and moved it to the end of the room where he had access to the phone jack and an extra power receptacle for the laptop's battery charger.

Baylor was stretched out on one of the two lumpy beds, the back of his forearm across his eyes while he faded in and out of sleep. At the moment, he was awake, listening to the Wozniak's banter as he explored the contents of his new toy.

"Ouilette hasn't said I work for him yet," Baylor replied.

"Foregone conclusion, my lad. You've the right stuff for this kind of work. I suspect you know that as well."

"Then why is he keeping us on the outside?"

Wozniak shook his head. "I don't see it that way, Ed. We, you and I, offer something Commander Ouilette really needs right now. Something like very special skills coupled with unpredictable behavior. Besides, we're connected to the core of the problem, which none of his other troops are."

Baylor sat up. "Doc, spell it out. What is the problem? What do you think is going on?"

Wozniak blinked. "You don't know?"

"What do I know? Damned little and I'm guessing at the rest. I want to hear your opinion."

"Very well, my friend. *The World according to Wozniak.* The Chao have been investing in the human race for eons. Marcus and I spoke about that actually. He said you once said, to Petersham I believe, that Linneow was a mission for seventy million years."

"Yep, I said that."

"Did she actually tell you that?"

"Well...sort of. She said she had been on Earth for seventy million years and understood much about us. Or something like that.."

"The mission part...?"

"My words, I guess. Did I overstate the situation?"

Wozniak shook his head. "Possibly not.. Do you recall context? What prompted you to believe it was a mission?"

"I don't know. What else could it be? Why is this important?"

The scientist folded his arms over his ample middle. "Marcus made an excellent point earlier. The Chao and their friends the Vithri, have astutely analyzed our potential as a resource against a tyranny that traces it roots beyond time itself."

"Potential? We're hardly more than plant-life compared to the Chao."

"Not so, my friend. I will admit our ally and her people have a huge head start, technologically speaking. But they're not so bright, you know."

Baylor's expression transformed into one of disbelief, so Wozniak added, "I'm a scientist, Ed and I've studied their history.

"Linneow and her ilk are intelligent enough for mammalian carnivores. But, they're pastoral in nature and tend to accept the status quo until events overtake them. They are a pragmatic people and lack the creative sizzle that has allowed mankind to make great leaps forward. Unfettered by the Oo'ahan, we might surpass Chao science in a few hundred years."

"C'mon, Doc! I can hardly believe we'd create an intergalactic starship anytime soon."

"That's Vithri science, Ed...and an entirely different proposition. The Vithra are the brains in this alliance, and they're much more impressive."

"What do they need us for, if they're so smart."

"Such a lovely question, isn't it?" Wozniak said with a smile. "And why start seventy million years ago when we've been around for only two? There's something missing here, my friend. Something that our allies wish to keep hidden. Because that intrigued me from the very moment when Marcus posed the question, I've spent a lot of time trying to resolve the answer."

"Which is?"

"Don't know. May never know. I still need the data in the crystal to confirm much of what I've learned from our debriefing with Linneow, so here's a preliminary view. It is a fact that the Vithra were well established as an intergalactic species. They govern twelve thousand star systems, Ed."

"Inconceivable."

"Nearly so," Wozniak agreed. "But, the Prides of Vith did not build Rome in a day. Have you any idea how long they live?" At Baylor's negative expression, Wozniak added, "The lifespan of an average individual might exceed six thousand years."

"No shit!"

"And our little clock runs down in a matter of decades. While Vithri progress in the sciences was exceedingly slow, they had all the time in the world. And, there's something else. They take naps. Long ones."

"What are you implying, Doc?"

"Vith, their planet of origin existed in a complex system comprised of binary stars. Three pairs of them."

"Six suns! They must have slept during an endless day."

"During the off season, actually. The Vithri are reptilian. Prior to their diasporas, they fell dormant for periods lasting decades...when several of their suns receded simultaneously. A winter, if you will. It took them forty-thousand years to orbit their own planet once they decided it was necessary."

"Whoa! But, they've come a long way since then."

"Science resembles a pyramid, Ed. The broader the foundation, the taller the structure. Building the foundation takes time and, unfortunately for us, we've run short."

"I'm getting that feeling also. In what way? You have an idea about what's coming?"

"The alliance against the Oo'ahan routinely invests in any promising species they discover. Remember my point about seventy million years verses two million and our question about that warrants an answer. However, their opposition periodically slaps the constructs of the Chao and their friends to tatters. They did that here, but long before our time. And now they're planning to do it again. All the little clockworks of the last two millennia are in jeopardy."

"You know, Doc, that's exactly what...you've painted it just as I imagined. That's a horrible prognosis. I hate it so much I don't want to believe it. In fact, it's almost impossible to keep the faith. How can you be so sure you're right?"

Wozniak pursed his lips. He rolled his wrist over and glanced at his watch. With his pen, he pointed at the TV. "Get a dose of reality, Ed. Six o'clock news. Tune in on the world. I don't think you're going to like what you see."

"Good idea." Baylor retrieved the remote control for the television. He pushed the power button and within a few seconds, sound and images appeared on the set.

The news anchors at the local station had a full plate. The first scenes depicted a full-scale invasion of India by combined Pakistani and Chinese troops. Sixty divisions swarmed across the border, driving the tattered remains of India's front line assault forces before them. India was calling up reserves and making ominous threats about the use of *extreme measures* if the invaders did not immediately withdraw.

In Arabia, the Kingdom of Al-Saud was no more. Both the United Arab Emirates and Oman had also fallen to the spreading wave of a new fundamentalist movement. Iran had opened its arms to the new regime, promising weapons, technology and support of its allies, chiefly China.

New developments in Europe, particularly today's crash of the French economy, had shattered the bonds of a united currency. Both Britain and Germany hastened to distance themselves from the problems that beset the French government where high unemployment and rampant inflation had undermined the commercial sector until the entire structure collapsed. Without capital, as foreign investors ran for cover, French industry ground to a halt in a matter of hours.

On the domestic scene, the states of California, Arizona and Nevada formed a coalition called the Western Commercial Alliance. The first act of the WCA was to order a tariff on produce imported from outside the zone. The federal government immediately stepped in to declare these tariffs unconstitutional and ordered the WCA to withdraw them. Within hours, however, southern and central states joined in a protest that included penalties and counter-tariffs on computer products and citrus exports of the WCA. The United States Congress called an unprecedented recess as various senators and representatives hastened homeward in an attempt to ease rising discord from their constituents.

In a new development of the bizarre helicopter crash in the nation's capital yesterday, the pentagon today released the name of the pilot who died in the accident. It was believed that Navy Lieutenant Karen Royce, who was not a trained pilot and unauthorized to fly a helicopter, was willfully ferrying nearly a half-ton of cocaine when she lost control of her craft. Sources close to the White House said that the U.S. Navy has been recently implicated in an undercover and renegade organization of which Lieutenant Royce was a part.

The news feed flashed the photo of Karen Royce on the screen. The picture stunned Baylor. His jaw dropped and his eyes bulged. "Bullshit!"

Startled by his response, Wozniak glanced at the screen and back at Baylor. "You knew her?"

"Shush!" Baylor waved the scientist to silence, but the television station switched to sports and weather. He changed channels and found more of the same. In disgust, he pressed the power button.

"I can't believe this! The world is falling apart and all these people want to tell us is that the Red Sox beat the Yankees and it's seventy-four degrees in Minneapolis." Baylor launched to his feet. "Damn! I've got to call Ouilette. He needs to know about this!"

"Get a grip," Wozniak said. "Ouilette's instructions said no contact while at this hotel. What put the bee in your bonnet, anyway?"

"That Navy Lieutenant. She's one of us. She works for Ouilette, only her name's not Royce, its Reeves. Adele Reeves."

"Yeah, like your name is Ryerson."

Baylor sat down suddenly. "Shit! You're right. What do I know? Damn it all to hell. I liked that lady." He stood up again. "I can't stand this, Doc. Something's rotten about the whole thing. I need to talk to Ouilette."

Baylor stood again and began to pace the room.

"Did you hear? They talked about the Navy and a rogue organization. That's Petersham, Ouilette, me, and Reeves or Royce or whatever her name is or was. We're being painted as drug lords. They can hit us anytime, anywhere, no questions asked."

Wozniak motioned with his hand, palm down. "Ease up, my friend. No telling how thick the walls are."

Baylor sat down again, the volume of his voice greatly reduced. "You're right again. This is going to drive me crazy." Baylor stood again. "I can't sit around."

"Take a walk or a jog, or whatever. You're making me dizzy and if I'm dizzy I can't think. I need to finish these programs and you're not helping the cause."

"Sorry, Doc. I'll go for a run. If I see a phone booth I'll call in and find out what's going on."

Wozniak waved him away then dropped both hands back to the keyboard. He pounded furiously, oblivious to Baylor's departure.

Baylor spotted his third phone booth just about the time he figured he had covered three miles. Unlike the first two, this phone still had a handset. He even heard a dial tone when he snatched the handset from its cradle. He punched in his access code and dialed the number.

"Base."

"Ryerson. Grant, please."

"Sorry, Mr. Ryerson. Mr. Grant is unavailable."

Baylor swore silently then asked, "Are you sure? This is kind of an emergency."

"He's off-site, sir. Can I help?"

Baylor thought it through for a moment, cognizant of the need to avoid a security blunder. "Maybe. One of our people was on the news, tonight. I'd like to know the truth."

Silence emanated from the handset for several seconds.

"Bad data, Mr. Ryerson. That's all I can say."

"Not true?"

"None of it, sir. Is there anything else?"

Baylor felt the moisture well in his eyes. "Bless you, no."

A hint of friendliness entered the voice on the other end. "Thank you, Mr. Ryerson. We felt the same way." With a click, the line went dead.

Baylor felt like there were springs in his shoes during his run back to the hotel. As he approached, he also felt a little guilty about leaving Wozniak with the search for Weber. At least he could have helped with the brainstorming of how they were going to spring him loose from wherever the opposition had installed him.

He knocked and turned the key at the same time. Wozniak was still furiously tapping out a rhythm on the keyboard. He glanced up momentarily and continued without a pause. "Feel better now?"

"Heaps. She's not dead. The report's hogwash."

Wozniak lifted his face, interested. "Really? I wonder why?"

"They got it wrong somehow. News-people muck-up."

"I don't think so." Wozniak leaned back in his chair. "You say she's one of Ouilette's people. Yet, her picture hits the major news media. That's the worst thing that could happen to a covert agent. They say she's dead when she's not, so they want everybody on the outside of the organization to think so. They really smear her. Why?"

"She pissed somebody off? They're holding a grudge?"

Wozniak shook his head. "The opposition wants to immobilize her. Everybody who has seen her will be calling the cops. She can no longer move around in public. They're trying to isolate the lady. That's what I think."

"Why the smear job? They could just offer a huge reward and get the same effect."

Wozniak picked at his lip with a forefinger. "You said you know her. What's she like?"

"Smart, sassy. Upbeat, warm. But she doesn't tell everything. I think she bopped one of the opposition, when he was tailing me. That was before I knew the score."

"She killed him?"

"Put him to sleep for a while."

"That's probably where they caught on to her. She have any family?"

"I don't know. I didn't know her long enough to get invited home for dinner."

Wozniak grinned. "Let's find out." His fingers flew over the keyboard. "Royce, right?"

"Yeah. Karen Royce."

"Royce, Karen, US Navy, Lieutenant. What else?"

Baylor shrugged again. "Nothing...wait! She said her name was Adele."

Wozniak raised an eyebrow. "Can't hurt." He typed a few more strokes and sat back. The screen flashed several times and he smiled.

"Bingo!" He turned the laptop around and Baylor read aloud.

"Martha Royce, 52, d. 10/16/18, survived by husband Jonathan and three children, Karen Adele, a Naval officer, Cynthia Ann, and Jonathan Jr. The Funeral is scheduled for tomorrow at Winter Gardens, Lenexa Kansas.

"Jeez, Doc. That's stunning. The date is kind of old, though. Let's see if we can find the father."

Wozniak spun the laptop around and typed away. After a minute, he read the results. "Jonathan Royce was recently promoted to telecommunications manager at the JC Penny catalog order center in Lenexa. This happened less than two months ago, so it's probably still accurate."

Wozniak tapped the computer. "Which brings me to the other thing we were supposed to do. I've found Sam Weber."

Baylor sat on the bed. "No shit? Where is he?"

Wozniak nodded. "About fifty miles from Mr. Royce in the city to the north of Lenexa. It's called Leavenworth, Ed. Weber's locked up in the maximum security section of the federal penitentiary at Fort Leavenworth."

Baylor dropped backward on the bed with a groan. "Damn! We couldn't get him out of there with an army. Even an army with tanks."

Wozniak replied, "That's right, Ed."

Something in his tone caused Baylor to bend his head so that he could see Wozniak from his horizontal position on the bed.

"You think we can create a diversion, or run a scam?"

"Something even better."

Baylor sat up. "Doc! This is Leavenworth we're talking about. They don't make a tougher nut to crack. There's no way we can force our way inside, let alone break Weber out."

"A different plan is required. Something unique, an operation that's never been done before. It should work once anyway. And then, well, someone else will have to come up with a better idea."

Baylor picked up a chair and dropped it next to Wozniak's. He lowered his frame into it and leaned over the makeshift desk.

"I'm all ears, Doc. Fill me in."

Wozniak smiled at him. "You're about to get a crash course in the dark side of computing. Inside every software engineer resides a Mr. Hyde who is counterpoint to our everyday Dr. Jekyll appearance. A savage hacker, Ed. The more brilliance displayed at the keyboard, the greater the discipline required to walk on the bright side. I'm among the best, my friend, the very best. And now, I shall cut loose the leash." Wozniak twisted his face into an exaggerated leer. "Mankind will never be the same."

"Doc, you have my attention. Let it out."

"We're going to design a virus. Not just any old virus, but a Trojan horse. Inside of this polymorphic, multi-partite virus we'll—"

"Whoa, whoa...what's this? A polymorphic something? You're losing me."

"In layman's terms then. We design a hollow virus. We pack the interior with nifty tools to change things we need changed. Like schedules, or assignments, or whatever. We pack it with ferrets to search out things we need to know and pigeons to send us the information the ferrets discover. We add a trap-door so we can climb in when we want to and a bomb to blow the works sky-high when the time is right."

"Blow the works! What in a prison would...oh, I get it. Disrupt the computer systems."

"Yes. We might need a few other things inside our Trojan horse as well, but when the virus is done we embed it in a document. Any document will work, as long as it's innocent in appearance. A letter, say, to the warden from his church or something like that."

"Won't the prison's virus prevention software detect it?"

Wozniak smiled. "That's why the discipline part is so tough, Ed. A new virus is a preemptive strike. A virus used for the first time is difficult to detect because anti-virus software works on pattern recognition. Oh, there's some behavioral stuff to watch for but I can avoid that. Anyway, if the pattern is new, the AV software is often not engaged. Even so, there are some things we can do to stealth the virus.

It's possible that I might unintentionally duplicate some patterns previously written so we'll test pretty thoroughly before we launch."

Baylor shook his head. "Doc, you're a menace. How come you never did this stuff before?"

"Who says I haven't?"

"What! You mean…nah."

Wozniak just raised and lowered both eyebrows, a crooked grin bending his lips.

07:22 CDT, 14 May, Minot AFB, ND

Will fading, her focus slipping, Linneow turned to techniques the Vithri had taught her and emptied her mind of thought while flexing the various muscles in her body, one by one. The process was to exercise neural patterns she could sacrifice while the deadly elements coursed through her cortex. Nearly thirty-six units the humans called hours had passed since the Oo'ahan drone had injected her with his poison. She could feel its effects gradually consume her strength and control. Her legs suffered the worst. Even if freed of her bonds, she could not cross the room unaided.

For a day and a half, Linneow had struggled against the urge to sleep; a prodigious effort for a Chao whose nervous system and metabolism demanded short but frequent periods of rest. She believed she had now fixed a preponderance of the heavy metals to the neural pathways serving her body's muscular control. She must feign a limited degree of confusion lest the drone inject her again. She knew she would be incapable of managing the dispersion of a second dose.

The human named Pigott proved a diabolical opponent. She guessed the human part of his consciousness was not so capable, that the Oo'ahan suggestive implants remained the greater risk. Nevertheless, she had detected an overlay of ego that drove the host to fanatical lengths in support of the group-mind controller. He pressed their plans forward with a zeal she had not witnessed to this degree in humans before.

Pigott had, however, unknowingly aided her in her efforts to defeat his dosage. His strategy of sleep deprivation, with the flashing lights, the circling fans, and the random buzzers, had provided the only means by which she remained conscious long enough to misdirect the poisons. She had finally reached the limits of her ability. She closed her eyes and let her limbs relax. The hiss and whir of the fans assumed a roar as consciousness faded. Her subconscious, long deprived of outlet, surged upward.

Linneow closed her eyes and touched her forehead to the cool, silvered surface of the display. It could not be! In all time and space – fate would not, could not be so callous. Her extended talons raked furrows in the composite surface of the desk. Could she rend the iridium-laced ceramic of the hull, she would have. Let in the void. Absolute zero might chill the searing torment.

Cassione, the first-born. A statuesque, silver-maned warrior of the wing. Among the best the Chao could field. And as if that were not enough, so too the pair-born siblings, Sionine and Luestus, who nipped at their brother's heels. Intellect and humor. Strategist and scientist. Female and male. Pride and joy.

The recording looped again. Again, the ice moon smashed through every conceivable defense and struck Tassone. At a distance, a graceful merging – a deadly embrace.

Cracks radiated around the equator of Fortress Tassone. The crust fractured and heaved and magma erupted in violent waves. The shattered fortress stretched into an ellipsoid as the moon thrust to its core. Again, the combined mass exploded into pyrogenic fragments, most spinning off in myriad trajectories.

Defeat. Death. Destruction on an unthinkable scale.

Linneow strove to contain the agony in her breast. Sionine and Luestus. Cassione. All dead. And what of dearest Massia? She recognized that anguish would be no stranger amongst the Chao this day, but this fact did not lessen her pain.

An alarm chimed at the entryway to her quarters and the portal irised open with a metallic hiss. A leader of six to the second, a Ki'stor, strode through. Another warrior of the wing, and one of proven valor. He dropped to one knee and offered his neck.

"Word from the fleet, Mistress," he said. "They've recovered some of our own from the orbital batteries."

"Massia," she breathed.

"He lives. Injured, as most are, but he will recover."

Linneow controlled her breathing with difficulty. She must show strength. Position demanded strength, and civility, above all else. This was almost too much to ask and she turned away to save face. "Inform my lord Sassineue I shall join him on the command deck."

The warrior stood and struck his breast. "My lord commander requests your presence, Mistress, not on the command deck, but in the launch bay." When she whirled, he straightened and added, "We soon sally against the enemy."

"What madness is this?" she whispered.

Intra-ship transportation spanned the distance to the flight deck in a matter of moments, but the passage seemed interminably long. The lift opened into the mammoth volume of the primary bay where nine beak-nosed, droop-winged Saarks, all that remained of a once mighty complement, huddled in the center of the deck like discarded fragments of an abandoned puzzle. Sassineue stood with the last of the Chao, and little doubt remained of the Ki'stor's claim for her lord and all his companions wore flight suits.

Anger eroded Linneow's composure when she approached and he seemed to sense this for when she drew within earshot, he turned to his warriors and said, "Board your craft."

They dispersed, well conscious of the coming storm.

"You've received news of Massia," he began.

"One child in four still lives. We are defeated. It is time to withdraw."

"The enemy has not yet accomplished his goal."

She stood close and lifted her gaze to his. "My lord, we are defeated. Must we risk all? What then of the future should the Chao vanish from this domain? We must withdraw." Linneow trembled with desperation, but her plea could not sway him. His magnificent mane swung in the negative.

"All we might save is worth less than what we would lose." His baritone sent shivers through her frame. When she sought to reject his claim, he gently pushed her muzzle to his throat. "There is no one I trust more. Save the cradle, else all we've sacrificed is in vain."

"Pride of Siturn—"

"Sayla, my love, my life. The Vithra will not sustain against the enemy. This you know as well as I."

She pressed her talons into his back, purposely drawing blood and bringing a flicker of surprise to his eyes. "Your pain is mine," she sobbed. "Your life is mine. You must not face the sphere alone."

Sassineue held her at arm's length and gently shook her smaller frame. "I'm not alone. Two flights of Saarks launch with me."

"Saarks! What chance of victory is that!"

He inclined his head. "The mother of my children knows we seek only time enough to end the threat. The honor of victory I bestow upon you. Save the cradle, Sayla."

The greatest Mi'stor among the Chao, a legendary leader of six to the sixth drew himself to full height, bared his fighting fangs and bowed. With grace and power, he swept up the side of his Saark and slipped into its cockpit. His violet eyes remained locked with hers until the descending ceramic canopy severed the link.

In the screens on *Ammonte's* command deck, nine tiny dots erupted through the launch bay iris. Linneow's despair mounted as they dwindled. Delay, he said. At what cost? The Oo'ahan consumed all who faced them. None would survive, this much was certain. The antimatter-powered jewels bent away, turning into the wake of the cruiser as it hurtled sunward. Alone now, Linneow confirmed the great vessel's trajectory into the inner system. When the warship's gestalt confirmed time enough remained, she assumed the command chair and rocked to and fro, humming a mantra of reconciliation.

Time flowed into the fountain.

Sunsong faded and seascent soothed the troubled brow. Finwings swirled and sailed and spun in lavender vaults above the soft sigh of the eventide surf. Cynnion-spiced plumes whispered from webvine fires set by early revelers gathering along the shoreline. Darkentime gently approached, and with it the time of union – of joy. Rheia – the state of bliss. Two times through brightentime before the end. She did not fail him then. Once again, honor was hers and she would not fail him now.

The first of the melodious warnings trilled unheeded.

Time flowed out of the fountain.

Into the abyss of stellar night – the cold and still and silent void where peril steals swiftly close on feather-soft soles. Where death comes at a ruthless, studied pace, and decay, not at all. Where eternity beckons and serves the unwary, careless or unfortunate with equal and implacable disdain. Where fate might still the aching heart, cool the wretched flame and end the endless pain.

Smaller and swifter than *Pride of Siturn*, the Chao cruiser rapidly closed upon the Vithri ship and the eight Collective destroyers that pursued her. When the enemy began its attack, Linneow traced patterns of force throughout the volume of the tactical tank, securing remnants of shattered Fortress Tassone. She directed these blasted lumps into converging trajectories with the pair of moons far ahead.

The sons of Vith would not prevail, he said. And why? Because of civility? A Vithri trait the Chao tried most to emulate? And why not? We live among them, a caste apart but seeking confluence with our sponsor race since the destruction of our beloved Cha so long ago.

If the Vithra, with all their might, could not best the foe, then what methods might the Chao employ? Perhaps civility was not the answer. What then? The antithesis? Reversion? Cast away one hundred billion years and return to the savage roots? *Unthinkable.*

Whatever the plan, it must first destroy the enemy. And then, with Vithri aid, divert the calamity now in motion.

Strategic warnings illuminated within the tank, but *Ammonte* remained well out of range. Far ahead, *Pride of Siturn* bent around the limb of the largest marauding moon. The Vithri cruiser began its bombardment by hurling chunks of rock against the moon's barren surface. *Ammonte's* gestalt initiated an analysis. The Vithri had power to spare and their calculations, superbly accurate. If not for the enemy, they would turn that moon away from the cradle. The second, but smaller moon presented a lesser problem.

First one and then a second Collective destroyer flashed in to strike the Vithri warship. The other six turned away, recognizing the threat a Chao ship represented and looping back toward her battlecruiser. Focused on pummeling its target, *Pride of Siturn* paid no heed. When the destroyers' attack drove ribbons of flaming debris from the Vithri ship, Linneow extended her talons into the padded arm of the command chair. Still too far for beam or missile.

As the range narrowed, the Vithri vessel showed signs of distress. It still lobbed its missiles with unerring accuracy but fewer of them and those with less velocity. The gestalt's analysis evolved. Unaided, *Pride of Siturn* could no longer prevent either moon from striking the cradle.

Combat warnings flooded the command deck when *Ammonte* entered extreme range and at that moment, something miraculous happened. An unknown vessel flashed into existence ahead, and in the moments that followed, all six approaching destroyers flared briefly into minor suns – an impressive display of incredible power. Her ship dashed past the intruder, a gleaming streamlined silver ship of a type never seen before. There was no time to spare for greeting, or even acknowledgement for now the remaining destroyers urgently pressed forward their destruction of the Vithra ship.

Linneow slipped into her pressure suit and donned the virtual command helmet. She configured missile launchers to her claws and the spinal laser to her fangs. Secondary weapons were synched to her eyes. Each blink would fire the batteries. Finally, she assigned the deflectors to her hands and subsequent screens to muscles on her shoulders, back and legs.

Chao were no match for the Vithra in abstract methods of warfare and the logic of consequence was a game where the Oo'ahan reigned supreme.

Swift, random, deranged response? Exploit a weakness often exhibited in Saark to Strike-ship encounters? But these were Fleet Destroyers. Immensely capable and she outmatched two to one. The Vithri Web...it might be the only answer. Linneow connected to her vessel's gestalt. The ship around her disappeared when she engaged the I-link.

Knee-high Tessgrass erupted from a bowl-shaped savanna. Windwire trees thrust into a violaceous sky around the periphery of the glade. A screech eagle issued its challenge and she could not resist a reply. Her high-pitched snarl ended in a base rumble that echoed across the plain.

The Chao hunting cry went unanswered.

This time she was alone – a chilling reminder of a probable future. Of loss – of that which was – and of that which was to come. The thought filled her with agony and, in the lower tongue, she screamed into the void.

Despoiler, come to me! Taste my wrath!

Across the glade, the female beastcat turned away from a ponderous frondcow. The male still tore into its bleeding flanks.

Linneow unhinged anger's gate. Fury flared fulgent.

Long and lean and lethal, the beastcat streaked toward her. She leapt to meet it and, as they closed, she reached out and slashed the enemy with extended claws. She raked it again and a third time. Sparks of light flew inward. She brushed at them with her right hand and half winked out of existence.

Rage consumed her. Filled her limbs and mind with prodigious purposeful power. Her scream of challenge burst across the glen.

The screech eagles dove for cover.

A herd of knothogs stampeded into the silkbrush.

Songdoves scattered in all directions.

Racing across the verdant savanna, she angled toward the enemy, increasing her pace with every stride. Her gleaming ivory opponent slowed, flattened its ears, extended both claw and fang.

Filled with splendiferous savagery, Linneow flashed alongside the enemy. In passing, she raked and savaged it with claw and fang, oblivious to pinpricks of heat stabbing her shoulders.

She did not turn nor break her stride. The enemy fell rapidly behind, its momentum lost. She bore down upon the second foe, now standing over a helpless prey, shaking her fallen ally in its teeth. Linneow drove directly toward him and he veered away, fearing collision.

She tore at his tail with fangs, ripped open his back with claws. She struck his haunches, tearing flesh and sinew. The enemy screeched in agony and tried to turn toward her. She leapt upon his back, gouging, raking and pummeling until bones and muscle fell away in blood-soaked ribbons.

Stabs of pain stung her with increasing frequency, a signal the female now closed, desperate to deflect her attack. Linneow slipped beneath her screaming, bleeding opponent, using his body as a shield. She lifted her feet, extended claws and disemboweled the enemy. At his death cry, she reached in with her fangs and tore out his throat. When the corpse flared with heat, she leapt clear and closed upon the remaining beastcat.

Behind her, the stricken enemy burst into a glorious glimmering globe.

Linneow struck the female with unquenched fury. Claws ripped hide and fangs tore muscle. Her violence overwhelmed the female's courage and it turned to flee. Driven to exultant heights by combat's heady brew, her war cry pealed across the glade. Filled with mindless instinctive ferocity, Linneow held nothing back. She slashed the enemy until one hind leg was torn to ribbons and the second sundered from its body. She savaged wounded, bleeding flanks until the beastcat could no longer turn with her. She mauled its hindquarters until it dragged rent and crippled legs through phlegm-flecked furrows filled with gore.

She leapt upon its back and stabbed her talons deep. Ribs snapped. Muscle flayed. Crimson mist jetted into the void. She grasped the female's spine with fang and jaw, snapping viciously left and right. Bone and sinew cracked and tore asunder. The beastcat screeched in mortal agony. Linneow sank her fangs into its neck and ripped savagely from side to side. The enemy sagged and fell silent.

Linneow heaved free of the virtual helmet and staggered out of the command chair. Her legs would not sustain her and she collapsed to the deck, where she sought to clear away rivulets of sweat stinging her eyes. Acrid smoke and the smell of burning insulation filled the command deck. Alarms sounded throughout the cruiser. In the tank, the last enemy ship lay dead – three sections drifting apart.

Linneow touched the comm for the cruiser's gestalt. "Damage report!"

A mellifluous voice responded, "Moderate and severe damage to after shielding. Primary and secondary energy weapons sustained minimal damage. Aft missile launchers inoperative. Spinal laser severely overheated. You should heed my admonition about rate of fire, Linneow."

"Had I, we'd still be sustaining damage. What of *Pride of Siturn*?"

"The Vithri vessel is gravely injured. Drive inoperable. Deflectors inoperable. Main armament destroyed. Secondary armament, inoperable. Limited life-support. Eighty percent of the ship is open to space."

"Can you contact them?"

"On channel four."

A screen sprang to life on the forward bulkhead depicting only a shadowy haze sporadically lit by flashes. No sign of the great saurian masters.

"Counselor Rhian, this is *Ammonte*," she called. "Can you hear me?"

"We see you, Linneow of the Chao. Pride-kin Rhian is deceased. Peace follows his path. We shall not survive far beyond his time."

"Transfer to *Ammonte*, honored kin. We have room to spare."

"Linneow is alone and yet the enemy has fallen. Perhaps Linneow has too well learned the art of war."

Castigation or complement? The web, of course. Universal among Vithri-built vessels, of which *Ammonte* was one. They would have seen it all as if through her eyes. What now of vaunted civility? And worst of all, it was the counselors of Siturn who witnessed her fall from grace. The warrior caste of Chalin might have understood. Linneow inclined her head and softly replied, "My decision, honored kin, faulty though it may seem was to give instinct full reign. Perhaps this is sufficient."

"We have seen, and so, believe. Pride-kin will not transport to *Ammonte*. Time is insufficient to save both the nest-world and ourselves. We choose the nest-world and you must assist."

Linneow recalled her mate and his squadron, still engaged with the last Oo'ahan spheres. "The enemy still threatens, honored kin."

"The enemy is close, Linneow of the Chao. Our unknown ally engages them. The danger is also here, as are we. To the task we must attend."

Linneow resisted the compelling Vithri undertones. "Should I delay, my mate will perish. You cannot ask me to ignore his peril."

"Decision comes now upon the Chao. Consider well before you act, for our time here ends and yours begins. Should you avoid your destiny, there will be only endings and the Oo'ahan shall prevail. We know they have taken your children. We know calamity befalls our nestlings. Our colony is lost and we are lost, but you may begin again. For this reason, the *Prides of Siturn* bequeath the cradle to you, Linneow of the Chao. Raise again your young. Defend this world as your own."

Agony banked its infernal fire. Her lord was right. She might save more than they lost. But what of Sassineue? Cradle or mate? Could she – should she choose life for one over the other? What of a future without her mate? And what of a future where sacrifice had been futile. This decision might wound her spirit. To choose wrong would destroy it.

"Speak to me of the task, honored kin."

"We shall designate targets and you must hurl the missiles. Time is insufficient for further discussion. Let us begin."

Linneow climbed back into the command chair. The virtual helmet descended and she stood alone on an obsidian plane facing a pair of silvered icy moons that slowly approached.

A red dot illuminated a chunk of rock and then selected a precise spot on the larger moon's surface.

Seventeen hundred kirods!

The voice spoke into her mind. She grasped the indicated rock and threw it precisely at the indicated position. Ammonte staggered as drive systems coped with hurling an equivalent mass at the approaching moon.

Time flowed from the fountain, and the bombardment continued.

Linneow exhausted the Vithri horde of missiles, and the larger moon had been transformed into loose collection of molten debris. The smaller, a pockmarked erubescent sea.

The cruiser's gestalt issued another report that confirmed her fears. While the larger moon was shattered and broken, and the trajectory of the majority of its mass had slowed and turned, the changes were still inadequate. The smaller moon had slowed but was still intact.

In the tank, the cradle loomed close, an unfulfilled promise for the future. If she could not divert the impending collisions, this world might soon suffer a fate similar to that of the Fortress Tassone.

But nothing further could be accomplished at the moment.

"Honored kin, all missiles are expended until we intercept those I sent earlier. You may transfer now without endangering the cradle."

There was no reply.

"Honored kin, please respond."

Ammonte's gestalt replied instead, "There is no life aboard their ship. *Pride of Siturn* is dead."

Linneow bent her head and whispered, "Forgive me, Pridekin of Siturn. Peace follows your path."

With surgical precision, she carved up the battered hulk of the dead warship and launched each section on a trajectory her own gestalt provided. Soon afterward, and with the magnificent sphere of the cradle swelling nearby, Linneow intercepted the debris she had launched before her battle with the Oo'ahan Collective destroyers. Another extended bombardment ensued until all projectiles were again expended. She again reviewed her gestalt's analysis.

Some fragments of the larger moon had gone astray and several angry crimson scars marked planet-fall. The smaller moon, slowed but still intact, struck with cataclysmic effect. Sensor readings indicated burgeoning changes in the atmosphere and analysis concluded the biosphere had been devastated but probably not destroyed. The Prides of Vith must determine if she had saved or slain the cradle.

She turned *Ammonte* away from the blue-white sphere, engaged the cruiser's drive to maximum capacity and surged outbound, back toward another conflict raging behind her. The mysterious silvered ally, alone and unaided, had engaged two massive Oo'ahan capital ships, a mighty firefly swatting away their combined offensive power. In the next moment, one of the two globes lost its protective shell. An instant later, the exposed latticed construct erupted into a brilliant ball of destruction, mortally injuring its twin.

Ammonte's sensors depicted a launch from the silvered ship that veered away from the conflict. A moment later, both that vessel and the remaining globe vanished in a blaze of light.

Linneow gasped with surprise. *Such prodigious power! Who were these people?*

The sensors warned of another approach. Vithri ships, this time. Of the original six, two remained. Linneow was thankful to find *Pride of Chalin* among the survivors. After the councilors of Siturn, that great ship possessed the most able and brightest minds she knew of among the Vithra.

While relieved, Linneow's pain of loss did not abate. Her mate spoke the same words over and over again...words whispered into the back of her mind. She believed she would hear them for all eternity.

Use the I-link, my love...

She arched her back and screamed his name, "ARDE!"

The I-link...

Pigott turned away, frustration evident in his features.

"Hopeless. It's completely confused."

Rotts nodded. "What's this Arde and Saark?"

Pigott glanced at him and clamped his jaw. "Pray you never find out."

As the two men walked through the exit doors, Pigott continued, "Tell the medical team to desist with the deprivation routines. We'll try again tomorrow without them. And Phil..."

"Yes, sir?"

"I think it's time to reduce some risks. Send a secure message to Leavenworth. Tell them to terminate their most recent guest."

Rotts frowned. "These are unprecedented steps, sir."

Pigott paused in his stride. He waited until Rotts faced him.

"Colonel, these are unprecedented times or haven't you noticed?"

"Yes, sir. We all have. I just don't see the connection."

"They're connected all right. There are forces at work that we can barely conceive of, let alone understand. Our task, fortunately, does not require understanding, only prevention. Weber will not support us. We cannot let him become a resource to the enemy."

"How can they get to him in Leavenworth, sir?"

Pigott turned away and started walking, drawing Rotts along with him. "Oh they'll get to him, all right. One way or the other, they'll get to him. See to it, Phil. Make sure he cannot help them."

Baylor climbed back into the Jeep after trying without success to reach Ouilette. Wozniak was engrossed with the computer again. Attached to a short antenna, a cable ran across his lap to a receptacle at the back of the unit. The antenna clung to the passenger's window with two small suction cups.

"What have we here, Doc? Looks like a radio hookup."

"Cellular modem, Ed. I want to check on the progress of the virus we uploaded this morning. Roland Bishop, the warden at Leavenworth should have read his mail by now."

Baylor started the engine, pulled out of the gas station and returned to Interstate 70. He accelerated down the eastbound ramp and merged with traffic.

"Here we are," Wozniak suddenly said. "Yes! I'm in! The trap door is inside the Warden's user code." Wozniak could not contain his excitement. "This guy can go anywhere, no passwords required."

"Hey, Doc. If you're messing around in there while the warden's logged on, won't they catch on to you?"

"Not likely. My routine resembles a detached process, gathering some report data. Time to call home the pigeons. Video feeds first. Cell 2011A. Good Lord! That's a huge file! They've at least one camera running in this cell all the time."

Wozniak scrolled through countless frames, all of them showing the backside of a man sleeping in his bunk. "C'mon. Roll over or something. Hold it, here comes dinner, oops, breakfast I mean. Now he's up. Look this way, man. Got him!" Wozniak froze the frame and pivoted the laptop toward Baylor.

"That's our boy, Doc. Now all we have to do is get him out of there."

Wozniak nodded. "Been thinking about that. I've another ferret collecting mail on our subject. I'm going to scan what we find until I locate the authorization that admitted Weber to Leavenworth."

"Then you'll un-admit him, right?"

"Something like a psychiatric examination at a clinic in Kansas City comes to mind."

Baylor switched on his cell phone. "I'll call Ouilette. We're going to need some backup on this one."

"Wow! Catch this! Pigott sent Weber down here. They have him on thiopental sodium, dosed to the gills through his food. Pigott has designated no visitors, absolute quarantine. Anybody who tries to see him is to be apprehended immediately. Lethal force authorized."

"Well, I'll be damned. It's bloody fortunate we didn't try to confirm his presence. Pigott must be one of the bad guys."

Wozniak nodded. "I never liked that asshole."

Baylor dialed Ouilette's number while steering with his knee.

"Base."

"Ryerson. Mr. Grant, please. Imperative!"

"Yes, sir. Standby."

In a few seconds, Ouilette answered, "What have you got?'

"Your target, sir. We know where he is and who sent him there."

"I can guess who. Where are you? Direction and distance from your lodging, please."

"About two hundred and fifty miles east."

"How far to the package?"

"Four or five hours, sir. He's right on the river, slightly north." Several seconds passed before Ouilette responded.

"Understood, Mr. Ryerson. Well done. Can you brief our team before the extraction? Our people will be on the ground at 0200."

"A direct effort, sir?"

"That's the plan."

"My colleague may have a better idea. I'll let you speak to him." Baylor passed the cell phone to Wozniak.

"What's on your mind, Doctor?" Ouilette asked.

"From what Mr. Ryerson tells me, there will be the devil to pay with your method, Comman…er, Mr. Grant."

"I expect a difficult task. You've an alternative, perhaps?"

"Possibly. I'm inside already, in a manner of speaking. I can influence the environment to a large degree, perhaps even to moving our subject off-site."

"Doctor, if you can arrange that, I would be most grateful."

Wozniak had been tapping keys while he talked, the phone captured between his shoulder and jaw. Suddenly he tensed. He pounded the keys in an agitated manner. Finally, he swore and said, "Mr. Grant, the matter has become urgent. How soon can your people arrive?"

"The earliest is by air at 0200, local time."

"Not good enough. A termination order has been issued for eleven p.m., tonight."

"Can you delay it, Doctor?"

"Delay isn't an option, Mr. Grant. Confirmation after the event is specifically required. We might be able to change the location, but we'll need support soon afterward…and impressive support at that."

"Spare no effort, Doctor. Keep me advised. Please put Mr. Ryerson back on the line."

Wozniak handed the phone to Baylor.

"Mr. Ryerson, I'll trust in your resourcefulness today. I've still another task for you, on top of what you're already engaged in."

Baylor smiled and said, "Final exam, Mr. Grant?"

"You've already passed any test I might devise. You're strategically placed and one of my people is in trouble. I cannot move resources quickly enough to support her. I need you in the arena by 1600."

"Where, sir? The father?"

Ouilette paused. His voice betrayed surprise when he continued. "Had there been a test, you would've just passed it. Affirmative, your last. Locate her, but do not make contact. Shadow until 1900, at which point an SOG team will take over."

"That's cutting it a little fine, sir. We're needed up north shortly afterward."

"I've no alternative. I expect that you and your associate will accompany the 0200 extraction team back to base."

Baylor grinned. He poked his fist at Wozniak with a thumb pointing toward the roof. The scientist simply looked perplexed for a moment and then returned to his computer.

Ouilette continued, "A modification to field methodology, Mr. Ryerson. For today only, you'll switch on your cell phone from 1600 to 1900 and again from 0100 onward. Understood?"

"Yes, sir. I'm to expect a call?"

"Perhaps. We'll also need to know your location." Ouilette broke the connection.

Baylor folded his phone and pocketed it. He glanced at Wozniak momentarily while he passed a series of semis. "How are we going to play this, Doc? We might need to split up."

"I sincerely hope not, my friend," Wozniak replied. "Together we make a good team. You know...brains and brawn?"

"Doc! You know how to make a guy feel like a slab of meat. What happened to my degree in critical thinking and analysis?"

Wozniak sobered. "All joking aside, Ed. I'll not forget that climb on the stairway. If there's ever a way to reciprocate, I'll do it. That's a promise."

Baylor grinned. "Lighten up, Doc. It was nothing."

"It was a lot more than nothing, Ed Baylor. I'll stick by my word."

"Doc, help my girlfriend out of a jam and I'll be happy."

"Miss Royce?"

"No, I'll have to tackle that one alone, I think. My other girlfriend. The one with the silver pants."

Wozniak's cheeks, neck and the tips of his ears turned bright red. He broke into laughter. "I did infer that, didn't I? *Touché*. I'm worried about her. If Pigott's willing to execute Weber, maybe he was also involved with Petersham's death and the report about Miss Royce. What are his limitations? How come we've not heard from Linneow? It's been four or five days since everything went to hell."

Baylor shook his head with emphasis, once to each side. "I can't think about that, Doc. I'm a linear kind of guy. Take out the closest threat and move on to the next one." He turned to the scientist and grinned. "Maybe we make a pretty good team after all. You set the priorities and I'll nuke 'em." Baylor thumped the steering wheel. "No afterburner! This is a damn slow way to travel."

15:14 CDT, JC Penny Catalog Center, Lenexa, KS

"Whom are you visiting, Mister, er...Ryerson?" the receptionist asked. An officious-looking woman in her fifties, she wore a blue blazer and gray slacks. A silver badge over her left breast pronounced her as security, the nametag below it as the shift supervisor.

Baylor lifted his eyes from the visitor's pass he was completing.

"Mr. Jonathan Royce, ma'am. The telecommunications manager."

"You have an appointment with Mr. Royce?"

"No, ma'am. But my contractor says I'm supposed to check with him before I begin the upgrade on the switching systems. He might have some special instructions for me."

"Your contractor is?"

"Rockwell Electronic Commerce, ma'am."

"Be sure you note that information on your visitor's pass. I'll ring Mr. Royce for you now."

The receptionist picked up a handset and dialed a four-digit number.

"Mr. Royce? There's a Mr. Ryerson in the lobby to see you." After a short pause, she added, "No, sir. He says he did not have an appointment but his employer, Rockwell, told him to contact you before he begins work on your equipment."

"Yes, sir. He's standing right here. You want to talk to him?"

"Yes, sir. I'll do that. Thank you, sir."

Baylor tried to hide his disappointment when she returned the phone to its cradle. The receptionist allayed his fears in the next instant when she said, "Mr. Royce is sending someone down to fetch you. He thinks there must be some mistake, but he wants to speak with you anyway. You can have a seat if you'd like."

Relief washed through him. He nodded and stepped backward toward a low couch placed between two large ficus trees. Instead of sitting, he placed the briefcase he had borrowed from Wozniak upon the glass-covered table in front of the couch. He slowly turned around. The lobby was of an ultra-modern design. Textured concrete slabs, trimmed with heavy oak beams ran at angles to the floor. They intersected far over his head, creating a pyramidal spaciousness that was aesthetically pleasing as well as timeless in concept.

"Mr. Ryerson?"

Baylor turned toward a slim man dressed in a white shirt and tie with navy blue slacks. The newcomer extended his hand as he approached.

"That's me," Baylor said, shaking the proffered hand. He picked up his briefcase.

"Joe Marks. Where's your tools?"

Baylor hefted his briefcase. "Tapes. Software upgrade, not hardware."

"Oh, no. That means a long night. We'll have to test every function. Are you sure this was scheduled?"

Baylor shrugged. "You got me. I just follow orders."

Marks laughed. "Yeah. I know how that goes. Well, we've a long walk."

Baylor followed Marks through the lobby and into an elevator that dropped three levels. They descended a staircase and entered a subterranean corridor of exceptional width. One half of the corridor was filled with motorized conveyers, now still and silent. They entered a cavernous warehouse that was dark and empty.

"Running low on stock?" Baylor quipped.

"Not hardly. This is a transient holding area. By tomorrow morning, this place will be packed to the gills. All the orders received today are inbound. Comes in all night long, goes out all day."

"Wow!" Baylor said, impressed. "That's a lot of space to fill with phone orders."

Marks nodded. "The Spectrum Switch passes fifty thousand dollars a minute in orders." Marks glanced at Baylor. "Exactly why we cannot afford to take chances with unscheduled changes. If Mr. Royce approves, we can let you have the standby node at five p.m. Once we test the changes you can upgrade the reporting node. When the operators close down, we'll switch one of those to call routing and test it all night. If it works, then you get the last node. Are you ready for a long night?"

Baylor considered the tasks facing him and replied, "That I am."

The two men walked through a fire door and into another warehouse space. This one was lit with fluorescent lamps. Marks led Baylor to a steep and narrow stairway equipped with a wooden railing. At another fire door with a keypad switch, Marks rapidly punched a five-digit code. He pushed the bar handle and the door opened. Baylor stepped into a brilliantly lit room, the center of which was occupied by a row of black cabinets trimmed with purple. The door clanged shut behind him. He shivered in air so dry and cold that, compared to the warehouse outside, he might have been transported to Alaska.

"Welcome to my kingdom," Jonathan Royce said, stepping forward from a table before the computer array. A tall man, and thin, with ample traces of gray invading his short, tightly coiled hair, he extended his hand. "You must be Ryerson. You're a new one. You've not been here before."

Baylor shook his hand. "No, sir. Lots of other places but not here."

"What other places?"

Baylor hesitated. "Mostly government places, sir."

"Baltimore?"

"I've been there."

Royce whistled. "Now there's an installation. How's the Social Security System doing these days?"

Baylor shrugged. "About as well as can be expected, given the state of things." He began to sweat, even in the cool environment. He needed to change this subject before his string of luck ran out.

Royce replied, "I know what you mean. At least in the private sector we use our own money. If we decide to spend it, who's to say no?"

"Yes, sir. I'd like to review the changes with you, Mr. Royce. Can we use your office?"

"Sure. This way."

Royce led him to a small office, ushered him in and shut the door. He leaned against the backside, all trace of joviality slipping from his face.

"All right, just who the hell are you?"

Baylor turned, surprised by the sudden shift. Royce continued, "Don't give me any shit about upgrades, either. I'd be willing to bet you don't know squat about computers. Rockwell didn't send you. I checked."

Baylor inclined his head, a rueful smile flickering at the corners of his mouth. Before he could reply, Royce continued, "I thought not. Well, whatever your name is, come clean and quick. I'm in no mood for bullshit and if that's all you have to offer, I'll throw your sorry ass out of here so fast and so far you'll wish you'd never heard of anyone named Royce."

"It's not likely I'd ever wish that, sir."

Royce squinted. "What the hell do you mean?"

Baylor dug into his wallet and fished out his military ID card. He slipped off his ring and passed them to Royce. The older man clamped his jaws and his eyes narrowed. He placed both items on the table in front of him.

"So what? You people have been pestering the hell out of my family these last few days. I've no use for the lot of you. You and all your damned lies."

Baylor's heart lurched. "You know it's a lie! You've talked to her!"

Royce blinked once, then shook his head. "I think you better leave."

"No, sir. It's best I stay." As Royce bristled, Baylor hurried on. "Look, Mr. Royce, I know you've no reason to believe me, but if you'll hear me out you might find one. Adele and I are on the same side."

"Adele?"

"Adele Reeves and Karen Royce are one and the same. Adele saved my bacon less than a week ago. Now our boss, hers and mine, wants me to cover her back until he gets a team in here to extract her."

"What's the boss's name?"

"You know I can't tell you that, sir."

"Where'd you meet my girl?"

"Andrews Air Force Base, sir. About a week ago. She danced my legs off."

For the first time since they had entered the office, Royce smiled. "I can believe it. How did she save your ass?"

"I was a target, sir. Much like she is now. She unhooked the bad guys and gave me an exit. I think they might have caught on to her in the process."

Royce leaned his head back against the door. "So now you feel the need to even the score, is that it?"

Baylor smiled. The old guy was shrewd. "To tell you the truth, sir, I'm not exactly looking forward to meeting your daughter again. She's going to flay me alive."

Royce looked perplexed. "Why's that?"

"Well, sir, she sort of loaned me her car. I kind of lost it."

The older man tried to withhold a smile. "Kind of lost it? What does that mean? Stolen?"

Baylor sighed. "No, sir. There were these two guys with automatic weapons. They were trying to fill me full of holes and keep my buddy locked in a laboratory with a huge bomb in the basement. I dove through the doorway and ducked behind the car. They shot it up a little."

Royce was grinning now. "Shot it full of holes?"

"Yes, sir. But your daughter had a shotgun in the trunk and I filled the gunmen full of holes. Anyway, my buddy made it out of the building, but we couldn't move the Porsche because it was shot up pretty bad. Wouldn't start. We ran for cover and the bomb went off."

"Let me guess," Royce said, shaking with pent up laughter. "The Porsche was blown to hell and back."

"Well, sir, it hasn't come back yet."

Royce burst out laughing. He bent over and slapped his knee. Baylor couldn't help himself and joined in. The old man laughed even louder. "Man, oh man. You are in trouble. You better save this story for a time when you're at least a thousand miles away."

Royce sat down, tears streaming down his face. He pointed at Baylor but still could not stop the laughter. "You have to be on the level. No one could invent a story like that. What kind of shotgun was it?"

"Mossberg, sir. Model 590. I still have it."

"That's my girl's trouble gun all right. That's what she called it. I tried to give her a pistol once, when she moved to Washington. She says to me, 'What do I want that little old thing for, Daddy. I got my own trouble gun.' She pulled that bad-ass shotgun out and I felt a whole lot better." Royce pointed to a second chair. "Sit down Mr. Ryerson, or whatever your name is. I'll bet it's not Ryerson, though."

"No, sir. The Military ID is legit. I think it would be best not to mention my name out loud, though. The guys we need to avoid might have this place bugged."

"With our security? No way. We're here twenty-four hours a day and I know every man on this team. Not one of them is anything but the most loyal employee possible. No one can get into this place unless one of us agrees and then we have to log him or her in and out. Any visitor is under escort one hundred percent of the time. No, sir! This is probably the only safe place to talk."

"All the same, sir, I need to know where Adele...I mean, Karen is. In about," Baylor checked his watch, "three hours, a hotshot team of commandos will pick her up and move her safely out of town. I'm supposed to hover around until they arrive. Sort of like a wild card in case the bad guys close in first."

Royce turned sober. "What are you going to do if that happens?"

Baylor glanced at his feet. "I don't know. I'll think of something."

"You better, Mister. Because, if you let my baby down, she won't be the only one after your hide. I'll be leading the charge and, believe me, that is something you don't want to see." Royce leaned over and scribbled on a sheet of paper. He handed it across the desk.

"This is the place. That's the phone number. You better get a move on."

Baylor stood and scooped up his ring and ID. He reached out his hand. "It's been a pleasure, sir."

Royce shook it. "Well, I think so too, Mr. Ryerson. You two went dancing, huh?"

Baylor smiled sadly. "Yeah, about a thousand years ago, seems like."

16:08 CDT, Minot AFB, ND

Rotts knocked once and stuck his head into Pigott's office. The general leaned back in his chair.

"Sir, we've found Wozniak's Jeep!"

Pigott stood and stretched. "Outstanding. How?"

"We tapped the national surveillance network in New Mexico first, and when that didn't pan out, expanded the coverage. Eventually we picked up this from a toll booth just outside of Topeka." Rotts passed across a black and white photo of a dark colored Jeep Cherokee with two occupants inside. The shaded windshield hid their identity, but the license plate was clearly displayed. "There aren't many of that model around since production ended in 2001."

"This one has Minnesota plates," Pigott objected.

"We ran them all...on every Cherokee we found. This one turned up as an unissued plate number. Reported missing on the same day as all their recruiting began."

"Excellent, Phil. You run it to earth?"

"Yes, sir. We did."

"And the Doctor?"

"No, sir. We spotted the same Jeep at Jonathan Royce's place of employment and verified the VIN. It's Wozniak's Jeep all right. A black guy we didn't recognize drove it out of there."

Pigott turned toward his computer monitor. He stood with his arms crossed, one hand supporting his chin. After several seconds, he pivoted back to Rotts.

"Here it is. Royce covers Wozniak as part of her assignment. We know she was there because of her Porsche, the wreckage of which we dug out of that hole in the ground. She ensconces the doctor away in some safe house and lights out for Kansas City, using his Jeep, when our story breaks."

Rotts nodded. "Makes sense. Who's the guy driving it now?"

Pigott shrugged. "Boyfriend maybe. Get a photo of him and send it in. Meanwhile, don't loose the Jeep. If we're careful and cautious, he may lead us to Royce."

17:40 CDT, Kansas City, KS

Baylor exited the Parallel Parkway and headed north on 59th street. After several blocks he turned left into an older subdivision and slowed the Jeep. He found the address and drove right by it. A block farther up the street he turned into a driveway, backed out and parked on the opposite curb from the stately old house bearing the address Royce had given him. He dug out his cell phone and dialed. The phone rang once.

"Yeah?"

"Doc, I'm in place. What's happening?"

"I'm working on it. I don't like the car you got me. Too hard to climb in and out of it."

Baylor chuckled. "Doc, you need to go on a diet."

"Bite your tongue! Can you be here by nine p.m.?"

"I'd say so. See you then."

"Right."

Baylor broke the connection and dialed a second number. This time the phone rang a half dozen times before it was picked up.

"Hello?" The voice was a young woman's but not Adele's. Baylor had put some thought into this call on his drive up from Lenexa.

"Hi! I can't talk very long right now, but I have a message for your friend from the Navy."

"I - I don't know what you mean."

Baylor softened his tone. "Just tell her to sit tight. Mr. Grant will invite her to his house around seven. I'll call back when the time is right. Have you got that?"

"I - I'm not sure what—"

A second woman's voice cut in. "Affirmative." She hung up.

Baylor smiled. Now that was Adele.

At the end of the street, four blocks away, a gray Crown Victoria pulled up to the curb on a cross street. One of the two men in the back seat rolled down the tinted glass part way and clipped a window mounted spotting scope to the edge of the glass. He dialed the Leupold to maximum power and focused on the Jeep.

"Isn't he going in?" the driver asked.

"Negative. He's just sitting there, using a cell phone."

"I don't like it. What's he waiting for? Backup?"

The passenger in the front seat shook his head. "This guy's no pro or he wouldn't be using that vehicle. He probably just thinks he's guarding the house. Can you get a picture from here?"

"Sure," replied the spotter. He clipped an adapter to the eyepiece of the spotting scope and shot several frames. After removing the camera, he checked his quarry again.

"Why don't we just hit the back door while he's out front? It's likely he'd never even know."

"We sit," the passenger up front replied. "We don't know which house and I'll give our friend credit for sense enough not to park directly in front of it."

At twenty minutes to seven, Baylor's cell phone chirped. He opened it and punched the call button.

"Ryerson."

"Right Claw Six. You've got the package?"

"I'm close by."

"Contact the package and send it east on Parallel Parkway. Leave your phone on." The connection was broken.

Baylor dialed the number Royce had given him. She picked up the phone on the first ring.

"Reeves."

"You've transportation?"

"I do."

"Follow the Jeep." He hung up. In a few seconds, an athletic-looking blonde came out of the house and climbed into a pale blue Corolla in the driveway. Baylor started the Jeep. When the Corolla's backup lights illuminated, he pulled away from the curve and drove past the driveway. He slowed slightly, until the Corolla backed out and turned to follow him.

"He's rolling!" the spotter announced.

"Anybody with him?" the front seat passenger asked.

"No. Wait! Another car is backing out. It's headed in the same direction. The driver's a blonde though."

The man in the front seat grunted as the Jeep and the Corolla rolled past their Ford. "That's her! And he's working a leading tail. This guy's better than I thought. Wait until they turn on 59th and then follow them." He pulled a cell phone out of his pocket and punched several numbers.

Baylor turned east onto the Parkway. Almost as soon as he had completed his turn, his cell phone rang again. When he connected, someone on the other end spoke without waiting for a greeting.

"Turn north on 51st."

"Right. What am I looking for?"

"Green Caravan in a Walgreen lot. Drive right by. What's the package wrapped in?"

"Pale blue. Foreign issue."

"Good enough. When it turns off, you keep going." The connection broke again.

Baylor flicked his turn signal for the left turn and swore when a full-sized gray Ford cut him off and turned in front of him. The green arrow remained lit long enough for both the Jeep and the Corolla to make the turn. He missed the next light and slowed to a stop as the first vehicle in line. In the rear view mirror, he studied her face.

Adele had dark circles under her eyes and her hands gripped the wheel with a tension that showed in her whitened knuckles. Her head never stopped moving, her eyes roved from side to side. The light changed and he led the Corolla across the intersection where the street narrowed.

"Are they in position yet?" the front seat team leader asked.

"A hundred yards behind the woman. Nobody in between. They're in position."

"Let's do it. Let the Jeep pass and cut her off. Disable her car but we need the woman alive. If the guy in the Jeep becomes involved, take him out."

The driver of the Ford eased his gearshift into low. He crept to the edge of the residential driveway into which he had backed.

Baylor tapped the brakes lightly when the passenger car ahead rolled toward the end of the driveway. He thought it might pull out in front of him but evidently the driver had seen him. He shifted his focus forward, looking for indications of the drugstore ahead. The sound of squealing tires, followed a moment later by the report of a heavy pistol, wrenched his attention to the rear. The passenger car, the same gray Ford he'd seen before, now blocked the road. People were jumping out of all four doors. They were armed.

He stomped on the brakes. The Jeep slid to a stop. He ratcheted the shifter into reverse and mashed the accelerator to the floor. As the Cherokee rocketed backward, one of the men stepped into the street and swung an assault rifle in his direction. Rapid flashes appeared at the muzzle. The rear window dissolved in a shower of glass. Two bullets punched into the dash, one through the opposite headrest and something tugged at the collar of his jacket.

Baylor slammed the brake pedal again. He groped for the shape of the shotgun, which he had left on the floor behind the front seat. For one panicked moment, he could not find it. As his fingers curled around its grip, he glanced again through the shattered rear window. The rifleman was inserting another magazine.

Beyond the Ford, he could see the Corolla, sideways in the street. Adele had tried to reverse and escape in the other direction, but a large white suburban blocked the street behind her. The rear tires on the Corolla were flat. In the moment he had, he saw one of the assailants from the Ford use a shotgun to shoot out the front tires.

Adele's head, minus the blonde wig, popped up from behind the Corolla's right front door. Her pistol, a government forty-five by the sound of it, barked once and the man with the shotgun was hurled backward onto the hood of the Ford.

Baylor had no time to loiter. The assault rifle swung up again. He hastily pointed the shotgun through the shattered window and pulled the trigger. The weapon bucked upward, its muzzle bouncing off the headliner. His aim was low but the charge of buckshot ricocheted from the concrete surface of the street. It caught the gunman in the knees and knocked his feet out from under him. He fell with a clatter, his weapon discharging into the air.

Baylor shifted into four-wheel drive. He aimed the back-end of the Jeep directly for the rear quarter of the Ford. Just before impact, he slouched in his seat to provide support for his head. The Jeep smashed into the Ford and slowed. The Ford was a heavy car, but the Jeep was more robust and had momentum. The Ford spun, offering a partial opening into the gun battle developing beyond it.

The windshield shattered under a stream of bullets and Baylor ducked below the dash. He kept his foot pinned on the accelerator, the tires squealing in protest as they slowly pushed the Ford farther and farther around. With a screech of metal, the Jeep tore free of the Ford. Baylor swerved in the general direction of the Corolla. He jammed his foot on the brakes, sliding to a stop. At a momentary pause in the automatic weapons fire, Baylor sat up. He swept the shotgun forward, knocking out the remains of the windshield. One of the gunmen stood near the Ford's front bumper, frantically jamming a new magazine into his weapon.

Baylor laid the shotgun across the top of the dash and squeezed the trigger. The gunman flung his weapon away and pitched backward on the grassy lawn behind him. Baylor worked the action and fired again, this time aiming at a silhouette of head and shoulders above the back fender of the Ford. His opponent dropped out of sight when the buckshot punched a dozen holes in the side of the car. Baylor reached over and unlatched the passenger's door. He kicked it open and launched himself across the console, dragging the shotgun behind him. When he hit the surface of the street and rolled upright, he found Adele calmly reloading the magazine to her Colt Commander.

She stared at him with amazement.

"Heaven above! It's Pilot Ed!"

Another burst of weapons fire from the suburban forced them both downward.

He jacked another round into the shotgun as he replied, "I thought I'd take you dancing."

Adele leaned around the edge of the Jeep, using the front bumper as a brace, and fired two rounds. She cleanly caught the remaining gunman behind the Ford as he stood to take aim. Her target toppled backward.

She dropped behind the Corolla as a score of bullets from the suburban thumped and clanged into both the Jeep and the Japanese car. "So what is this? A warm up before the main event?"

"It will be if you don't get your cute butt out of here. These guys are sure to call in a lot of backup. Take the Jeep. About a half-mile down the street is a Walgreen's. Look for a green Caravan. That's your team."

"What about you, hotshot? Are you planning a one-man war?"

Baylor lurched to his feet. He triggered the shotgun four times in rapid succession, first driving his opponents under cover and then taking out both tires on the right side of the suburban. He ducked down to avoid return fire.

"I have another job to do. Go on now, woman! Get your ass out of here!"

She grinned, kissed him on the forehead and launched herself into the Jeep. She jammed the shifter into gear and stomped on the gas pedal. The battered Cherokee surged past the Ford, careened off a tree and disappeared down the street. Baylor counted his remaining rounds, reloading from the speed-loaders in the side of the shotgun. He scrambled around the end of the Corolla and fired twice at the suburban. He hesitated a moment. One assailant showed himself, swinging his weapon to bear. He spied the ready shotgun and tried to leap backward. Baylor triggered twice more, his first round bringing a yelp of pain.

In the momentary lull, Baylor pushed away from the Corolla and sprinted to the side of the nearest house. He peered around the corner in time to see three men preparing to chase after him. He fired his last round, driving them to cover and then dashed into the backyard. He leapt over a waist high hedge into another yard. In seconds, he flashed between the opposing houses and out onto the street beyond.

Baylor dialed up the speed, thankful he had decided to wear his Nike's instead of his loafers. As he passed a dumpster, he pitched the empty shotgun inside and continued onward.

About ten blocks up the street he met an elderly man standing by his rock garden, trowel and rake in hand. "What the hell's going on back there? Sounded like world war three," the oldster asked.

Baylor replied without altering his pace. "Couldn't say, my friend. Maybe someone's celebrating an early Fourth of July."

Far behind him, three men slowed to a walk then stopped. They gasped and coughed. One sat down on the lawn behind him. They watched their quarry disappear around a corner a dozen blocks up the street.

"Geez! Who was that guy? The six-million-dollar man?" the man on the lawn asked.

Still standing but too tired to reply, his superior just shook his head. After a moment, he turned around and waved his hand. He coughed as he rasped out, "C'mon. We've left a mess back there. You guys get your DEA identification ready. The place is going to be swarming with cops by the time we get back."

Baylor kept a steady pace for most of thirty minutes. His running sweats provided the perfect disguise for a man who wanted to escape on foot. Police cars hurtled by him in both directions, sirens wailing and lights flashing. None paid any notice. He turned east on Leavenworth and jogged into a Shell station a few minutes later where he spotted a sign for a public phone.

On the first ring, the phone rattled loudly. "Doc? Is that you?"

"Thank God! Sorry, I dropped the phone. The news reports are talking about a drug war. I even saw—"

"That was us in the gun battle. The opposition caught on and were laying for us just before we reached the pickup team." Baylor paused. "Uh, Doc…about your Jeep?"

"That's what I was going to say. The news is plastered with pictures of my Jeep. It's all bashed up and full of bullet holes. One witness said a woman jumped out and fled. There was no mention of you but they did say two men were killed and several wounded. I was going nuts."

"Hey, Doc, I'm glad you care."

"Cut the bullshit, Ed. If they had you, they would soon know about our plan for Weber, which I'd never be able to pull off alone. I was getting ready to scramble when you called. Where are you, anyway?"

Baylor told him and added, "I'm going to catch a cab to the airport and rent another vehicle. I should make it to the hotel a little after nine."

"Great. We need a van…one from which we can remove the seats. It has to be big enough for a stretcher to fit in the back."

"You've got my attention, Doc. You mind telling me the plan?"

"No time for that." Wozniak hung up.

Baylor guessed the scientist was more than a little upset. He dialed information, obtained the number for a cab company. He promised a large tip if the driver was prompt. Less than five minutes later, a red and white Chevy Caprice, with the emblem of Target Cabs painted on the doors, rolled into the filling station. "Appropriate," Baylor snorted as he climbed in.

20:20 CDT, Minot AFB, ND

Colonel Rotts intercepted Pigott immediately outside the conference room where the briefing was taking place.

"What's the problem, Phil?"

"I can handle what we're covering inside, sir. I need your help on another matter. The pickup team got clobbered, sir."

Pigott's lips thinned. "Tell me," he finally said.

"It started well enough. They intercepted and isolated Royce from her escort. She was armed and resisted capture. Her escort re-engaged and all hell broke loose. We've two dead and three wounded, one critically. The first team took the brunt of it. Royce fled while the escort pinned our second team. Backup arrived in less than four minutes, but it was over by then."

"Did they suffer any casualties?"

"No, sir. Not that our people could tell."

"How many in their escort?"

Rotts licked his lips. "One, sir."

"One man did all this?"

"He tipped the balance, sir. Royce accounted for both fatalities. Head shots, thirty plus yards, with a handgun. If we send people against her again, they should not be force-level restricted as this team was."

"Forget Royce. Ouilette's people have retrieved her and she has undoubtedly contacted her family. The program is busted."

"Yes, sir. There's one other thing."

Pigott narrowed his eyes, but said nothing. Rotts continued, "The pilot, Baylor? The one who ducked us in DC? There must be more to his background than we can discover."

"Why, Colonel? He's regular Navy, a fighter jockey."

"That's what the record says. However, he was part of the inner circle that Ouilette was putting together. He did lead the Chao to this base and, therefore, had nearly six hours of contact prior to everyone else. He did not react as expected when we started a program on him. In fact, he made immediate contact with the Royce woman and vanished. Now he turns up in Kansas City."

"What!" Pigott injected. "Baylor's in Kansas City?"

"Yes, sir. That's what has me concerned. His action as the escort for Royce is outside any reasonable profile for his service record."

Pigott waved Rotts to silence. "You're telling me that Baylor was the man who smashed the pickup operation?"

"Yes, sir."

Pigott pursed his lips. "Baylor is in Kansas City. So is Royce. Are they a team?" Pigott asked the question in a manner that led Rotts to believe it was rhetorical.

"I don't like it, Phil. They could be after Weber and we've read this all wrong. Contact Leavenworth via secure electronic link. Weber is to be terminated immediately."

Rotts nodded. "Yes, sir. I'll also pull our resources in Kansas City back together and send them up to Fort Leavenworth. If Ouilette's people try for breakout, maybe we can bottle them up and inflict some major damage."

When Rotts turned toward the conference room, Pigott asked, "Who was leading that pickup team?"

Rotts flipped through his clipboard. "Agent Rozermann, sir. One of the wounded men."

"How badly?"

"Legs are full of buckshot. He'll be laid up for months."

"How fortunate. I've no use for incompetence. Make sure he has access to a workstation. I have some material I want him to read."

21:02 CDT, Holiday Inn, Leavenworth, KS

Baylor knocked on the door to room 212. "Doc. It's me."

The door wrenched open and Wozniak, moving at uncharacteristic speed, reached out, grabbed his arm and pulled him inside. "Ed, we have a crisis. A message hit the warden's in-basket less then twenty minutes ago ordering Weber's immediate termination. We must go in now." Wozniak pointed at a uniform lying on the bed. "Climb into that and put this on." He handed Baylor a black leather security belt, complete with a holster and handgun.

Baylor unsnapped the flap and pulled it out. "Where in hell did you come up with the Glock?"

"It was in the briefcase with the computer. Come on, Ed. We've got to move!"

"No time for a shower, I guess."

"Give me the keys. I'll load the van while you're changing."

"We'll load the van together when I'm done." Baylor shucked his sweats and tossed them into a duffel bag. "You can brief me while I'm changing."

Wozniak placed his briefcase on the floor and leaned back against the wall. "I've been in the Warden's user account all evening. I altered the execution command somewhat. I specified that it should be done off-site as part of a psychiatric examination, an accidental interaction of drugs during therapy. My memorandum detailed that an SOG team, that's us, would retrieve Weber at ten-thirty and take him, under armed guard, to a facility outside Lawrence where the dirty deed would be done. So far my Trojan Horse has worked flawlessly. It intercepts all mail to the Warden, backtracks and deletes any carbon copies and sends a delivery receipt to the sender."

Baylor buckled the holster around his waist. "So I'm the security guard. Where did you find the uniform?"

"Rental agency. Anyway, with this new message, I had to move forward the timetable for the pickup. We're now expected at nine-thirty." Wozniak checked his watch. "In fourteen minutes. I'm worried that someone will call down asking if the job is done yet. If that happens before we arrive or while we're inside…"

"Our goose is cooked," Baylor replied. "And so is Weber's. I get the picture." Baylor hefted his bag and opened the door. "Let's go, Doc. I'll call Ouilette on the way into the prison. He'll need to know about our new timetable."

20:28 MDT, Desert Range Experimental Station, UT

Ouilette paced the room, limited in his strides only by the umbilical of the coiled phone cord from the desk-set to the receiver he held to his ear. "No, Mr. Ryerson. We cannot launch early. It's still daylight and we have a satellite overhead. There is no way I'm dropping an aircraft in here before 2200, our time. We're twelve hundred miles away, so you see the nature of the problem."

Ouilette paused.

"Yes, we can do that. Do you have an alternate site in mind?"

Ouilette shook his head.

"Let us worry about it then. By my calculation, your cell phone battery cannot have much time left. Turn it off except to call in. When you have Weber and are clear, call back." Ouilette broke the connection.

"DAMN!" He slammed the receiver into the cradle.

Captain Andrew Meisner, USMC, Recon, peered up at him. "Sounds like the fun's started already."

"Shouldn't surprise me. Plans seldom survive first contact. I'm glad we got KR back safely but that little fiasco is probably the reason this mission has jumped off early." Ouilette checked his watch. "When is the satellite clear?"

"There are several, sir. Our window begins at 21:33 and lasts until around 23:00. That's the only one until the day after tomorrow."

"So we could get off about a half hour earlier."

"Yes, sir. But it's still daylight at this latitude. Even 22:00 is pushing the envelope a little. If there should be an aircraft over-flight, it would be tough to explain why a Herky-bird is nesting in a Forest Service tree farm."

"It's a risk, Andy, I'll give you that." He rubbed his chin and then replied, "Our Talon has the Q70 aboard. Is it operational?"

"Yes, sir."

"Realistically, we could bring the aircraft into the area. As soon as the satellites drop over the horizon, sweep for any aircraft close enough to be a problem."

"But, what about the Q70's radar signature? Everything within three hundred miles could read it."

"How long would it take to establish range and bearing on every target once we illuminate them?" Ouilette asked.

"Not my area of expertise, sir."

Ouilette pointed at the workstation on his aide's desk. "Use the database, Andy. That's what it's there for."

The marine officer sat up suddenly. "The computer network is up already? When did this happen?"

Ouilette grinned. "Don't feel put out. That's what I was coming to tell you when Ryerson called. Reynolds had three of six nodes online within a couple of hours."

Meisner's fingers flew across the keyboard. The screen flashed the results almost as soon as he finished. "Lord above! This puppy is fast. The answer to your question, sir, is three and a half to four seconds. That's the illumination time required for three hundred-sixty degrees, zero to one hundred thousand feet. Computed and analyzed results in milliseconds."

Ouilette smiled. "Since the Q70 is spectrum-mobile, we change frequencies constantly during the sweep and let the computers figure it out. Nobody with a set-frequency receiver would see more than a few milliseconds of emission."

"I'll dial up one of the Talons and get it airborne."

"Do that, Andy. Also let the other teams know we're moving up the schedule by twenty-seven minutes."

21:37 CDT, Fort Leavenworth Penitentiary, KS

"Your admittance papers, sir." The security guard at the entrance gate reached out his hand. Wozniak passed a letter-sized manila envelope, which the guard opened. After scanning the contents, he glanced upward.

"Mr. Ryerson, this authorization says you are armed."

Baylor, sitting in the passenger seat, leaned forward. "Yes, sir."

"You'll not be permitted inside with your weapon," the guard replied. He added, "You may check it here, or at the main lobby and retrieve it when you exit."

Wozniak intervened. "That won't be necessary. He can wait with the vehicle. The prison's security staff will be escorting our prisoner all the way out. Mr. Ryerson will take over once the prisoner has been released to us."

"I understand, Dr. Wozniak. Your escort will be waiting at the lobby."

Wozniak nodded. "Thank you." When the steel gate lifted, he pulled away from the guard station.

Baylor stared at him. "Brazen, aren't we? Using your own name and all. Where did you get all that entry paperwork? I'm impressed."

Wozniak glanced momentarily at his passenger and then peered straight ahead. "Actually, I'm scared to death. Unlike you, all I have is my own identity. I don't think Commander Ouilette foresaw the possibility that we would actually become the team to free Weber."

Baylor laughed. "Don't worry about the fear, Doc. I can tell you from personal experience that it fades when the shit hits the fan. Pretty cool documents you handed those guys, pictures of you and me and Weber. How did you do all that?"

"Downloaded all the files, faxed the authorizations from the Warden's office directly to the hotel, merged it all with pixel editors. Pretty mundane stuff actually."

Wozniak turned the Dodge Grand Caravan into the visitor's lot. He spun the wheel and backed into the nearest space to the lobby. He handed the keys to Baylor.

"If something goes really wrong, I mean sirens going off, guards running all over the place...you should split."

Baylor raised his eyebrows. "Stick in the key and drive away?"

"I think that's best, don't you?"

"Doc, if they catch on to you, I'm unlikely to get very far. If something goes wrong, we're in a heap of trouble. So see that it doesn't, okay?"

"Yeah, right." Wozniak opened the door and stepped down. Without a backward glance, he walked toward the lobby.

Two guards, accompanied by a woman, met him at the reception desk. The woman glanced at her clipboard. "Doctor Wozniak, I'm Helen Radcliff, Warden Bishop's administrative assistant. According to our transport notification, you were supposed to be accompanied by an armed escort."

"Yes, Miss Radcliff. I have a security guard. He's remaining with the vehicle so we wouldn't have to fiddle with checking his weapon. You can escort the prisoner all the way through to the vehicle, can't you?"

"That won't be a problem, Doctor. If you follow me, we can stop at the Warden's office and complete the transfer paperwork and then I'll take you to the hospital, where your prisoner is."

"Is something wrong? Is he ill?"

"No, Doctor. Routine outbound examination. We are required to certify the prisoner as healthy when we deliver him into your care."

Wozniak looked for traces of sarcasm but found none. Helen Radcliff probably had no idea of the intentions for this prisoner. They started to exit the lobby when Radcliff directed Wozniak toward the metal arch over the corridor leading to the prison interior.

"Please, Doctor, you need to pass through the metal detector."

Wozniak followed her instructions. She led him into a featureless white corridor without windows or exits. The hall sloped downward at a modest angle but the length of it convinced Wozniak that he was descending into the bowels of the earth. When the four of them reached the far end, he discovered he was mistaken. They stepped out into the fading twilight and Radcliff led him to a vehicle that appeared to be a converted golf cart.

"It's a long walk, Doctor. I thought you might appreciate a ride."

Wozniak nodded but remained mute. He reflected that the word penitentiary could not convey the same image delivered by a view of the place, especially when one stood behind the twenty-foot walls topped with razor wire, surrounded by squat towers with searchlights and armed men. His mouth dry and a rubbery feeling in his legs, he climbed into the vehicle. The cart whined smoothly away from the only tunnel to the outside world.

After a five-minute ride, Radcliff pointed to a pair of imposing buildings straddling a courtyard. "Our maximum security section. The Warden's office is just beyond."

A couple of minutes later, the cart pulled up in front of a more modern structure. The stainless steel-framed glass windows seemed distinctly out of place, better suited to an office building than a federal prison. Once inside, Radcliff led the way to an elevator that whisked Wozniak and his escort to the second floor. A moment later he was ushered into Roland

Bishop's office. The Warden stood and extended his hand in greeting.

"I'm glad you've come, Doctor. Employing your clinic is a sensible solution if you ask me."

Wozniak cleared his throat. "No sense in unneeded complications, Warden. I'd like to conclude this matter with dispatch." Wozniak rolled his wrist over to check his watch. "It's a long—"

The phone rang, interrupting. Bishop snatched it up, jolting Wozniak with his catlike spring for the instrument. "Bishop."

"No, not yet." He covered the mouthpiece with his hand and whispered, "Minot."

Wozniak could literally feel the blood drain from his face. His stomach churned as the warden continued, "We're tending to it this very moment. I said I would confirm when the matter is complete. Don't you people read your mail?"

Bishop pulled the phone away from his ear and shook his head. After a moment, he spoke into the receiver. "I'll call you later." He hung up and peered at Wozniak. "Idiots! I should make them wait until morning."

Wozniak managed a smile. "It would serve them right. They drop a hot potato in your hands and then expect you to dance to their tune while holding it."

Bishop frowned then shrugged. "Anyway, let's get on with it. Here are the transportation forms and the transfer authority. Technically, he's yours as soon as you sign these."

Wozniak bent and scribbled his signature on both. He stood upright and glanced from Bishop to Radcliff. "As I was about to say, it's a long drive."

Bishop nodded and motioned with his head to Radcliff. She turned toward the door. "Please follow me, Doctor." She preceded him into the elevator and from there, to the first floor and deeper into the building. Wozniak could not ignore the nagging fear, which grew stronger with every passing second, that Bishop might be calling Minot at any moment. He could only hope that call would be postponed until they had Weber safely transported through the main gate.

A large plaque, proclaiming they had just entered the hospital, roused Wozniak from his distraction. Radcliff led him to the infirmary where he immediately spied Weber lying upon the center bed of the three available. The agent was strapped in with an intra-venous drip hanging by his side. Weber turned his head toward the disturbance as they entered and Wozniak felt alarm stab through him. Weber's reaction might unravel the ruse. He had no cause to worry, as aside from a slight widening of his eyes, Weber evinced no other response. He simply turned his head away.

Wozniak walked directly up to the attending physician. "Is my prisoner ready to transport?"

"Quite, er...Doctor Wozniak. I'm Doctor Amos Nobling." After they shook hands, Nobling lifted the chart lying between Weber's legs. "This prisoner's chart includes directives for medication to control his behavior. He seems exceptionally alert considering the dose he had taken earlier." Nobling glanced toward Wozniak. "I wondered if you might not want us to re-administer the drug to be certain that he's quiescent during the drive south."

Wozniak paused, pretending to consider the idea. He shook his head. "No, Doctor. I don't think so. We don't want any unpredictable drug interactions when we begin our work in the clinic. If he's securely strapped, all will be well. I have armed escort traveling with me."

Nobling replaced the chart and nodded. "Very well. The man is a homicidal schizophrenic, just so you know."

"I'm aware of his nature, Doctor. No doubt, he's a dangerous man, but I think we have the situation under control. I would like to get started and I think Warden Bishop would as well."

A phone rang at the infirmary reception desk and an orderly called out, "Miss Radcliff, it's for you. Warden Bishop."

For the second time, Wozniak felt his world spin. Beads of perspiration sprung from his forehead as Radcliff took the call and glanced at Wozniak as she spoke. She hung up and walked briskly over to the scientist. "I'm sorry, Doctor Wozniak. There's been a major systems crash. The Warden needs my help to sort things out. These guards will convey your prisoner to the hospital's emergency entrance on the third floor. From there they can transport him to your vehicle via ambulance."

Wozniak nodded, relieved that evidence of his computer system tampering had just evaporated with the self-destruction of his Trojan horse. Radcliff hurried away as the orderly and Doctor Nobling lifted Weber's stretcher from the bed and deposited it on a gurney. Wozniak and the orderly wheeled it out of the infirmary, down the corridor and into the elevator.

They soon reached the emergency entrance and loaded Weber into a waiting ambulance. Wozniak climbed in beside him, as did the two prison guards. The ambulance pulled out from under the canopy, circled upward to the security gate. Wozniak felt a third of the weight on his shoulders drop away. The ambulance drove around the prison complex until they reached the parking lot in front of the lobby. The driver leaned backward.

"Which one's your vehicle, Doctor Wozniak?"

"The gray Caravan."

The ambulance swerved to the left and then backed up. The driver leapt out and opened the rear doors. He and Wozniak eased the gurney backward until the wheels dropped. Baylor stood behind the orderly, the signs of tension gradually fading from his face.

Wozniak nodded to him. "Ed, why don't you pull the van forward. We can load our passenger and be on our way."

Baylor ducked his head, jumped in the van and drove it forward about thirty feet. He popped the release for the lift gate. As soon as the gate swung up, the orderly and Wozniak loaded Weber aboard. Wozniak closed the gate and turned to the guards.

"Thank you, gentlemen. You've been a great help."

He turned to the driver's window of the Caravan and motioned to Baylor to lower the window. He leaned close and muttered, "I'll drive. You should be tending to the prisoner."

Baylor scurried into the back of the van as Wozniak climbed into the driver's seat. The scientist rolled up the window, shifted into drive and eased away from the lobby. He twisted his head toward the back.

"Were you getting nervous?"

Baylor replied, "Doc, I feel like shit. I can hardly keep my eyes open. I had to walk around the van to stay awake. That and my sense of time has been blown way out of whack. I thought you were in there for hours."

Wozniak nodded. "Adrenaline hangover. I've heard of it. Never had a chance to experience it though. Must be your lifestyle, Ed. Maybe you need to take it easy for a while."

Weber's laconic voice cut in. "You hombres going to jawbone all night? How about turning me loose?"

"Not yet, my friend," Wozniak replied. "We still have the main gate to worry about. And we're coming up on it now, so act like a prisoner."

Weber mumbled something Wozniak couldn't hear, but Baylor just patted the agent on the shoulder.

Wozniak slowed the van and idled under the floodlights at the guard station. He rolled down his window and passed the transportation documents to the guard. After a few minutes of review, the guard stepped out of the building, unclipping a flashlight from his belt.

"Open up, Doctor."

"Is there a problem?"

"Not that I'm aware of. We check all outgoing vehicles."

Wozniak pushed the button to release the lift-gate. The guard shined his light into Weber's face and then Baylor's. He closed the gate and approached the front of the van. Before he could open his mouth, three vehicles hurtled down the driveway toward the main gate from the far side. The guard narrowed his eyes and said, "Just a minute." He walked across to the incoming roadway, unclipping the flap to his holster. He joined his teammate as they waved the vehicles to a stop. Wozniak could hear him clearly as he admonished the driver of the lead vehicle.

"You gentlemen are driving on government property. Stay within the posted speed limits unless you want some real trouble. State your business."

The driver passed over an ID card that Wozniak could not make out.

The guard nodded. "Sir, while the FBI has access to the prison, I'm still required to ask why you are here. Who is it you wish to see?"

"The Warden," the driver answered. "We've reason to believe a breakout may be in progress or soon to begin."

The guard passed back the ID card. "Very well, sir. I'll phone ahead. The warden is still onsite. He'll greet you in the lobby." The guard waved the vehicles through. They spurted down the road, completely ignoring the earlier warning. The security guard returned to Wozniak.

"I'm sorry, gentlemen. Because of the nature of this development, I'm must ask you to return to the lobby until the Warden personally clears your passage."

Wozniak shook his head. "He's already done that. This paperwork is signed by him."

"I'm sorry, sir. I need a verbal confirmation. Please back your vehicle—"

Wozniak tried again. "I can understand your position. You're about to call the Warden anyway. Tell him that Doctor Wozniak is still at the main gate and it's imperative we continue. I'm under contract to the U.S. Government who had directed Warden Bishop to deliver this prisoner for testing."

The guard started to shake his head when his partner handed him the phone. "I've got the Warden, Barry. You could ask him."

After a moment, the security guard returned. "I'm sorry for the delay, gentlemen. Have a good evening." He pressed a button on his console and the heavy iron gate retracted.

Wozniak shifted into gear and drove through it. Two hundred yards down the road, he whispered, "I think I'm going to be sick."

Baylor ripped away at the Velcro straps that restrained Weber. The agent sat up and Baylor passed him a gym bag that contained a flannel shirt, jeans, belt, socks and tennis shoes. Weber silently changed out of the prison garb, and then climbed stiffly into the front seat. He looked at Baylor and Wozniak in turn. "That was the slickest breakout ever conceived, especially for a couple of amateurs." Weber slapped his palm on the dash. "We need to get rid of this van, though. Pronto."

Baylor and Wozniak peered at each other. Baylor spoke first. "There's another car at the hotel."

"How far?" Weber asked.

"Five minutes," Wozniak replied.

"Or we could rent a third one," Baylor added.

Weber turned toward him. "Did you use your cover ID to get into the prison?" Baylor nodded and the agent continued, "Then that's out. I'm not complaining, it was an exceptional piece of work. Let's find the other vehicle." Weber glanced at Baylor again. "You carrying?"

Baylor patted his holster. "A Glock 22."

"Ever use one?"

"No sir." Baylor grinned. "I'm afraid my skill runs toward shotguns."

"I'd say so," Wozniak replied.

"In that case, Ed, would you feel offended if I tend to the Glock?"

"Not at all." Baylor shucked the holster and passed it to Weber who withdrew the pistol and its spare magazine. The agent shoved the pistol into the back of his jeans and tossed the security rig to the rear of the van.

"You're pretty spunky for a guy who's supposed to be taking thirty milligrams of Pentothal every day," Wozniak interjected.

"Figured it out a couple of days ago and flushed the stuff."

"You haven't eaten for two days?" Baylor asked.

"If we grab some grub real soon, I'd be appreciative."

Wozniak turned into the Holiday Inn parking lot. He pulled up beside the car Baylor had rented for him earlier, a Buick Riviera. Weber asked, "Who's got the keys?"

"I do," Wozniak replied. He dug them out of his pocket. Weber stepped out of the van and groaned. He stretched his legs and leaned in through the window. "I'm getting too old for this kind of life. Look, we can't leave the van here. They know where you stayed and if we don't move it, we'd be leaving a telegram that we switched vehicles. There's a twenty-four hour grocery store back up the street a few blocks. Follow me, and we'll dump the van there." Weber turned away, unlocked the Riviera and climbed in. He backed up and drove briskly out of the hotel's lot, the Riviera's tires chirping in protest.

Baylor nodded to Wozniak. "Let's go, Doc. I feel better already."

When they pulled into the shopping mart's lot, and parked beside the Riviera, Weber stepped out and handed Baylor the keys.

"Mind driving, Ed? I'm a little shaky."

Baylor nodded and climbed into the driver's seat, Weber across from him. Wozniak eased his bulk into the back seat.

Baylor turned the Riviera out toward the road. He paused about thirty yards from the exit.

"Where to?"

Weber's eyes widened. "You're asking me?"

Wozniak interjected, "Our plan only extended to getting you out of the prison, Mr. Weber. I think there's some kind of mix up on Mr. Grant's end of things."

Weber turned to face him. "Who's Grant?"

Baylor replied, "Sam, there's a whole lot of stuff you need to know. Let's decide on a direction of travel first and then we'll fill you in."

Weber nodded. "Fair enough. Where're we headed?"

Neither man could answer him. At their blank stares Weber asked, "All right, where's Marcus?"

"We don't know," Wozniak replied.

"God bless!" Weber muttered shaking his head. "Since we're in Kansas, we travel westward." Weber unfolded the Avis map and studied it for a moment. "Turn left, Ed. We'll take highway 73 to 192 to 4 and drive down toward Topeka."

Baylor pulled out of the lot and accelerated up the road in the indicated direction. Before they passed the turnoff into the prison, three cars hurtled past them, traveling in the opposite direction at a high rate of speed.

"The FBI guys, I'd bet," Weber quipped. "They're headed for your hotel. Let's not dally, Ace."

21:35 MDT, Desert Station Experimental Range, UT

Shouting over the high-pitched whine of the turbines and the buzz-saw roar of the propellers, Ouilette asked Meisner, "Everyone on board?" He had to shield his eyes from the driven streams of dust whipping past the fuselage of the huge aircraft.

The Marine captain gave him a thumbs-up, so Ouilette pointed at the ramp behind the C-130 Hercules. "Let's roll!" he shouted. Both men trotted up the ramp, which immediately began to retract. Inside, the sound of the props was slightly muted, the air still, but hot, close and reeking with the sweet smell of jet fuel. Finding his way in the dim red light, Ouilette gripped the cargo webbing along the inner fuselage surface as he navigated the narrow space between the aircraft's hull and its cargo. He patted the bulky shape that occupied most of the aircraft's interior.

"A stroke of genius, Andy."

"Thank you, sir," the marine replied.

Ouilette added, "I'm not real happy about risking so many of our assets, but this gives us the mobility we'll need on the other end."

"And the firepower, sir."

"That too," Ouilette replied. He found a seat near the forward end of the aircraft and buckled in. He glanced at each of the eight men and women arraigned in two opposing rows, meeting their grins, nods and smiles with one of his own. The Hercules lumbered across the desert floor, bumping and swaying over the rough surface. Ouilette could feel the aircraft turn to the right and suddenly the sound of the engines changed.

The buzz-saw snarl dropped away as the pitch of the propeller blades increased. The engines assumed a deep, urgent hum that transmitted itself throughout the airframe. Augmented by persistent acceleration, the sway and bump turned into a jolting vibration as the C-130 gained speed. Suddenly, the nose of the aircraft pitched steeply upward and, seconds later, the ride turned steady and smooth.

Ouilette listened to the whine, thump and clunk of landing gear and flaps. He felt weight in his stomach from the upward surge as the Hercules gained altitude. The aircraft banked sharply to the right and his ears popped from the change in cabin pressure. He glanced at his watch. 2139. A good, fast start.

22:48 CDT, Minot AFB, ND

"Put it over there," Rotts commanded. He added, "Set up each line for a different agency. I want every one of them manned at both ends." The colonel turned away from the phone installer, toward his projector and snapped on the switch. He unclipped the laser pointer from his breast pocket, picked up the remote control and strode to the podium at the front of the room. When he turned to face his response team, he noticed that Pigott had just entered the auditorium. He nodded at the general and then rapped the wooden surface of the podium with his knuckles.

"Listen up!" When he had everyone's attention, he continued.

"We're right behind these guys so let's not slip up. We don't know where they are but we do know where they aren't. They cannot use the airports, railways or bus stations. We have the van they used and we know that they've rented a late model Buick Riviera from Avis. The plate number is Kansas 214 GLC. This vehicle is metallic tan in color. Get that out to each of the agencies you're covering as soon as we conclude.

"Based on the time they left the main gate, we know they did not head for or enter Kansas City. We've secured all major and minor routes in that direction. That still leaves a lot of choices." Rotts clicked the remote and a map appeared on the screen. He clicked it again and a grid superimposed upon the map. One more click turned the center of the grid, which was focused on the penitentiary, bright red.

Rotts continued, "They have a forty minute head start. This red zone represents practical limitations of travel by vehicle given the condition of the roads and the expected traffic patterns at this time of day. It is likely that our quarry is still in the red zone."

The colonel clicked the remote again. A yellow zone illuminated all around the red patch. "This is our focus. I want intensive search in this yellow zone. This is where we stand the greatest chance of making contact. As time passes, this zone will continue to expand, stretching and then overtaxing our resources. The earlier we can cover this the better. Your responsibility is to manage state, county and local resources in the yellow zone to which you are assigned." While Rotts swept his pointer around the map, both the red zone and the yellow zone shifted, growing slightly in size.

"That's all, gentlemen. Get to it."

As Rotts left the stage, Pigott beckoned him. He joined the general and the two men stepped out of the auditorium.

Pigott spoke first. "I like what I see, Phil. A solid tactical approach. What do you need?"

"More air assets, sir. As the circle gets bigger, we'll need faster eyes to cover the increased territory."

"I'll see what I can come up with. How did they do it, Colonel? I understand they used no force at all."

"Sir, we're trying to reconstruct the method. It's clear that someone, probably Wozniak, subverted the prison's computer system. I'm amazed at the combination of luck, guts, and skill these two guys showed." Rotts shifted his feet. "Sir, I want to use lethal force. Particularly now that Weber has joined them."

"Go ahead, Phil."

Rotts continued, "General, we have a unique opportunity. These three men represent most of Ouilette's inner circle. I cannot believe they are operating without his support. Ouilette has to be out there somewhere."

"What's on your mind, Phil?"

"Fight fire with fire, sir. Ouilette's people, if Weber and Royce are any indication, are all paramilitary. I would like to back up my contact team with something comparable. If you take the Kansas City debacle as an example, I don't want to send police or intelligence operatives in against elite military types. Let's use light infantry. Rangers or something similar."

"Good idea. I'll arrange it," Pigott replied. He turned away.

"Oh, general! I almost forgot. We have another casualty. Rozermann, the supervisor of the pickup team that failed with Royce?"

Pigott nodded. "What about him?"

"He died tonight. Hospital staff says he had a brain aneurysm while reading his E-mail."

Pigott evinced no emotion. After a moment, he simply said, "Justice prevails." The general turned and walked away, leaving Rotts wondering about the meaning of his words.

23:31 CDT, US Hwy. 24, north of Topeka, KS

Baylor dialed Ouilette's number. He glanced toward the Buick. It was barely visible even when he knew where to look for it. While parked in the shadows of the closed Shell station, Weber had advised him to call in and get an update. Wozniak and Weber poured over the map of Kansas, trying to find a route that would avoid most heavily populated areas.

"Base."

"This is Ryerson."

"We're very glad you've called Mr. Ryerson. We were worried because we hadn't heard from you."

"My cell phone's dead. Weber didn't think it was advisable to stop in any well lit or populated area," Baylor replied.

"Mr. Weber is correct. Our intelligence tells us the opposition has geared up to a full-scale search. They've found your van."

Baylor grimaced. "Do they know what we're driving now?"

"Uncertain but likely. Can you change vehicles?"

"I don't see how. Where's Mr. Grant?"

"He's en route, Mr. Ryerson. Where are you now?"

Baylor reported his location and then asked, "How will we know where to meet him?"

"Keep moving west. Call back in ninety minutes." The line went dead.

22:40 MDT, 22,000 feet over Colorado

Meisner leaned over Ouilette. The Navy officer had his head back, his mouth open. He was sound asleep. Meisner shook his shoulder. Ouilette's head snapped forward.

"What's up, Andy?"

"Baylor called in, sir. They're still clear and moving. Close to Topeka."

"Where are we?"

"Over Leadville, Colorado at the moment, sir. Kansas state line in forty minutes."

Ouilette glanced at his watch. He looked up in surprise. "So soon?"

The pilot told me he's picked up a heck of a tailwind, sir. Almost ninety knots."

Ouilette nodded. "I'll take every gift we can find."

Meisner replied, "One other thing, sir. Baylor's cell phone is dead. He's supposed to call in ninety minutes from now."

00:29 CDT, 15 May, Wamego, KS

"Turn right at the next intersection," Weber said. The light turned green before they reached the junction of 99 and 24, so Baylor kept his speed and swung north.

"We need to start thinking about gas. Only a quarter of a tank left." Baylor glanced at Weber. "Should we have turned so soon? The signs are telling about a lot of hotels and gas stations just a few miles ahead."

Weber shook his head. "Too many eyes. We'll trust there's an all-night gas station up the road."

In a few minutes, they entered the small village of Louisville. Directly in the center of town, bright fluorescent lights illuminated a Texaco station that was still open. Baylor turned in and pulled close to the pumps. Weber climbed out, turned around and said, "Fifty buck's worth. I want out from under these lights."

Baylor nodded. He inserted the nozzle into the filler spout as Wozniak clambered out of the back seat and headed for the washroom.

Weber opened the screen door, stepped through it and stretched.

"Long drive?" a gray-haired elderly man, sitting on a stool behind the counter, asked.

"Long enough." Weber replied.

The oldster snorted. "Look at you. What're you going to do in twenty years, when you catch up with me?"

Weber walked up to the counter, leaned on the edge and dropped a fifty on its surface. He grinned and said, "Maybe I'll buy your place and welcome strangers into town."

"You wouldn't like the hours."

"A lot of traffic through here at night?"

"Nary a car. Yours is the first in almost an hour. Lots of diesel though."

"Trucks?" Weber asked.

The old man shook his head. "Tractors. This time of year, the crops are going in. Twenty-four hours a day until the job is done. Farmers come from miles around 'cause they know I'm open. Fifty is all you want?"

"That'll do it." Weber straightened, turned and sauntered out the door. Baylor had just finished pumping and climbed behind the wheel. Wozniak shuffled from the washroom and lowered himself into the back seat. Weber eased his door shut and said, "Let's roll."

Billie Dunham nudged his cousin Odie in the ribs as they flew southward through the village of Louisville at nearly sixty miles an hour.

"Hey! Hey! Lookee there, Odie. Could that be...?"

Odie's head swiveled as they swept past the town's only gas station. The Buick Billie had pointed at slipped into the darkness, but not before Odie caught a glimpse of it.

"I reckon it could. Let's check it out." Odie stomped on the brakes. The heavy cruiser slithered on the road, its tires squealing. He shifted into reverse and backed up, spinning the rear end of the car into the gas station. He shifted back into drive, switched on his overhead lights, and stomped on the gas. The Pottawatomie County Sheriff's cruiser slung gravel all the way across the apron. It rattled on the glass, bringing a shouted curse from the old man. The cruiser rocketed northward.

"You want me to call it in?" Billie asked.

"Let's check the plate first."

Weber turned around in the seat. "All good things must end." He leaned toward Baylor. "Listen up, Ace. When he pulls in behind us, ease off the gas and move toward the shoulder. Use your turn signal, but don't leave the pavement."

Weber turned to Wozniak. "Scoot down, Doc."

The agent reached up and dropped his visor. He slid down into his seat so that his head was not visible from behind. He adjusted the mirror until he had a good view of the road behind the Buick.

The Sheriff's cruiser quickly overhauled the Riviera. When it closed to within a car length, its red and blue flashing lights filling his mirror, Baylor put on his turn signal and pulled to the edge of the pavement.

Billie Dunham could scarcely contain his excitement. He unsnapped his holster flap. "It's the right plate! Omigod! We caught them, Odie! We did it!"

Odie frowned. "There's only one guy in the car. There's supposed to be three. You don't reckon the other two are back at the gas station, do you?"

"How the hell should I know? Let's get this guy cuffed and check it out."

"Now you just take it easy, Billie. The report says armed and dangerous. Remember what I taught you. Turn on your spotlight and aim it through the back window, got it?"

"Yeah! That's right!" Billie fumbled with his light. Odie reached down and picked up his mike. He switched it to loudspeaker and adjusted the volume to eliminate the squeal.

He turned to Billie. "Open your door and step out, but remember to stay behind cover."

"I know. I know." Billie climbed out and Odie did the same from the opposite side of the cruiser. He keyed the microphone.

"Step out of the car. Place your hands on top of your head." The electronically amplified voice sounded especially loud in the silence of the night.

"They're both standing outside the car," Weber said. "Pull forward about thirty yards. Stop and shift into reverse."

Baylor complied.

"They're getting away!" Billie shouted. He clawed at his gun.

"Get in the damned car!" Odie yelled. He dropped into the driver's seat, shifted into drive. Before Billie had even closed his door, Odie stomped the accelerator to the floor. In the glare of the spotlights, he missed the flash of backup lights as the Buick shifted into reverse.

"Gas it!" Weber ordered. A half second later, he yelled, "Brace yourself, Doc!"

The Buick lunged backward. Just before contact, Odie slammed on his brakes. The nose of the cruiser dove. The two vehicles collided at a combined speed of almost thirty miles per hour. The rear bumper of the Riviera slid up and over the forward bumper of the police car. It smashed through the grille and radiator, driving a mass of metal, plastic and glass into the forward end of the engine block. Drive belts and hoses shredded. The cooling fan exploded. The water pump cracked. A huge cloud of steam enveloped the forward end of the cruiser.

Billie broke his nose on the dashboard. Odie banged his head so hard on the steering wheel that he saw stars. The rear end of the Riviera crumpled inward, the trunk flying upward as its latch sprung.

"Go! Go!" Weber shouted.

Baylor shifted into drive and punched the accelerator. The Buick lurched forward trailing shattered glass and plastic.

Over the rumpled hood of his cruiser, Odie watched his quarry speed away. He jumped on the gas to follow. The cruiser leapt after the Buick, a horrid rattle and vibration emanating from the engine compartment.

Odie glanced at his cousin, the younger man bent over and moaning.

"Where are you hurt, Billie? Can you use the radio?"

Billie continued to moan and rock back and forth. Odie watched the Buick pull away from him, gaining distance despite the souped-up engine under the bent and twisted hood of the police car. Within another half mile, the cruiser slowed dramatically. The oil light began to flash on and off. With an ominous knocking and a final clank, the engine quit. Sheriff's cruiser number two coasted to the side of the deserted road.

Chapter Seventeen
01:04 CDT, 15 May, Minot AFB, ND

"Contact!" shouted one of the enlisted men. The noncom's fingers flew over his keyboard. On the screen above the stage, the map view zoomed in to greater detail. A flashing black 'X' icon appeared on route 99 just above the dot marking the village of Westmoreland. The 'X' cloned itself at the next junction, one symbol traveling east, the other continuing toward the village where it split again, this time traveling both north toward St. George and south toward Fostoria.

Rotts stood in front of the large screen for several seconds.

"All right!" he shouted. Without looking away from the screen, he added, "Move our people from Leavenworth westward along US 36. Send two teams down 63 and US 77." He stepped directly up to the screen and tapped the lower portion with his index finger. "Move all the troopers up from the interstate to US 24. Let's send the response teams in Salina to US 81. Seal all entrances and exits on 36, 24 and 81." He turned around. "We'll drive them into the box, gentlemen."

01:31 CDT, 22,000 feet over Russell Springs, KS

"Andy, why the sour look? Ouilette asked, looking up from his team briefing.

"Weber's group has been spotted, sir. I'm afraid we don't have a lot of time."

Ouilette stood. "ETA?"

Meisner stretched a map across the crate Ouilette had been using for a desk. He pointed to an area forty miles north of Salina. "It will take us about forty minutes to arrive here. This area is remote and sparsely populated, consisting mostly of empty fields. That satellite data shows most of them as fallow. We should cross US 81 right about here," Meisner tapped the map. "Directly afterward, we'll shed altitude from three thousand to less than five hundred. Inside of three miles, we turn north and drop down onto this unimproved road. It's a six-mile stretch, sir. Flat as hell and no utility poles. We can taxi into one of the fields, shut down the Herk and then unload."

"How do we locate Weber?"

"Mike Reiss from intelligence at the base had a good idea. Once we're down, Simmons, the pilot, will use the Q-70's receivers as a scanner. We should be able to latch onto the opposition's chatter as they zero on Weber. Hopefully, we can get to them first."

"We'd better, Andy."

01:52 CDT, Highway 16, just east of Tuttle Creek reservoir

Weber finished lacing the trunk lid down using a section of wiring he had stripped from the smashed taillights. When he climbed back into the Buick, Baylor jabbed his thumb toward Wozniak.

"Doc thinks we should head north. US 77 is just over the bridge."

Weber turned toward the Scientist. "Why north, Doc?"

"Too many roads down here. Too many places to cut us off. Nebraska, especially northern Nebraska, is a lot more open."

Weber nodded. "Maybe you're right. Not on US 77 though. Too much traffic. Maybe we can slip across the state line on one of these county roads. Let's roll, Ace."

Baylor shifted into gear and started across the mile-long bridge over the reservoir. Once they reached the western side, they could see the traffic flowing south along US 77. A quarter mile ahead, a lone police car sat at the junction of 16 and US 77, its lights flashing.

Baylor swore. He turned to Weber. "What now?"

"Don't slow down. Try to time the light so it's green."

When they had approached within two hundred yards, the patrolman, who had been standing next to his cruiser, leaned in through the driver's window and switched on his spotlight. The Buick swept through the beam, galvanizing the officer. He wrenched the door open and started to climb into his patrol car. Simultaneously, the lights in the intersection changed, turning green for traffic approaching from highway 16.

Weber rolled down his window and eased the Glock from his belt. The front tires of the cruiser churned, struggling for traction. Unfortunately for the patrolman, he had parked on the shoulder. The loose sand and gravel foiled his attempt to block the passage of his quarry. He decided to ram instead.

"Gas it!" Weber shouted. He braced his hands against the doorframe, aimed low, and snapped off three quick shots. The Buick surged past, missing the patrol car's onrushing bumper by inches. The cruiser spun out of control and drifted into the ditch, the left front tire peeling away from its rim. The Riviera swept across the highway and hurtled into darkness on the far side.

"That was close!" Wozniak said, a tremor in his voice.

Weber clamped his jaw, shoved the Glock back into his belt and turned to the scientist. "Can't outrun his radio."

01:59 CDT, Minot AFB, ND

"About time!" Rotts shouted. "Pull everybody west of US 77." He tapped the map with his finger. "Move this team up 119 and block the end of 16. It's clear these guys are armed and willing to shoot. Connect me directly to Air-ten." Rotts studied the map a little longer. "While you're at it, bring this unit up to block the end of route 80. They have National Guard support, do they not?"

"Yes, sir," an aide answered. "A mounted unit with a Bradley APC."

"Good! That's the anvil. Has Air-ten reported in yet?"

"Line two, sir."

02:08 CDT, County road W, south of Rice, KS

The huge black aircraft drove a whirlwind of debris before its propellers as the blades reversed. The pilot had no trouble stopping his craft's forward motion in little more than a quarter mile. He immediately killed the landing lights. Two commandos dismounted, ducked around the spinning blades and located an access road into the field on the left. One of them bent his lips to the mike attached to his collar. "Claw seven says it's fallow, sir. It'll take our weight just fine."

Guided by the second commando, who waved a green glow-stick, the Hercules eased forward, turned sharply to the left and taxied a few hundred yards into the field. The ramps extended and the pilot shut down all but one engine.

"Any trouble with Air Traffic Control, Andy?" Ouilette asked.

"No, sir. They bought our private field story."

Ouilette nodded and turned to the remaining six commandos. "Dismount and unload. We're up against the clock, gentlemen." Ouilette turned back to his aide. "Andy, until we're set up, I'd like you to stay with the air-crew. Try to get a handle on our boys' location."

Minot AFB, ND, at the same moment

"Air-ten says the target vehicle beat the team coming up from US 24 to the juncture with highway 16. They turned right, headed straight up 119."

"And straight into our southbound task force. It's almost over, gentlemen. Stay sharp."

"Sir! Air-ten reports that they just turned off 119 onto route 80, traveling at a high rate of speed."

Rotts tapped the map. Is the reinforced unit in place at this end of 80?"

"Yes, sir. With the barricades up. The National Guard unit has dismounted and is deploying along the road, sir."

The colonel glanced once more at the map. "Tell Air-ten to overfly Morganville. I want to know if they remain on 80 or turn north."

02:19 CDT, Morganville, KS

"Which way?" Baylor asked.

"Straight ahead. We'll turn north at the next intersection," Weber replied, twisting in his seat to peer out the rear window. "We've company coming. Don't let the grass grow, Ace."

"How far back?" Baylor asked, unwilling to shift his eyes from the road while the Buick tore through the town at nearly one hundred and ten miles per hour.

"A couple of miles. Maybe we'll get lucky and shake them at one of the next two intersections."

Minot AFB, ND

"Air-ten says the target continues west. I can patch the chopper into the speakerphone, sir."

"Do it!"

The whine of a turbine, underscored by the repetitive thump of rotors, filled the room. Rotts stood closer to the microphone.

"Air-ten, this is Colonel Rotts. Can you hear me?"

"Yes, sir. Loud and clear."

"Where are you, relative to the fugitives?"

"We're a thousand feet up, sir. Trailing by about a quarter mile."

"You have a shooter aboard?"

"Yes, sir. An M60 door gunner."

"Excellent!" Rotts replied. "When these boys see our welcoming committee they're likely to panic. I think they'll stop and talk it over. When they do, I want you to pin them to the spot. Disable that vehicle, Air-ten. Don't worry about taking prisoners. Do you understand?"

"Yes, sir. Lethal force is authorized?"

"You got it! We're leaving the mike open on this end. We've got them bottled. Finish it."

"Yes, sir."

In the field south of Rice

Meisner's feet thudded across the sod. He shouted while he was still fifty yards away, his tone urgent, tense. "We've tapped into the tactical channel the opposition is using. They've just authorized lethal force. Our boys are only fifteen miles from here."

Ouilette stiffened. "Wind her up, Andy. Let's get airborne." He pointed at two of the eight commandos standing close by.

"Steiner, Jossman! You're elected. Climb aboard."

Both reacted swiftly, wordlessly, securing their weapons and grabbing their gear. Ouilette listened to first one and then another turbine spin up on its starter. A muffled thump followed by a muted roar told him it was time to join the rescue team.

02:27 CDT, the Republican River, KS

The short span of the narrow bridge over the Republican River featured a prominent arch in the roadway near its mid-section. Because of the Riviera's high rate of speed, the minor hill heaved the Buick airborne for several car lengths. The car landed with a crash that rattled its passengers and prompted a curse from Wozniak.

"Hey, Ed! What use trying to escape if we die in the process?"

Baylor had eased off the gas as they approached a second rise in the road just beyond the river.

"Sorry, guys. I didn't think that we—Ho! Shit!"

Baylor jammed on the brakes, frantically trying to control the Buick as it slewed around, the tires protesting. He had just topped the second rise. About two and a half miles to the west, the horizon was filled with a mass of flashing red and blue lights.

"Back up! Back up!" Weber yelled.

As soon as Baylor fought the car under control he shifted into reverse and floored the accelerator. Both he and Weber heard the rotors of the helicopter at the same moment.

Minot AFB

The speakerphone crackled with the sound of an automatic weapon operating in the background while the pilot spoke. "Air-ten is opening fire on the suspect vehicle. The vehicle is backing rapidly. It's taking hits. It appears to be out of control."

The windshield shattered and several holes were punched through the roof. Baylor and Wozniak shouted at the same instant, Baylor from shock, the scientist with pain. Baylor's side window imploded and he felt the sting of flying glass across his face and neck. The left front tire was blown to ribbons and the Riviera spun sideways. The Buick slid into the ditch on the right side of the road, the front end dropping into a trench. The car rocked up on its side, hung for a moment and crashed down on its wheels. Another burst of machine gun fire stitched across the road and several bullets pounded into the trunk and drove through the roof. The sound of the turbines approached even closer.

"Those guys aren't taking prisoners," Baylor yelled.

"Looks that way, Ace," Weber replied. He kicked the door open, jerked his Glock out and shouted, "Maybe I'm lucky twice." Weber hurled himself outward, rolled in the grass once and came up shooting. He concentrated on the Plexiglas panels in front of the pilot's feet, emptying the magazine with a rapid stream of fire.

"We're taking fire! We're taking fire!" The speakers in the auditorium reverberated to the sound of the pilot's voice, raised in both pitch and volume.

Rotts straightened. "Air-ten are you damaged? Air-ten?"

For a few seconds, there was no answer.

"Air-ten! Say your status, damn it!" Rotts roared.

"We're fine. We took a few rounds through the windscreen. I banked away to clear us out of danger. One of those guys just popped out under me and cut loose with a handgun."

Rotts shook his head and muttered, "Weber." He raised his voice. "Re-engage, Air-ten. Pull back out of range of the handgun and re-engage."

"Out of the car! Move it!" Weber yelled when the police helicopter banked away. He ejected the spent magazine from the Glock and inserted the spare. Baylor tumbled out but Wozniak remained bent forward, swaying back and forth. Weber wrenched open the rear door.

"C'mon, Doc. We've seconds only."

Wozniak glanced up, his face white and his teeth clenched.

"I'm wounded. The pain is really bad."

Weber reached in and pulled the scientist's hands away from his calf. A large caliber bullet had inscribed a deep furrow down his right leg. Weber ducked his head to check on the helicopter. It was turning around about three hundred yards to the south. He grasped Wozniak's lightweight coat at either shoulder.

"Hang on, Doc. I'll drag you out. Your wound isn't as bad as it feels. If you stay in here, the next one will be worse." Weber heaved backward. He barely moved Wozniak to the edge of the seat. Baylor grabbed the scientist's belt and together the two of them dragged him from the car.

"Head for the ditch!" Weber shouted. Baylor nodded and all three men slid into the deep grass in front of the wrecked Riviera.

Columns of dust leapt from the edge of the pavement. Amid the clang, thump and occasional whine of bullets, they could hear the heavy rattle of the machine gun over the sound of the helicopter. The Buick rocked to the repeated impacts, glass shattering, trim hurled away. The trunk lid sprung upward and then twisted to the left as one hinge was shot through. Two more tires blew out. The smell of gasoline filled the air.

Baylor wrinkled his nose and turned toward the agent.

"Time to split!" Weber shouted.

"No shit! But where to?"

Weber indicated they should crawl back toward the river. He tapped Wozniak on the shoulder and pointed in that direction. The scientist nodded and, ignoring the flaring pain in his leg, crawled as swiftly as he could on all fours. Weber and Baylor followed.

They had barely managed twenty yards when a bullet smacked into the pavement behind them, sending a shower of sparks under the crippled Buick.

With a thump, a bang and a flare of yellow light, the bullet-shredded gas tank exploded. The concussion drove the vehicle nose down into the ditch.

"The target vehicle has exploded. It's engulfed in flames. Just a minute! We have motion to the right. The fugitives are now afoot! We're re-engaging."

"Get down!" Weber shouted. He had seen the helicopter shift its position, turning toward them.

"We're in range and locked on, sir."

"Do it, Andy! The air assets first and then the bridge!" Ouilette shouted above the roar of the wind coming through the side door, the whine of the twin turbines and the pounding beat of the heavy rotors.

"Selecting one! Firing one!" An intense flash of light engulfed the left side of the MH-60 Nighthawk helicopter.

The speakers in the auditorium reflected surprise and sudden fear when the pilot spotted the flash and streak of light that curved away from it. The streak bent around and arrowed toward him.

"What the hell? Incoming missile! Incoming mis—"

A burst of white noise was followed by a hiss of static and then silence.

The phone operator clicked his receiver several times and then shrugged. Rotts' jaw hung open with shock and surprise. He turned toward the map trying to comprehend what had happened. He spun around.

"Get someone on the line! Anyone! Find out what happened to Air-ten."

"Selecting two! Firing two!" A second missile streaked away from the banking Nighthawk. It arced upward, nosed over and dove. Meisner kept the laser illuminator centered on the middle span. The Hellfire missile flashed into the target and exploded, blowing a twenty-foot crater in the pavement. The structure groaned and sagged slightly, but did not collapse.

"Colonel Rotts, sir! I have the commander of the Guard Company on the line. He says that a second helicopter has attacked and destroyed Air-ten. It's now working over the approaches to the Republican River Bridge. He wants to know if he should engage, sir."

"He has anti-aircraft capability?"

The operator spoke for a few seconds into his phone.

"No, sir. But he says his Bradley fighting vehicle is equipped with a laser sight and a 25mm chain gun."

Rotts swore and pounded his fist on the table. Ouilette! It could be no one else. Who would have believed he would show up with an attack helicopter.

"Send him in! Send in the infantry! Send in everybody! I want those three men dead!"

Meisner glanced at Ouilette as he banked the Nighthawk.

"It needs another one, sir. We only have two left."

Ouilette nodded. Meisner depressed the button on his stick.

"Firing three!" This missile streaked directly in and detonated. Fragments of girders spun into the air. A thirty-foot section of the bridge twisted and crashed into the river below.

"Good shot, Andy. I prefer a one-front battle."

Meisner banked the helicopter again, this time back toward the burning vehicle.

"Got 'em, lieutenant. Right above the wreck!"

"Open fire!"

The discordant roar of the chain gun drowned the clatter of the Bradley's tracks as the APC thundered down the road.

"Low! Low! Bring it up!" Lieutenant Davies yelled at his gunner.

The first twenty rounds tore into the flaming Riviera, dismembering it. Before the gunner could correct his aim, Meisner flicked his stick forward and yanked the collective upward. The Nighthawk vacated the space just before half a hundred high explosive shells clawed the air.

"Track at nine o'clock!" Steiner, manning one of the door guns, yelled.

Meisner shook his head, glancing at Ouilette. "Sorry, sir. That was a dumb move. I should have checked the other end first."

"Can you use the last missile on the track?" Ouilette asked.

"Yes, sir. I'll move out of range of their gun and we'll let fly."

"Yeah! We drove them off!" The gunner yelled as the helicopter sheered away.

Davies dropped down into the hull and slapped the noncom on his helmet. "You dumb shit! They're setting up for a missile launch. Make smoke! Give it all she's got, Mikey." Davies yelled his last words at the driver.

The Bradley began a high-speed charge toward the flaming auto. Davies jumped up into his cupola and craned his neck around, searching for the Nighthawk. He yelled into his mike, "Slow down! I can't hear a thing." The APC ground to a stop. In the deep gloom of a moonless night, the black helicopter had an edge. A flash of light, twenty degrees forward of his left flank drew his attention. Horror swelled to near panic when he realized the source of it.

"Reverse! Reverse!" The Bradley leapt backward, diving into a cloud of dense smoke. Davies ducked into his cupola just as the missile struck and exploded twenty meters in front of the retreating fighting vehicle.

"Dammit!" Meisner swore. He leaned toward Ouilette. "The laser lost acquisition in the smoke. I guess that makes it an even fight."

"What do you mean?" Ouilette asked.

"I'm going to guns. We carry a 25mm chain gun, same as the Bradley."

"Yeah, but he has armor," Ouilette replied.

Meisner grinned. "If the track was an Abrams that might matter. To the 25mm, a Bradley is tin foil, same as us."

Ouilette nodded. "All the same, a track can take more damage than a chopper."

"Yes, sir. And it's a lot easier to hit. Let's give him something to think about."

"Where is the bastard? Can you see him?" Davies asked two infantrymen who closed up on the stationary Bradley.

"No, sir. Can't hear his rotors either. Do you think—"

A strident hum and a string of explosions from the police vehicles at the end of highway 80 cut off his words.

"Guns! He's gone to guns. He must be out of missiles." Davies bent down into his cupola. "Reverse, Mike. Take us back—"

"Incoming!" someone along the road shouted. A rapid series of explosions rippled upward from the pavement, marching down the road toward the APC. Infantrymen on both sides of the road opened fire into the air, some of them sweeping their weapons from side to side. The Bradley's gunner followed suit, even though nothing appeared in his sight.

Meisner grinned as he banked the MH-60 around to the right and then reversed again. He lined up on the Bradley and dove the helicopter earthward. The chopper closed to optimum range in seconds.

"Cease fire, damn you! There's nothing out there! CEASE FIRE!" Davies yelled at the top of his lungs. When the infantry and the Bradley's gunner fell silent, the only sound he heard was the thump and whine of an approaching helicopter. It came from his left.

"TRAVERSE LEFT!" he shouted, knowing all too well the battle was lost.

Meisner depressed his firing stud. The Nighthawk shuddered as the chain gun cycled. Twelve rounds ripped through the thin armor of the Bradley, detonating its fuel and ammo. The turret blew off, as did the left track. Flames shot skyward from the empty hole in the upper deck.

Meisner swept his gun along the road. Facing the awful firepower of the phantom chopper, the infantry faded into the fields on either side of the highway. To a man, they dove for cover.

Ouilette tapped the marine officer on his shoulder. "Enough! You've made the point. Let's pick up our people and get the hell out of here.

"Yes!" Baylor shouted when the Bradley exploded.

Weber glanced at the pilot. "They're our boys, Ed."

Baylor nodded without taking his eyes from the burning APC. Both men stood on either side of Wozniak supporting the injured scientist between them.

Finally, he returned Weber's stare. "I'm not a sadist. But now I know how it is to face the enemy on unequal terms. I don't like it one damn bit."

Wozniak peered around at the smoking bridge, the glowing remains of the burnt out Buick, the still-burning wreckage of the police helicopter and, finally, the explosions and flames leaping from the destroyed Bradley.

"This is just the beginning, isn't it?"

Weber nodded. "Reckon so, Doc." He pointed his chin at the dark bulk of the settling MH-60 as it descended scarcely fifty yards away. "Let's head for the ranch."

Two commandos leapt down from the chopper and rushed toward them. They each grasped one of Wozniak's arms and hustled him toward the helicopter. Baylor and Weber followed. Baylor leapt in but Weber, still stiff and weak from his old wounds, groaned as he lifted himself onto the gun deck. The Nighthawk surged upward and banked away.

Ouilette slipped back among the trio. He slapped Baylor on the shoulder. "Welcome back, hero. You want to sit up front with Andy and learn a few tricks about this flying machine?"

Baylor's eyes lit up. "Damn straight!" The pilot edged his way toward the cockpit.

Ouilette turned toward Weber. "What do you say, you old dog?"

"Good to see you, Marcus."

Ouilette bent down to Wozniak who was sitting on the floor as one of the commandos bandaged his leg. "Doctor Wozniak, I think I can speak for us all when I say we're extremely grateful. You've performed a miracle here." Before Wozniak could reply, Ouilette asked the commando, "How bad?"

Jossman glanced up from her effort.

"To a commando, it's just a scratch. For a world-renowned scientist, something more than that." Jossman finished the bandage. "Is that how you see it, Doc?"

Wozniak smiled in spite of himself. He studied Ouilette and said, "One more to go."

Ouilette sobered. "It'll take everything we have."

Weber shifted position to peer up at Ouilette. "When are we going after her, Marcus?"

"We begin tonight. Six man team. A HALO drop."

Weber nodded. "I should be jumping with them."

Ouilette laughed. "You've got some mending to finish first."

"Reckon so. This team is the advance unit?"

Ouilette nodded. "It is that, Sam. Not to worry. When the main show starts you'll be right in the thick of it."

"Count on it." Weber yawned and sank down by Wozniak.

The MH-60 settled into the field beside the Hercules moments later. Weber eased his frame from the deck as he muttered, "I need some shuteye. Wake me before the jump, will you Marcus?"

03:41 CDT, Minot AFB, ND

Rotts stood alone in the semi-dark expanse of the stage. The hushed and urgent words of the operators echoed around him but he heard none of them. The map remained dark and he did not expect it to change anytime soon. When footsteps approached, he glanced around. For a few seconds he said nothing. "I'm sorry, General. I truly am."

"I watched the whole thing, Phil. Nothing more you could have done."

"Not true, sir. We made our mistake early. Right at the beginning."

"How's that, Colonel?"

Rotts glanced at his feet. After a moment, he lifted his head and met his commander's eye. "We considered that Ouilette was running a covert operation. We based all our decisions on that assumption."

"So what's wrong with that?"

"Commander Ouilette is waging war. Every time he needs to win, he throws in whatever it takes. We need to think about that, General."

Pigott nodded and then smiled. "That's why I brought you in, Phil."

The General turned away and left the auditorium.

03:44 MDT, over NW Nebraska

In the frigid air at five and a half miles above the blackness of the Nebraskan prairie, six men poised near the edge of the C-130's cargo deck. The cargo hatch was secured over their heads. Ouilette stood at the edge facing forward, Weber beside him, both men on oxygen. A light on the bulkhead above his head turned green. Ouilette turned to face the commandos who were all intently watching him. He nodded. Weber lifted his fist, thumb pointing upward. The commandos walked forward and stepped off into space. There was no sign of a parachute.

The hatch ground downward and, when the aircraft was sealed and pressurized once more, heaters strained to warm the C-130's interior. Ouilette and Weber joined Wozniak and everyone stripped off their masks.

"Where's Baylor?" Ouilette asked.

"In heaven," Wozniak replied. At the confused looks, he added, "Captain Meisner came back and asked if Ed would like to be checked out in a C-130. I guess your pilot put in a lot of hours tonight and could use the help."

When Ouilette nodded, Wozniak asked, "What just happened back there. You called it a HALO drop?"

Weber answered, "High Altitude, Low Opening. The team will free-fall all the way down. They open their chutes under a thousand feet. Sometimes a long way under."

Wozniak stared at Weber for several moments. Finally he said, "You guys are strange people, you know that?"

Flying from the right seat, Baylor pulled back on the wheel, letting the Hercules flare out a few meters above the grass field. The heavy aircraft sank through the ground effect and quit flying. With a soft thump and a rumble the main gear touched, followed a moment later by the nose wheel.

"Nice one," the pilot, Cliff Simmons, said. He slipped a lever forward on the console, reversing the pitch of the blades. Baylor advanced the throttles.

The aircraft slowed, but not as quickly as the navy pilot expected.

"Where's the hook?" he asked with a grin.

"With this baby, you plan ahead. Try your brakes, you'll be surprised."

Baylor did so and the aircraft slowed abruptly. He pulled the throttles back to an idle. By the two thousand-foot marker, the Talon stood at rest. Simmons reached up and flicked two switches. The outboard engines spun down. He feathered the props and jerked his thumb to the left.

"Taxi over to the farthest hanger."

Baylor reset the propeller controls and advanced the remaining two engines. The Hercules resisted at first, but with a brief surge in turbine RPM, it began to roll. Baylor taxied toward the indicated building. As he approached, the hanger doors began to open.

"Kill your lights," Simmons added.

Baylor did so, guided in the darkness by a ground-crew with a pair of lighted flashlights. The two red cones waved him forward with rapid strokes that slowed as he approached. Finally, when the cones crossed, Baylor stopped the aircraft's motion and set the brakes. He reached up to the switches for the inboard engines, but Simmons said, "Leave them running. You've a nice touch, Ed. Maybe a bit impatient with this old truck, but you're precise. I like flying with you."

Baylor grasped the offered hand. "Thanks, Cliff. I like the Hercules. It feels heavy but...solid. The roll rate takes some getting used to, though. He added, "This isn't your final destination?"

"The Herk would stick out like a sore thumb up here. While you guys stow the chopper, Andy and I'll zoom down to Salt Lake. The rest of you will travel by surface to the base."

"Why start here and not from Salt Lake City?"

Simmons shrugged. "People, I guess. Less here and more there."

Baylor unbuckled, climbed out of his seat and left the flight deck. In the cargo bay, a pair of electric winches were hauling the Nighthawk down an extended ramp. Once the helicopter was grounded, the ramps retracted, the Hercules' engines built up speed and the C-130 lumbered away. The two remaining commandos hitched a tractor to the Blackhawk and towed it into the hanger. Baylor glanced around. "Where's Mr. Grant?"

Weber pointed toward the hanger. "Arranging for our transportation, I reckon."

Only when the hanger doors had completely closed did the lights flicker to life within the building. There were no windows, but Baylor could see bright slivers delineating the base of the hanger doors and escaping from ventilation grills in the walls near the roof.

Ouilette returned a few moments later behind the wheel of a crew cab pickup truck. He leaned out the window.

"Climb in. We've a long road ahead of us."

Weber helped Wozniak to his feet and into the rear seat. Baylor climbed in front. A few moments later, one of the commandos returned. He opened the rear door and jumped in next to the scientist.

"All set, sir. Pop is relieved and sends his appreciation for bringing his creation back without a ding. He wondered about all the expended ammo."

Ouilette grinned. "What did you tell him?"

"I told him to read the papers."

At that moment, the C-130 roared past, its shape discernible against the dark gray backdrop of a predawn sky. The Hercules climbed swiftly, banked to the east and disappeared from view.

Ouilette looked at his watch. "Sunup in forty minutes." He shifted into gear and drove away from the tiny field. Several miles down the road to the south, he pulled in behind a semi sitting on the shoulder, its four-way hazard lights flashing.

Baylor groaned. "Oh, no."

Ouilette laughed. "What else did you expect, Mr. Ryerson? By the way, I think we can retire that name now."

"Don't you guys travel by any other method?" Baylor asked.

"We're damn near invisible using this form of transportation. Since we're presently building our resource stockpile, we had trucks all around the country. The perfect bus line."

Ouilette pulled in behind the semi and honked his horn. The rear door opened and a power lift tail gate dropped to street level. The commando in the back seat exchanged places with Ouilette while Wozniak and Baylor climbed out of the cab.

Ouilette leaned close to an open window. "Post-flight the chopper. Refuel and rearm it. With Pop and Anjanet helping, you should be finished by noon."

"Yes, sir. Then what?"

"Catch a ride on the truck from Minnesota. It'll show by then."

Steiner nodded, shifted into gear and, after executing a U-turn, pulled away from the semi.

When the power-lift tailgate raised the four men to the trailer's deck height, they discovered a narrow passage between two rows of cartons. The passage extended toward the front of the trailer but the far end was not visible in the darkness.

"A conspiracy," Wozniak muttered as he followed Ouilette into the opening.

"What'd you say, Doc?" Baylor asked.

The scientist craned his neck part way around to the navy pilot who followed him. "I said all this is a conspiracy against those of us who have indulged in life."

"All what, Doc?"

"Everything! Bombs in the basement, midnight warfare on the prairie, climbing in and out of helicopters and tractor-trailers. Somebody is trying awfully hard to convince me that I need to diet."

Baylor prepared his comeback, but before he could open his mouth, they stepped out of the narrow corridor into an opening that consumed the full width of the trailer and extended nearly a third of its length. Behind them, the door rumbled down and they could hear the diesel start. Ouilette snapped on the lights. A small ice chest and a bucket of fruit stood in the corner, but what caught the flyer's eyes were the mattress pads on the floor.

"Man, oh man! What a welcome sight!"

He plopped down on one and stretched out, kicking off his Nikes. "Wake me in a thousand years."

Wozniak trundled over to a second pad, groaned as he lowered himself and again as he reclined. He muttered something unintelligible as he rolled onto his back, his forearm over his eyes.

Within minutes, both men were sound asleep.

Ouilette hung up the intercom phone to the cab and glanced at the two men on the pads. "I was going to update those two, but I guess it can wait."

"Let them sleep, Marcus. They earned it." Weber pulled a bottle of Sam Adams from the cooler and dropped his frame into one of the chairs. He twisted the cap free and upended the bottle, draining half the contents in a single draught.

He let out his breath with a long sigh. "Hallelujah!" When Ouilette sat in another chair, Weber turned his head. "You might update *me*, though. Start with that toy you used tonight."

"The MH-60?" Ouilette asked.

Weber nodded. "Hell of a lot smaller than any Blackhawk I've ever seen."

"A special project Andy concocted about two years ago. He's been working with a retired airframe engineer up here in Wyoming. The guy's name is Everett McPherson, but everybody just calls him Pop. Anyway, Andy secured a wrecked standard-issue Blackhawk. Pop rebuilt it from the ground up. Shortened it, relocated and redesigned the tail section, chopped and lowered the fuselage. They welded the whole thing back together and added a lot of special hardware."

"Why go through all the trouble?"

Ouilette took a swig from his beer and replied, "A helicopter is slow and short-ranged so Andy came up with the camel approach. Instead of refueling in-flight, which limits the response to the top speed of the helicopter, why not carry the chopper inside an air-cargo airframe. He picked the C-130 because there are a lot of them and they are readily available. The Hercules has more than twice the speed and five times the range of a Blackhawk. This particular Blackhawk was reconstructed to fit into the available space."

Weber drained the last of his beer. He stood and retrieved a second bottle then returned to his seat. "So you added a lot of hardware from the Pave Hawk program and ended up with a sharp mission platform."

Ouilette nodded. "Andy says the flight characteristics are not the best, but he manages well enough." He shifted in his chair. "Did Baylor and Wozniak fill you in on Pigott and his crew?"

"They did. What does he hope to gain?"

Ouilette raised his bottle to make a point. "Don't make the mistake of thinking Pigott's operating independently."

"Who's pulling his strings? The president?"

Ouilette grinned. "You know better than that. I wouldn't be surprised to find Pigott at the top of the human heap on the other side, but that still doesn't mean he's running the show."

"He seems to have carte blanche with every state, local and federal organization I've ever heard of. About the only people not chasing us was the IRS."

"Our general sicced them on Baylor."

"There you go."

"He's not on top because the scope is too wide. There's far more underway than any one man could manage. You'll see what I mean tomorrow evening."

"What happens tomorrow?" Weber asked.

"Theater update, mission profile, campaign description. Whatever you want to call it," Ouilette replied.

"Who's involved? Which teams?"

"All of them. Everyone except the advance group we dropped in tonight."

Weber set his bottle on the floor of the trailer. He leaned back in his chair with his hands behind his head. "This must be the big one, Marcus. What *Night Tiger* was designed for."

Ouilette shook his head. He stared past his outstretched legs, his eyes distant and his tone subdued. "No, my friend. No one, the designers of *Night Tiger* included, ever considered what we face today."

11:42 CDT, Minot AFB, ND

General Pigott had barely begun to power up his workstation when the door to his office rattled. Before he could turn his head or call out an invitation to enter, it snapped open. Colonel Rotts thrust his head through the opening.

"Trouble on the alert pad, sir. You may want to see this for yourself."

Pigott stood, picked up his hat and turned toward the doorway. On the way out he asked, "The XT craft?"

"Yes, sir. I've just received a radio report that it's powering up."

"A reaction to anything we might have done?"

"No, sir. All of our installations were pulled back five hundred yards from the craft after the last incident. Maybe it's the Chao. Could she be controlling it?"

As the two men slammed through a doorway onto the flight-line, Pigott shook his head.

"No, I don't think so. Its mind is disrupted. I'm afraid I might have given it too large a dose. I was just about to check on that when you dropped in."

Rotts and Pigott climbed into a humvee. Rotts gunned the engine once and shifted into gear. He floored the accelerator and the utility vehicle lurched forward and sped toward the alert pad. Two minutes later, they approached the barrier where several marines stood peering at the Sikt through glasses.

Pigott climbed out and strode over to the commander of the marine detachment.

"What's the story, Lieutenant?"

Lieutenant Alvarez passed his binoculars to the general. "Six minutes ago, we noticed a lot of dust and gas blowing off the concrete around the craft, sir. We could hear the blast from here. About a minute ago, the head came up. We're pretty nervous about that as we're exposed should that thing go on a rampage. Maybe you should withdraw, general."

Pigott held the binoculars to his face. He could see waves of heat flaring from the tortured pavement under the craft. The neck joints had shifted the head slightly higher than the fuselage.

"No, lieutenant. I think I'll stick around and learn something." Pigott had barely finished when the faint roaring sound suddenly increased in both pitch and volume. It rose to a continuous thunder that visibly shook the vehicles around them. Pigott felt the vibrations in his chest.

Rotts cautioned, "General? Maybe we should—"

In the next moment, the craft lifted from the pavement. Its skids retracted. It started to rotate on its vertical axis, swinging toward them.

"Everybody down!" Alvarez shouted. The lieutenant dove behind his humvee, leaving the general as the only man standing.

Pigott watched the craft swing through one hundred and eighty degrees while hovering about three meters above the pavement. Its nose inclined further. This time, the entire fuselage pitched upward until the fighter stood poised at a sixty-degree angle, pointing into the heavens.

"General, sir! Please take cover!" Alvarez pleaded.

Pigott waved away his concern, shouting over the roar, "There's no danger, lieutenant. The Sikt is leaving us."

In the next instant, the craft sprang upwards. Not with the slow majesty of a missile launch, nor the graceful acceleration of a powerful military fighter. With a crash of sound and fury, the Sikt streaked into the clouds, dwindled to a dot, and vanished. A sonic thunderclap rolled across the vacant field.

Pigott had lowered his glasses to watch the departure. He smiled and shook his head. When Rotts climbed to his feet and approached him, he said, "Phil, we must have this technology. That was the most inspiring thing I've ever seen."

"Where do you think it went, sir?"

Pigott turned to face him. "The cruiser has returned. The mother hen calls home its chicks. The question is, what happens when it discovers that one little chicken remained behind?"

Baylor bent down, braced a hand on the edge of the trailer and dropped to the gravel surface below. Compared to the air-conditioned environment within the trailer, the air outside felt like a furnace. He stretched his legs and glanced around. There were a total of six tractor-trailer rigs gathered nearby. Each was painted with a different brand or logo upon its cab or trailer. Despite the difference, Baylor intuitively believed that all were headed for the same destination. As he peered around the edge of the trailer he had dismounted from, a blatting staccato drew his attention toward the road behind him. Two more trucks appeared, compression braking as they approached. Their turn signals flashed and both pulled in behind the rest.

"Looks like a bloody convention," he muttered.

He turned and strode toward the cab. In front of the tractor, he found Ouilette and Weber in conversation with a dozen other men.

Ouilette glanced up at his approach. He clapped Baylor on the shoulder. "This is the resourceful fellow of whom I spoke. His name is Ed Baylor, lately a Lieutenant Commander in the United States Navy."

"You make that sound past tense, sir," Baylor remarked as Ouilette introduced the other men. They were all military, from every branch of the service and career men by their rank, both noncoms and officers.

"It is." Ouilette did not elaborate. "I was just giving these fellows a new timetable. Previously, we were supposed to run right on down to the base this evening but our friends in Minot have different ideas. They've redirected several satellites from the Southern Hemisphere to overfly CONUS. We can only believe this development is their effort to locate us. No doubt they're looking for something unusual, such as aircraft where there should be none or activity where none is expected.

"Anyway, we can no longer enter our base before nightfall. The last satellite pass occurs at 21:40. Before that time, I don't want any truck closer than thirty miles and no more than two vehicles parked in any one spot. Stay on US 6 until 21:45, then highball it home. Everybody got that?"

At the wave of nods, Ouilette added, "Good. Move out. I have another bunch to brief and we already have too many vehicles clustered together."

When the group broke up, each pair of men turning to a different truck, Baylor asked, "Where did you find all the rolling stock?"

Ouilette replied, "We bought them. Almost eighty rigs in all. We probably drove the used truck market up a few points about ten days ago."

"You guys must be rolling in dough. The taxpayers fund all this?"

Weber kicked at a pebble as he replied, "Indirectly. Under the provisions of the foundation, which sponsors this plan, certain federal and state general funds are tapped from time to time. Idle assets are invested until called upon by the owner of the fund, at which time they are quietly and immediately replaced. What you see here is profit returned from those investments."

"Wow!" Baylor exclaimed. "I'd like to talk to the broker you used."

Ouilette replied, "You would be disappointed, Ed. Our investment strategy was extremely conservative. You see, we could invest an awful lot of money for very long periods. We didn't want an aggressive plan nor did we need its risk, given that we often had to pull from the investment to replace the owner's funds."

"I must be thinking too small. How large is large? How long is long?"

Ouilette smiled. "Billions and decades."

Baylor's jaw dropped. "This little exercise has been planned that long?"

Weber nodded. "A beneficial legacy of the Joe McCarthy era."

The same moment, Damman Oil Fields, Saudi Arabia

"We're ready, Sayyid." The technician lifted his gaze from a control panel.

The mullah asked without turning, "How long until the sun rises?"

"Fifteen minutes, Sayyid. The timers are set for twenty."

"All of the devices are prepared?"

"The Kuwaitis and our brothers in Abu Dhabi await your signal."

"Then you may begin."

The technician's fingers flew over his keyboard. He picked up a phone and called several numbers. Each conversation was short, a few words at most. Finally, he put down the phone and turned toward the mullah, a fine sheen of perspiration showing on his face. "It is done, Sayyid. May Allah have mercy upon us."

The holy man bowed. "Inshallah."

"We must depart. To remain here is death."

"I will conduct Salat where I stand." When the technician's eyes widened in horror, the mullah continued, "Today we cast off the foreign yoke. I lead my people toward the past, to a time of righteousness. It is fitting that I should consecrate the ground where we return to the ways of the one, true God."

The mullah read the fear in his servant's features. "Only those who wish to be called to Allah need remain."

22:39 MDT, Desert Range Experimental Station, UT

Baylor leaned forward in the cab. He rode up front with the driver, Ouilette. The semi rolled down a narrow two-lane paved road toward the southeast.

"The truck ahead just turned out its lights!"

Ouilette replied, "As will we in a moment. We've reached the turnoff."

Ouilette braked and downshifted. He switched off his lights and then leaned forward, willing his eyes to adjust to the darkened road ahead. In the starlight, augmented by a crescent moon far to the east, he could barely see the edges of the pavement where the blacktop contrasted against the sand at either side of the road. Movement ahead quickly resolved itself into a man waving a green glow-stick. The figure gestured to the left. Ouilette shifted into low and turned immediately before the traffic guide. The truck swayed as it rolled over an unpaved and scarcely definable path that could hardly be called a road.

When the tractor-trailer topped a low ridge and began its descent into the valley beyond, Baylor could discern a single structure in the middle of an open plain. The building, about two hundred feet in length and less than half as wide, stood immediately before a line of moving vehicles also visible against the brighter backdrop of the desert floor. As the fourth semi disappeared into the building, Baylor rubbed his eyes.

"That's a hell of a magic trick. That building can't possibly hold more than two of these rigs but I just saw at least four enter."

"No magic, Ed. Unless you want to count the construction as such."

In a few more minutes, their truck reached the entrance to the building. As the semi rolled into the opening, it pitched down an incline and Ouilette switched on the lights. In the few seconds he had, Baylor could see that the internal floor of the building had retracted, uncovering a ramp that led into a subterranean passage.

The truck rolled down the ramp and into a long darkened tunnel that terminated in a glare of brightness at the far end. When the tractor-trailer wheeled into the light, Baylor found himself inside an immense structure that bore all the earmarks of a massive warehouse. At least sixty over-the-road rigs were parked in several orderly rows. Dozens of people, men and women both, were handling cargo with powered and manually operated forklifts.

A man with cone-covered flashlights, like those used in airports, blew a whistle at Ouilette's approach. He pointed at their truck and then to the left, signifying that they should turn in front of him. As Ouilette slowed and began his turn, their guide recognized the driver and snapped a crisp salute. Ouilette nodded as he twisted the steering wheel to the left.

Farther along the row they had been directed into, a second guide pointed to an open slot between two trucks. Ouilette wheeled his rig around and backed into the opening. Watching through his rear-views, he backed up until the guide blew a whistle. He stopped, shut down the engine and engaged the brakes.

"Home, sweet home."

Baylor had been twisting his head around, trying to take it all in. He snapped around to Ouilette. "What can I say? This is astounding!"

Ouilette reached into the console and withdrew two pairs of gloves. He tossed a pair to Baylor and stuffed his hands into the second pair.

"There's a lot more to see, but first we need to unload this baby."

Ouilette climbed down from the cab. He met Weber, Wozniak and the original driver at the power lift-gate. Weber was supporting the scientist while Wozniak stood on one leg. An electric cart pulled alongside a moment later.

"Sir! The dispatcher said you had wounded?" the driver asked.

Ouilette pointed to Wozniak. "This gentleman has a flesh wound. Run him down to the infirmary and, when they've cared for him, take him to his quarters." Ouilette turned to Wozniak. "Doctor, we'll fetch you for breakfast in the morning, if that's all right?"

Wozniak's face was drawn and pale. He simply nodded. Weber helped him hobble to the cart and then turned back toward Ouilette.

"Pass me a pair of gloves, Marcus. You could use my help."

"We could but we won't." Ouilette glanced at the driver. "Take this gentlemen to the infirmary as well. I want a complete rundown on him. He needs to achieve battle status in forty-eight hours. Make sure the doctor knows that."

"Marcus, there's no need—"

Ouilette cut him off. "Give it up, Sam. If you want in on the party, you'll play by the rules."

Weber nodded and sat beside Wozniak. The cart whisked both men away.

Baylor and Ouilette turned their efforts to unloading their trailer.

04:22 CDT, 16 May, Minot AFB, ND

Pigott sat with his arms crossed and the barest glimmer of a smile as he watched the military news feed. Rotts stood a pace closer to the monitor, tension evident in every feature and in his stance.

On the screen, a BBC reporter was reiterating the main story of the hour. Several nuclear devices had been detonated in various Middle Eastern oil fields. A nuclear physicist, serving as an expert commentator, confirmed what seismologists had reported nearly six hours earlier. Seven explosions, far below ground level, had simultaneously occurred in the United Arab Emirates, in Kuwait and in the old Saudi Kingdom that had, for two days now, called itself the Arabian Republic of Islam. The effects of the blasts could not yet be determined, although damage to wellheads in the immediate vicinity of the detonations was severe. Several hundred people had been killed and thousands more injured in flash fires or eruptions directly related to the explosions.

There was an unconfirmed report of radiation poisoning coming out of Kuwait. Military forces of many western nations rushed to the area, fearing the worst. But thus far, no additional nuclear devices had been detonated. The Brotherhood of Islamic Nations, established last week in Tehran, condemned western technology as the source of great evil and barred entry into the stricken area by any western military or relief organizations. There was no attack on population centers and the threat did not seem to be ethnically motivated, as Israel remained unscathed.

Rotts turned to Pigott. "What in heaven's name is going on over there? Have those people lost their sanity?"

The general punched a button on the remote control and the set went dark. He glanced up at his deputy. "No, Phil. They just made a decision that some things are more important than money. A major shift in the economic world is underway. I think a lot of people are in for some nasty surprises."

At the same moment, Desert Range Experimental Station, UT

Meisner leaned back in his chair. He swiveled it to face Ouilette who sat on the edge of his aide's desk. "I don't get it, sir. This is outside any scenario we've played with."

Ouilette shook his head. "I don't think so. The opposition is going for the jugular, my friend. If anything will disrupt this country's cohesiveness, it's this."

"Care to fill me in, sir?"

"Not yet, Andy. Let's surf around the dial for a spell. I need some more information.

Nearly four hours later, Meisner knocked quietly on Ouilette's office door. Hearing no answer he opened the door part way and poked his head inside. Ouilette was slouched back in his chair, his feet propped up on his desk and very much asleep. Meisner turned to Wozniak, who had prompted this visit.

"Give us a moment, Doctor." Meisner slipped through the entrance and closed the door behind him. He shook Ouilette's shoulder gently.

"Commander?"

Ouilette responded immediately, jerking himself upright and dropping his feet from the desk. He glanced at the clock on his desk and rubbed his face.

"Must have dozed off. I need a shower and shave." Ouilette stood. "Thanks for the wake-up call."

"Sir, Doctor Wozniak wants to see you. He says the matter's urgent."

"Show him in."

Meisner opened the door and beckoned the scientist inside. Wozniak took one glance at Ouilette and smiled. "You look like I felt last night. Did you sleep at all?"

"I grabbed a few minutes now and then. Andy tells me you have something that requires my attention?"

Wozniak nodded. "I've been surfing the channels this morning, trying to catch up with the world. I wish I hadn't. What's got me worried is the Wall Street thing. I'd like to spend some time with your information technologies manager to discuss it."

Ouilette blinked. "Maybe I didn't sleep long enough after all, Doctor." He turned to Meisner. "You have any idea what he's talking about?"

"Yes, sir. The market opened this morning for only forty-five minutes. Because of the Mid-East crisis, it took a nose-dive. Computer algorithms were supposed to cut in and level the trading, but the entire network crashed. Things got worse after that."

"That's right," Wozniak interjected. "The major houses tried to withdraw from the market and failed. Their computers started misbehaving very badly. Random data dumps, crashes, disk wipes, that type of thing. The SEC called the whole mess to a halt right then. What has me worried is that the computer problems are still spreading. It's like some super-virus has contaminated the Internet and rabidly infects every system or server that connects to it. This is what I want to talk to your information technologies manager about."

Ouilette laughed. "Well, Doc, if you want to talk to him...look in the mirror. Nobody else comes close."

Surprise flooded Wozniak's features. Before he could respond, Ouilette continued, "And while you're working out that problem, I have a top priority request. The director of this illustrious organization, and that happens to be me at the moment, needs to pull together a global briefing beginning at 1700 today. I'll need your crystal readers online by then and news feeds depicting every major event in the world. You'll be co-hosting with me."

"Me!" Wozniak's head swiveled to Meisner and back. "What can I add? I don't know anything about what your people need."

"On the contrary. You're the featured presenter. I'll be reviewing current events as a warm-up. From you, Doctor, we're going to learn about the history of the Universe."

Chapter Nineteen
10:20 MDT, 16 May
Desert Range Experimental Station, UT

Ed Baylor slept longer than he should have. He made up some of that lost time in a mad scramble to get dressed and promptly lost it again by losing his way in the massive complex. Conscious of closing satellite windows and limited time to accomplish his required objectives for the morning, each wrong turn and subsequent backtrack began to wear away his already thin patience.

As he dashed past an open doorway, he spotted Weber seated alone at a table sipping a cup of coffee. He reversed course, passed through the doorway and discovered he was in the chow hall, something he'd given up on almost a quarter hour ago.

"Thank God!" he breathed. When Weber glanced upward, he added, "I'm totally lost."

Weber cracked a smile and said, "Take a seat, Ace."

"I can't. I'm supposed to report topside for—"

"You've got time. Take a seat." When Baylor did so, Weber raised his voice, "Biscuits and gravy, side of bacon, and coffee! How do you like it?" he asked the sweating aviator in a milder tone."

"Black. Do I have time for this?"

"Make that black!" the agent shouted. "And pronto."

Weber studied the man across from him for several seconds and then said, "I'm not often wrong, Ace, but when we first met, I figured you for ninety percent ego and the rest mouth. You did a mighty fine job out there and seeing how I was the beneficiary, I owe you one. Thank you."

Before Baylor could reply breakfast was delivered by a hustling server, who also happened to wear captain's bars. At Baylor's incredulous glance, Weber said, "We all take a turn serving those who've just returned from missions. You came to the right place."

Baylor laughed at that and dug into his meal, which lasted only minutes. When he finished, he said, "It's a mask, you know...a shield."

Weber caught the inference. "For what?"

"Strapping on something like a Black Widow would, and should, terrify any rational being. We're no different. We just hide it behind bravado, causing some people to think we're chauvinistic assholes strutting around like our shit doesn't stink."

"Who are you hiding it from?"

"The guy in the mirror." Baylor laughed at that. "It works, but not all the time. And not for very long." He sighed and added, "You can pay me back by telling me where that magical elevator topside is supposed to be."

"No magic there." Weber reached into his breast pocket and pulled out a map. "Keep this with you for a day or two and after that you won't need it." Weber glanced at his watch and said, "Time's getting tight, Ace. Better scoot." He pointed toward the doorway by which Baylor had entered. "Go left, two rights, then follow the map."

Baylor peered at the map as he hustled along a corridor marked 16W. He was only a couple of minutes late but each intersection added its own small delay in the large and labyrinthine facility. Finally, he found the right hallway and turned the corner. Within seconds, he spotted the man he sought as one of two standing just a short way down the corridor.

Both men stood before a polished steel door set into a concrete block wall. On the floor by their feet lay two black canvas satchels.

"Last night, Captain Meisner said I should report to you here at 1045, sir. He said I should be prompt," Baylor said.

"Accurate on both counts." Ouilette pointed at the satchel to his left. "This is your gear bag, commando. You're going topside in seven minutes. There's a small-arms range on top and you have almost two hours to qualify on two principal weapons." Ouilette nudged one of the bags with his toe. "This contains a Sig-Sauer P226 and a Heckler & Koch MP5, both in 9mm. It also contains your personal body armor. I'd suggest you suit up."

Ouilette turned to the second man. "This gentleman is Henry Tyson. We call him 'Tyke' for short. He'll be your partner and mentor for the next few months." Ouilette turned away and left without another word.

Baylor towered over the other man, but when he shook hands with him, he could feel impressive strength in his arms. "Hey...didn't we meet back—"

"The guy with the target on his cheek. I hear you're good with a shotgun," Tyson said.

"More lucky than good, I'd say."

"Works the same way. Don't knock it."

A tramp of running feet interrupted them as Baylor struggled into his body armor. A troop of two dozen commandos, composed of both men and women, rounded a corner at a run and bore directly toward the two men.

Baylor, his vest over his head and shoulders, pushed his bag out of their way with his feet. To his surprise, the crowd of newcomers did not pass by. They lined up directly behind Baylor and Tyson. In four more minutes, the elevator door opened and Tyson gestured Baylor in before him. Half a dozen other commandos followed them in before the doors closed and the lift surged upward. After a thirty-second climb, the doors opened again. Baylor and Tyson followed the others out into a tunnel carved out of rock. Immediately beneath his feet ran a pair of rusty rails. When the elevator doors closed, Baylor could see only slabs of rock where the opening had been. He had to peer very closely to find any visible seam.

"Let's move it," Tyson said. "We've only got a hundred and twelve minutes until the next satellite pass."

Baylor followed the smaller man out under a glaring sun. When he peered back at the tunnel he was surprised to see what appeared to be an old mine shaft entrance. A sign nearby warned of imminent danger of collapse if any trespassers were so foolhardy as to enter.

Tyson led him along a narrow footpath over a low ridge and down into a natural hollow. The smaller man bent to pick up several pieces of lumber that appeared to be discards from some old mining camp. The pieces precisely fitted together to become a table.

"Lay out your gear on this and we'll get started."

The MP5 turned out to be the simpler weapon to master. With its sling and shell catcher, it was well balanced. Its mild recoil shifted Baylor's point of aim only slightly and Tyson showed him how to adjust for the effect. Baylor learned to tear down and refurbish the MP5's silencer in less than four minutes. The long-snouted suppresser was easily removed and replaced, requiring no tools and little attention. Tyson assured him that, with a little practice, he could even do it in total darkness.

"Why a scope for such a minuscule round? Especially on an automatic weapon?" Baylor asked as they dismantled the MP5 and prepared the handguns.

Tyson bared his teeth as he pressed several rounds into his Sig's magazine. "That sight has a lighted reticule and the MP5 is surgically precise. You'll use it single tap, in the dark, more often than not. We stay with the 9mm to keep the projectile sub-sonic. Otherwise the silencer's useless."

A loud crack sounded from around the ridge. Several more followed. Tyson grinned. "Unlike them folks, we work up close and personal. If you hose down the county, your silencer fades fast. Then you find yourself in a heap of trouble."

Baylor nodded, thinking as he did so, that the fire button on a joystick sounded better and better all the time.

He had more trouble with the handgun.

"The damn thing shoots low. It must be the sights."

"The damn thing shoots where you point it," Tyson countered. He held out his hand. Baylor handed across the Sig. With movements nearly too fast to follow, Tyson dropped the magazine, racked the slide back and emptied the chamber. He dismounted the slide and barrel and eyeballed both. Then he reassembled the firearm, racking the slide and then inserting the magazine. He flicked the safety off and handed it to Baylor.

"Take careful aim. Squeeze off one shot. I want you to take particular care to watch what happens."

Baylor nodded. He sighted on the bull less than twenty yards distant. He squeezed the trigger. The striker fell on an empty chamber but his wrist jerked downward all the same. He gritted his teeth and shook his head.

"Anticipation," Tyson said. "Now you know why you're shooting in the dirt. Gun control is derived from mind control. Remember that and work on it awhile."

After another hour, Baylor finally passed the qualification standards Tyson had set for him. By the time he was through with both the MP5 and the Sig, his canteen was emptied and he felt an unremitting thirst take hold.

"The sun's a killer up here. I'd hate to spend an entire day in this armor."

Tyson nodded. "I hear you. Luckily, we work mostly at night. Sometimes a mission requires us to work in close during the day. It takes a little more time to train for that, though."

"I don't doubt it. You've been doing this a while?"

"Long enough. I'm a career ranger. Light infantry. Or was until this jaunt started. How about you?"

"U.S. Navy," Baylor replied.

"Well you couldn't be a SEAL or you wouldn't need me. What did you do?"

"Black Widow driver." Baylor moved his hand in front of his chest in aircraft fashion.

"No shit!" The smaller man glanced upward, awe on his face. After a moment, he continued to knock the impromptu table apart and then picked up his bag. He added, "I'll make you a deal."

"What's that?"

"I'll train you in the best tradition of special operations. Someday, if you ever get the chance, you can return the favor."

"You want to learn to fly?"

"I'll settle on a ride. Just a ride and maybe a little work with the weapons."

Baylor grinned. "You're on. But somehow I think you're going to come out on the short end of the stick."

Tyson led the way back up the slope, talking over his shoulder. "Always have. Probably always will. They don't call me *Tyke* for nothing."

Both men had nearly returned to the mineshaft when a single shot rang out. A loud cheer followed it.

Tyson twisted around. He glanced back at Baylor. "C'mon. You gotta see this." The diminutive warrior led Baylor down into another ravine, this one very wide and shallow. As they closed on the group clustered around a single table, another shot was fired, the blast accompanying the concussion spoke with deep and impressive authority. A man crouched at the table, peering through a spotting scope held his thumb in the air and another cheer erupted.

Out in front of the table by a dozen yards stretched the slim body of a single shooter in a prone position. Alongside the shooter, another man crouched behind a spotting scope on a tripod. Baylor could barely hear the drone of his words. He was chanting out numbers.

"What the heck is going on?" Baylor asked one of the men standing close to him. The commando was peering through a pair of binoculars at the far bank of the ravine. He dropped the eyeglasses from his face.

"KR's punching good-luck charms. Take a look." He handed the binoculars to Baylor who put them up to his eyes and adjusted the focus.

"What am I supposed to be looking at?"

"Just below the top of the ridge … a line of bright spots."

"No…Oh, yeah! I got them." Baylor could just make out a line of three silver dots in the eight power binoculars. The rifle bellowed again and the leftmost dot disappeared. Only two remained. The group around the table cheered again.

Baylor handed the binoculars back.

"Good Luck charms?"

"You bet! Everyone who has one ducks the bullet meant for them."

Baylor laughed. "It takes a bullet to make one though. What exactly are they?"

The commando reached into his pocket and drew out a silver dollar. A hole, slightly larger than a quarter inch, had been cleanly driven through the coin near its center.

"Jehoshaphat! That's what those dots are? He can hit them from here? That's a quarter mile or more."

"Five hundred yards. There's nobody better. You want one?"

Baylor nodded. "Who's to say luck doesn't count."

The commando stretched himself up on tiptoes. "Hey, KR! The nugget would like a taste of your magic."

The man crouching beside the shooter turned around and picked up a radio. He spoke a few words into it and then lifted his earmuff and listened. He nodded and then spoke again. The shooter lifted the muzzle of the rifle skyward and opened the bolt. In the distance, a tiny figured climbed over the ridge and ran up to the target area. After a moment, he returned to his cover.

The man beside the shooter yelled out.

"Page is out of silver dollars. All he had was a quarter."

A murmur of appreciation rippled through the commandos.

Baylor's companion said, "You lucky dog. If KR drills that one, you'll become immortal."

Baylor pointed at the crouching man beside the shooter. "What's that guy up to? Is he calling out the range?"

"The wind. See the flags? Manning is the coach. He reads the wind and continuously calls out adjustments. KR moves the sights according to his calls. When it's right...pow!"

The rifle bellowed again. At the back of the group, a man peering at his watch called out. "Twenty minutes! Twenty minutes!"

When Baylor glanced at the caller, his companion with the binoculars said, "Don't worry. That's a lot of time. We'll finish before the next satellite pass."

"What kind of rifle can shoot a hole in a silver dollar a quarter mile away?" Baylor asked.

"KR uses a custom, long-action M24 in 7mm STW. Lot's of velocity. Shoots flat. Hits hard. A hundred and twenty grain solid projectile zipping at close to 3700 feet per second."

Baylor shook his head. "I'll take your word for it."

The rifle blasted again and another cheer rolled out.

"This is really great. KR's poised for a clean sweep if she nails your charm. It's never happened before."

Baylor glanced at the commando. "KR is a woman?"

"Oh, yeah! But not one to mess with, if you know what I mean."

Baylor laughed. "I ran into one like that not too long ago."

"Okay, here we go."

In the sudden hush, Baylor could hear the droning chant of the coach. The long, dark tube of the extended barrel seemed frozen in space. A minute passed and then a second. Deep into the third, the barrel jerked backward. Dust blasted from the surface of the ground and the heavy report rolled across the canyon.

"Bingo!" the commando with the binoculars said.

"All right!" Baylor laughed. His attention was drawn to the shooter who suddenly launched up from the ground. She slipped her arm from the sling, folded her bipod and tossed her hat in the air.

"Yeeoow!" she screeched.

When she turned around, Baylor was struck speechless for he faced the auburn tangle and pixie features he remembered so well. KR was none other than Adele Reeves. Karen Adele Royce, he reminded himself. He joined in the applause.

She spotted him at that moment and handed her rifle to her coach. She marched directly toward him, her face forewarning of less than pleasant intentions.

"Uh-oh!" said the commando with the binoculars, suddenly giving Baylor plenty of elbowroom.

Baylor's smiled faded. "At least she gave up the gun first." He raised his hands as she approached. "It was an accident. How was I to know—"

She struck him across his left cheek, turning his head with the force of the blow. Her eyes flashed with fire and she was breathing heavily.

Baylor bowed his head. "Will you let me explain how—"

"Do you know how long I saved for that car? Do you have any idea what it meant to me? You could put up your fancy fighter pilot pay for three years and still not replace my baby. How could you be so reckless when I trusted you with it?"

Baylor rubbed his jaw and smiled. "I don't know, Adele. Trouble has been following me around lately. Why, there's an Avis rent-a-car in Kansas that will never be the same. I think the act-of-war cause on the insurance policy will take effect on that one. And look at poor Doc Wozniak's Jeep. What choice did I have there? Sometimes you have to make tough decisions."

Her lips formed the beginnings of a smile. "Was it a tough decision, Pilot Ed? Sacrificing the Jeep?"

He grinned. "That one was easy. The Porsche was tough! Oh, yes. Real tough! A huge bomb in the basement. Set to go off in seconds. Two guys with machine guns pinning us inside the building. Our friend down with a head wound, the fate of the world in our hands."

She advanced on him again, and he backed a step.

"It was hard, Adele. Really it was."

Her arms snaked around his neck and she kissed him, directly on his lips. After a moment, he encircled her waist and pulled her close amid rousing applause, cheering and catcalls.

"Five minutes! Five minutes!"

Baylor broke the clench. "Sorry, girl. Not enough time."

She rubbed his jaw where she had struck him. "Poor Ed. Always playing second fiddle to a clock." She grinned at him. "You won't always be so lucky, you know."

"Don't be so sure. I've a new charm that says different."

"It says you duck the bullet. It says nothing about ducking me." She turned away, retrieved her weapon, and double-timed it up the slope towards the cave entrance.

14:11 CDT, Minot AFB, ND

Rotts whacked his pointer against the screen and tossed it on the table in front of him. "That's the lot of them, sir. Every blessed pass since yesterday morning and not a damn thing to show for it! It's like they dug a hole and pulled the sod in after them."

Pigott rubbed his chin. "Impressive work, Phil. In my opinion, you've left nothing uncovered." He stood and walked toward the projected image on the screen. It showed a vast expanse of prairie and mountains. Pigott stood before it for several seconds before he asked, "Do you remember Agent Orange?"

"Who doesn't? Strip away the jungle cover so we could follow the enemy's traffic more closely."

"Precisely. Our enemy is hiding in a different jungle. We need to defoliate it, Phil. And I think our Moslem friends have given us the means."

Rotts raised his eyebrows. "Full scale restriction of transportation?"

"Start with commercial air and private vehicles. No travel by either for the next ten days. Position it as conservation of the national petroleum stockpiles. Leave trucking and rail alone for now."

Rotts whistled. "The President will go for that?"

Pigott let a mild smile invade his features. "He's depending on us to manage this situation. He'll back us."

"Trucking offers the enemy some major possibilities, sir. Should we include the OTR rigs in the restriction as well?"

"Not yet. Establish inspection stations at all major interstate junctions. That would help a little."

"What happens after ten days, General?"

"We're moving south, Phil."

Rotts sat on the edge of the table. He crossed his arms and waited. After a moment Pigott added, "Houston. I think the LBJ Space center should work."

"When did you make this decision, sir?"

"Just now…while you were showing us how well Ouilette has covered his tracks. We need to think long term, Phil. This little outpost is too remote. All of our supply lines are at risk if we remain up here. In south Texas, we'll find more resources, namely oil and croplands. The latter may prove especially important. We'll also have an outlet to the ocean. The energy budget is much lower. All in all, an ideal solution, Phil."

"When, General?"

"Tomorrow. Tonight. At the earliest moment."

"The alien, sir? She goes or stays?"

Pigott clenched his jaw. "It comes with us. That creature holds the key to the albatross around our neck." Pigott pointed straight up. "Up there is the enemy's most important asset. To use it, they need the Chao. To capture it for ourselves we need her. As long as we control the key, we control the situation."

"We could eliminate the creature, general. It would save us a lot of time."

Pigott shook his head. "It would save us effort, but not time. If we gain access to its technology, *that* would save us time. We'll keep it whole for a while yet."

Rotts lifted himself from the table. "I'll need to move the lab and the support services. I'll also need to arrange a location to receive them. That will take some time. In the interim, we should upgrade our security support. I'd like to organize resources capable of handling anything Ouilette can throw at us."

"What did you have in mind?"

Rotts paced across the room and back. "Since the XT craft has left us, let's get some air support in here. A flight of fast movers to start and then I'll take a page out of Ouilette's handbook. I'll order up Apaches, gun-ships for ground support."

"Sounds good. What else?" Pigott asked.

Rotts chopped two fingers against the palm of his left hand. "We're set for infantry in the marine units. Let's add some mechanization. Some Bradleys and maybe even a couple of heavy tracks." Rotts turned to face Pigott. "General, I'd also like to put us on full alert until we lift for Houston. Twenty-four hour patrols. Airspace watch. That sort of thing."

Pigott nodded. "Whatever you need, Colonel. Just don't delay our exit by a single hour."

15:30 MDT, Desert Range Experimental Station, UT

Ouilette glanced around the conference room. Weber sat to his right and Wozniak across the table. Adjacent to the scientist, Baylor fidgeted in his seat. Captain Andrew Meisner stood at the far end of the table, shuffling through some files.

Ouilette returned his gaze to Wozniak.

"Doctor Wozniak makes a good point. He's about to deliver a most important message, but the messenger is still in jeopardy. On top of that, Captain Meisner brings us some disturbing news. Go ahead, Andy."

Meisner cleared his throat and lifted a sheet of paper from a folder. "As of 1400 today, the FAA suspended all non-military flights over the Continental U.S. The ICC, acting under an executive order, placed a similar restriction against private transportation on American roadways. Satellite search patterns have intensified to the point of continuous coverage over this base for the next seven days. There is no break over any part of the U.S."

"Where are our transports?" Ouilette asked.

"We've two MC-130 Talons at Bear River Refuge, north of Salt Lake City. Our original plan called for them to launch at 1800 tomorrow, retrieve Black Magic and its resources before vectoring to this base. I don't see how that's possible, sir."

"We'll work on it. What else?"

"Right Claw has inserted. They reported about a half an hour ago via laser-link and landline. They won't have another chance until tomorrow. The report says that Minot is landing heavy-cargo aircraft and operating under increased security measures. The incoming aircraft are C-17s, which brought in mechanized reinforcements and at least two attack helicopters. More importantly, the C-17s did not leave. It looks like they're being staged for a major loading. And one last thing, sir. The XT craft is missing."

Ouilette stiffened. "Are you sure?"

"Yes, sir. The report says the alert pad contains burnt-out vehicles and smashed power units but no Sikt."

Ouilette glanced over to Weber. For several seconds, their eyes locked. Weber spoke first. "He's bugging out."

Ouilette nodded. "And we're expected."

Weber kicked back in his chair. He stretched his arms over his head and locked his fingers behind his neck. "Marcus, this sounds like a one-way trip."

"Don't it though."

Baylor glanced from one to the other. "You guys aren't getting cold feet are you? We're still going after her, aren't we? We need her!"

Wozniak leaned forward. "I agree. After scanning the crystal all day, I think I know what's coming and it isn't pretty."

Ouilette raised a hand. "We're acknowledging the risks, not avoiding them. Unless we remove Linneow from her captors, any effort to free her is senseless. First we need to find out if she is still on the base. If so, where is her craft? If they've moved her, or she's escaped, a mission to retrieve her makes no sense."

Ouilette turned to Meisner. "Andy, tell Right Claw to verify Linneow's presence at Minot. Without verification, there's no way I can authorize *Tiger-Bright*."

"Sir, I can't reach them until 1400 tomorrow. The timetable's impossible."

Several seconds of silence passed. Finally, Ouilette shook his head. "I'll need some time to think about that as well." He rubbed his eyes with his knuckles.

"No!" Wozniak said.

Ouilette lifted his face. "Pardon, Doctor?"

Wozniak climbed to his feet and walked to the whiteboard. He picked up a marker and turned toward Ouilette. "You've a bandwidth problem, Commander. In ninety minutes or so, you must stand in front of the troops and tell them what this mission is all about, what the whole affair is all about. You need to inspire them, to gather their enthusiasm, their force of will and focus it. In short, you must lead them. No one else can.

"It's up to the rest of us to act as your strategy team. Captain Meisner and I can assume responsibility for the tactical issues."

Ouilette glanced at Weber who just shrugged. Ouilette raised an eyebrow and said, "What's on your mind, Doctor."

Wozniak turned toward the whiteboard and drew two small circles in opposing corners. He wrote Minot in one and Base in the other. He turned and said, "Item one. We must position our forces closely enough to strike quickly after we ascertain where Linneow is located. Let's assume she's still at Minot. We cannot direct the advance team to locate her until 1400. They may not be able to confirm for several hours. What's closer to Minot than this base? A friendly place."

"Wyoming!" Baylor said. When Wozniak glanced at him, he repeated, "Wyoming. We landed there before we transferred into the truck."

Wozniak nodded. "I remember, sort of." He drew a circle closer to Minot and labeled it Wyoming. "This is the staging area. Under cover of darkness, we move our forces to Wyoming and then, when Linneow's presence is confirmed, we launch from there."

Ouilette shook his head. "Takes too long to fly from here to Wyoming after dark. We'd never get set in time."

"Then we stage tonight. Return the aircraft to the safe zones and call them in after dark tomorrow. If no-go, they take us home again."

Ouilette leaned backward, his face blank. Meisner stood and walked to the board where he drew a path across the circle labeled Wyoming.

"If we could avoid this satellite, we could bring up all of our resources at the same time."

Wozniak drew a series of Xs across the path. "My task will be to send that particular satellite on a wild goose chase."

Weber asked, "You can change satellite coverage parameters?"

"If he can't, no one else can," Ouilette said. "He programmed the damn things."

"At taxpayer expense, I might add," Wozniak said with a smile. "All I need to know is which satellite needs orbit modification."

Ouilette interjected. "Air traffic control. Only military missions allowed."

"Talons fly NOE, Nap of the Earth, Meisner responded. "Underneath the coverage."

"What about the opposition's air support?" Weber asked.

"Q-70. Confuse them, defuse them." Meisner snapped back.

Ouilette stood. He walked around to the other side of the table. "I like what I'm hearing. Andy, you and Doc polish this will you? When you think it's ready, launch it. By 1830, my global briefing will have concluded. You two can update me. I'll make the final call then."

Meisner stepped away from the board. "Sir, there's one problem yet to solve." He glanced at Baylor as he finished.

"And that is?"

"Cliff Simmons and I can fly the Talons to Shirley Basin easily enough." He turned to Wozniak. "That's the field in Wyoming." Meisner then glanced at Weber and Ouilette again. "And afterwards we can even ferry them to the jump-off point where we launch Black Magic. But from that point on, sir, we're short on pilots. Someone's going to have to bring the second Talon forward for the extraction."

Baylor grinned. "Looks like I get my wings back, eh, Doc?" He nudged the scientist with his elbow.

Ouilette frowned. "Do you have enough time in type?"

"I think so."

"So does Simmons, sir," Meisner added.

Ouilette nodded. "So be it." He glanced at his watch. "Fifty-five minutes, gentlemen, in the auditorium. Don't be late."

16:55 MDT, 16 May
Desert Range Experimental Station, UT

Baylor stepped through the entryway into the auditorium and paused in mid-step, seized by surprise. Back to front, several dozen steeply inclined rows of seats were nearly packed with people. Voices filled the capacious hall, which could have served as a respectable theatre. Before he ambled down the ramp toward the front, he searched for a familiar face in a sea of bobbing heads.

By counting rows and columns, he tried to estimate the hall's capacity, which had to exceed more than two hundred people in total. He stopped near the front rows, which were elevated about two meters above the stage platform, still undecided about where he would sit. While he was looking toward his right, a soft, warm arm hooked through his own.

"This way, Pilot Ed. I've saved you a front-row seat."

"Adele! Or should I call you KR?"

She wrinkled her nose. "Adele. C'mon." She tugged his arm. "It's almost time."

Baylor had just claimed his seat when Andy Meisner bounded up the stage stairs on his left. The marine trotted to the lectern at the center of the platform, drew a chrome traffic whistle out of his pocket and blew one short blast.

"Attention on deck!" he shouted.

Accompanied by the rest of the crowd, Baylor sprang to his feet. A muffled series of quick-paced steps traveled past on his right but he kept his head rigidly facing forward. Ouilette entered his peripheral vision, jogged across in front of the section where Baylor stood and mounted the same stairway Meisner had used.

The Commander was dressed in commando blacks, his uniform unadorned with any semblance of rank or insignia. He strode to Meisner, shook his hand and then stepped behind the podium.

Directly over Ouilette's head hung a large screen measuring nearly five meters square. Two others flanked him, each mounted about a meter lower. All three remained dark. Ouilette moved close to the microphones.

"At ease. Be seated." He waited until the rumble and squeak of the chairs ceased. "My name is Marcus Ouilette. Some of you know me only by the signature appended to the orders you received a dozen days ago. Others, a little better than that. It's my privilege to serve this organization as its director. Today, it's the only rank I hold."

Ouilette leaned forward. "That's enough about me. I want to talk about you. Who you are and why you're here. Look around. Meet your neighbor and his or her neighbor. Study them well for that man or woman you see is quite remarkable. The faces may seem commonplace but I can assure you the opposite is true. And now you'll learn why."

The stage lights faded. The center screen brightened, depicting in silent black and white an old news film of what appeared to be a Senate hearing.

"In the early fifties, a junior senator from Wisconsin initiated a vendetta against real or imagined subversion within the United States government. During a four-year campaign of accusation and indictment, this Senator challenged the integrity of some of the highest-ranking politicians and military men of the time. Ultimately, he was discredited and then condemned by his colleagues."

The center screen turned dark and the one to the left brightened, depicting a military tribunal seated with members of Eisenhower's staff.

"That historical episode led to a new series of war-games that assumed Senator McCarthy was right. A chilling scenario soon became apparent. If subversion of our government began at the highest levels and involved key members of the U.S. Military, it appeared that our constitutional republic could be in grave danger. A concept developed out of those games gained momentum because forward thinking individuals formed a group, which designed something new and unique to prevent any such nightmare from happening. Out of that concept evolved the program called *Night-Tiger*. That's you, ladies and gentlemen."

The left screen faded to darkness.

"My predecessors created an external force unbounded by the normal chain of command, a force designed to use whatever means necessary to disrupt a coup targeted at the government of the United States. They formed a foundation to support it and began recruitment to sustain it. Admirals and Generals initiated a studied and secret process to select the best of the best. They designed a process unlike any before or since."

Ouilette paused. "Have you ever wondered why you received so many offers from private industry? From academia? From the political establishment?

"Yes, I know about them. Every person in this room, including me, was the target of an intense recruiting effort. There were many forms of persuasion. Most sought to engage your services as consultants, counselors, aides, professors, executives or what-have-you? Remember those offers? They were pretty good, weren't they? C'mon admit it! Some were damn good, were they not?"

Amid the laughter and hum of agreement, Ouilette continued. "But you declined them all. All the money, the condos, the perks, the fabulous lifestyles of the rich and famous. Why did you turn your back on all that pomp and splendor?

"You like dining at the chow hall? Or maybe you enjoyed that unannounced inspection on Saturday morning. Perhaps you cherished the alert drill twenty minutes into a date with a man or a woman you would die for."

To override the roar of disagreement, Ouilette leaned close to the mike. "Nothing in this world measures up, does it? Call it what you want. A job. A calling. A career. A life."

Ouilette let several moments of silence pass.

"The program's recruitment effort runs in reverse. You weren't recruited into this program. You're the people that could not be recruited out of it." Ouilette swept his hand across the audience. "Two hundred and twenty one. Eighty-six women and a hundred and thirty-five men. Care to guess how many we started with? No? Well, I'll tell you anyway. Fourteen thousand, give or take a few. All of them were, at one time, every bit as good as the best of you.

"To some, the enticements of civilian life meant more. Others wanted to marry and raise families. Some suffered erosion in morals or ethics. Some were injured or their skills declined. Some died in Somalia, in Bosnia, in Haiti, in Indochina, in Panama, in the Persian Gulf or the Balkans, in Iraq, Afghanistan, or Guatemala."

Ouilette paused for a second. "The point, ladies and gentlemen, is that you're all that's left. And the fate of the planet now depends on you."

He punched a button on the lectern.

The center screen changed to show flaming oil wells against a desert landscape. The sky was black with roiling, oily clouds to the far horizon. Most of the derricks lay on their side, crumpled or twisted. The surface of the ground was etched with a patchwork of gaping fissures oozing steam and smoke. The aerial shot panned. The only people in sight had fallen prostrate, lying still and silent. In the middle distance a dark and lifeless city withered under sheets of flame and a pall of smoke.

"Kuwait. A modern-era nightmare. Less than twenty-four hours ago, three nuclear warheads detonated deep underground, each within ten kilometers of the city. These devices were evidently cobalt-enriched war-shots, purposely constructed to form the dirtiest, most radioactive weapon known to man. One of them was not planted deeply enough. The Sheikdom of Kuwait can no longer sustain life. Early assessment tells us that most of the oil reserves in the area will not be usable as petroleum products for decades...perhaps centuries."

The screen to the left of the lectern flashed to life showing hundreds, perhaps thousands of corpses. Some wore military uniforms, but most did not.

"Faisalabad. This morning, within hours after the nuclear devastation in the Mid-East, India fired several dozen biological and chemical weapons into Pakistan." The right screen brightened. It showed a border outline of both countries. A tide of red crept into India from Pakistan. "Earlier this week, a conventional war between these two antagonists led to major losses by India.

"As Pakistani forces drove south, India threatened reprisal, claiming dire but undefined consequences if the coalition of Pakistani and Chinese troops did not withdraw."

The red flood turned blotchy. Several sections disappeared.

"Pakistani forces, augmented by Chinese divisions, suffered grievous losses as they were unprepared for the use of chemical weapons."

Three bright, white sparks expanded into circles inside India.

"This is their response," Ouilette added.

The upper screen faded to another scene, a hideous smoking ruin clearly recognizable as a city devastated by nuclear assault. Both side screens showed similar views, the lack of recognizable details, the charred and smoking rubble inciting its own brand of horror.

Ouilette lifted his gaze. "Calcutta, Mumbai, New Delhi."

All three screens faded to black. The left one lit again. It showed another city, one in the throes of a riot. The camera panned backward. The riot stretched onward for hundreds of city blocks. Entire buildings were aflame. The press of people in the streets invoked images of stampeding cattle or lemmings rushing to destruction.

"This morning, the Nikkei failed to open. Speculation about a crash turned ugly with the resulting run on Japan's national banks. The financial collapse ignited a volatile atmosphere induced by the oil crisis. Japan, as you know, imports eighty percent of her energy needs. This film was taken about mid-day and the chaos in Tokyo continues to escalate."

When the screen on the right illuminated, it seemed like the same city until the camera panned past the Eiffel Tower.

"The three-day old conflict in Paris shows no sign of abating. All services in the city have long since disappeared. There are reports of wide-spread looting and raiding into the suburbs and countryside by armed and mobile mobs as food in the metropolitan area runs low."

The upper screen brightened to show rows of trucks and armored vehicles moving along a major highway. It changed to a railway station where trains were loading with troops and a moment later shifted to another scene where two squadrons of Tornado's raced down the runway.

"Unified just a week ago, Europe now approaches a degree of polarization not seen since just before World War Two. These are scenes from Britain and Germany. With the collapse of the Euro, both countries face severe economic problems. They're desperately attempting to stem the tide that overwhelmed France."

The images on all three screens faded. In a rapid sequence, the leftmost depicted a tank, a Russian T-80 by its shape and markings, firing at another of the same type. The second tank spectacularly exploded. The center screen showed a crippled, smoking aircraft spiral into the ground. On the right screen, a burning, listing warship rolled over, its propellers still thrashing.

On the left screen, the tank battle switched to a view of infantrymen launching mortar rounds. Ragtag street clothes revealed that they were not military but civilian antagonists.

The center screen showed the facade of an office building blown to fragments by the combined cannon fire of several tanks. In the right screen, two men threw objects from the third story of a tattered building at a passing APC. The wheeled armored vehicle swept the windows with machine gun fire. One of the men toppled forward, hanging from the opening.

In the next instant, the objects exploded upon the APC, engulfing it in flames. It careened into the side of the building. The rapid sequence continued, but the content never altered.

"There has been no official transmission from the Republic of Russia. Its army, long neglected and seldom paid, seems to have fractured along divisional lines. By all appearances, the Russian people are engaged in their second civil war in less than a hundred years."

The sequence faded, the outer screens darkened but the center one zoomed backward from the torch of the Statue of Liberty. It panned across the skyline of New York. The left screen flashed a split image picture of LaGuardia and JFK, both airports silent, filled with motionless aircraft.

The right screen illuminated the darkened halls of Wall Street where the only occupants were pigeons. The center screen switched to a view of Interstate 95, across the George Washington Bridge and northwards. Only a handful of semis rolled along the highway. Manhattan was a ghost city.

Left and right screens flashed an endless stream of CITGO, Mobil, Shell, Texaco, Amoco, and Sunoco gas stations—all closed.

The center screen switched to a motionless tractor in a field. An ambulance at the side of a road with its hood raised.

A fire truck where the fireman was refueling from a gas can and a long line of city police cars behind a single pump where a sign read *No Gas*.

All three screens darkened and remained unlit. Ouilette bowed his head in silence. He switched off the lectern's light and stepped out from behind the podium. The stage lights brightened to half intensity. He walked to the forward edge of the platform.

"In the last fifteen to twenty years," Ouilette began, "I've accepted at face value that this nation needed to lend its strength to less fortunate peoples who aspired to our way of life. The ideals we cherish are universal. Every sentient being in every part of the universe deserves no less than what we have. When it is in our power to promote these concepts, advance liberty and justice and the pursuit of happiness, we should. I don't think a man or woman in this room would disagree.

"I watched with dismay, and I'm sure that many of you did also, when this wonderful willingness to help, to sacrifice, to support and to befriend was ill-applied because of cloudy vision. Somalia and Bosnia represent the worst of muddy thinking. Guatemala was, perhaps, the best example of insightful purpose. The rest lie somewhere in between. What I've shown you just now is a nightmare of a world in chaos. You might look at all that calamity and wonder what can be done. What does it all mean?

"It comes down to cause and effect. Everything I've shown you thus far represents an effect. These symptoms are not widespread calamities brought about by diverse and unrelated events. As unfathomable as it may seem, there is but a single cause lying at the root of all of it...which is fortunate because it means that we, you and I, can make a difference. Our mission, called *Tiger-Bright*, may or may not launch. If we go, it will be because we have a clear and achievable objective, one that is worth the cost in lives and equipment it requires us to spend. I'll revisit this mission later tonight. Right now, you need to learn about our opposition, the true enemy of the United States...and of the human race."

Ouilette shifted his gaze above the audience and toward the back of the room.

"I'd like to introduce a man of significant accomplishments. *Magna cum laude* from Massachusetts Institute of Technology, Physicist fellowship to Cal-Tech, Doctorate of Applied Intelligence Systems from the University of Michigan. The man who programmed the Callisto probes, the Europa lander and a host of other accomplishments, which the hour begs we illuminate another time.

"Whatever your opinion of learned men, when you see this man with a cane tonight, it's because he stood in harm's way, as would you and I. On a recent mission, he provided the underlying strategy, a pivotal solo performance that saved the life of one of our best, and all of the pre-op intelligence. His escape vehicle came under fire by airborne assets of the enemy. Before our extraction team could intercede, he was struck by direct fire from an M-60 machine gun."

Ouilette bent close to the mike and added in a deeper, softer note, "A civilian did all this."

After a pregnant pause, he said, "I'm proud to have him on our side. Please welcome Doctor Stanley Wozniak." He walked to the edge of the stage and began the applause.

Wozniak limped down the carpet pathway and the applause continued while he painfully negotiated the stairway up to the stage's surface. Once up, he hefted the cane in his hand and strode purposefully toward the lectern. The applause gained in volume while Ouilette withdrew.

In a few seconds, the tumult diminished. Wozniak leaned toward the mike and said, "Now you know why I was wounded. I mean, how could they miss?" When the level of laughter and applause built again, he waved it down and held up his cane.

"Since I'm in Special Ops now, I don't need this anymore. It was only a flesh wound, right?" He tossed the cane across the stage and into a corner. More applause surged from the audience and Wozniak waited the moments it took before they fell silent. He leaned forward against the lectern and placed both his arms across the top edges. His voice and demeanor lost its humorous edge. With a lower, softer pitch, he began.

"Have you ever stopped to watch kindergarten kids having a good time on a playground? Sliding down slides. Swinging on swings? Teeter-totters and jungle gyms and merry-go-rounds? Hopscotch, dodge ball, tag?

"They have a great little world. Simple, self-contained and safe. No atomic submarines or nerve gas or earthquakes and floods? The real world is out of sight. Beyond their knowledge, understanding and experience. With their young eyes and unsophisticated minds, they gaze through our world and never see it. They live right in the middle of it, unaware, happy and secure."

Wozniak slowly swept the audience with his gaze. Baylor sat near the front, a pretty woman on his arm, leaning close. The scientist locked eyes with him, bent toward the microphone and said with a hushed voice, "Reality is different, isn't it?"

When Baylor nodded, the woman glanced at him and whispered something in his ear.

Wozniak continued, "Earth is the playground, we are the children, and childhood's end is upon us." On the center screen, a silver arc appeared in the upper left corner. Subtended by the edges of the screen, it gradually expanded to cover the entire square.

"This video feed is derived from a carbon crystal, a data cell, an archive created by an unknown entity. A friend of the human race provided this crystal as a history lesson."

Wozniak pointed to the right screen. "This red ellipse defines a circle of one astronomical unit, the distance from the Earth to the Sun, as seen from thirty degrees above the elliptical plane. The left screen shows the same view but from a point of one light year's distance. The red circle is not visible."

On the overhead screen, the silver edged circle appeared to shrink. Two others accompanied it, and the perspective cleared. They were spheres, hanging motionless in space while the viewpoint retreated from the globes. More and more spheres entered the screen, until there were hundreds then thousands and, finally, tens of thousands.

The orbs became points of light, forming a hollow sphere. Immense at first, it too shrank until the globe of lights occupied less than a third of the upper screen.

"When, you might ask," Wozniak said. "Perhaps a trillion years ago. That's right, not a million. Not a billion. A trillion years ago at an undefined point in space and time. We don't know where or exactly when, but they obviously do."

He pushed a button on the lectern. A row of red zeros filled the bottom of each screen. "Because this is a recording, I can control the speed of the event. There are twenty-four zeros to the right of the decimal point. In total, they represent one second in real time, our time…each zero, one septillionth, a trillionth of a trillionth. Don't blink."

A few chuckles subsided. Wozniak lifted his remote control and, with an exaggerated motion, pressed the button. The zeros at the far right of each screen scrolled into a synchronized blur. The zeros for thousands cascaded into millions and into billions. A white dot appeared at the center of the right screen.

Wozniak leaned into the mike. "Time reference accelerates as the event develops."

Tens of billionths became hundreds. The white dot swelled into a visible sphere. It grew rapidly. When the twelfth zero marking one trillionth, halfway across the screen, flipped to a one the brilliant mass occupied more than half of the space within the ellipse. It was now irregular in shape. A white dot appeared in the center of the screen on the left. Another three zeros turned into scrolling numbers. The left screen filled with blazing, churning light.

"One nanosecond…an event of duration scarcely measured in our fastest computers. Diameter of the event horizon now exceeds six hundred million miles," Wozniak said.

Ten nanoseconds passed into twenty, and then fifty. The swelling amorphous shape quickly filled the left screen. When the zero representing one hundred nanoseconds changed to a one, the left screen also drowned in a sea of white. In the screen over Wozniak's head, a white speck appeared in the center of the globe of lights. The dot expanded, its brilliance overreaching that of the spheres, which appeared to flee from the encroaching violence.

"One micro-second and ten light-years in diameter," Wozniak intoned. The last zero scrolled from one to nine. All three screens churned with violent light. They faded to darkness.

He stepped away from the lectern and approached the forward edge of the stage. "In the beginning...darkness was on the face of the deep...and light was made.

"We've witnessed the emergence of new energy into an immeasurably old and cold, dark domain. A few decades ago, we used to think of this moment as the *Big Bang*, and to its result as the observable universe. A few centuries before that we believed our universe consisted of the sun and planets out to Saturn. As always, our understanding of the cosmos continues to evolve, significantly. More on that later.

"At the end of the first second, our event seems to have inflated to five hundred thousand light years in diameter. I say *seems* because such inflation, being faster by far than the speed of light, is not possible. Instead, what we are seeing is an expanding area of interaction between two domains in our complex and infinite universe. Think of it as two mountains, one inverted, colliding at great speed, peak to peak. As they merge, the area of interaction expands with dramatic speed."

Wozniak glanced around at his enraptured audience. He raised the volume of his voice. "In a thousand years, matter takes on form and structure. The average temperature is just a million degrees. Density is now only a millionth of a gram per centimeter in a volume of space over one hundred million light-years in diameter. Of course, some spots are still very dense and very hot.

"A million years pass, and then a billion. Galaxies have formed, comprised of large and very hot stars. The average temperature is just over a thousand degrees. Average density is now a meaningless number. Five billion years pass. Many of the hot young stars have exploded.

"Longer-lived, second-generation suns form from the dust and gas of remnants, pushed together as if by some cosmic broom from the light pressure of the survivors. Solar systems evolve where a star does not eat its brood in a few short millennia. The clock ticks away another three or four billion years."

Wozniak waited in silence, emphasizing the immense passage of time before he toggled his remote. The center screen lit up with the hazy irregular shape of a luminous cloud. The view zoomed in until individual specks of light assumed definition.

"Not stars," Wozniak cautioned. The zoom continued inward until it focused on a single point, which swelled to become a galaxy. Wozniak stopped the zoom and retreated until the original representation of the cloud reasserted itself.

"Remember the spheres at the beginning? Did they suggest artifacts? Constructs assembled by some sentient entity? By the symmetry of their grouping, one would assume this the case. If so, where did they come from? And how? An enigma, no?

"This record tells us the spheres belong to the Oo'ahan. The Builders. That's what the word meant in the tongue of another old race, a race of competitors who no longer exist." Wozniak paused to let that fact stand forth. "Fifteen billion years after the eruption of new material into their domain, the Oo'ahan possess a substantial head start in monopolizing the resources. Any competition would have to evolve from primordial muck on some planet, possess the good fortune to survive through untold and innumerable catastrophes. Comprehend, master, apply prodigious sciences, and *then* go exploring.

"The Oo'ahan are represented in red." Wozniak pushed a button on his remote. The cloud took on a pink hue. "Not quite everywhere, but then a domain is an awfully big place. I tried to count the elements they controlled using my new toy, a six-node computer cluster of the latest design. The cluster ran out of horsepower before we reached a measurable proportion of one percent.

"Using a different tack, we sampled clusters of galaxies, hoping to gain some idea of the density. We think the Oo'ahan controlled nearly four percent of this volume. That's an immense number of galaxies and an inconceivable number of star systems, but...they were not alone.

"There's a host of other species in the record but only a few that achieved any significant growth. None of them rival the Oo'ahan. Peace and prosperity for all? With over ninety-five percent of this domain unaccounted for, you would think that highly evolved, intelligent species could work in perpetual harmonious accord. Except for one fact, they probably would have."

All three screens faded again. Wozniak held up three fingers.

"Early in the twentieth century, there were three mainstream models of the universe. We called the first an open model. After a supposed *Big Bang*, things keep expanding forever. The second was called a flat model. Expansion ends at some finite size and then everything just hangs around until entropy sets in and it all decays to nothing. Both of these first two models have lifetimes so long as to be called infinite. Lastly, there was the closed model, where expansion stops and gravity pulls all the mass back into a pinpoint. A *Big Crunch*, if you will. All of these models have flaws and we were never able to refine them.

"Our history lesson is a library loan from the Deneb Crystal Archives and for those of you who are less than proficient at astronomy, I'll add the fact that Deneb is over fifteen hundred light-years from Earth.

"You may have noticed I've used the word *domain* several times. One of the facts we discovered in the archive is confirmation of more recent human theories that portrayed a universe much larger and more complex than those in the previously accepted observable models. According to the archive, the universe is indeed infinite, and is composed of multiple dimensions, many of those possibly similar to our observable three-dimensional domain. *Big Bangs*, as we previously understood them, do not occur. Instead, over immense periods of time, possibly even trillions of years, at some point some planes of the universe interact with others. A couple of decades ago, our theorists called those planes, membranes, or *'branes* for short.

"From the Deneb Archives, we learn that people with a far-more-advanced perspective than our own, call them *domains*, which might give you a hint about where I came up with the term.

"When domains interact, merge or collide, the result is violent beyond all imagination. Inconceivable quantities of energy erupt in both domains, hurling them apart and creating a new bubble of galaxies, stars, nebulae, planets and peoples within each. Each point of interaction establishes a new event in an old domain – in our case, an event represented by a volume of space, which became our observable universe."

Wozniak paused, drew a deep breath.

"I'll admit that a billion years might seem infinite but that's only on the scale of human events. In some regards, a combination of old theories about the flat universe and the expanding universe fits rather closely to what happens next in our newly populated domain. Expansion continues today and in the far future, hundreds of billions, maybe even trillions of years, entropy wins. The domain will be come cold and dark once more. Maybe. Or maybe another domain will interact first and wreck everything already in progress. Or maybe after lying fallow for trillions upon trillions of years, said other domain would re-ignite our fires of life once more.

"What's important to remember is that if it doesn't happen in our neighborhood, it certainly will elsewhere. Probably already has, over and over again along the long infinite hallways of distant space. Infinite. A tough word to grasp."

Wozniak pressed his remote. All three screens darkened. At a nod from the scientist, Meisner turned up the lights so that Wozniak could clearly see his audience and they, him.

"There's no script to this record. I've no omniscient guide to tell me what's happening or why. Given a lifetime to study this recording and a host of experts to counsel with, I might establish an ironclad, indisputable theory. We have neither so we have to employ reasonable methods. We take what we can in the limited time we have and build a hypothesis. We formulate plans and actions while evolving the hypothesis...adding to it...modifying it. Eventually, with luck and perseverance, we'll be able to predict future results and our hypothesis will become theory.

"I'm about to portray my hypothesis. It leads to the inevitable conclusion that we, the Earth, the human race and the United States, are under attack. This hypothesis helps us understand our assailant and shows some of the reasons why they've chosen to assault us."

Wozniak pointed at Meisner and returned to the lectern. Meisner dimmed the lights and the scientist brought the pink cloud up on the left screen.

"The domain, nine billion years after emergence of new matter, of new building materials. The Oo'ahan own it all at this point and about two percent of the galactic population bears evidence of their influence. Evidence of steady and accelerating event expansion is obvious."

An image flickered on the center screen.

"A couple of billion years later. Note the concentrations near the periphery. There are three of them. I'm now going to advance about two hundred million years at a crack for the next five or six frames."

The image flickered again.

"There are now five concentrations; the early ones now quite dense."

The image changed again.

"Seven of them. Note the position shift in these two. They are two of the first three formed. Let's zoom in."

The screen showed two galaxies in collision with several more approaching a common locus.

"I cannot conceive of the force it would take to steer galaxies, but this is no accident. The Oo'ahan are building something on a scale capable only by a type IV civilization...a civilization attempting to become the masters of their universe...a practical application of the concept of God."

Wozniak paused for a moment.

"Somewhere around seventeen billion years, something goes awry. There is conflict...but with who? Who could possibly contend with the Oo'ahan? Let's examine this bright spot at seventeen billion years. If we zoom all the way down to the stellar level, we discover the reason for the increased luminescence. All along the interface, there are no less than one hundred and forty-one novae and supernovae...evidence of antagonists detonating star systems during the confrontation."

Wozniak paused and sighed. "Blowing up stars."

He shook his head and continued, "When we advance another six-hundred million years, we find more than nine thousand different points of contact. This battle makes interstellar warfare look like *Trivial Pursuit*. A billion-year war. Think about that."

Both side screens faded.

"After that conflict concluded, a trend becomes clear. Expansion and entropy continues until, three hundred billion years later, there are no habitable systems remaining.

Everything has decayed into formlessness in a once more cold, dark, domain."

Wozniak pointed to a faint haze in the center of emptiness. "Care to guess what this is?" He zoomed the view inward. The haze resolved into specks, which grew to silver spheres, thousands upon thousands of them.

"Whatever these are, they were present at both the beginning and the end. I think they are habitats of some sort, a sanctuary capable of sustaining life, or at least preserving it, until the next interaction between domains.

"What evidence we can decipher leads toward a possible conclusion. The Oo'ahan tried to prevent inevitable expansion and entropy. In this, they failed, perhaps because someone opposed them."

Only the faint cloud of spheres remained. In front of the darkened screens, Wozniak lowered his voice. "I suspect they're not about to let that happen again. Anyone and everyone with ability or potential is an enemy, and that evidently includes the human race."

He paused for effect before adding, "The Oo'ahan have returned. Not in a gigantic silver sphere with overpowering weapons and technology as is so popular with science fiction and horror entertainment. That may come but probably only if their current effort fails.

"This time they've launched a clandestine war. They undermine our systems, corrupt our governments, and turn our own strengths against us. We don't know where they are, what they look like, or how they work. If we were alone, it would be a hopeless battle. We'd have no way of detecting our enemy before they overwhelmed us.

"But, we're not alone. Forces opposing the Oo'ahan have sent a Chao among us. The Chao have a history that, when compared to the other species on record, is least unlike our own."

"Chao worlds were destroyed long ago in this conflict, but a large percentage of the population lives on. This record contains no evidence that the Chao have resettled anywhere. In fact, it almost appears as if their culture has been assimilated into the Vithra Dominion...an ethnic subset scattered throughout that civilization not unlike our Jewish population before modern-day Israel."

On the screen, the star-field dimmed and faded. It was replaced by an image of the Sikt grounded at Minot AFB. To the left, was the familiar shape of an F-27 Black Widow. The pilot stood about ten yards in front of his aircraft peering across the intervening space. Another man joined him.

"An Air Force pilot had an inspiration to engage his gun camera allowing us to capture this historic moment where human meets Chao. You might recognize the F-27 pilot." Wozniak zoomed in on Baylor's face.

Out in the audience, Adele stiffened. "My God! You knew all this stuff?"

On the screen overhead, the Sikt canopy opened. The Chao climbed out and a buzz of conversation erupted throughout the auditorium.

Adele swiveled toward Baylor. "You've got to be kidding! Female, right?"

"No doubt about that. There's more to come."

On the screen, Baylor took the supine form of Weber from the Chao's arms and carried him away from the craft. When the Chao removed her helmet, Wozniak zoomed in and froze the frame.

"Ambassador Sayla Linneow provided the crystal archive we've reviewed today and she initiated an extensive joint-study effort with our scientists. We've cooperated on a plan for a major technology transfer and you don't need me to tell you which way. The Chao-Human relationship was off to an excellent start."

Adele elbowed Baylor's ribs. "So this is the woman with hair on her face. You told me she weighed two hundred pounds. I'd say more like a hundred and ten."

Baylor leaned closer. "You'd be wrong. Dense musculature, boron skeleton, entirely different internals. She tipped the scale at one-ninety-six."

Wozniak tapped the mike. The thumps emanating from the speakers restored silence to the auditorium. "Now for the bad news. The enemy has seized the Chao ambassador. Corrupt human elements, in league with Oo'ahan insurgent forces already on-planet, control the landing site and the ambassador. Evidence exists that indicates they have not yet gained access to the ambassador's craft or her technology.

Wozniak paused and leaned over the microphone. "I think you begin to see the nature of the problem. Locate the Chao Ambassador. Free her from Oo'ahan influence and control. Remove her to a secure location. Clear, concise objectives necessary for our survival. Director Ouilette will provide the operational details."

Wozniak walked out from behind the lectern and left the stage.

This time, there was no applause.

Adele leaned against Baylor's arm.

"My God! How can we ever...I mean, this is beyond anything...." She couldn't finish.

Baylor nodded. He folded her fingers into his own. "One day at a time. Set aside what you don't know. Just think about our goals for tomorrow."

She nodded. As Ouilette climbed the stairway to the stage, Adele leaned her head upon Baylor's shoulder.

The commander strode to the lectern. He scanned his audience, giving them a moment to digest Wozniak's last words. After several seconds, he spoke into the microphone.

"*Tiger-Bright* is our first major offensive. Any reasonable expenditure of manpower and resources is justified as long as we accomplish the mission objectives.

"The primary role of *Night Tiger* was to be clandestine in nature. Survival of this organization, under the scenarios envisioned by its founders, was always the top priority. Unfortunately, the founders never foresaw this situation or anything like it. Unless we can free the Chao and provide for her security, our survival is meaningless."

"*Tiger-Bright* will consist of two elements. As usual, *Right Claw* will assume the extraction objectives. An alpha team of six is already on-site. Alpha team will ascertain the exact whereabouts of the Chao and the nature of her containment. Two additional teams of six will join the Alpha team for the extraction. I'll brief *Right Claw* elements in detail at 2100.

"*Left Claw* is the cover force and will include *Black Magic* and *Little Paw* plus four twelve-man teams. We expect the enemy to deploy both air support and mounted infantry and they know we're likely to come. They don't know when and they don't know what we know about them. *Left Claw's* goals are to sow confusion and disarray among the defensive forces.

"Captains Barth and Meisner, responsible for respective ground and air elements of Left Claw in the field, will also brief their teams at 2100.

Ouilette stepped out from behind the podium and walked to within a meter of the forward edge of the stage.

"One third of our strength, along with all of our air resources, will engage the enemy. In your quarters, you will find team selection details. Two out of every three will remain behind. For the next four days, these units have another task. It's possible some of our *Tiger-Bright* force will fall into enemy hands. If that happens, we must assume the opposition will discover our base.

"The reserve units, almost a hundred and fifty of you, will engage in a second operation called *Sanctuary*. This crucial program establishes a subterranean colony in a remote wilderness location designed to assure our long-term survival. Doctor Wozniak will lead this operation. His briefing also commences at 2100."

Ouilette glanced at his watch. "It's 1820. You've a little over two and a half hours. Use them well."

Meisner took a step away from the edge of the stage where he had been standing with Wozniak.

"ATTENTION ON DECK!" he shouted, and everyone leapt to their feet.

Ouilette strode to the stairway, descended and jogged toward the exit.

Meisner waited until the commander had left the auditorium before he said, "*Right Claw* meets in the wardroom. *Left Claw* in the cafeteria. *Sanctuary*, right here. Dismissed."

Baylor strolled toward the exit, scarcely conscious of the light grip on his arm. He tried to fit what he'd learned tonight with the discussion earlier in the day. Because Meisner would fly the MH-60 and Simmons the ferry craft, that meant the other C-130, his aircraft, would deliver the *Left Claw* team. The Nighthawk could lift almost a dozen troops, so it was likely that the chopper would perform the actual extraction once Linneow was freed.

Did that mean he was part of *Left Claw*, the offensive team? He couldn't decide.

Adele gripped his arm more fiercely. "Are you worried?" she asked, her voice subdued.

Baylor glanced at her. "More confused than worried. I'm wondering how I'll fit into this operation." He wrapped an arm around her waist and tugged her closer as they walked toward a corridor that led to private quarters.

"You have this all figured out, I'll bet," he said. "This Special Operations Group routine is old hat to you."

A flicker of a smile touched her lips and vanished. When they approached a cross-corridor, she started to turn right and he left.

"I'm in 2303," he nodded his head toward the left.

Adele disengaged. "I'm the other way." She stepped back, her eyes large and luminous. "See you later, I hope." She turned away and quickened her pace, her arms wrapped about her middle.

"I hope so," Baylor muttered. He trotted to his room, opened the door and stepped in. A white envelope lay on his bunk. He stripped off his shirt and then tore the end from the envelope. A single sheet, typewritten, designated him as *Left Claw*. A capsule summary of his responsibilities showed that he would fly the C-130 to a spot to be designated, land, and assist in disembarkation of the strike force. His job after that would be to protect and defend the aircraft until the strike team returned.

"A bloody bus driver is all," Baylor muttered. "Why the hell did I need to mess with guns?"

He resolved that he would speak with Meisner about it later. He stripped off the remainder of his clothing, stepped into the bathroom and turned on the shower. He adjusted the water to very hot and climbed inside the cubicle. After the spray struck the back of his neck for several minutes, he soaped up and then cooled down with a cold-water rinse. Baylor shut the water off, stepped out and toweled dry. He threw the damp towel over the edge of the shower stall and snapped out the lights. He planned to grab about an hour of shut-eye. It would be a long night if Ouilette decided to launch after the briefing.

Baylor opened the door and stepped into darkness. He didn't remember turning off the lights but it didn't matter. The room was small and he knew where the bed was. As he approached it, he smiled for despite his shower he could still detect a trace of Adele's perfume. He flipped the covers back and flopped onto the sheets. His thigh, hip, shoulder and arm struck something that made him bolt from the bed.

"Jehoshaphat!" he exclaimed.

She laughed softly and whispered, "Come back to bed, Ed. I need to be held."

"I...I'm not dressed, Adele."

"People don't shower with clothes on, Ed. If you won't come to me this instant, I'm out of here, clothes or no."

Baylor needed no further urging. He slipped into the bed and her arms immediately wrapped around his neck, her legs entangling his own.

"Adele, are you sure about—"

"Shush. The next two hours may be the last chance we have. I can't bear the thought of spending them alone."

Chapter Twenty-one
20:45 MDT, 16 May
Desert Range Experimental Station, UT

Weber knocked once, opened the door, and thrust his head inside. The room was dark so he swept his hand across the wall near the door, seeking the light switch.

"Hit the deck, Ace. Time to rise and shine."

Just before the lights illuminated, he heard the shower running and so the stunning sight on Baylor's bed was completely unexpected.

"Glory be!" he murmured.

Adele lay on her stomach, dozing. She stirred at his comment and, recognizing Weber in the entryway, yanked at a sheet to cover her body. In an irritated whisper, she said, "Close the damn door!"

Weber stepped inside and complied. With an appreciative nod, he said, "Nice to see you, KR."

Adele reached over the side of the bed, picked up one of Baylor's Nikes and hurled it at him. "I meant with you outside, rat."

Weber ducked the shoe, whisked open the door and exited. He closed the door and leaned against the wall outside, chuckling. A moment later, Adele stepped out beside him. She held her shoes in her hand and her blouse hung loose over her belt. She dropped the shoes on the floor and jammed her feet into them while tucking in her blouse.

"Sort of robbing the cradle, aren't you?" Weber asked.

"Why Mister Weber, what can you mean?"

"Ace knows his business in the cockpit." Adele rolled her eyes at his choice of words, but Weber was unfazed. He added, "But taking a lover in Special Ops is another matter. He's wet behind the ears in this kind of work."

Adele snapped the top button on her jeans. "He's a big boy." She trotted down the hall toward her quarters.

"You ought to pick on someone your own age," he called after her.

She twitched her buttocks in exaggerated fashion. "Eat your heart out, Sam," she said over her shoulder.

Weber murmured as he entered Baylor's door again, "I am, darlin'...I am." He stepped into the room just as Baylor opened the door to the bathroom, a towel over his head.

"All yours," he called out.

"Don't need it," Weber replied.

Baylor yanked the towel from his head, embarrassment flooding his features. "Where...? Did you...?" he ground to a halt.

Weber just grinned at him. "We need to visit Ouilette before you brief with Andy."

A few minutes later, both Baylor and Weber followed Meisner into the director's office. Wozniak stood beside Ouilette who sat on the surface of his desk. Simmons sat in Ouilette's chair. Wozniak appeared to be uncharacteristically perturbed.

Baylor grinned at the scientist and said, "Hey, Doc. What's up?"

Ouilette answered first. "Doctor Wozniak is agitated by my announcement. Tell the troops, in your briefings, that Doctor Wozniak has been promoted to deputy-director. If anything should happen to me during our engagement, he'll assume overall command of *Night Tiger*."

Weber ducked his head. "Quite a call, Marcus."

Ouilette turned to his friend. "Sam, this campaign will encompass much more than military endeavors. *Night Tiger* was conceived to respond to a coup. We face a whole lot more. We're talking about a long-term struggle that involves scientific, social, and technological elements. No member of the military establishment is up to that challenge. In my opinion, if Doctor Wozniak operates only as my advisor, those elements will never receive the attention they deserve. I think Stan should form his own organization, staff it to address these concerns and use our military contingent as just another method to project the organization's will.

"Von Clausewitz," Wozniak murmured. "A flawed treatise."

"If it were not for the Oo'ahan, I'd agree," Ouilette replied. "I'll retain the role as commander of the military forces and serve as an advisor to Doctor Wozniak on how best to use these resources when and if they should be deemed necessary."

Wozniak shook his head. "This is premature. For me, it's also unsettling, particularly in view of what we need to accomplish tonight. I think we should table this discussion until after the operation."

"Spoken like a director." Ouilette turned to Baylor. "Ed, we need to touch upon another element. Earlier tonight, we said you'd be carrying the *Left Claw* troops because Cliff cannot fit them in with Black Magic. We've since determined that the only effective delivery of those troops involves a maneuver that shouldn't be tried for the first time in a combat situation. Since Cliff has no experience, we need to know more about your combat training."

Simmons interjected, "*Right Claw's* alpha team is going to take out the enemy's search radar. The instant it goes down, Minot will realize our attack has commenced." To Baylor, he said, "Your delivery must follow at the first possible moment thereafter."

"Talk to me," Baylor said with a shrug.

"The maneuver is simple but requires precision. You approach on the deck, only fifty or sixty feet up. As soon as your Talon equipment indicates radar acquisition, you give the signal for the alpha team to bust them. If they fail to acquire your aircraft...even better. We think they'll see you about six or seven miles out. In a Herk with the pedal to the metal, that's one minute away.

"When the radar goes down, you pop up to five hundred feet. You'll traverse the base at precisely this altitude, with no variation in course or speed. Even if they throw the kitchen sink, you can't duck. Our guys go out the back. Their chutes open less than a hundred feet up. They're down and engaged in ten seconds. We've drawn up a path that takes you over most of the critical areas we need to control while *Right Claw* does its thing. If you change course or speed, or if you fly too low or too high, the whole operation's a bust."

Baylor dipped his head. "Got it. One of the delivery programs aboard the F-27, uses a similar method. We pinpoint conventional or nuclear weapons without radar emissions to guide us ... a passive-attack profile. It uses a combination of inertial and terrain-following guidance that allows the pilot to approach the target at supersonic speeds right on the deck, just as Cliff says." He nodded toward Simmons. "Since our staging flights and initial approach are all NOE, Nap of Earth, I should have a real good feeling for how the Herk responds by the time we need to implement this maneuver. I don't see a problem."

Simmons gave Baylor a thumbs up.

Ouilette stood. "That's exactly what Cliff said and it's good enough for me. At 2200, we unload Little Paw topside. Andy will fly you and Cliff to Bear River. He's already sent a message to have the Talons prepped. You should make it back here by 2345. The strike teams load up and we launch by midnight. Any questions?"

Baylor and Simmons shook their heads.

"The teams await your briefings, gentlemen."

Everyone scurried for the door, Wozniak trailing. Just before the scientist stepped outside, Ouilette claimed his seat and called, "Doctor?"

Wozniak stepped back into the room, closed the door and leaned against it. Several seconds of silence passed between them before he said, "You're worried about the mission."

"My professional opinion is that we've a reasonable chance of success." Ouilette leaned back in his chair. "What comes afterward has me worried."

Wozniak limped over to the chair beside the desk and groaned as he gingerly lowered his bulk into it. He leaned his head back against the wall, closed his eyes and sighed. The coming years, decades and perhaps even centuries opened like a chasm, at first glance appearing as a bleak and inhospitable future. Without opening his eyes, he said, "It may be difficult to believe this, but I was a jock in my younger days. I'll be twenty-eight in a few months, and about a decade ago, the weight began to increase. No amount of exercise or diet had any effect." He opened his eyes and peered at Ouilette. "It's a genetic mutation, a disorder I now medicate for, but the best I can achieve is a stalemate. I lost my life as I knew it, Commander."

"Stan...it's Marcus...please."

"Old habits die hard. The point is, we play the hand that's dealt us. It's likely the human race will lose everything built in the past five thousand years."

"Shit!" Ouilette softly murmured.

"Succinctly put," Wozniak replied. "And in that light, we should discuss some items that have been on my mind today as they are both relevant and essential. Currently, we're mostly elite paramilitary types, and while that's necessary for defense, the knowledge base is unsuitable for an extended effort." At Ouilette's sudden frown, he added, "How do we analyze new threats we're likely to face? How do we develop countermeasures? How do we manufacture them? Over the years, decades and perhaps centuries to come."

"I get the point. What do you suggest?"

"Maybe you were right earlier. Perhaps I should recruit an organization, and perhaps we shouldn't put all our eggs in one basket either. I'm thinking about two remote locations. Two *Sanctuaries*, if you will. I've a couple of locations in mind. Would you like to hear about them?"

Ouilette held up a palm. "Not until after *Tiger-Bright*. Are they geographically suitable?"

"As much as possible, I believe. Inaccessible except by air...and water, in the case of the second. I'm thinking of the latter as a research and development facility. Subterranean, hardened, and highly invisible."

"How would we communicate?"

"Suborn a satellite or two. Laser linkages. Ground-wave transmissions. Whatever. One of the easier problems to solve, most likely."

"Why a separate place?"

"You're going to hit the enemy. If they hit back, you can defend. We won't have that luxury. And you won't want us getting underfoot either. In the meantime, we should be able to give you some nice toys to wage battle with. Perhaps even give you a definitive edge during your likely confrontations."

Ouilette slowly nodded. "Stan, I'm glad you're here. What's the long-term prognosis?"

Wozniak sighed again. "With the Chao's assistance, perhaps we can turn the corner in a century or two. Those of us left after they've done their worst must rebuild. It will take a millennia, but we shall rebuild."

"That's the way I saw it, too."

"It's a burden better carried by a few, so we should keep that view to ourselves. This also." He reached into his shirt pocket, retrieved and passed a flash chip across the table.

"What's this? Ouilette asked, inserting the chip into his workstation's receptacle.

"Some footage I didn't show tonight."

The screen brightened and a scene of destruction unfolded. Black ebony teardrops contended with sleek ivory ships and silvered latticed globes.

"Vithra and Oo'ahan," Ouilette guessed. "When and where?"

"Here. Out near Jupiter. Sixty-six million years ago."

"The black ships are the good guys?"

"Yes."

"They're getting their asses handed to them."

"At first," Wozniak replied. "Back up a little." When Ouilette reversed the display, and after a moment or two, he said, "Stop. Go forward. Stop. Right there. Freeze it."

Ouilette did. He studied the screen in detail. "Four Oo'ahan ships. Look like someone blew them apart."

Wozniak leaned back in his chair. "Because of the detail, I believe this is actual combat footage rather than rendered history."

"You might be right," Ouilette replied, studying the fragments spinning away from each detonation. "Your point?"

Wozniak captured the mouse from Ouilette's fingers. He pointed to a bright spot on the screen and zoomed the view. He highlighted the object and expanded it again.

"That's a ship!" Ouilette exclaimed. "Belonging to?"

"Somebody very powerful."

Ouilette sat back in his chair also. "But not Chao, or Vithra, or Oo'ahan. Who then?"

"The question of the moment. Something even our allies seem adverse to share."

"They appear to be on our side though and stronger than both the Chao and the Vithra."

Wozniak nodded. "So it seems. Especially in later scenes. One must wonder why they have not been discussed, mentioned, or even named." He shrugged. "A question for another time perhaps."

"Until then, this is for you and I, alone?"

Wozniak inclined his head. "I think that's best." He groaned and stood. He strode to and opened the door, where he turned and said, "We *are* alone at the moment, Marcus. Humanity, I mean. We'll lose a lot, perhaps all. But, look at it this way, my friend. *Tiger-Bright* is a nepenthean solution. If we succeed tomorrow, the triumph will ease our pain."

22:42 MDT, Bear River Migratory Refuge, UT

Meisner banked the AH-6K in a tight turn, nearly standing the nimble little helicopter on its rotor ends. The fuel gage registered more than twenty-five percent remaining and he tapped it with his index finger.

"This thing is reading high. I'll refuel and prepare to load while you two get the Talons cranked. I'll be stowing aboard your bird, Ed, so stay close to the hanger. Start only your outboard engines."

Baylor nodded. Meisner zoomed across a dry lakebed, lifted briefly over a low ridge and dropped into the shallow basin beyond. At a hundred and fifty knots, the lithe black helicopter closed the distance to a pair of battered hangers situated on the far edge. Flying at ten feet above the surface of the sand greatly enhanced the sensation of speed. Baylor felt a sense of unease and mild anticipation at the same time. He sincerely wished the hangers contained a different type of airframe, one equipped with an afterburner.

Once within several hundred yards of the two buildings, Meisner pulled back on the stick. He lifted the collective and pumped the tail rotor pedals, dumping speed. At less than forty knots, he wheeled the AH-6 around a hundred and eighty degrees and then dropped into a hover only inches off the ground. The chopper settled with a light bump to the right of one of the hangers.

Meisner reached over his head, flicking switches and breakers. The turbine shut down and the main rotor began to slow. He unlatched his door, hopped out and wrenched open the door to the rear compartment. Baylor climbed out while Simmons exited from the left front seat. The massive doors on both hangers slowly retracted. A beat-up old pickup with a fuel tank in the cargo bed rattled across the gravel surface toward them.

Simmons pointed to the closest hanger as both he and Baylor jogged across the intervening distance. "Two forty-seven's your bird. Start her up as Andy said, but don't taxi out until he gives you the signal."

Baylor nodded and angled away toward the first hanger. Within its cavernous interior, he could barely make out the outline of the Hercules. He ran up to the crew-hatch on the port side of the aircraft and climbed inside. An officer standing in the cargo bay turned at his entrance.

"Commander Baylor?"

"Affirmative."

"I'm Lieutenant Jennisette, Paul Jennisette. I'm your copilot. This is Ricky Yates, the loadmaster. I understand we'll pick up the rest of the crew at the base?"

Baylor shook hands and nodded. "You got it. Are we ready to roll?"

"Yes, sir. We've just finished the interior check list."

"Good. Let's do a walk around together. You can point out the details as I don't have a ton of time in type."

Baylor and Jennisette completed their external inspection and then climbed into the flight deck. They spent five or six minutes stepping through the preflight checklist and then Baylor cranked number one engine. The whine of the starter was especially loud inside the hanger but the drone of the prop soon drowned it out as the engine came up to speed. Baylor switched to number four and soon the second engine's roar resonated with the first. Vibration thrummed through the controls into his fingertips.

"All right!" he muttered. So it wasn't a fighter. It was an aircraft and a respectable one at that. He slipped the headphones over his head and switched the radio to the tactical channel Simmons had told him to use.

Meisner's voice crackled in his ears.

"*Bright Hawk One*, *Little Paw*. Pull it out and we'll load up. *Bright Hawk leader*, stay in the nest."

Simmons voice responded first. "*Bright Hawk lead*, roger."

"One," Baylor replied. He slid open his side-vent and waved the ground crew to pull the chocks. He stepped on the brakes until they were clear and then advanced the throttles for the outboard engines. He released the brakes but the Hercules sat, reluctant to move. Jennisette added more pitch and Baylor nudged the throttles briefly. The surge of power started them rolling. They eased into the dim moonlight, a crewman walking before them with a signal light. When the ground crew crossed his wands, Baylor stepped on the brakes and backed the throttles to an idle. He reduced pitch to the minimum.

Jennisette unbuckled. "I'll give Yates a hand with the chopper." At Baylor's nod, he climbed out of the right seat and dropped into the cargo section. Baylor glanced out the right side panes just in time to see the pickup tow the small helicopter, its skids now on dollies, toward the rear of his aircraft. Meisner had already folded the five rotors and secured them to the tail boom.

Less than fifteen minutes later the copilot returned, Meisner right behind him. Meisner dropped into the right seat and Jennisette settled in the flight engineer's position. Meisner slipped on his headset and switched to the tactical frequency.

He turned to Jennisette. "Buttoned up?"

"All green," Jennisette replied.

Meisner switched on the radio.

"*Bright Hawk leader*, bring her out. Immediate departure, 190 magnetic, NOE."

Baylor reached over and flipped the switches for number two engine. When the turbine spun up, he immediately proceeded to number three. With all turbines at an idle he glanced around at Jennisette and received a thumb's up.

The other MC-130 roared by on his left, a windstorm of sand trailing behind its straining engines.

Meisner flicked his index finger forward and Baylor advanced the throttles. When the blades reached full speed, Meisner adjusted the pitch. The snarl of the props turned to a muted roar and the Hercules began to accelerate. In less than twenty seconds, the lumbering craft reached flying speed. Baylor pulled back on the wheel. The nose pitched up and, after a moment's hesitation, the aircraft vaulted skyward.

He eased the wheel forward immediately, and gently banked to the right, swinging the huge craft through forty degrees to the correct course. The altimeter said a hundred and ten feet. He dropped a few yards to a hundred feet even and then raised both gear and flaps. As the airspeed passed two hundred and forty knots, he caught sight of Bright Hawk leader, about a mile ahead. Baylor advanced the throttles again and closed the distance.

Twenty minutes later, Simmons' voice crackled over his headset.

"Coming right to 225. Speed 350."

Baylor depressed his mike. "Roger. 350 on 225." He followed Simmons around in the turn, maintaining minimal separation. Less than a hundred yards of empty space existed between their wing tips. Because Simmons' aircraft was inside on the turn, it was now slightly ahead. Ten minutes later, Simmons came back on the air.

"Coming left to 210. Reduce speed to 190. Switch to ILS."

Baylor turned on the Instrument Landing System and keyed his mike. "Roger, 190 on 210. ILS engaged."

Simmons kept his power dialed up when Baylor slowed his aircraft. The lead Hercules gained several hundred yards in separation and then swung to the right. Simmons continued his wide turn decreasing his power setting as he swung around behind Baylor. From a half-mile back, he called again.

"Slow to 140 knots and take her in. No lights. Let the ILS put you over the runway and then take it from there."

"Roger, slowing to 140 on 210." Baylor turned to Meisner. "Call the list."

As Meisner stepped through the landing checklist, Baylor's throat felt scratched and dry. He could not see the ground the altimeter said was only eighty feet below. He wasn't sure exactly where he was, even though the ILS indicated the Hercules was directly on its glide slope. A low ridge slipped by so close he nearly flinched. A lone building covering the truck entrance flashed by on his right. A few seconds later, he could see the shapes of clumps of grass and scrubs zipping by on his left. When the ILS indicated ten feet, he switched it off. He eased the throttles, pulled back on the wheel and let the Hercules settle. After a series of light thumps, it quit flying and dropped into the sand for good.

At first, Baylor thought he had made some dreadful mistake. The aircraft lurched and heaved and rattled. He overcame his apprehension and reversed the pitch of the propellers and advanced the throttles. When his airspeed dropped to seventy knots he stepped on the brakes. In less then ten seconds, the ride lost its savage jolting characteristics.

The aircraft swayed and dipped as it slowed. Baylor backed the throttles and changed pitch again. He poured on some power to negotiate a turn at the end of the short field runway where a ground crew stood waving two flashlights to the right. A hundred meters further another beckoning flashlight sent him right again.

A moment later, the second Hercules flashed past on his right, headed in the opposite direction and driving a sandstorm before its propellers as it landed.

When he approached the beginning of the runway, he spotted several trucks and a pair of ground crewmen signaling with their flashlights. Baylor completed two more right turns, lining up on the runway upon which he had just landed. He shut down the inboard engines, dropped the others to an idle and set the brakes.

Meisner bounded out of his seat and said to Jennisette as he dove out of the flight deck, "Drop the ramp."

Jennisette flicked two switches and then grinned at Baylor.

"What do you think?"

Baylor raised an eyebrow. "If you live through it, flying in the dark can be fun."

Outside, Meisner trotted up to Ouilette. He watched the troops of *Left Claw* as they double-timed it up the ramp. After a moment, the director turned to him.

"So?"

"Very smooth."

"Glad to hear it. We can always use good pilots."

Meisner nodded. "Speaking of which, I'm putting Jossman in *Little Paw*."

"Walker's not your wingman? I thought you said he was the best."

"We'll be air-to-air on this fight. Against Apaches. Which is why I need him in the left seat on *Magic*."

"Your call. This change your briefing?"

"I'll make the adjustment on the way up. Both chopper crews are flying up with Simmons and the *Right Claw* troops."

Ouilette watched as the ramp lifted on the first C-130. The inboard engines spun up and, a few seconds later, all four engines snarled at full power. The snarl faded to a roar and the Hercules gathered speed down the runway. Simmons' craft, its ramp already declining, swung into the vacated spot. Ouilette and Meisner joined the rest of the strike force as they trundled aboard. Three minutes later, the second MC-130 hustled down the runway and surged into the air.

16:10 CDT, 17 May, Minot AFB, ND

Michael Zwickey switched off his transceiver. He spent the next six minutes edging the map out of his breast pocket, buried deep inside the ghillie suit. With his face only four inches from the sod, he studied the fine detail of the layout and then, ever so slowly, raised his head. *Yep, this was the place.*

The drainage ditch was a long hundred yards away. Once in the ditch, he could make much better time. But up here, in plain view of the front offices it was slow and easy. Ninety minutes, maybe a little more, to the ditch. Another thirty to the latrine. Consuming almost half a minute, he crept forward another ten inches.

Zwickey considered again how much he hated changes to operational plans, especially those in the midst of execution.

More than two hours passed and Lance Corporal Dennis Wright was having a bad day. His duty shift seemed even worse than the night before. At least in the rack he managed some sleep between bouts of diarrhea. For most of the afternoon, however, he could only hunch over in the chair at his desk and try to keep his mind on the routing forms for all the material now scheduled for shipment to Texas.

Every fifteen minutes or so, a rumble in his gut forced him up, out the door, and off to the latrine at a quick trot. The knowing snickers and leering grins from his accomplices in yesterday's twenty-four hour bash stirred his suspicions that those *Granny's brownies* were somehow related to his suffering.

Distressed called again. He puckered his sphincter as best he could and began his quick march for the door. Wayne Trenchman, one of the most probable culprits if there was a conspiracy, asked when he passed, "Need a good book?"

Wright responded with an appropriate gesture and quickened his pace. When he rounded the corner of the building, he noticed that the pile of dead grass less than ten feet from the entrance had been removed.

Something done right for a change.

When he flipped on the lights, his expression changed. Whoever had picked up the debris outside had dumped it square in the middle of the latrine. Outrageous!

Wright's breath exploded from him when the mound rocketed from the floor. A fast moving, blunt object drove deep into his solar plexus, doubling him over. Something hard chopped the back of his neck and the lights went out.

Zwickey stepped over the marine's body and locked the latrine from the inside. He shucked the ghillie suit and started to undress the unconscious man. After a moment, he sniffed. "Oh man! Did you have to shit your pants?"

Working even faster, he stripped his victim's trousers, relieved to find no trace of the effluvium had yet penetrated the undergarments. He dragged the marine to the only stall, carrying his own field pack in his teeth. Zwickey bound and gagged him, tied him upright and gave him a shot of Pentothal that would knock him out for several hours.

He locked the stall from inside and slid out under the barrier. Satisfied with the view from outside, he changed into the marine's clothes and bundled his own uniform inside the ghillie suit, which he jammed into the rafters over the door. He put the transceiver into a breast pocket, unclipped his earpiece and stuffed it in afterward.

Zwickey left the latrine and walked towards the building the plans had designated as the medical labs. He strode through the door like he owned the place and walked directly up to the receptionist's counter.

"Can I help you?" asked a white-smocked woman with lieutenant's bars on her shoulder.

"Yes, ma'am. I'm supposed to inventory the equipment in the lab that's due to be shipped out tonight."

"They never tell me anything." Her lips twisted into an irritated scowl. "Which lab?" she finished.

Zwickey let his surprise show. "More than one's gonna ship? I didn't know…"

She waved him silent. "No, no. You're right. The XT lab. End of the hall, turn right. Here, you'll need a badge. And you'll have to sign in." She handed him a snap-on badge and a clipboard with a sign-in sheet affixed to it. Almost as soon as Zwickey started to fill out the sheet, the phone rang. She answered it.

"What! Look, I'm short-handed as it is…all right! Five minutes."

She hung up the phone. "Listen, I have a minor emergency to handle. Just leave the sheet when you're done."

Without waiting to see if he understood, the officer turned away and hurried down the hall in the opposite direction.

Zwickey smiled, turned the sign-in sheet over and slipped the clipboard under his arm. He sauntered off in the direction the receptionist had indicated. When he turned the corner, he spotted two armed marines in battle dress uniforms. He walked directly toward the door they barred. As he approached, one of them glanced at the other and then both stiffened. The first one lifted his weapon from the floor.

"No farther, buddy. No one's allowed beyond this point."

Zwickey shifted his eyes from one to the other. "What the hell do you mean? I'm supposed to inventory the stuff in there."

The marine shook his head. "No one goes in there without the General's permission."

Zwickey took a chance. "Look, the General wanted this stuff shipped by air. How the hell can that happen if we don't know what's supposed to be shipped?"

The marine looked at his partner and then shrugged. "Hey, man, we follow orders and our orders are no one goes in there as long as that thing's inside. You want in, you need the General to approve it personally. You want me to give him a call?"

Zwickey forced a double take. "The creature's in there?" When one of the marines nodded, he added. "Hey, forget it. I'm not going in there. How do I know there's not some fatal disease? As long as it's in there I'm not going in, I don't care who asks."

"Come back tomorrow then. We ship it out tonight, around 0300."

Zwickey nodded. "Thanks, bud. See you around." He started down the hall toward the reception. He walked past the reception area and dropped the clipboard on the desk. On his way back to the latrine, he passed another soldier coming the other way.

"If you're going to take a shit, don't bother," the other man said. "Some asshole's camping out in there. Stinkin' up the place, too."

Zwickey nodded. "Thanks, but I'm just taking out the trash."

Inside the latrine, Zwickey yanked the top off one of the two trashcans. He lifted out the bag inside and dumped the contents back into the empty can. After replacing the lid, he retrieved his ghillie suit and stuffed it into the black plastic bag.

Whistling an old Polish melody, he strolled out of the latrine and walked along the drainage ditch, bending down every now and then to pick up some small piece of trash. In about eighty yards, he arrived at the spot where he had stashed his weapon. He placed the bag beside it, glanced around and then slipped the silenced MP5 into the bag. He reached into his breast pocket, pulled out his earpiece and then scratched behind his ear. In a single deft movement, he inserted the earpiece.

Zwickey switched on the transceiver.

"Two, four."

"Yeah."

"Positive. Until 0300."

"Got it."

Zwickey waited a couple of minutes. "What now?"

"Can you make your way to the flight-line?"

"Sure...and?"

"We need an obstacle at the fast movers."

"The Falcons?"

"Affirmative."

"No sweat," Zwickey replied. He added, "Check out the janitor with the trash-bag."

"I see him. Is he a threat?"

"Negative. He's me."

"Cool one, Zwick. You're good."

18:10 MDT, Shirley Basin, Wyoming

Meisner stepped over and around half a hundred sleeping bodies before he found Ouilette, leaning against a wall next to Sam Weber. Both men glanced upward at his approach.

"I hope it's good news, Andy," Ouilette drawled.

"Yes, sir! She's still on site. They move her at 0200, our time."

Ouilette stood. He waved for Weber and Meisner to follow him. As he marched across the hanger, he pointed at the helicopters.

"Are they ready?"

"Yes, sir. We can load them in twenty minutes."

"Tell me about the weapons."

Meisner quickened his pace.

"Two Hellfires on *Little Paw*, Four on *Black Magic*. We also have air-to-air stingers on the MH-60. And the chain gun. The AH-6 also carries stingers and a minigun."

"A little light, but it'll have to do." Ouilette led all three men to an office where a map covered one wall. He tapped a position on the map representing the refuge in Utah. "Two hundred and sixty miles. How long?"

"Kind of mountainous coming this way," Meisner replied. "That will slow them down. Say fifty minutes, an hour at the outside."

"They launch at 2200. Arrive at 2300. We load and depart in, what, thirty minutes?"

"Can do."

"All right. 2330 out the door. Four hundred miles to Minot."

"Three-seventy to the IP, sir. An hour and twenty minutes. Another twenty to unload and prepare the choppers. Twenty more to get up and over the target."

"0230 local." Ouilette shook his head. "Not good enough, Andy. Something goes wrong, any little delay or Pigott moves up his schedule and we're dead. Worse than that, we expend our best stuff for nothing."

Meisner shrugged. "How can we change it, sir?"

Ouilette looked away from the map. "Call Doctor Wozniak. Tell him we need to launch our Talons at 2045. He needs to cover them on the flight up from Bear River. Take out that satellite."

20:20 MDT, Desert Range Experimental Station, UT

Wozniak adjusted his browser. "I don't like it, Tim. Look at this huge block of memory. Something's in there. Something big and mean. We can't access it without giving ourselves away."

"So what? The satellite tasking code isn't even connected to it. Your task list is exactly as you described it, right down to the code-names."

"I don't like that either. Anybody with a lick of sense would have changed those after my little charade in Leavenworth."

"Maybe they've got too much on their minds. You said they were planning on moving from Minot."

"And maybe this is some sort of trap. Tell you what. Call the operator at the switch in Denver. Keep him on the line. If we get in trouble, he's to pull the plug. I don't want anything tracing us back here."

"Do we have time?"

"Just enough…if you call him now."

In four minutes, Reynolds nodded. "He's ready."

"Here goes nothing." Wozniak tapped out a command string, duplicated it and appended an execute command. He sent it.

"There it goes. The satellite's responding. Five minutes more and we'll be out…oh, shit." Wozniak's hands flew over the keyboard. He re-entered a command and then re-entered it again. He scribed out a repetitive batch macro and appended it to the copied command. "Take that, you pig."

"What's going on?" Reynolds asked.

"That big block of code woke up when the satellite changed course. It countered my command and so I repeated. Then we had a little tug of war. Finally, I sent an imperative and batched it. See this, we've used up all available memory and we keep spawning commands as fast as that clunker can delete them. Okay, the satellite is off course. They can't restore it on this orbit. Let's get the Talons..., Good God! What is this? Look at that thing! What kind of code is that?"

"What do you see?" Reynolds asked.

"Some really weird shit is self-extracting from that memory block. Time to leave Dodge, I think." Wozniak typed the log-off command. As soon as his prompt returned to the WAN in Washington, DC, another stream of cryptic characters broiled onto his screen.

"Get out! It blew right through the network firewall! That stuff is tapping my trace!" Wozniak raced across the keyboard, jumping up two levels, backing out as fast as he could. Each time, the screen filled with garbage.

"It's some kind of worm. Tell Denver to pull the plug. Now!"

Reynolds spoke urgently into the phone. With alarm in his face, he said, "The guy says he did, but the system won't go down. The battery backup took over and he doesn't know how to shut it off."

Wozniak never glanced away from his screen. "Tell him to take an ax to it if he has to. Tell him he has less than ten seconds before his worst nightmare comes true. Tell him anything but get that damn thing switched off-line." A few seconds passed.

"Yes!" Wozniak shouted. "He did it! Wow, that was close."

Reynolds swallowed. "The operator said he had to shoot it."

"He what?"

"He used his sidearm to shoot out the power supply."

Wozniak studied the window several screens back showing the foreign code lines. "Good thing. I don't think anything human wrote that stuff."

He swiveled his chair around. "Now, back to the main event. Call up the Talons and tell them it's safe to launch.

Baylor flexed his shoulders, trying to shake echoes of the adrenaline rush after the thrilling blast across the mountains of Wyoming, the southeastern prairies of Montana and the charge across the Little Missouri National Grasslands.

The steady, forgiving feel of the Hercules was growing on him. A few hundred meters behind and slightly to the right of the lead craft, his MC-130 had bored through the sky only a couple of hundred feet above the earth for more than three hundred miles. Their path took them away from the cities, the towns and villages below. Meisner had penned a route that avoided all major highways and population centers for the last eighty miles of the flight.

A hurtling black bulk outlined in the moonlight ahead, the lead Talon casually dipped a wing to the left and slid northwards. Maintaining radio silence, Baylor followed Simmons around. The two heavy aircraft zipped across the seven-mile stretch of Highway 85 between Watford City and Arnegard. Only thirty meters above the waving fields of wheat, both aircraft flashed over the broad silver expanse of the Missouri, nearly three miles wide at this point because of Garrison Dam below Lake Sakakawea.

Thirty seconds later, Baylor followed *Bright Hawk Lead* into a steep turn to the east. Simmons flashed his clearance lights twice. Thirty-five miles and six minutes to go. At the five-minute mark, Baylor turned to Jennisette. "Let them know."

The copilot flicked a switch near his console.

In the cargo bay, a green light blinked out. The red night-lights illuminated. Loadmaster Yates shouted, "Five minutes! Five minutes!"

Army Captain Mitch Barth stood and bellowed, "Left Claw! Stow your gear. After we land, exit the aircraft on the double. Do it in the bushes if you need to but don't wander away." He patted the nose of the AH-6. "As soon as we offload this bird, I want everyone's butt back on board."

Both MC-130s zoomed across Highway 8 four miles south of Belden. Mile after mile of waving grain sped past scarcely fifty feet under the bellies of the ponderous craft. The dark line of an empty road swept by, followed a dozen seconds later by another. Off his right wingtip, a glow of lights from a small town cast an orange hue into the gloom.

Simmons flashed his lights again, three repetitions this time. Baylor pulled his throttles back, stepped through the checklist with Jennisette and dropped both gear and flaps. The Hercules lost its smooth and steady ride as turbulence from the appendages buffeted the aircraft. The lead Hercules dwindled in the distance and then disappeared in the darkness.

Baylor let his speed drop to a hundred and forty knots before adding more power. Three or four minutes later a long dark strip bearing to the east appeared. He centered his aircraft above the road and let the Hercules sink until it floated about five meters above the gravel surface. About a thousand meters ahead, a red highway flare gleamed in the darkness. He nodded to Jennisette who gripped the pitch controls. Baylor dialed back the power.

"Touchdown," he muttered. The main gear of the aircraft slapped down directly on top of the flare. It shattered, spreading sputtering sparks along the gravel surface. He dialed on the power after Jennisette reversed pitch. A light touch of the brakes slowed the Hercules to thirty knots.

Baylor continued to taxi along the road until the bulk of the lead craft loomed in the night. He braked to a halt and shut down his inboard engines. Jennisette fired up the APU, the auxiliary power unit, and then killed the remaining engines. Baylor glanced at his copilot. "Time for a little pow-wow. Can you manage?" When Jennisette nodded, Baylor ducked into the cargo bay. Two dozen troopers heaved the AH-6 down the ramp. They dragged it clear and began to unfold the rotors. Baylor found his way to Captain Barth.

"You set?" he asked.

"Yep. Want to run through it one more time?" Barth asked.

"Just the first part. Zero-time starts when I hit the fence. I'll switch the light to green at that moment."

"Got it!" the ranger replied. "My teams jump at the intervals we've designated."

"If you run into trouble at extraction," Baylor cautioned, "and can't contact Black Magic, shout at us on tac-four. We'll work something out."

The burley captain gave him a thumb's-up, checked his watch and strode to the Talon's ramp.

"Mount up!" he bellowed.

Baylor could hear the whine of turbines as the MH-60 cranked up its engines. Jossman folded herself into *Little Paw's* cockpit and moments later, the AH-6's rotor started to spin.

The *Left Claw* teams scurried aboard, forming two rows of twenty-four on either side of the cargo bay. Yates reached over his head and flipped a switch. The ramp began to lift. Moments later, the light helicopter surged into the air.

Baylor glanced at the luminous dial of his watch. 0040. Time to crank up again. He climbed into the cockpit and buckled in. He turned to the two technicians manning the Q-70 package.

"You guys on-line?"

"Yes, sir. *Black Magic* and *Little Paw* are five by five. They're on the way," one of the controllers replied.

Up ahead, the lead Talon powered up its inboard engines and slowly taxied forward. Baylor cranked number one. It wound up smoothly and he continued the sequence until all engines idled. He glanced at his watch again. Four minutes. He toggled his crew-control net to life.

"Controllers, what have you got?"

"Lot's of search pulse Doppler from Minot. Nothing else. The choppers are really low. We're losing them in the clutter already."

The lead aircraft disappeared in the gloom ahead. Baylor knew that Simmons would taxi forward until the second Talon had plenty of room to take off from behind. He glanced at his watch again. One minute.

In the road ahead, a crewman switched on two flashlights and waved them in circles over his head. Baylor nodded to Jennisette and advanced the throttles. In seconds, all four engines wound up to full military power. The Hercules surged and swayed like some beast with an urgent desire to lunge. The two flashlights steadied, pointing vertically. The crewmen walked to the edge of the road and off to the side until he was clear of the wing. Baylor watched the clock tick down to zero. At that precise moment, both flashlights snapped forward, pointing down the road. Jennisette adjusted the pitch, changing the snarl of the props into a roar of thrust. The Hercules surged forward.

"It's no cat shot," Baylor murmured. He let the speed build and, at the proper moment, eased the wheel back. The nose lifted. Three seconds later, the MC-130's main gear left the roadway. Baylor banked to the left and leveled the aircraft at the same moment. His altitude was eighty feet so he let the Hercules sink a little while he raised the gear and flaps. Airspeed continued to build. They crossed Highway 52 at three hundred knots and sixty feet of altitude.

01:05 CDT, 18 May, Minot AFB, ND

Pigott leaned back in his chair.

"I don't like the satellite problem, Phil. I know it's quiet, but somebody was in that system before we lost it. I think it was Wozniak and I think he needed to eliminate this pass."

Rotts shrugged. "What do you want me to do, sir? We have the alert crews standing by. We can lift in three or four minutes, max."

"Send two of the choppers up now. Launch a Falcon, too. Rotate air cover until we fly out. Were you able to move up the schedule?"

Rotts raised his index finger after he dialed a number on his cell phone.

"*Banjo team, Pinnacle,* launch one of your fighters and put two Apaches on a racetrack pattern over the base. No, we've no contact. This is precautionary."

Rotts hung up and nodded. "Yes, sir. Our C-17 departs in forty-five minutes. In fact, you should gather what you want to bring and make your way to the transportation center, sir."

"In a few minutes."

01:07 CDT, Alert pad #2, Minot AFB, ND

Army Ranger John Nesbitt steadied the crosshairs of his sight on the Apache. A heat signature continued to build as the rotor spun faster and faster. He had a solid lock and his missile was ready to go.

"What do you think? Do we let him lift?" he asked his partner, Tom Shaughnessy.

Shaughnessy nodded. "What else? Show's not started yet."

01:10 CDT, MC-130 Talon #247

"Search radar is vectoring! They're swinging our way. They're ranging and have gone to acquisition mode. They see us, sir!"

Baylor nodded to Jennisette. "Let *Alpha* know."

Rotts burst back into the room he had just left.

"Red Alert! Inbound bogey right on the deck! Five miles out!"

Pigott stood. "I knew it! Launch every—"

A double explosion shook the building, shattering the glass in the hallways. The lights went out. A siren that had started to build in volume fell silent. Two more explosions sounded in the distance. A flare of orange and yellow light leapt skyward near the alert pad. Pigott and Rotts ran out into the hallway, gingerly picking their way through the broken glass.

"I called in the two that got away. Take out the remaining chopper and we'll go help Zwick. He's got his hands full."

"Right," said Nesbitt, punching the button. His second missile streaked away, reached across the concrete and plowed into the remaining helicopter. With an ear-splitting crack, the warhead detonated. Flaming fuel and munitions soared skyward. The two commandos scurried backward, unaware of the danger from above.

"*Banjo leader*, I got them! A missile team. Targeting."

The trailing Apache skidded around and dove.

"Radar's down!" one of the controller's yelled. Baylor pulled back hard on the wheel. The Talon streaked upward. He leveled at five hundred and thirty feet and then adjusted his altitude downward just a little. The fence flashed by under him eight seconds later. He flipped the light in the cargo bay and said to Jennisette. "Drop the ramp." He turned the big aircraft onto its new heading and eased the throttles to slow the airspeed to two hundred and forty knots.

Air Force Captain Richard Lenkiss kept his nose against the concrete. His flight-leader, Major Ross Fulbright lay less than ten feet away, a bullet through his neck. Somewhere, out in the darkness, a sniper pinned him like a captured butterfly. The two F-16 Falcons might as well be a hundred miles away.

"Eleven! Twelve! Thirteen...*Beta*! Go!" Barth shouted above the roar of the slipstream. A dozen commandos, six from either side of the aircraft leapt into space, their ripcords fastened to an overhead wire.
"Sixteen, Seventeen, Eighteen...*Gamma*! Go!"

"*Black Magic, Bright Hawk*, I have two bogies. One is vectoring on us. Bust him, pronto!"
"Roger, *Bright Hawk*," Meisner replied. "*Little Paw*, cover the Herk. We need to drop our team before we join the dance."
Jossman's voice, pitched even higher than normal, responded, "On him, *Magic*. Firing..." In the distance, Meisner could see a streak of red light up the sky from the AH-6's minigun.

"Break! Break! Break!" The stream of tracers passed so close to the Apache, neither crewman could understand how they were unharmed. The pilot swung the AH-64 in a tight circle, looking for his attacker. They forgot about the Hercules for the moment.

Clods of dirt exploded around Nesbitt. He heard Shaughnessy cry out and then something massive struck him from behind. He was smashed to the ground and everything went dark.

"Dead missile team! *Pinnacle* says we have an enemy chopper landing near the labs. Top priority." The gunner of the AH-64 switched from his 30mm chain gun to missiles.

"What kind of helicopter?" he asked.

"Nighthawk! That's what they said, anyway," the pilot replied.

"No shit! Do me a favor. See them first."

"Twenty-eight, twenty-nine ... *Omega*! Go!" Barth leapt with the last team. Yates dragged all the tethers aboard and secured them. He picked up the intercom and yelled over the slipstream, "All teams are away!" He flipped the switch to close the hatch. A violent turn by the Hercules threw him against the fuselage where he clutched the cargo nets for support. He heard the flare canisters fire from either side, three times each.

"Missile! Missile! Jennisette yelled. "Two o'clock, low!"

"Heat seeker! No emissions!" One of the controllers shouted.

Baylor jerked the wheel around and stomped on the rudder, turning into the missile. He fired three flares. When the missile veered to correct, he swung the other way and lifted his right wing. The missile streaked by underneath and exploded behind them.

Jennisette's pale face turned toward him. Baylor grinned and flicked his eyebrows. Jennisette swallowed. "You played chicken with it?"

"Doing the common job. Too bad I can't shoot back. You can bet there's one shooter down there sweating bullets."

"What do you mean, down there? I'm sweating bullets."

Baylor chuckled. "First rule of the game is to shoot first."

"So?"

"So, the second is don't miss. If you miss, you might as well let the other guy shoot first."

"*Banjo One*, get your butt up here and peel this asshole off me!" The AH-64 dove and turned to the left, narrowly avoiding yet another burst from the unseen but persistent threat from behind.

"*Banjo leader*, this is one. I have a priority call from *Pinnacle* for support at the lab. You'll have to stick it out alone, Captain. Sorry."

Zwickey edged to the left. The Bradley had blocked his line of fire momentarily and now the F-16 pilot was climbing to his feet. Zwickey touched off a three-round burst, his MP5 silently coughing as it bucked against his shoulder. He folded the stock and rolled rapidly to his left. The Bradley must have seen his muzzle flash as its turret swung in his direction. Just as he dropped into the drainage ditch, the pilot tumbled, clutching his calf as he fell. A brilliant stream of cannon fire tore into the field on his right.

As soon as both *Right Claw* teams hit the ground, Meisner lifted the collective and spun the MH-60 over the labs. A voice crackled in his earphones.

"*Black Magic*, break left! Break left! Bogie at your eight!"

Meisner reversed his direction and triggered his cannon even as he started swinging.

The stream of 25mm tracers startled the gunner. He was expecting an easy kill as the Blackhawk turned away. Suddenly it reversed and swung around firing even as it lined up. He launched his missile prematurely and it streaked under his target, exploding harmlessly behind it.

When the C7 charge ripped a hole in the wall, Weber tumbled through, rolled to his feet and spun. The room was clear. He tossed a flash/bang through a far doorway and yelled, "Go!" Two more team members launched themselves through the same door. Four commandos followed Weber into the next room. He pointed at the two exits at either end of the hallway. Two commandos crouched along the walls to cover them. The rest of the six-man team slipped forward with Weber past the receptionist's station. As they approached the next intersection, a tee-shaped junction where a cross-corridor intersected with their own, Weber heard running feet coming from the left. He waved his team into two pairs. They crouched against the walls.

A squad of marines burst into the opening, trotting toward the right. Several glanced in their direction but only a noncom reacted. He whirled, bringing his weapon to bear. The MP5s of the pair of commandos on the left chuffed and the marine dropped with a clatter. Someone around the corner yelled, "Ambush!" The corridor echoed with the thunder of un-silenced automatic weapons. The marines' fire, unready and surprised, was wild and erratic. The commandos picked their shots and escaped back to the receptionist's area unscathed.

Weber silently hand-signaled the two commandos at the exits to join him as he ran out of one end of the building. He slipped the sling of his MP5 over his neck and leapt up to grab the eaves. He swung his body upward and then helped the other two commandos up. All three trotted across the roof and dropped to the ground on the far side. One of the two reached into her pack and passed strips of plastic explosive. Working quickly and quietly, Weber formed another circle on the wall. He stepped back and whispered into his mike.

In the hall below, the remaining four commandos unscrewed their silencers. Two of the commandos tossed flash/bang grenades up into the juncture as the other two cut loose a volley with the un-silenced MP5s. They drew immediate but ineffective counter-fire.

Weber selected three-shot bursts on his MP5. He detonated the explosives, blowing another hole in the wall during the exchange of gunfire. He rolled through the opening, coming to his feet as two marines turned from the double doors at the end of the lab. His MP5 bucked twice and both men dropped, one loosing a stream of fire into the ceiling from his M4.

Two more commandos jumped into the room behind him and took up positions at either wall. Someone shouted from the far side of the door and started to push it open. Weber tossed a second flash/bang through the opening. The door slammed shut as a voice yelled. "Grenade!"

Zwickey muttered into his microphone, "This is *Alpha-four*. I'd like a little assistance with the tin can on the taxiway. They're not playing fair."

Jossman broke away from the Apache. The AH-64 was extending anyway and she was loath to use one of her two Hellfires on a low percentage shot. She spun the AH-6 toward the alert pad.

"Hey, Twicky! Where you at?" she called.

"Dollface! I hear a turbine. Are you airborne?" the commando replied.

"Youbetcha!" She spotted the Bradley sweeping the field with its chain-gun. "The track by the fast movers? That's the bad boy?"

"He's the one."

Jossman zeroed her sights. "Fox one!" One of her Hellfires streaked away, flashed down to the APC and blew it to fragments. She drove the AH-6 over the flaming wreckage and banked away.

Zwickey peered over the edge of his battered refuge as the chopper roared overhead and disappeared. "Baby, I love ya," he muttered into his mike.

Ouilette pointed toward the labs in the distance. "KR, I want two long rifles for cover. Set up out here and direct the team this way as they withdraw."

"They're overdue, sir."

"Minor problems, so far. Weber's inside but he had to take a detour." He pivoted around. "I'm taking two of your team forward to the extraction zone. We'll dust it and then pass the word."

Two hundred yards inside the main gate, four commandos strung wire backward from the roadway. They ducked behind the berm as their team leader twisted his detonator. A subdued concussion shook the air and the ground slapped their bellies. The explosives ripped a ten-foot wide chasm in the narrow bridge across the drainage ditch. Floodlights pivoted toward them from the guard station ahead, but the commando team had already retreated into the darkness.

A dull thud, followed by another and then a third, preceded a long string of explosions across a line of fuel bladders. A half-dozen fuel trucks joined in the fireworks and two large storage tanks blew up, lighting up the night sky for miles around.

Baylor banked the Hercules away from the sudden glare.

Jennisette turned toward his pilot. "Wow! That ought to wake them up. I wonder where their fighters are, not that I miss them?"

"Let's hope we don't find out," Baylor replied.

One of the controllers called, "*Black Magic*, you have two bogies inbound. One at nine o'clock and the other at seven. Suggest a turn to port and engage former."

Rotts returned to Pigott who had changed into his flight-suit.

Pigott looked up as he zipped the suit closed. "Where are the Falcons, Colonel? And where is the detail I sent after the XT?"

"Our pilots are down, sir. One dead, the other wounded. The birds are still on the ground. Evidently, they had infiltrators on base before the fun started. We lost two choppers and both pilots in the first minute."

"And the XT?"

"Unknown, sir. There's a heavy volume of automatic weapons fire coming from the lab. I've sent in mounted relief and one of the heavy tracks."

Pigott clenched his jaw. "Send the second toward the fighters. And find some more pilots. I'll take one of the Falcons up if I have to."

"We have two more qualified F-16 drivers, sir. But we can't move transportation in to pick them up. The enemy has two fire teams blocking the roadway across the base. Also, General, they cut the bridge to the outside."

Pigott nodded. "Take me to the second track."

Meisner listened to the soft beep of the seeker head on his air-to-air stinger. The tone steadied and he fired. The Apache fired simultaneously.

"Missile!" Walker shouted.

"I see it!" Meisner replied. He hauled the collective upwards and yanked the stick to the left. The missile arced around but not far enough. A thump sounded aft and a flash of light loomed ahead.

"Got him!" Walker yelled.

"Scratch one bandit," Meisner replied. He kept the turn constant, swinging toward the second Apache.

"Designating target two," Walker called out, using his FLIR to acquire the other helicopter. He never saw the sudden flash from below and behind.

"*Black Magic*, break left! Break left! Missile launch!" the controller screamed. Baylor banked the Hercules toward the encounter. He was almost ten miles to the north, out of imminent danger and at a range where the Talon's Q-70 system could help without endangering the platform.

"Missile, five o'clock low!" shouted the door gunner. Meisner started his turn, but ran out of time. A tremendous crash sounded immediately behind and above. Panel lights illuminated across the board. A ragged screech issued from the right side of the helicopter.

"Fire in number two!" Walker yelled, flipping switches.

Meisner gritted his teeth. He turned power in the port engine all the way to the stops. "Get it under control, Mike."

A stream of shells stitched across the sky from the AH-64. They found the Blackhawk. Amid the clang and thump of impacts, Meisner saw a red fountain erupt from his copilot's chest. Walker slumped forward. A shower of sparks erupted from the panel overhead. The stick wobbled in his hand. The Blackhawk was loosing altitude. Meisner tried to block out the screams from the wounded gunner behind him.

"*Little Paw*, *Bright Hawk*! *Magic's* in trouble. Can you assist?"

Jossman listened to her radio as she spun her craft away from a truck full of reinforcements that she had left burning near one end of the lab. As she pulled up, an ominous shape thrust the wreckage aside. It turned the corner and swung its massive turret around. "Oh, shit!" she muttered.

She keyed her mike. "On the way, *Magic*. Where are you? *Black Magic*, are you up?" she repeated. In another second, she spotted the MH-60 descending, a banking Apache above and behind it. The AH-64 was lining up for a kill shot.

Weber ripped away the Velcro straps. Linneow tried to move away from the canted table but her legs failed. Weber slipped in close as her left arm snaked around his neck.

"Are you injured?" he asked.

"Not injured, my brother. Oo'ahan puppet Pigott injects Linneow with heavy metals."

Foreboding nipped at Weber's spine. "Sayla, darlin, you told me that makes your people insane."

She inclined her head. "Linneow sacrifices to save her mind. My legs are immobile, my brother."

Weber slung his weapon and muttered, "If I see that snake-eyed...unnhhh!" He grunted as he swept the Chao into his arms. He staggered to the ragged opening in the back wall of the lab before he placed her on her feet and helped her lean against the wall.

"You're definitely an armful, sweetheart. Saunders!" he shouted, "Give me a hand." One of the two commandos lifted Linneow's other arm and shared half her weight. Together, they eased her through the opening and trotted along the wall outside of the laboratory.

"Fall back!" Barth shouted. He led both *Omega* and *Gamma* teams after the fuel dump exploded. His combined units had been whittled away by the constant fighting-withdrawal in the face of superior forces. Two Bradley's, recently arriving made further resistance futile. The commando team retreated toward the escape zone.

As Barth dropped back through his *Delta* team, he counted his casualties. Seven dead, five wounded. Three of the wounded still fought. The wounded and dead, they carried. "You've tracks inbound, Monty," he yelled over the rattle of small-arms fire.

"We'll slow them down, sir, but you need to shake a leg."

Jossman swore as a streak of fire lanced away from the Apache before she could close the range. It ripped across the intervening distance and struck the staggering, smoking Blackhawk. The MH-60 piled into the ground, tumbled and erupted into a ball of flame.

"YOU BASTARD!" she screamed, holding down the fire button. The mini-guns roared with her anger and fell silent, out of ammunition.

"Holy shit!"

"What the hell!"

The pilot and gunner yelled together as the former banked the Apache to the left. A hail of bullets chewed at his craft, starring the armored screens, buckling the ceramic plates around the cockpit. The right engine changed in pitch, turning ragged.

"Losing oil pressure in number two," The gunner called out. "It's that damned Loach again."

"Where? Where is it?" The pilot's head swiveled to the right and above.

On the right! Coming forward! Look out!" The Apache pilot had been turning left and then banked right to meet his attacker when the AH-6 flashed out of the night, and passed directly in front of him, up on its rotor tips. The gunner jammed the trigger down but the nimble helicopter had already passed. 30mm cannon shells arced out into the night.

Two dark shapes rushed toward him.

"Peters!" Weber called. The lone unencumbered commando swung around from her trailing position to assume a front guard. The mike buzzed in his ear.

"This is three. We had to withdraw."

Weber waved the rest of his team in.

"What's cooking," he asked.

"We've got an Abrams working the far side. Time to scoot."

Over the sporadic fire around the base, Weber could hear the heavy rumble of tracks as the main battle tank edged down the far side of the building. He peered out into the field.

"That's the wrong direction." He changed frequencies.

Jossman pulled the stick all the way back and then banged it hard to the right. With the throttle twisted to the stops and the six hundred horsepower turbine screaming in protest, she yanked the collective up and then drove it down. The little helicopter executed the equivalent to a hammerhead stall and dropped down behind the jinking Apache.

"Take him!" Wilbur Montgomery patted his dragon shooter on the shoulder. The missile launched, streaked over the intervening runway and smashed into the Bradley. The APC exploded, its hull ripped open and the turret blown upward. The other fighting vehicle spun to the left and accelerated. The second and last Dragon missile ripped from its launcher and struck the APC low and forward. A track blew off and the Bradley slewed around, smoking. Its crew and mounted infantry bailed out and took cover.

"Fall back!" Montgomery bellowed again. He turned on his transceiver.

Baylor banked the Hercules around in a tight circle, turning back toward the base. In the distance, the bright glow of flame from the fuel dump illuminated a pall of dense smoke that rose several thousand feet.

"Are you sure?" he asked the controller. The technician nodded, his features numb. Baylor switched frequencies. "*Bright Hawk leader*, *Hawk One*. We need you, buddy. *Magic* is down."

"*Lead* copies. Cranking."

One of the controllers called out, "I have *Left Claw* calling for extraction. That's us, right?"

"Was," Baylor replied. "Tell him to sit tight or stay loose, whatever works for him. We'll figure it out."

Jossman tuned up her second stinger. The Apache had ducked the first one, but could not shake the little chopper. "I should've finished you the first time, you son of a bitch!" She bored in, closing the distance. She gripped the stick with light, practiced ease and let her instincts guide her motions, second-guessing the enemy pilot, cutting his turns and closing.

The Apache zigged to the left but not very far. Jossman flicked her stick right and pressed the firing button. The AH-64, hoping to feint away from the AH-6, reversed and swung directly into the Stinger's path. The little missile arrowed into the right exhaust and detonated.

The warhead was not very large, but it severed the main-shaft of the turbine, which spun away at twenty thousand rpm, smashing into the transmission and turning that vital assembly to junk. The rotors snapped off and the Apache cratered.

Zwickey gazed up from the wreckage Jossman had delivered less than a hundred meters away. When the AH-6 buzzed by overhead, he glanced again at the flaming debris from the attack helicopter and muttered, "Shouldn't have pissed her off. I could've told you that."

Ouilette pressed his receiver. "This is *Right Claw Lead*."

"We have her Marcus. Can you send *Magic* over to the backside of the lab for a pickup?" Weber asked.

"Sorry, my friend. Andy's bought the farm."

A few seconds of silence passed. "That's a pot of bad news, Marcus. We're down two, and need help with an Abrams."

Ouilette grimaced. "You never give me easy ones, Sam. I'll see what I can do." Ouilette changed frequencies.

Baylor also changed frequencies.

"Captain Barth, can you hear me?"

"Yeah! Who's this?"

"*Bright Hawk*. Are you in the specified position?"

"Not any more. We can't sit still and stay alive. What's on your mind?"

"Turn due north. About a thousand meters away, you'll find another abandoned parking apron. *Bright Hawk Lead* is on the way in. You've six minutes. He can't wait."

"Bless you, my son. I used to be a pastor, you know that?"

"No, I didn't. Lean on your good will with the Man upstairs. Things are turning rotten all around."

"*Little Paw*, this is *Right Claw Lead*."

"*Little Paw*, sir. I'm here."

"What's your status?"

"Mini-guns are dry. One Hellfire and one Stinger remaining. Less than twenty minutes of fuel. Can I go home now?"

Ouilette laughed. "Sure, just a little favor before you leave."

"What have you got?"

"Our extraction team has the package but they're cut off."

"Sir, how many?"

"Four plus the package."

"I can lift them, director. I'm light on fuel and ammo."

"Do what you can." Ouilette broke the connection.

Linneow whispered into Weber's ear. "Are we losing this struggle?"

"Not while we have you, we're not."

With Linneow slung between them, Weber and another commando raced across the field. Two more followed behind, scanning the back-trail for signs of pursuit. They found a low depression and tumbled to the earth just as the hulking shape of the Abrams turned the corner. Its turret swiveled toward them. It lurched to a stop and the main gun fired with an ear-splitting crack.

The shell shrieked overhead and exploded a thousand yards beyond them.

One of the commandos raised his head and asked with a grin, "Was that a warning shot?"

Weber grinned back. "Why don't you ask him?"

"Twelve o'clock! Above the track!" another commando called out.

The AH-6 dove at a steep angle. One of the supporting infantry must have warned the tank's crew because suddenly it lurched into motion. Its turbine shrieking, it accelerated out into the field.

"You can run, but you can't hide," Jossman whispered as she pressed the firing button. The Hellfire arrowed earthward, struck the turret directly on its flat upper surface. With a bright, white-hot glow, a clang like a dinner bell rang across the field. Sparks flew upward and the tank skidded to a stop. A muffled explosion echoed from within its hull, followed by a second. The AH-6 pulled out of its dive, skimming directly over the commandos and the Chao. Jossman pulled the helicopter up and spun it around. She zoomed back toward them as she clicked on the mike of her loudspeaker. The AH-6 settled into the sand about thirty meters distant.

"Come to mama," she said.

Ouilette watched the MC-130 accelerate across the apron over half a mile away. Its nose pitched up and the Talon lifted into the night. He could barely make out its form as it banked to the north and disappeared. He eased his breath. *Left Claw*, what was left of them, had escaped.

Baylor craned his neck toward the controllers.

"They're away clean? No pursuit?"

"No, sir. Nothing in the air but us and *Little Paw*."

"Tell the director that we'll put down on the taxiway and roll right up to him."

"You little bitch!" Jossman shouted, thumping her fist against the dash, "You lied to me!" The turbine stuttered again and then quit. She had just enough time to execute a partial hover before the helicopter pitched into the sand, snapping off two blades. The unbalanced remainder threatened to overturn the craft but had not the velocity. She clicked her mike.

"*Little Paw* is down. I'm two clicks south of *Right Claw Lead* and out of gas." She turned to the trio in the back compartment. "End of the line, folks. Sam, will you help me with the funeral?"

The commandos climbed out while Jossman and Weber prepared two charges of C7 inside the airframe. Jossman unloaded the remaining Stinger from its launcher and then waved in the direction the helicopter was pointed.

"That-away, about a mile."

Weber and a commando named Pryke carried Linneow between them. They had managed about three hundred paces when the charges in the chopper detonated. There was no flame, only two thumps in the darkness.

"HEAT!"

"Up!

"Traverse left! Steady. Steady. Target!"

"Identified!"

"Fire."

"On the way!"

The tank's main gun recoiled. The shell arced across the three-thousand-yard interval in two seconds. It passed in front of the MC-130's nose by less than ten meters and exploded two hundred yards away and forward of their direction of travel.

"Yo! What the hell was that!" Baylor shouted. The Talon had just touched down. Ouilette's voice, edged with tension suddenly crackled in his ears.

"*Bright Hawk*! You're under fire by an Abrams!"

Baylor needed no further warning. He shoved the throttles to the stops.

"Fire!"

"On the way!" The next shell struck behind the Talon.

"What the heck, Lieutenant? That should have been a direct hit."

"He's accelerating again. The enemy units are still on the ground. Let's get at them."

"How much longer?" Pigott asked the crew chief. He stood at the nose of one of the Falcons, watching the weapons crew off-load the air to ground rockets and the cluster munitions. Two other crews worked on the main gear.

"We'll have you loaded for air to air in about twelve minutes, sir. The tires will take a little longer. We have to plug them because there are no spares on the base. Not exactly by the book, General. Maybe twenty-five minutes in all."

"Did you find me a wingman yet?" Pigott asked, turning to Rotts.

"Yes, sir. Major Wellsley. He's suiting up and we'll drive him up from briefing in about ten minutes."

"It's looking grim, Marcus. The long rifles have isolated the track. But, there's damn little we can do to slow it down."

Weber wiped the back of his hand along the right side of his jaw.

Jossman trotted up. "Sir, she…the…, What' s her name, again?"

"Linneow," Weber replied.

"Yeah! She wants to talk to Baylor."

Ouilette shrugged and passed his radio to the commando. He glanced at Weber. "We need to pick up and move again, Sam. They'll be getting our bearings if we sit still too long."

Weber nodded. He turned away, but not before Ouilette noticed just how dog-tired the agent appeared.

"Is Pilot Ed listening? It is Linneow who calls."

Baylor's heart lurched. It seemed like a century had passed since he'd heard that throaty whisper.

"I'm here! I'll find a way down, I promise."

"Pilot Ed, you have a powerful transmitter in your craft?"

Baylor glanced over toward the controllers. "What can we crank out, guys?"

They both shrugged. One answered, "Depends on the freq, sir. Up to forty-thousand watts on some bands."

Baylor depressed his mike. "Forty kilowatts, Linneow."

"Tune your carrier to eighty-seven hundred million cycles per second, frequency modulated. You will do this, Pilot Ed?"

Baylor had patched her voice into the aircraft intercom. One of the controllers tapped out a sequence on the keyboard. He turned toward Baylor and nodded.

"All set, Linneow. What do you want me to transmit?"

"Connect me to the transmitter, please."

With two more strokes, the controller nodded again.

"You're patched in."

"Do not interrupt, Pilot Ed. This is very important. You agree?"

"Go to it," he replied.

"Thank you." She paused for a moment. "*Delanka-ami. Codetts-ka. Te Setti corsonui amatesh. Te kaasch onta codetts.*"

Again she paused.

After a few seconds, she continued, "*Delanka-ami. Codetts-ka. Te Gassinae onta codetts. Staa!*"

"You may turn off the transmitter now. You must withdraw from this airspace."

"I can't, Linneow. My friends are in danger—"

"They are not. I offer my neck. Will you believe?"

Baylor grinned as he banked the aircraft away from the base. He keyed his transmitter again. "An offer I can't refuse."

"Sir! The Herk turned away. It's headed north."

Ouilette clenched his jaw. As much as he hated to see the last link to freedom vanish, Baylor had made the logical decision. Unless his people could defeat that damned tank, any extraction was not in the cards.

"All up, sir. Weapons checked green." The avionics technician descended from the cockpit.

Pigott turned to Wellsley. "We hunt down and destroy the C-130 first. Then we'll mop up the units still on the ground. "You got that, Major?" Pigott's last words carried a hard edge.

The other officer had his head twisted to the left, one ear cocked. He glanced at Pigott. "What's that sound?"

"Left! Left! Target! Far hill."

"Identified!"

A sharp crack upon the exterior of the terrain viewer startled the tank commander. "Damnation! Right in the bloody periscope! Somebody out there is one hell of a shot."

"Don't I know it! The radio doesn't work anymore. Neither does my IR search-light."

"Be glad they're not driving a tank. Switch to AP."

"Anti-Personnel, up!"

"Wait a minute! The aircraft is coming back. Unload."

"Unloaded."

"HEAT!"

"Up!"

"Wow! That thing's no Herk! It's engaging the Bradleys and ripping them to shreds!"

"Target!"

"Identified!"

"Fire!"

"On the way!"

The Abrams rocked to the recoil. "Go! Go! Go!" With a scream of its turbine, the M1A2 rocketed out of the shallow ditch and dove behind a hill.

"Hit or miss?"

"Miss, I think. It was swinging around. Crap! There goes another Bradley."

"HEAT!"

"Up!"

"Fire!"

"On the way! Direct hit! No effect! Impossible!"

"No! No! The pill blew up on the way in!"

"Left! Left! Traverse hard!"

As if from a massive hammer, a heavy metallic clang reverberated throughout the Abram's hull. "Damn! That was an anti-tank round! The thing's a flying tank! Switch to silver bullets."

"Sabot!"

"Up!"

Linneow turned to Weber.

"What type of vehicle is that, my brother?"

"An Abrams main battle tank, Sayla. Made in America."

"To survive a strike from the mass-driver, this American tank is a strong weapon. See, now, how the Sikt adapts. It recognizes the principal threat and ignores the others. It fights the tank first, I think."

"Where! I lost it!"

"Traverse right, Zeb!"

"I got it! Target!"

"Identified!"

"Shoot!"

"On the way!"

"Clean miss!"

"Sabot!"

The gunner never gained the time to reload the M1's cannon. The Sikt swung broadside of the Abrams and opened fire from three hundred yards. All four mass drivers ripple-fired into the hapless vehicle, blowing the treads into flying chunks, the skirt into flashes of bright, liquid steel. The main gun was sheared away twelve inches in front of the carapace. A half dozen bright sparks flew from the turret before it was penetrated, the hatch blowing upward.

The Sikt swung sideways and hovered behind the dead tank. It drilled a dozen more rounds into the back deck. Ammunition and fuel detonated, lifting the turret fifty yards into the air. It fell with a crash onto the hull of the tank and bounced into the sand along side.

The extra-terrestrial fighter circled the smoldering tank twice more, without firing. It hovered for ten seconds and then leapt back toward the hill where the commandos had gathered.

Ouilette pointed toward the apron from which *Left Claw* had departed.

"Let's go, people. Call Baylor and bring him in. I want out of here before they recover."

Pigott climbed back down the ladder from his fighter. He watched the Sikt hover over the far apron, a looming hulk slightly darker than the moonlit landscape. Wellsley also climbed down and walked over to him.

"Sir?"

"We wait."

Baylor touched down again and taxied at full speed toward the alert pad. He gaped at the broken and flaming vehicles scattered around the landscape.

"It looks like a tank battle took place out here." When the C-130 turned onto the apron, he nodded. The Sikt. No wonder Linneow wanted him well clear. The craft was using the AI to maneuver and it might not reliably distinguish friend from foe.

He reversed the pitch on number one and revved number four to help turn the Hercules on its own length. Jennisette lowered the ramp and Baylor shut down the inboard engines. He unbuckled and jumped from his seat.

"Mind the fort, would you?" At Jennisette's nod, he dashed out into the cargo bay. A lithe shape in black swept toward him."

"Adele! Thank God!" Baylor wrapped his arms around her waist, lifted her and spun her once. He set her on her feet and breathed, "I'm glad you're still in one piece."

"Did you see it? That incredible aircraft? What am I saying? Of course you did! You brought it here! My God! The power..." Adele spoke so swiftly the words were jammed end to end, like an adolescent splattering out what she wanted to say before someone interrupted.

"C'mon!" Baylor grabbed her hand. "I want you to meet her."

The two of them slipped through the press of troops tramping up the ramp into the interior of the Hercules. A hundred paces away, the Sikt stood silent above a circle of steaming pavement.

"Over here, Ace!"

Baylor turned toward the sound of Weber's voice. Weber and Ouilette stood with the Chao supported between them. Baylor led Adele up to the two men. The Chao spoke first.

"Linneow finds joy to see Pilot Ed, again. Will you carry me to the Sikt?"

Ouilette motioned Baylor forward. "You and Weber help with her craft. I need to get the rest of the group squared away."

When Baylor replaced Ouilette under Linneow's left arm, the director trotted toward the Hercules. Baylor turned to the Chao. "What now, Linneow?"

"Take me closer."

They walked toward the Sikt until Linneow told them to stop.

"Wait now, while I secure our safety." She turned toward the fighter.

"*Delanka-ami. Codetts-ka. Staa! Te Setti, tesh l'Ardenue!*"

With a hiss of escaping vapor, the upper half of the goose-head clam-shelled open.

"What did you say?" Baylor asked.

"Linneow first invokes life-form eminence. Next is the identification sequence known only to me. Linneow reminds Sikt I am Sethkean and mate for life to my love, Ardenue. We are safe from harm. Will you carry me to the Sikt?"

Weber and Baylor hustled across the pad toward the craft. Adele followed behind. Alongside the Sikt, Weber reached in the forward cockpit and retrieved Linneow's helmet. She lifted it over her head and, with the help of both men, slid into the cockpit's envelope.

"You've no flight suit!" Baylor exclaimed.

"Not so important, this is."

A bullet ricocheted from the hull of the Sikt, causing both men to duck. Adele merely turned in the direction of the shot, her eyes narrowed. "We'll see about that," she murmured. She switched on her starlight scope, un-slung her rifle and trotted toward a low rise near the edge of the apron.

"This female warrior, she is your mate, Pilot Ed?" Linneow asked.

Baylor's head snapped around. "Ah...I..., we haven't..." he fumbled.

Weber chuckled and said, "She is."

Adele's rifle cracked in the background.

Linneow craned her neck to Weber. "In the access panel behind you, my brother, withdraw the sphere you find inside."

Weber complied. He returned to the cockpit with a gray sphere the size of a tennis ball. He handed it to Linneow. She raised a small lever in the upper surface and removed the top half. Nestled inside were four obsidian pellets, each the size and shape of an almond.

"Listen carefully, my human friends. These are biotes, which have been engineered to coexist only with selected humans. When you swallow one of these, it will protect your body at the cellular level."

"Protect how?" Weber asked.

"Against invasion by parasites, against chemicals or radiation. Abnormal cells are eradicated. Each strand of your DNA will replicate precisely as it is now, for as long as the power of the biote lasts."

Baylor lifted one of the pellets. It felt heavy and warm to the touch. "So we cannot die by poison, bug or snake bites, or radiation. And no cancer. Sounds good to me. What about bullets?"

"It cannot prevent physical damage but repair of less than fatal injury is greatly accelerated."

"There are four of them. Who are they for?" Weber asked.

Linneow ducked her head. "One each for Wozniak, the Scholar and my brothers, Sam and Ed. One also for Flight-leader Ouilette."

"Which is which?" Baylor asked.

"It does not matter."

"Can I take it now?"

"If my brother so chooses."

"Cool!" Baylor quipped. He popped the pellet into his mouth and swallowed with difficulty. "Quite a horse pill. And quite a gift."

"I hope my brother feels so in the future."

"Linneow—" Baylor began.

She raised her eyes. "It is proper for my brother to call me Sayla."

Baylor rubbed his jaw and glanced at Weber, his eyes filling. The agent grinned and nodded. "It gets to you."

Baylor agreed. He returned his gaze to the Chao. "Sayla, will you recover? Can you manage alone, wherever you're going?"

She inclined her head. "*Ammonte* has technology to return my health. Much time will pass. Remember always that I will return."

"How long?" Baylor asked.

"I cannot answer this question." The Chao lowered her gaze and said no more. Baylor glanced at Weber who simply shrugged.

Adele's rifle cracked once more. She then stood, slung her weapon and hustled back toward them. As she approached, Linneow sealed the sphere and handed it to Weber who pocketed it. Baylor stepped away to meet Adele.

"What is her name, my brother?" Linneow asked Weber.

"I call her KR. Ed calls her Adele."

Linneow blinked. "So proper! Like Chao. Sam, my brother, you will care for Ed? Difficult times lie in his path, but he is essential to the future of your world and to another."

Weber grinned. "You bet!"

"Then, I must leave you now." She reached toward the consoles at the right and left of the cockpit, touching several illuminated sections in rapid order. Weber backed away and stood beside Baylor.

Linneow swiveled her gaze to Adele. When she beckoned, Adele glanced at Baylor. He nodded and she trotted forward to the edge of the cockpit.

Linneow said, "You have chosen among the most unique of human males."

Adele smiled. "I hope he stays chosen. Men can be difficult."

Linneow hissed, inclining her head. "Bear him many children. This is important!"

Adele frowned. "Why?"

"For the future. Something portentous may happen."

"Like what?"

The Chao reached over the cockpit sill and gently touched the back of her hand. "This knowledge is for you alone. If the Oo'ahan succeed, you will lose this world, just as your forebears lost their home-world seven billion years ago. Humankind may even perish, as they perished. To persevere, humankind needs what he carries in his genes. The heritage of the Elliner and that of the Danua. The fate of the Cradle may rest in your loins."

"Ed knows about this?"

"He knows not. The gift is his, but you must bring it forth."

Moved almost to tears, Adele softly answered, "I will, I swear it."

The Chao bared her feline fangs and hissed. "My brother has chosen well. I must now depart. Tell your man to move his aircraft to safety."

A whine from the body of the Sikt increased in pitch. The upper half of the goose-head began to descend. Just before it closed, Linneow touched her helmet in a gesture of farewell.

Adele joined Weber and Baylor.

"What did she say?" Baylor asked.

"Woman talk. She's a neat lady, if that's a proper term for a Chao."

"Woman talk? Like what?"

Adele turned to face him. "None of your business, nosy." She pointed to the Hercules. "She did say you need to move your airplane, though."

Weber pulled Baylor and Adele toward the MC-130. A rush of vapor flowed around the base of the Sikt. All three sprinted towards the transport. They dashed in behind Jossman while the commando half-carried and half-dragged a companion. The man was drenched in sweat and obviously exhausted. He gasped as he dropped to his knees just inside.

Jossman kicked him gently with her toe. "C'mon Twicky. You ain't done yet."

Ouilette glanced up as Baylor, Weber and Adele boarded.

"He's the last. Let's scoot," the commander said.

Baylor nodded and clambered up into the flight deck. Jennisette already had the engines running and as soon as Baylor buckled in, advanced the throttles. The Hercules began its takeoff roll. Thirty seconds later, it lifted into the black backdrop and banked away to the west.

One of the controllers raised his voice.

"I have airborne search radar. Ranging now, trying to acquire us."

"Where's the aircraft?" Baylor twisted around, sudden alarm flooding him.

"Still on the deck at Minot."

General Pigott motioned the ground crew to remove the chocks. He lowered the canopy and turned his attention to the fire-control radar. Pigott bracketed the fleeing MC-130 with his radar acquisition hash marks. He pressed the button, acquiring a solid lock. In the next second, the huge, black shape of the Sikt materialized out of the night. It hovered directly in front of his Falcon only thirty meters away.

Pigott heard the Chao's voice whisper in his helmet.

"For Arde."

The rippling fire of the mass drivers tore the Falcon to atoms. Flaming debris engulfed the second Falcon and it also exploded. The Sikt pivoted, angled upward toward the heavens and vanished.

An hour later, while the Talon was hurtling through the mountains of Montana, Baylor pointed through the windscreen.

"Check out the shooting stars!"

Jennisette could only shake his head. Ouilette entered the flight deck a moment later and said, "We've just received a long-wave message from Doctor Wozniak. Every satellite capable of ground surveillance has been inexplicably eradicated."

Baylor laughed aloud. "Or maybe not-so-inexplicably. Did you take your pill?"

Ouilette nodded. "I did."

"How do you feel?"

"On top of the world."

Epilog
August, seven years later
Slategoat Mountain, Bob Marshall Wilderness

Mid-morning had come and gone before Ouilette scaled the last of the ladders to 3C, a old-new nickname for a hollowed out cavity deep within the bowels of the mountain. Command and Control Center. Not that there was much to command and control. Not yet. That would come in the decades and centuries to follow. One could always hope.

He wiped the sweat from his brow and zipped open his jacket. Captain Barth glanced up from the engineering plans as Ouilette entered the dimly lit cavern.

"Morning, Commander. I trust your journey from the Colony went well."

"Better than usual," Ouilette replied, "now that aircraft seem to be a thing of the past. Weber call in yet?"

"Twenty minutes ago. He'll be along shortly."

"Outstanding." Ouilette peeled off his jacket. "Hell of a climb."

"Yes, sir, it is. We're tunneling as fast as possible given the power budget, but it will be a number of years yet before we have the lifts operational. Look on the bright side."

"There's a bright side?"

"Monty says he'll have the cable grid up in a month. We'll be zinging from center to center without the long climb down and back."

Ouilette approached and peered into the natural abyss that penetrated the mountain fortress along its axis. Even the carbon-arc floods could not completely penetrate its stygian depths. They had been lucky twice in this. Silvertip was long known for its caverns and fissures. But the internal chasm in Slategoat had been a complete surprise, and a true gift.

All along both sides of a fissure seventy meters across, three hundred deep, and almost half a mile in length, lamps glimmered—marking construction sites for barracks, armories, storage centers. Seven years. And they had barely begun.

Barth joined him and, as if he had read his mind, softly said, "The long view...damn hard to keep the faith without it."

"That it is, my friend."

"You gents planning to jump?"

Ouilette pivoted. Weber had silently sprawled in a chair at the table under the central lighting fixture. "Damn it Sam, you're always the ghost. No one ever sees you come or go." Weber wore his forest dispersal-patterned battle dress, both Ouilette and Barth their covert blacks.

"Old habits die hard, Marcus. Take a load off."

Ouilette joined him and motioned to Barth. "Call the others in and we'll get started."

When the entire staff had assembled, Ouilette turned the floor over to Weber, who spent the next forty minutes delivering his report. To call it grim news would have been an understatement.

Ouilette finally pushed back from the table and stood. He paced the length of the cavern twice before he asked, "What's the chance they can come up with a vaccine? Or that the virus will run its course?"

"Nature of the beast," Weber replied. "Incubation period is six weeks, and it's contagious the entire time. Doc sealed Drummond Island up tight over a month ago." Weber pushed a package across the table. "His operational plan to salvage what we can."

"You've read it?" At Weber's affirmation, Ouilette added, "Summarize it for me, then. What should we do?"

Weber clasped his fingers behind his neck. "It's another engineered virus, Marcus. And this one's lethal as hell. As with the others, it began in Africa and spreads by common contact, by insects, by who knows the hell what. We've no distribution system left so even if they came up with a vaccine, it would make no difference."

"So what's the answer, Sam? Tell me there is one."

Weber indicated the package. "Plans for a quarantine center. Your boys build it, we fill it."

"We?"

"You and I. Doc's got his hands full."

Ouilette nodded. "The biotes. We're immune. What about Ed?"

Weber shook his head. "Doc needs him for the Evangel project. No one else has the skills."

Whom do we fill it with?"

"Doc made a list. We round them up. Soonest too, while we still can."

Ouilette returned to the table. He pushed the package to Barth. "Priority one, Captain." To Weber he softly added, "First the famines, then the nukes, and now this. What's next?"

The tall, gray-eyed agent met his gaze directly. "Worse is yet to come, Marcus. No doubt about that."

Weber paused in mid-swing, shielding his eyes from the glare of the sun. After a moment, he propped the ax against a growing pile of split rounds. The trail of dust at the foot of a distant ridge meant a man on horseback. He pulled his watch from his pocket, lifted his hat and mopped his brow. Weber hefted the ax one more time and drove its head into a log butt before turning away and striding toward the house.

As he entered the cool interior, he called toward the kitchen. "Angie?" When she stepped through the doorway, his saddlebags over her shoulder, he added, "Angie, darlin', you're reading my mind."

She stood on tiptoe and kissed his chin. "I'm not, Sam. I saw him through the telescope an hour ago."

Weber raised his hat higher on his brow. "Why didn't you say so?"

"We needed the wood split."

She placed the saddlebags over his shoulder and then handed him his canteen. "The transmitter is in your pack. Three days?"

Weber traced the route up to the glacier in his mind. For twenty-four hours, they would send a signal into the heavens and hope for a reply. "Time enough, I reckon." He turned to the doorway and paused in the entrance. "Adios." He stepped out into the warm spring sunshine.

Weber found his favorite sorrel tied to a post outside the barn, rifle in the scabbard and a pack rolled behind the saddle. He tossed his bags over the animal's rump and secured them. He untied the reins and led the sorrel past the house, waving at Angie's slim form. She waved back and retreated inside.

"Best one yet," he muttered.

Weber led the horse down to the fork in the trail where he waited the best part of an hour. He sat on a stump and chewed the end of a reed until the other rider showed. When the horseman straightened in the saddle and groaned, he drawled, "Howdy brother. You look a little peaked."

Baylor stretched his back. He leaned over the saddle-horn. "Sam, forgive me if I don't get down and greet you proper."

Weber's grin broadened as he stood. "Old age, maybe?"

"You should talk. You had a head start on me, even way back when."

Weber placed his foot in his stirrup and heaved himself into the saddle. He flicked the reins against the sorrel's neck and the two men started the long climb to the glacier. For a third of the distance, they could ride side by side.

Baylor brushed his hat back on his head. "You ought to come down once in a while, Sam. Things are really booming. New Boise has almost twenty thousand people now. The *ponics* farms are working wonders."

Weber shook his head. "You folks are too exposed for my comfort."

"You think there might be trouble?"

"You haven't forgotten what this is about, have you?"

Baylor glanced away. "Every morning when I look in the mirror, I remember."

Weber nodded without comment. After several moments he added, "Adelaide stopped by a few weeks back."

"You old cuss, why didn't you say something sooner? How's she doing? Where's she living?"

"Doing fine. Got a mess of brats up on the middle fork of the Flathead. Two new schools too. She's the spittin' image of Adele, you know. Near scared me out of ten year's growth when she rode in."

Baylor's expression turned somber. He looked away. "Yeah, I know."

Weber reached down alongside of his horse's neck and fetched a second stalk of grass. He munched on the end until it softened. "You never remarried, Ed. It would help if you did, you know."

Baylor faced him. "I don't know, Sam. I loved that woman so hard it hurt. To watch her grow old and die near ripped my heart apart."

"That's what the children are for. I've so many I can't remember their names, let alone those of the grand kids' and great-grand kids'. Angie's due again. By my count, that makes seventy."

Baylor grinned. "You're a randy old coot, aren't you?" He paused and added, "It's been two hundred and sixteen years, Sam. You still think she'll come?"

Weber lost his smile. "Reckon so."

Neither the beginning nor the end.

Thanks for purchasing and reading
Book Two – A Nepenthean Solution
By Rod Rogers

If you would like a complementary high-resolution image of the cover for your personal use, please contact the author: rod@mountainofdreams.com.

If you would to receive email updates on future works in this series, please send an email to the above address.

Printed in Great Britain
by Amazon.co.uk, Ltd.,
Marston Gate.

6165813R00216